Swords of the Imperium
Volume 2 of the Polaris Chronicles

Bryan Choi & Erica Carson

ISBN: 1-945882-01-8
ISBN-13: 978-1-945882-01-2

Swords of the Imperium is a work of fiction. Names, places, and incidents either are a product of the authors' imaginations or are used fictitiously.

Published by Delphinium Press, LLC.
www.carsonchoi.com

The Polaris Chronicles:

CONTENTS

Acknowledgments

Thanks to Shay, Whitney, Greg, and Colby for again being my faithful beta readers. I think you all must have read this entire thing four times back to back, suffering along the way. Thanks again to my onions and minions at Ninpocho Chronicles and Frequency Writer's Group in Providence for your support. And finally, I couldn't have done any of this without the skill, love, and sick burns of my coauthor, Erica. – Bryan

Thanks to everyone who encouraged me to stick with it, especially the Thunderdome team. Double thanks to me inimitable parents, abeonim, and eomeonim for encouraging and supporting our efforts. - Erica

1

Hadassah Mikkelsen licked the flat of her knife and smiled sweetly. "He's being difficult. Let's cut off his head, take his key, and open the chest already."

"I don't want to hang for fragging an officer," Draco Emreis said. He unwound a length of hempen rope from around his fists and drew it tight. "If we all rush him at once, we can hog-tie him instead. Besides, who's to say the key's actually on him? What if he hid it somewhere?"

Karma Gillette smacked the wide end of a leather-wrapped cudgel against his palm. "I bet he shoved it up his rear. It's like a hidden compartment for men."

"I'm *definitely* not checking that," Hadassah said.

"I'm in command," Captain Lotte Satou said. "I'll check."

Draco looked surprised. "Captain? You sure?"

Lotte nodded grimly and spat into her right hand. "Mikkelsen, hold him down. He'll feel more comfortable if women do the deed."

Taki Natalis clenched his jaw as he swept his squad with the muzzle of his pistol. With his promotion to cornet came the privilege of carrying a side arm within the Temple. The Herstal he had been given was a third-rate castoff pockmarked by rust, but it *worked*. Taki was grateful to have the weapon, especially while backed into a corner and facing unspeakable acts. The only problem was that he only had a single dirty round to his name. "For the *last time*," he said, "I'm not holding out on any of you! We are *out of bullets. That* is why you haven't been paid."

"Then go to the shrine and get more!" Draco flipped his hair in indignation. "I'll hold your hand if you're scared of being robbed."

"You think I haven't checked? There's no more grad in our coffers. Hecaton Mezeta's the one who fills our stores. She's been missing for a *fortnight*!"

"Don't we have savings?" Hadassah said. "Just give us our friggin' pay! I thought we were *friends*! Why do you have to be so *mean*?"

"I'm not being mean!" Taki replied. "And *you're* the one who wants to cut my head off or rape me or both!"

Hadassah sniffled and wiped at her nose.

Taki rolled his eyes. "Don't you dare!"

Karma shook his head. "Are you really making a girl cry?"

"Don't you feel bad about yourself, Natalis?" Draco asked.

For a moment, Taki considered shooting himself and trying to bleed all over everyone before he died. Hopefully, he'd make Hadassah throw up and Draco slip and break a rib. He wasn't Lotte—he couldn't simply beat them all to death—so suicide was the only alternative. He raked his fingernails against his scalp. "Oh, fine! This will definitely get me knouted, but fuck it. I'll open the box and show you all, if you stop trying to murder me."

"But I wanted to check!" Lotte said. Her fingers gleamed stickily in the torchlight.

Taki ignored her and holstered his gun. He knelt down, grasped the brass handle of a worn wooden chest, and dragged the chest over the stones until it was in full view of his squad. Then he reached into his leggings, grimaced, and produced a tarnished old key.

Hadassah gasped. "Was that in…in your *bung*?"

Taki shot her a vitriolic glare and turned the key. Slowly, he opened the lid.

"Damnation." Draco tossed his rope away.

"You all owe me an apology!" Taki's voice cracked, but his scowl held firm. The balding felt interior of the chest was completely bare. He slammed the lid shut. "I can't believe you all tried to brutalize me! You *know* I can't show you lot what's inside!"

"All right, we're sorry!" Draco looked at the others. "*Why am I the only one abasing myself here?*"

Taki crossed his arms.

Draco flinched. "You want me to kowtow to you? I'll do it, so long as you stop looking at me like that."

"That's enough," Lotte said. "I'm very sorry, Natalis. I shouldn't have let things get to this point. But the issue still stands! We need funds. We're hungry."

Taki sighed and sat back on the paybox. His expression softened, if only slightly. "Captain, you know the answer."

"Right. I'll sell Emreis to a cathouse."

"*No.* We have to find and talk to *Mezeta*. Without her, we starve."

Draco's eyes widened. "Wait a second. Let's not do anything rash! Leave her lordship out of this, aye? We can all get by for a bit longer. After all, these are blessed times. We're no longer in the kitchens, and most of all, that woman's gone and fucked off to God knows where! My virtue is a small price to pay for it. I'll make a *fine* courtesan. You know how good I look in a dress. I'll call myself...Dulcinea."

"Draco's delusions aside," Karma said, "didn't Mezeta vanish because of a promotion?"

"Yes, and it's just like her," Draco said. "She's the opposite of human decency! An ungrateful hag! Her Grace the Basileus appoints Mezeta the exarch's direct successor and what happens? The woman deserts!"

"Wait." Hadassah chewed a nail. "You're saying that being nice to Hecaton Mezeta makes her vanish? We've been going about this all wrong for *years*."

"No, and I'll tell you exactly why you're wrong," Draco said. "We're just stupid barbarians to that woman. We're not her loyal Polaris of the Temple. We're just shit-flinging monkeys she uses to troll the higher-ups for the sake of her ego. And even after we singlehandedly repulsed the Imperial horde while flying *her* standard, her way of saying thanks is to neglect to pay us. If trying to screw her and trying to appease her yield the same result, then I'd rather keep plotting her death. *If for nothing else, then for the sake of my dignity!*"

Hadassah cuffed Draco's cheek. "You're turning purple. And did you really just call me what I think you called me?"

"If she'd only dubbed our squad 'The Dung-Chucking Gorillas,' we'd all have been spared blasphemy charges and wouldn't have had to do nothing but peel potatoes for two whole years."

"So you *did* call me a poo-toucher! I *demand* satisfaction!"

Taki winced at the memory of punishment duty. Hecaton Mezeta was the squad's commander, but she acted more like its owner. She led in a style that was equally mean-spirited joke, blatant sedition, and part of a greater, if completely incomprehensible, plan. "Captain," he said, and shot Lotte a warning glance. "Enough dithering. Tell us what to do before we all resort to cannibalism."

Lotte groaned. "Do you have to always be so forthright?"

"Yes. I'm a commissioned officer of the Polaris of the Temple. Aren't *you?*"

"More sass, and I'll spank you."

"Go ahead. You'll all starve in the end, anyway."

Lotte looked wounded for a moment. "Fine. I think I know where Mezeta is. Come with me?"

Taki glared at her. "Is that your order, milord Captain?"

"If you're going to be that way, then yes," she said. "It's an order. Mikkelsen, come with us. Gillette and Emreis, go round up dinner. Here's the last of my funds." She took out her revolver, swung out the cylinder, and held out an unfired cartridge.

"Captain," Karma said, "I mean no disrespect, but there's a reason we're so poor right now. We've been eating market meat and fresh eggs at *every meal.* If we just restricted ourselves to the mess hall once a day, we'd save—"

Lotte mashed the lead nose of the bullet against Karma's forehead and twisted. "I'll kill us all before I eat another potato."

Karma shuddered, latched on to Draco's arm, and dragged the man away.

"Captain," Hadassah said, "did you have to be quite so flirty with the man? And are you sure old Hecaton hasn't just abandoned us for real?"

Lotte shook her head. "I'm afraid not. There's a stench coming from her quarters."

"I'm *not* toting her body." Hadassah crossed her arms and spat.

"It's not corpse flowers," Lotte said. "Now move along."

* * * *

Hecaton Kheiris Mezeta, formerly a major but now a lord principality of the Cloud Temple, had hung a cheery "Do Not Disturb" sign on the door of her office. The office was not only barred from within, but also protected by a retribution mandala. Taki discovered it when he attempted to force the door open with a shoulder check and ended up unceremoniously sprawled on the floor.

"Milord Principality!" Lotte shouted. "Open up! We know you're in there."

There was no response.

"You weren't kidding about the smell," Hadassah said. She scrunched her nose up at the smoky, cloying odor wafting out from the doorframe.

Taki groaned and slowly rose to his feet. He wiped away a thin stream of blood from his left nostril and reached out to cast a sutra. Before he could follow through, Hadassah kicked him in the back of a knee. He stumbled, lurched around, and pushed her. She riposted with an elbow to his gut, and the two started to wrestle.

"Out of my way," Lotte ordered. She knelt with palms upturned in supplication and started to invoke a sutra. *"The mind commands the body, and it obeys. I am become Walking Death. I eat the hearts of my enemies, wear their skins, and become cuter."*

Hadassah looked up from her efforts to drive her thumbs into Taki's nostrils. "Captain? What are you doing? We can't—"

Lotte inhaled and let out a roar before she lurched face forward at the door. Light lanced out from the wood to reveal a previously hidden mandala that blurred and dissolved under the assault. The door buckled and shattered like plate glass struck by a juggernaut, and Lotte careened in before coming to a stop in the center of the office.

Someone cackled. *"Om mani padme hum."*

Taki extricated himself from Hadassah's leg lock and limped into the office after Lotte. When he saw what lay within, his face scrunched in horror.

Hecaton sat atop her desk, cross-legged, with the tops of her feet flush against her thighs. A circlet of dessicated clover blossoms rested loosely across her brow, and she wore a robe of dirty, sweat-yellowed linen with a wooden begging bowl balanced in her lap. Before her, melted stumps of candles pooled wax across the wood and over the edge to form a stringy, multicolored waterfall.

"Milord Principality," Lotte said, out of breath, "I apologize for the intrusion and the door, but we were all concerned for you."

Hecaton smiled magnanimously. "My child, are you ready to shave your head and become a nun?" she asked.

"No. What's all this about?" She motioned with her head to the rest of the office. Stolen laundry lines crisscrossed above with deep-ochre-stained undergarments hung haphazardly in the fashion of prayer pennants. Books and scrolls were strewn around the floor unopened, their pages ripped from the bindings and spit-glued into lewd sculptures attached to the walls. Incomprehensible red squiggles danced across the walls, as if children had been given buckets of paint and promised protection from their parents' wrath.

"An offering, first." Hecaton pointed to a large, pewter spittoon overflowing with ash. A handful of fresh joss sticks pierced the gray mound. "I *am* a twice born, you know. I'm one who's entered the stream. If you give up your worldly desires and meditate every day, you can too."

Lotte looked at the other two. "Natalis, use your power."

Taki hesitated.

"Well, go on," Lotte said. "Eastern gods *eat the smells.*"

"You're sure, Captain?"

"Don't question her orders," Hadassah snapped. "Just do what she says! Wanna fight again?"

Taki shook his head. He edged closer to the spittoon with his arm stretched out, as if trying to avoid contamination. He flicked his fingers at the end of a joss stick but shook so much that the summoned flames missed their target entirely. The stick glowed feebly after a few more tries.

Lotte sighed. "Milord, there's your offering."

Hecaton nodded sagely. "Now, all of you clap twice and keep your hands pressed together. Bow at the waist and hold for ten seconds. I won't make you kowtow, since you're nonbelievers."

"Enough sacrilege!" Lotte said. "*You* answer *us* now. Why have you refused all contact, even from the exarch? What are you *doing* here? Have you fed *Babu*?"

Hearing his name, a rotund, tiger-striped tom half leapt, half pulled himself onto the desk next to Hecaton and let out a yowl. Hecaton shot an imperious glare at the tom, and he responded by flopping down in her lap. "The basileus has offended me greatly. So I will not see her cronies until she kowtows to me and retracts what she has done." She scratched Babu's ears, and he nibbled the folds of her robes.

Lotte frowned. "You are a principality of the Temple. You are the next in line to guide the flock, and you lord over even the Agia Triada. How in the hell does that displease you?"

"I didn't want it. I just wanted an egg—"

"Whether you wanted it or not is irrelevant. Besides, an increase in rank means more pay, more prestige." Lotte stepped forward around the repurposed urn and put her forehead to Hecaton's. "It means Her Grace wanted to *reward* you."

Hecaton merely licked the tip of Lotte's nose in repose. "That tastes like a lie!"

Lotte planted her hands on her hips. "Are you done playing dress-up? Can we move on?"

"You're insulting my people."

Hadassah waved. "Isn't a promotion just the kind of thing you want, though? You know, to be in control so you can piss around with people's lives and such?"

"All I wanted in life was to bake bread," Hecaton said. "My father and brother were bakers, you know. They were making scallion dumplings the day I went to the bihara. And now...*I don't remember how they tasted!*"

"Scallion dumplings are easy," Hadassah said. "I'll even be cute and teach you how. Does that make you happy?"

"No! They're made in a specific way, and none of you barbarians could possibly appreciate their refinement."

Lotte jabbed a finger at Hecaton's nose. "You're being rude."

Hecaton clasped Lotte's finger in her hands and peered at the tip while sucking her teeth. "Lieselotte, child, listen to me. I'm sorry, but you have leprosy."

"No one has leprosy!" Lotte snapped her hand back. "Now, with all due respect, shut the hell up and listen to me! You're acting like a godrotting child! If you're so unhappy with Her Grace's esteem, you can just *leave!* No one's keeping you here against your will. Go ahead and resign right now *so we can get paid!*"

Hecaton blinked. "But I don't want to. I like being around you dumb kids. Sometimes I think of you as my own."

"If you truly think that about us, milord Principality, then please respect our need to eat. Or else we'll all starve and possibly die."

"You can always eat the exarch. He's very fat and doesn't run fast."

Taki saw something wild cross his captain's face, and bile surged up his throat. "Beg pardon!" He stepped between the two women but avoided touching either. "If the basileus offended you, why don't you send a letter to her? Or even better, you can go *visit* Her Grace!"

Hecaton grinned and leapt from her perch to twirl around. "A splendid idea, my little regicide! We're off to see the basileus, the wonderful basil of Oz! And if she doesn't do what I want, I'll shove this promotion up her *ass!*"

She kicked the spittoon over and took Taki by the hips to whirl around in a clumsy, parodic waltz. Tears formed in Taki's eyes, and a thought crossed his mind: *It'd have been better to starve.*

"It's decided," Lotte said. She shook her head. "Accompany the Principality to Athenaeum."

Hecaton grinned and pirouetted while Taki scurried away. "Yes, come with me, my loyal onions, minions, or whatever you are! Company, to arms! And let us bask in obscene incandescence!" she said as she skipped airily out the door and left her choking subordinates in a cloud of ash.

"Wait, Captain," Hadassah said. "If we don't go with her, maybe she'll get lost and die in a ditch. After all, she's gone raving mad. We shouldn't squander this opportunity to be rid of her!"

Lotte cuffed the redhead gently across the cheek. "Idiot, this is a lucid moment for our tyrant. Now get your damned guns and off to the capital with you."

* * * *

Taki chanced a breath through his nostrils and immediately wished he hadn't. Effluvium coursed slowly down channels on either side of the boulevard he walked down and sent up an indescribable odor that cut his senses like a rusty shiv. Greenish-brown, the oily shit backed up everywhere and simply pooled on the cobblestones, making him step gingerly to avoid splashing it on his leggings.

The Argead Dominion, to which all Polaris of the Temple pledged their lives, was now a country only in name. A month earlier, the Osterbrand Imperium had overrun the borders in a sudden, brutal conquest. The surviving peerage of the Dominion now numbered less than a dozen, having been slaughtered in battle or hanged in front of their keeps. The assassination of the childless Basileus Niketas Palailogos had further destabilized the faltering nation, and his successor had been forced to offer terms despite an improbable Dominion victory at the capital's doorstep.

Because of that narrow win, Athenaeum had been spared a siege and thus was exactly the same as Taki remembered it: the smell of human waste intermingled with roasting harspud. Hecaton traipsed gaily ahead, still clad in her sweaty prayer robes, which dragged on the cobbles and smeared dust and filth in her wake. Taki shook his head at the sight and glanced at Hadassah, who was busy play-acting as a tourist and seemed indifferent to the smell.

"What?" she asked.

"Nothing," Taki said. He scrunched his nose up. "Well, what do you think of it? The jewel in the Dominion crown?"

"Disappointing. I expected more rubble and bodies falling from the rooftops. Or at least more fires. There hasn't been a single screaming woman or roasting child. There's nothing to loot, either."

"Why are you so preoccupied with looting? And with death and carnage?"

"Because I love shiny things and I'm not afraid to kill for them. Aren't I too perfect?"

"You're a criminal."

"We both are. Except I didn't, you know, kill the last of the Palaiologoi or nothin'." Hadassah slid a finger across her throat and let out a gruesome rattle.

"I didn't..." Taki began, but his words died in his throat. *I didn't what? Mean to do it?*

"Did you drown him in the tub? Or shank him on the shitter?"

"Nothing of the sort! Just...just shut up! Please!"

She wrapped an arm around his and squeezed. "Don't get me wrong, Natalis. There are lots of people out there who had it in for the old basil. And maybe some who'd call you a hero or a savior. So don't be glum.

The rest of us don't think ill of you, and even though you won't fess up to it, we know."

Taki blinked and unclenched his jaw. He let out a breath and murmured his thanks. "I appreciate it. I really do. I just need time to figure out some things."

Hadassah smiled. "Did you put something up his bung?"

Taki frowned and wormed his way out of her grasp. "Forget it! If you're just going to jape at me, then I have no further words for you."

"Your problem is that you're too damned uptight. You're so focused on your own stupid virtue that you end up being an ass most of the time." She took a too-large bite of a harspud ball impaled on a stick and started to pant.

"I hope you get the shits from that."

"Speaking of which," Hadassah said, "where's old Mezeta gone to?"

Taki swore and frantically looked around. The old woman was nowhere to be seen. He sprinted up to the edge of the square but realized quickly that finding her would be impossible in the crowd. He jogged back over to Hadassah, who hadn't moved an inch and was still chowing down like a yokel. "Damn you! She was just here! If you hadn't distracted me…"

He squatted and ran his fingers through his hair. Now he'd done it. The old hag had gone insane, slipped away, and would kill the new basileus for fun. He'd be a double-regicide now. Cries and gunshots erupted in the distance. The two Polaris looked at each other and took off running.

It wasn't long until they came up to the wrought-iron gates of the Mitripoli, only to be confronted by a line of bayonets and muzzles. Nearby, Hecaton stood with her hands on her hips, seething. A battle line of praetorians with rifles barred the way to the palace. From behind marched up a platoon of city garrison with brightly painted shields and spears, backed by crossbowmen. Taki raised his hands in surrender. There was no escaping now.

"Milord Principality," Taki said. "What happened?"

"One of them spat on my robes," Hecaton said. "I took offense and made them pay. Now the others will learn some proper respect. Because fuck turning the other cheek."

"Why didn't you wait for us?"

"You two were having fun. I didn't want to be a burden."

Taki rolled his eyes. "No, you wanted to ditch us and start a meaningless fight."

"Maybe?"

"What's the meaning of this?" Amilia Gillette said. She stood on the opposite side of the iron fence with her arms crossed and her brow furrowed. The ivory robes of the basileus contrasted with the brown of her hands and face and the silver of her hair. When she saw Hecaton, she sighed.

"Your Grace!" a praetorian shouted. "You must get to safety!"

Amilia shook her head. "Lower your weapons, open the gate, and resume your posts. I've been expecting this one and her entourage. I'll see you inside, Hecaton Mezeta. Be a dear and wipe your feet."

The praetorians slowly withdrew, disbelief written on their faces. One of them grudgingly unbarred the entry and pulled the gilded doors open. Hecaton strode nonchalantly inside without a word to her subordinates.

Taki slowly let his arms fall to his sides. They burned from being held up for so long, and he rubbed at his shoulders. He glanced at Hadassah. "Far be it from me to question the captain, but was it actually smart to bring Mezeta here? She's gone batshit!"

"It doesn't matter," Hadassah murmured. "She's going to do what she wants, with or without us. We're just her peons along for the journey. Now here, have some balls." She offered her snack to Taki, who finally, glumly, took a bite.

When they trudged into the throne room, the exchange had already begun.

Amilia, slumped on the brass eagle throne, regarded Hecaton with a bemused expression. "And for what purpose did you assault my men?"

"I want to escape the cycle of death and rebirth," Hecaton said. "Material attachments prevent me from doing so. Make them go away."

Amilia sighed. "I'm the basileus, not the Buddha, and definitely not God. Did you really waste your time coming here to hear that? Drop the bullshit religious act. It's self-indulgent."

"You've offended me, and I've lost my appetite," Hecaton said.

"Good. I wasn't going to throw you a feast, anyway."

"Then I ask you this. Why did you make me heir to the Temple without my consent?

"You make me sound like a rapist, and I resent that," Amilia said. "Exarch Niketas was a fair defender of the land in his prime. However, now that we are under Imperial control, it is time for new leadership. The old man's way of doing things nearly cost us our lives, though I don't aim to punish him for it. But I need fresh blood to replace stagnant."

"Then why don't you make one of the Triada take his place?" Hecaton asked, pacing all the while. "Or hell, just make lil' Karma do the job? He's *your* unlovable spawn."

"The Triada are idiots and blowhards. I'd execute them if I weren't concerned about rebellion. And Karma may be my son, but he is eminently unqualified for any position of power and prone to treasonous leanings. I often entertain the thought of having him killed. Prophylactically, you understand."

Hecaton grinned. "You are one of the few barbarians who understand good parenting!"

"Stop trying to flatter me and change the subject. I want *you* to run the Temple and appoint a new command. I want you to make us strong again."

Hecaton threw her head back and laughed. "No."

"I expected you'd say that. I'm prepared to offer you almost anything within reason in return for your acceptance. *How much?*"

"A million bullets and a pony."

"Will you take installments? The animal can be delivered immediately."

Hecaton glowered. "You don't do sarcasm, do you? I want nothing, and I won't accept."

"Then I order you to, on pain of death."

"Good! Just when I think you're getting boring, you prove me wrong again. If someone like you had been in charge a long time ago in my homeland, things would have turned out differently for Shastirch and I."

"All I hear from you is gibberish," Amilia said.

Hecaton inhaled deeply, exhaled, and smirked. "I know what you're trying to accomplish. Sadly, it's impossible. I am a 'twice born.' Do you know what that means?"

Amilia shook her head.

"Unlike most of you peons, I've been a human once before. This is my second birth, and because I've been such a good little arhant, I get to shoot lightning out of my cooter. Choniates and the Triada are *barely* twice born, and they'll just return as vermin when they die. Only the twice born among my people can manage this much power. I haven't seen it anywhere else, and I've traveled much further than you think I have. So I can't turn your Polaris into a bunch of little knockoff Mezetas. Not that I'd ever want to, anyway."

Amilia snorted. "Although I respect your power, you also display shocking levels of ignorance."

"Oh? Do explain."

"My order has nothing to do with your ability to control the elements or act like an arrogant ass. It has everything to do with preserving the people of this nation. And to do that, we will need to resist Imperial whims. We need to preserve our way of life."

"*You're* the one who offered the country on a platter," Hecaton said. "Besides, I've traveled their lands, and compared to the Dominion way of life, they're practically enlightened. No Imperial will accuse you of being a witch just so they can stone you and steal your house."

Amilia chuckled. "You act as if I haven't been accused of witchcraft before and haven't gotten my accusers boiled for slander. I offered a conditional surrender because my choices were to either sign a surrender treaty or reduce my own country to ash with the God Hand."

"That might have been preferable."

"I should have pressed the button then, but only for you."

Hecaton stamped a foot. "Why don't you nuke me right now?"

"Because it'd be a waste of a good relic. You're not that important."

"Clearly I must be, if I'm your only guard against the Imperium overtaking this shitty culture."

Amilia made a fist. "Mezeta, I despise many things about my own kingdom, and that's why I wished to change it. But the way the padishah sees it, each and every one of us is mere fodder for the machine of conquest. The man blathers on about parity between sexes and the primacy of merit through deed, but the reality is a shit pile. Men and women and queers all carry the same spear and turn into the same mincemeat to take some unimportant hill. Even *you* will meet that fate in his world."

"So be it. There's always someone stronger."

"And I aim to be smarter. So, will you accept?"

Hecaton rolled her eyes. "I'll think about it, if it gets you off my tit for a sodding second. Now, I need to piss."

She sauntered out of the chamber unbidden.

Amilia shook her head, rose from her throne, and dusted her robes off. She glanced at Taki and Hadassah. "I doubt the principality will return. In the meantime, I'd like a word with you, Cornet Natalis."

"Your Grace." Taki bowed deeply and tried to stifle his own trembling. *She wants to eliminate the evidence. Now is as good a time as any.* For once, he was glad that Hadassah was with him. *At least she'll get axed too.*

"There've been rumors of late," Amilia said. "Idle slander that I seduced a young Polaris of the Temple and that, in a foolish attempt to gain my favor, the young man killed our former liege."

"I know very little of these matters, Your Grace," Taki said. He swallowed. Sweat droplets formed on his brow.

"As basileus, it is my sacred duty to uphold the law and bring justice to the murderer. If it so happened that an ambitious but misguided young man raised his hand against Niketas Palaiologos, then he should be hanged, drawn, and quartered, and his parts sent to all corners of the Dominion to serve as an example for traitors."

Taki clenched his jaw. "Yes, Your Grace." *This is the end.*

"So you basically used him, and now you're gonna turn him into wieners?" Hadassah said. "That's pretty shitty of you."

Amilia cracked her knuckles. "Were we not alone here, you'd be flogged to death for your insolence, girl."

Hadassah seemed unfazed. "I just speak plainly, Your Grace."

"Just consider yourself lucky to be beneath my notice. As for you, Cornet Natalis, perhaps I'll speak plainly too. You're becoming a liability. But, as your wench pointed out, it would be untoward of me to simply have you killed."

"I'm *definitely* not his wench," Hadassah said.

Taki coughed and sputtered. "What will happen to me, Your Grace?"

"The safest thing for both of us would be to cut out your tongue, have you branded on both cheeks, and sever your thumbs before depositing you on the Ursalan border. You'd avoid execution, in any case."

Taki went pale. "P-please, Your Grace..."

"Luckily for you, another option has presented itself. For now, you'll simply need to wait...and to not do anything stupid."

Taki dug his nails into his palms. His knees wobbled, and he found it impossible to stand.

"I hope you understand my situation. I'm not a monster." With that, Amilia rose from her seat and pointed to the door.

Taki lowered his head and stared at the tiles on the floor. They formed a mosaic of Orestes tormented by the Furies: punishment for the murder of his betters. And yet because the deed had been instigated by a god, Orestes had been unable to even take shelter in any temple. Until he'd made impossible amends, his fate was always to suffer. Rendered in exacting detail with tiny precious stones, the ancient hero's face was caught in an eternal scream.

* * * *

Hecaton stood at the highest point of the Mitripoli, letting the wind whip her hair into disarray. Her prayer robes had been dumped on to a beggar in a side alley, and now she sported a gold-accented tunic that she'd swiped from Amilia's chambers. Wearing it was treason, but edicts were meaningless atop the fort's steeple. Athenaeum also smelled slightly better where she was.

"*Udaan uulzsangui shuu, Sirin*," Chronicler said. He perched on a buttress nearby, just out of arm's reach.

Hecaton tensed for a moment to hear her sworn nemesis speak her truest of names. Had anyone else addressed her with such familiarity—such intimacy—she'd have struck him down where he stood. Chronicler, however, was no stranger. She let out a sigh of resignation and continued to stare out over the city. Of the two of them, Chronicler was always the more physical, and trying to run from him would only result in more taunting. It was always better to cut the man down with words, anyway.

"I've made precious few mistakes in my life, Shastirch," Hecaton said, using the name deepest-graven on Chronicler's heart. "But marrying you was the worst by far."

"Have a care for my health, Sirin. Setting my heart aflutter like that is bad for my qi."

"Aren't you a little old to be scrambling on the rooftops like some idiotic basang?"

"The same could be said for you. That gray hair of yours is far too dignified. A head of shocking pink might fit better."

"You looked better wearing it, Shastirch. Now, are you done wasting my time, or have you come for some sort of useful purpose?"

Chronicler blinked. "Actually, I just wanted to talk you again. In person. Without the inconvenient need to slaughter each other on sight."

"I can't imagine why," Hecaton said. "Aren't you sick of my face?"

"Do you know how many years I searched for you? How many years of humiliation I had to endure for mere fleeting glimpses and missed chances?"

"You brought that on yourself. I never wanted you to come after me. Our romance was over a long time ago."

Chronicler laughed. "It wasn't out of sentimentality, I assure you. I wanted to take you back to the Ring for judgment. But now, I'm not so sure that's a good idea."

"I had my reasons. And I find it hard to believe the Sarang would allow you to abscond simply to look for me."

"Perhaps I wished to escape my service as well."

"Then we're both traitors without any right to return."

"So, what do you plan to do from now on, Sirin? Continue being a sellsword?"

"I'm thinking about carving out a swath of land for my own. You know, crown upon a troubled brow and all that. If you wish, you can be my consort. But no sex. I'm too dried out for that."

Chronicler laughed. "The offer sounds tempting, though I know you are merely mocking me."

"I really wasn't. How about you, Shastirch? Will you continue to be the padishah's dogsbody until senility?"

"I like to be on the winning side. And I have no intention of staying as a dogsbody."

"Hah! Now, that's the man I once knew. So when are you planning to assassinate your master?"

Chronicler shrugged. "I wasn't. I find him fascinating. He's certainly charismatic, as far as centuries-old demons go. He was actually around during the Fall, you know. Now he feels like it's his responsibility to lift mankind from the ashes. Through conquest, of course."

"Come, Chronicler, you're not saying you believe in his cause? World domination? How *trite*."

"It's not trite when he has the power to actually achieve his goal." Chronicler's eyes flitted from side to side. "He's set his sights on the Ring, and I intend to help him take it. Against his armies, even a thousand twice born don't stand a chance. And again, I want to be on the winning side."

Hecaton glowered. "What did he promise you in exchange for betraying our home?"

Chronicler shook his head. "I want to save it. I will rule in his stead there and make sure that what happened to us never happens to others."

"So, a dogsbody to the end."

"Call it what you want. I'll ask you one final time, Sirin. Will you join me and bring order to the Ring?"

Hecaton turned away. "No. You embark on a fool's journey. Try not to die on the way."

"The same to you, my dear. I advise you not to get in my way."

With that, Chronicler leapt off the top of the steeple and was gone.

2

Nestled in the foothills at the base of the Cloud Temple, the town of Sasori stood between the road up the mountainside and the old Egnatia Odos highway. Dead during the day, it revived at night for the arrival of younger Polaris eager to spend precious liberty exchanging cartridges for whores and liquor. The exarch tolerated the town's presence because relieving frustration kept the peace in his domain, and the villagers profited from the influx of milligrad while being protected from booze-induced destruction, thanks to the watchful eyes of the Black Cross.

Taki sipped at his tankard of beer and let out a satisfying, sour belch. Since the first time he'd gotten smashed on rotgut in the Duchy of Kosovo, he had grown more tolerant of alcohol. Now, he even enjoyed the taste of certain ales, though he still could not comprehend the appeal of wine other than as a cheap intoxicant. The louse-bitten hole he was currently drinking in was called the Dawnbringer. One of the larger swill houses in the village, it offered filling fare and nightly music. Drinking was also a great way to forget what had happened in Athenaeum. It had been a day since their return, but nothing seemed to have changed. At first, he'd thought of asking Lotte for advice but had quickly quashed the idea.

"Good showing, Natalis! I can smell you from here." Draco chortled as he fanned the air in front of his face. He reached into a wooden bowl and tore a piece of black bread away from a communal loaf before dipping it into a mash of chickpeas and sorghum.

"Just keep it coming," Taki grunted, and helped himself to a dollop of the sour dip. A wealth of food and drink was set before him on their spindle table. Normally, he would've been aghast at pissing away all of the squad's funds at the taverna, but considering the danger that loomed around every corner, he simply didn't care anymore. He was on his fourth tankard. Or was it the seventh? He'd lost count. Twanging chords from the zither-and-fiddle duo playing nearby drowned out any nascent misgivings.

"Hey, if the purser's not complaining, then we must be doing something right," Lotte said. Like Taki, she'd also drained more than her fair share of tankards. She grabbed a full one and raised it. "A toast, you minions!"

Taki raised his pint. "Er, to what?"

"To Tirefire the Lesser! May the glorious name of our squad e'er be—"

"Consecrated in shame!" Draco said, and drained his mug.

"Show some pride, damn you," Lotte said. "We're just as good as the other companies. Even though we, like, lost a castle and let a duke get killed and got our arses kicked by..."

"Heathen scum," Draco said with a laugh.

Lotte waved a sausage to Karma and Hadassah, who were in the process of furiously making out. "Hey! No fucking in public, you two."

Hadassah flashed a fig in response and drained her beer before returning her attention to petting.

"I *hate* couples," Draco said. "Happy people in love should just die."

"Sinners." Lotte ripped a chunk of sausage away with her teeth.

Draco grinned. "Say, I've got an idea, Captain. Why don't the rest of us poor saps all hit a cathouse?"

Taki raised an eyebrow. "You mean, hire a..."

"Good idea, Emreis," Lotte said. "I'm lonely enough to bang either of you at this point, and that's a problem."

"A true emergency!" Draco howled. "Off we go, then. I'm gonna choose me a wench who looks like Hundred-Arms Mezeta!"

Taki's cheeks reddened, and he turned away so Lotte couldn't see him. He still hadn't forgotten what it felt like to be kissed by her. He'd become awkward in her presence since that time but hadn't found the gumption to talk about it with her. But if she was lonely, and they were both drunk enough, perhaps there was no better moment.

And if I'm to meet my end soon, I might as well. For all the good it'll do. He reached for her. "Captain, a word?"

Before he could speak further, someone checked him from behind, and the contents of his tankard sloshed in his lap. His bolted from his stool and frantically tried to wipe the sodden mess from his leggings. Beer worked its way through the seams in the leather and chilled his manhood.

To have his clothing fouled was irksome, and for it to happen in front of his squad was embarrassing, if ultimately inconsequential. But to have it happen in front of Lotte burned in a way he hadn't predicted. To make matters worse, she laughed merrily along with Draco and the others. Taki whirled to face the cause of this disaster.

A burly man with a lieutenant's chain chuckled and started to walk away.

"Hey!" Taki said. "Apologize, you lout!"

The lieutenant turned and gave Taki a snort. "Shouldn't have been in my way."

"Lowly cur. I *said* apologize!" Taki grasped at the man's shoulder, only to be swatted off.

"You ready to back that up with steel?"

"I can do better," Taki said. Prana tingled at his fingertips. *Yes, this isn't the Temple. I can blast him.*

"Wait, I've seen you," the lieutenant said. "In Athenaeum. You were the old basil's catamite!"

"I wasn't a catamite!"

"What else could you have been? Certainly not a guard. Niketas loved boys, though."

"You bastard, I did nothing of the sort." Taki's face burned, and he clenched a fist. He needed to cow the arrogant ass in front of him, even if something rational within begged him not to. *"In fact, I'm the one who killed him!"*

Lotte's hand clamped over Taki's mouth. "That's enough!"

A small crowd had watched the argument out of prurient interest but resumed their conversations without missing a beat. The lieutenant shook his head and left to mingle.

Lotte eased her hand away. "How besotted are you?"

"S-sorry, Captain. I had too much," Taki said. He shook and tried to take a seat.

"Heaven defend our asses," Draco said, and grabbed Taki by an ear. "Hold your liquor, man!"

"Quiet, Emreis," Lotte said. She looked furtively around. "How many people heard?"

"You actually worried, Captain? No one would ever believe *Natalis* to be a regicide. I mean, he's not, right?"

Lotte peered at the crowd once more. "If that lieutenant really saw him in the capital, there could be trouble. We should leave."

"Then, to a house of ill repute?"

"Aye, wherever. Just get us out of here."

Before they could rise from their seats again, a nearby door opened, and three cloaked figures glided in and took their hoods off. Taki's bleary eyes opened wide in recognition at the man and especially the two women; his throat constricted, and his chest felt crushed in a vise. "Tirefire the Lesser, you are all a sodden mess," the man said, and crossed his arms.

Taki fought the urge to shit down his leggings at the sight of Aslatiel von Halcon, the Oberleutnant commander of Alfa Gruppe. Out of the millions of Imperial soldiers that made up the eastern hordes, Alfa were the most feared, respected, and hated. Their officers' faces were known throughout enemy lands, and each carried a sizeable bounty on his or her head. Any companies that had dared engagements with Alfa had all met grisly ends, save for Taki and his companions.

To Aslatiel's right was a sapphire-eyed, raven-haired beauty with a slasher smile. Even more feared than her brother, Lucatiel von Halcon had once reduced a hundred fully-armored chevaliers to oozing mincemeat with little more than her bare hands. Known from that encounter as the "Prince of Maladies," Lucatiel's odd title chilled the bones of veterans and fresh conscripts alike.

On Aslatiel's left was a blond woman Taki identified as Irulan Surenovna, Alfa's commissar and the Imperial padishah's eyes and ears on the front lines. With the authority to land even Aslatiel in the gulag for the slightest hint of sedition, she was possibly the most dangerous of the three. Taki also remembered that she was an excellent shot, to boot.

The tavern went silent for a moment and then exploded into whispers and pointing.

"Oh, for fuck's sake!" Draco said. He pinched himself before whispering in Taki's ear: *"Bad news. It isn't a dream."*

"Imperial pigfuckers!" someone in the crowd bellowed. "Get the hell out of here!"

Aslatiel ignored the jeers and bowed to Taki. "We meet again, Taki Natalis."

Taki grimaced and tried to make himself smaller. It was awkward enough to be approached by Imperials in a tavern full of drunken, restive Polaris sore from losing a war. But it was another matter entirely to have an enemy commander greet him personally in front of the same resentful crowd.

"Why do those bastards know shitty Tirefire?" another Polaris shouted.

Aslatiel put up a warning finger. "Our nations have signed an accord of cooperation and cease-fire. We are not your enemy. We're from the Imperium, and we're here to help."

Taki scanned the tavern. Many had now armed themselves with bottles, tankards, and knives. The wave of mounting anger was almost palpable. They had lost friends during the war. Vengeance was a right, treaties be damned. He returned his attention to the three Spetsnaz at the center. Aslatiel seemed unconcerned, but the two women behind him tensed for action. *Go away, dammit,* he thought at Aslatiel.

"Hey," the burly lieutenant from earlier said. He stared at Taki. "Didn't you say you killed the basileus?"

Taki's stomach turned. "I merely jested—"

"And now your Imperial masters are here to take you away! I didn't believe it, but God *damn.* You're a traitor! You're a regicide! Everyone, to arm—"

Lotte's fist crashed into the lieutenant's jaw and bowled the man over, but it was too late to stop the rallying cry from sounding. As if a hive of angry bees had dropped from on high, the Dawnbringer erupted into chaos.

Taki was rushed by two cornets and thrown across the table, knocking a heap of sausages and bread to the floor. Made slick by spilled beer and grease, he slid easily off the edge and crashed to the ground. A boot stomped on his midsection and turned the world into a blurry mess. He curled into a ball until the cornets were distracted by a thrown bench, and then he crawled his way through a tangle of snarled furniture and legs.

When he'd regained his wind, he sprang to his feet despite his throbbing belly. A chair smashed against his back, but the wood was rotted and it snapped without knocking him over. Taki wheeled on his attacker and smashed his fist into a scruffy face. The man stumbled back and was absorbed into the hateful melee within moments, earning Taki a moment of respite. He hopped on top of a grand table to try to locate his companions.

He saw Hadassah smash a stool into another woman's shoulder and knee another in the groin. Despite her triumph, a glass sailed across the room and smashed into her head, dropping her out of sight. Nearby, Karma ducked to avoid the swing of a broken bottle and swept at the feet of a lance corporal to knock him down before being kicked in the back and bowled over. A sergeant groped at Lotte's chest, and she pitched him out of a nearby window for his trouble.

With great cacophony, enforcers of the Black Cross stormed the tavern with shields and cudgels in hand. The brawlers forgot about the Imperials and each other and now fought the lawmen with relish.

A flailing man sailed through the air next to Taki, narrowly missing him. But someone was also trying to sneak up from behind him. There was no time for a sutra. He wheeled on the new adversary, aiming a solid kick at her midsection.

Lucatiel gave Taki a derisive snort as she caught his ankle in a joint lock and threw him to the wooden tabletop. His eyes widened as they met hers, and he yelped when he caught the unmistakable flash of steel in her hand. *Shit!* He tensed for death. With a dull thud, the fighting dagger sank almost to its hilt in the rough oak, right next to Taki's ear.

"That's for Pristina," she hissed, and eased her knee off of his chest. Another Polaris tried to tackle her from behind, only to be unbalanced and thrown off the side like discarded bread crust.

Taki patted frantically at his head to make sure that she hadn't simply driven the knife into his brain without his knowledge.

Lucatiel cuffed him across the cheek. "Stop flailing! Meet us in the alley nearby!"

"Why are you even here? Why are you people always trying to screw me?"

"Pissant! Do as I say, or I'll cut your balls off!"

Not wishing to inflame her further, Taki took a running leap from the table top and careened out of one of the nearby windows into the darkness outside. An earlier shower had made the ground muddy, and he slipped up on the landing and thumped his rear on the dirt.

Taki groaned, rolled onto his belly, and pulled himself to his feet. The night had taken one bad turn after another. Nothing could ever be simple or go pleasantly, at least not while he remained in Tirefire the Lesser. Even his plans to go to the cathouse had failed in spectacular fashion.

But if I'm to die anyway...

Taki reached into the small sack on his belt and came up with a pair of brass Lugers. They were more than enough to buy him admission to the Kitten Pile, which Draco had always raved about. He didn't need to listen to the insane Imperial woman. She was still an enemy, no matter what some treaty said. Furthermore, if the three Alfa hadn't shown up, perhaps things would have recovered in the end. He wouldn't have been outed in front of his fellow Polaris and might have ended the night correcting his most shameful character flaw. But now it had all turned to shit.

He couldn't change much right now, except for one thing. For a moment, he considered the slim possibility that Draco and the others were being lined up against a wall and shot by Imperial infiltrators. Or being cudgeled to a crimson pulp by angry Black Cross thugs. The images made him almost want to seek his squad out.

Oh, fuck them!

If his time with his companions had taught him anything, it was that the four were like roaches who always found a means to survive—or even prosper—amid chaos. They would be fine without him for a night. Taki smoothed his tousled hair and tromped off in the direction of the Kitten Pile.

* * * *

Later, he let out a quavering sigh and allowed himself to smile. The Triada Suite was the epitome of ostentatious luxury. He soaked in a cast-iron enameled tub large enough for four, with rose petals floating atop freshly boiled water scented with cardamom and citrus oil. Though he'd been advised to wait for a spell before entering the bath, he'd disregarded the instructions and immediately immersed himself. As a result, his skin had flushed to the point where he resembled a boiled crayfish, but he minded not. After such a terrible night, he needed this.

His thoughts wandered to his companions. They were either dead in a ditch or piled on top of each other in a prison cart. Either way, they were freezing, wet, and smelly. *Good,* he thought spitefully, and took a swig of wine from a glass nearby. In just a few minutes, the woman he'd chosen would arrive. Then, he'd be able to stop obsessing over a stupid kiss that didn't mean anything.

Taki heard the door unlatch. He smiled and kept his eyes closed while a pair of footsteps approached. There was no need to hurry things. Moments like this were meant to be savored. Someone sat nearby on the edge of the tub.

"Would you like to join me?" Taki purred.

In reply, a hand dipped into the water. Fingertips brushed over his chest and traced languid patterns across his skin. A woman—he could tell by a certain indescribable quality of her scent—leaned in close to his face, and her breath tickled his earlobe. Her hand wandered lower, down the center of his abdomen, ever closer to his sex.

Taki sighed with anticipation and slowly opened his eyes. It was time to behold the woman who'd make him a man.

Lucatiel grinned back at him. "What? Were you expecting some cute girl?"

Taki opened his mouth and let out a shrill scream.

* * * *

Later, he hurriedly toweled the luxury-scented bathwater off while silently fuming and cursing his rotten luck. Under other circumstances, he might have thanked his creator for the fact that Lucatiel hadn't turned him into a rosewater-scented corpse. But now there was only bile. His companions weren't free from his ire, either. In fact, he suspected they'd encouraged the Prince of Maladies to drop in and terrorize him in the first place. He threw on his rank-smelling shirt and emerged from behind the partition into the suite.

His squadmates were busy wallowing in crapulence brought on by the wine and food he'd paid for in the room he'd paid for. Draco was even neck-deep in the tub while Hadassah sat on the edge and soaked her bare feet. Periodically, she applied a pumice stone to the rough spots on her heels. To Taki, they might as well have been in their barracks, save for the fact that the deadliest fighters in the Imperium were within arm's length.

"I'll ask again," Aslatiel said. "What happened? Why were you all piss-drunk and getting into a barfight?"

Lotte shrugged and downed a glass of wine. "Why'd you think it was a good idea to walk into a tavern full of besotted Polaris who've lost friends to your kind?"

Aslatiel shook his head. "I concede that, but I thought Principality Mezeta had warned you of our arrival. I sent a letter by courier weeks ago. When we arrived at the Temple, we nearly had to fight your gate watch. We only ended up in this town by coincidence."

"That was your first mistake!" Draco said. "*Never* trust Mezeta. Hide her missives. Leave rooms when she is present. *That's* how you survive being *us!*"

Lotte shushed him with a gesture. "You wouldn't have known it, Imperial, but the principality is a fickle sort. She takes great pleasure from causing strife and hardship."

"I believe you," Aslatiel said, and shook his head. "Now, to the business at hand."

"Hold a second!" Draco waved frantically and sprayed water around him. "Sorry, Imperial, but this chance doesn't come every day. Now that you aren't trying to kill us, I want you to tell me why your armies haven't advanced past the ruins of Berlin. You know, the big pit of burning rubber. Why have your forces been doing nothing for years? Surely that's ruinously expensive? Are you saying we should've set more stuff ablaze to stop you?"

"*You're* the one who said they've got this animalistic fear of fire," Hadassah said.

"All animals fear fire," Lucatiel said. She rose from a squat in front of the small fireplace warming the suite and withdrew a poker from the embers. She then stood over Draco and fixed a scowl at him. Steam and sizzle erupted from the water when she plunged the red-hot metal in and let it hover right over his manhood. "I bet you do, too."

Draco paled and shrank away from her. "I said *atavistic*, not *animalistic*?"

"That's the same thing!"

"Dear sister, *not now*," Aslatiel said. "And unfortunately, Master Emreis, I cannot answer your question. That's classified information."

Lotte cleared her throat. "Now *I'll* ask again. Why are you here?"

"We came here to retrieve a member of your squad."

"Who?"

Aslatiel pointed. "Cornet Taki Natalis."

Bile rose in Taki's throat. He blinked, cowlike and stupefied. "Me?"

"Yes, you."

Lotte stepped closer to Aslatiel and bored her gaze into the top of his head; she was almost a hand's breadth taller than he. *"For what purpose, Imperial?"*

Aslatiel cleared his throat. "Come the morrow, Cornet Natalis will no longer be a Polaris of the Temple. He will be Spetsnaz in service of the padishah of the Imperium. I'm also permitted to conscript the rest of you as I see fit—"

"Whoa!" Hadassah said before losing her balance and falling backward off the edge of the tub. Her foot clipped Draco on the chin, and the pumice stone flew in the air to smash into fragments against a wall. She rolled to her feet and pointed accusingly at Aslatiel. *"Whoa!"*

"Dassa, what the *hell?*" Draco reeled and rubbed his chin.

"These guys tried to kill us!"

"Did you just realize that right now? And they are not 'guys.' There are two women and a man. Be polite."

"Don't sass me! This is really suspicious! Why are you Spetsnaz even here? Are you here for revenge? Have you come to do Natalis in the *butt?* He's a virgin, you perverts!"

"There will be no further aggression," Aslatiel said. "We have no scores to settle—"

Hadassah shook her fist. "Don't tell me we're supposed to go and follow your orders now. We listen to *our* captain, not *you*. I don't give a damn what colors I'm supposed to wear."

"Shut up," Taki said. His earlier shock was now replaced by realization. "He came for *me*, Dassa. You were there with me when we spoke with the basileus. Now I see what her 'other option' was." He let out a ragged chuckle. "Just never figured she'd go to these lengths."

"Natalis," Lotte said, "what the hell are you talking about? What's this business with Her Grace?"

"Oh, Captain," Taki said, "I'm being banished. I met with the basileus when you sent me to the capital. She told me I couldn't stay in the country but promised not to execute me all the same. So I'm being exiled. I'm sorry I kept it from you. I didn't want you to get involved."

"Is this because of…"

"Yeah."

Lotte grimaced and started to pace.

"I can assure you, Captain, that he'll be well treated," Aslatiel said. "I came here for a recruit, not a prisoner bound for the gallows."

"Tell me, Sir Aslatiel," Taki said, "am I right? Is this what Her Grace desired?"

Aslatiel smiled. "Your new liege wanted you sent to a forgotten outpost on the frontier. But when her request came to my attention, I could not ignore it. Luckily for me, *Ba'gshnar* listened."

"But why me?"

"Because although we first met as enemies, I was impressed by you, Taki Natalis. Impressed in a way I haven't been for a long, long time."

"So you *do* want his ass!" Hadassah said.

Taki wheeled on her. "Dammit, Mikkelsen, no one wants my ass!"

"Actually, a few girls I know and at least one of the guys do. You're just awkward and unlucky. And a kingslay—"

Lotte cleared her throat. "Do I have any say in this, Imperial?"

Aslatiel shook his head. "Even if you did, would you defy us and place Natalis in danger? This s the only way."

Taki averted his gaze. He did not want to see what was on Lotte's face. If he did, there was a chance that he would make a stupid decision that would end in his death. *But if I let go and start anew, especially under someone like Sir Aslatiel…*he balled his hands into fists. He'd miss Lotte, and perhaps even the rest of them, but his life and career were at stake again. He straightened his back. "Then I'm your man, Sir Aslatiel."

Aslatiel nodded. "I hoped you'd say that, Natalis. In the morning, you'll be given your severance papers and pension. The arrangements have already been made. And, as I've said before, I've also been given permission to conscript your squadmates. But only if they agree."

"Hell, no," Hadassah grumbled. "I'm *definitely* not fighting for the celestial glory of the Paddy-shaw or some nonsense."

"I won't go if she won't go," Karma said.

"The padishah is neither a god nor a megalomaniac, and he should not be regarded as such," Aslatiel said. "His dream is to enlighten all sentient beings through the Way."

"Great," Draco huffed. "Buncha fanatics after all. Count me out as well."

Lucatiel hit Draco with a gimlet stare, and he sank back down to eye level. *"Dassa, help. The Prince of Maladies is looking at me funny."*

"And how about you, Captain?" Aslatiel said. "I would welcome someone of your strength and prowess to our number. The Temple clearly doesn't respect your skill."

Lotte shook her head. "I can't do that, Imperial. I swore to serve the Temple and will do so until I perish. I cannot change my stars. Not now."

Aslatiel nodded. "So be it."

＊ ＊ ＊ ＊

The squad sweated out their hangovers trudging up the road to the Temple. The Black Cross's blockade had been lifted that morning, and a trickle of Polaris wound the ancient path like ants from a tankard of spilled beer.

Draco yawned and stretched his arms. His breath steamed in the mountain air. "The Imperials aren't coming with us, eh?"

"Well, there's no reason for it," Karma said. "After all, we're just here to see Natalis off. What're they going to do in the meantime? Go sightseeing? Get a blowie from the archangels?"

"Ew, Karma," Hadassah said. "I was actually feeling patriotic until you mentioned those creeps. Now I almost want to strip naked and dance in front of some Imperial altar."

"If you want to join up, I won't hold it against you," Karma said. "The padishah may have pretensions of divinity, but he controls half the known world. Our 'angelic' masters are a creep, an obsessive witch, and a thug who runs a prison for cursed children."

"You know," Hadassah said, "we *could* just tell the shrine that we're switching sides. Then they'd have to give us our discharges and bullets. We'd have our freedom and a sack of grad. We could be sellswords and travel the world!"

"Ye gods, Dassa, you're right!" Draco said. He smacked a fist into his palm. "Natalis, you won't rat on us, right? I mean, it makes no difference to you what we do from here on. We'd visit you, I swear!"

Lotte's boots crunched the gravel with extra emphasis. "It's far too early for this much treason. You mongrels can *run* the rest of the way up. On the double!" She swung her hands and smacked Draco and Hadassah on their rumps. They fled in terror, leaving a cloud of dust.

"But I didn't say anything," Karma cried. Lotte swung out her foot to kick him, and he bolted forward.

Taki shook his head, grateful that Lotte had spared him from yet another bout of harassment. In truth, he was now glad to be rid of the others. Once, he'd thought them his friends, but after the past few weeks of poverty and the accompanying nastiness, his esteem for them had all but vanished. A part of him had wanted to say "yes" to Hadassah's plan, but likely such a scheme would have led to everyone's executions. Melodic cursing echoed from above, courtesy of the rest of the squad. *Perhaps I like them a little bit. Just not enough to waste my life for.* Lotte, on the other hand, was a different story.

"Captain, I apologize for last night," he said. "I drank too much and acted rashly."

"You were stupid as hell," Lotte said. "I should whip you for that."

He gave her a cocky grin. "Are you even allowed to do that anymore?"

"Perhaps not. But I'll warn you that the Imperial Army is a harsh place. Their punishments are brutal, and they demand more discipline than the exarch. If you don't watch yourself, you could end up on the wrong side of a noose."

"Aslatiel doesn't give me that impression."

"On a first-name basis already?"

"No!"

"Taki. Listen to me," Lotte said.

He blinked. She'd never called him by his given name before.

She stopped and cupped his face in her hands. "Promise me you'll be careful. The Imperials are different from us. They'll want you to conform above all else. And for your sake, you'd better learn to see the padishah as not just your king but something more. Maybe even as your god. Learn from von Halcon, but remember that he's not your friend. None of them are."

"Aye, Captain."

"And, if things should ever turn awry, if the Dominion should ever seek to rebel, if you face me or any of us on the battlefield..." She trembled. "Make sure you kill us first."

His mouth was dry. "Cap—"

She shook him. "I'm not done yet! Just one last thing from me, and then you'll need to start your new life. You have great power but also a kind heart. I'm happier having known you. If you'd been older, or we'd been closer in rank, I might've...we might've..." A tear coursed down her cheek. "But don't worry about it now. Just promise me you won't settle for any old wench."

Taki felt his face tighten and his chest grow heavy. He clasped his hands over hers. "Dammit, Lotte, I'm sorry!"

"Don't be sorry. You—"

"I'm sorry I ever got dragged into that mess! I didn't mean to kill him. I just wanted to see things change. I couldn't get those villagers' faces out of my mind! I had to do something, and I got used like a tool and thrown away, and now I'll never see you again. Shit, I'll never see the others again, even though Dassa's kind of a bitch and Draco's a liar and Karma's a creeper..." He started to sob in earnest. "I'm so sorry!"

Lotte threw her arms around him and held him for a long time. Eventually, they trudged up the mountain in silence.

* * * *

On the opposite side of the barred window, a craggy-faced neokóros of the Shrine mumbled to himself while he stamped several pieces of vellum with a wax seal.

"Never thought I'd have the pleasure," the man said, and pushed them forward. "I always thought I'd prepare your warrants for the gallows, but this will do just fine. Here's for Cornet Natalis."

Lotte took the precious roll of vellum, unfurled it, and checked the seal. The exarch's signet ring had made a deep, clear impression in the wax, and only a few of the words were misspelled. The scroll was Taki's only proof that he was not a deserter and not immediately subject to hanging or worse. "And…you're free."

Taki smiled and marveled at his new possession. "Aye, feels good."

Lotte glanced expectantly through the bars. "Sir, aren't you forgetting something?"

"I don't believe so," the neokóros said.

"Now's not the time for jests. Where's this soldier's pension?"

The man cracked a smile of rotting teeth. "I thought you'd been apprised of that, milady Captain."

"Apprised of *what*?"

"Why, just a few bells ago, I was visited by Principality Mezeta herself. What a lovely and fearsome woman she is."

"Get to the point."

"Aye, milady. Well, the principality informed me that she'd personally take care of giving Cornet Natalis's payment to him. I had no right to question her, so I gave her the full sum. She also informed me that as of today, the squad disgracefully known as 'Tirefire the Lesser' had also been discharged from all duties as Polaris of the Temple. I was surprised that you only seemed interested in Cornet Natalis's walking papers, when I've prepared them for all of ye. Then, she took all other pension payments as well."

Lotte grew pale. "And where is the principality now?"

"Oh, milady, she gave me such a shock! After the principality received your funds, she disgracefully tore her chain of office from her neck and tossed it under the window to me. I believe she may have deserted and absconded with your milligrad. Naturally, I wasn't in a position to stop her."

"Wait a godrotting second," Taki said. "You mean that Hecaton Mezeta fired everyone and ran off with our money?"

"You could say that, young master."

Taki wrenched the bars so hard they shook in their casement. "You let her desert with *five hundred rounds and didn't tell anyone?*"

"Remove your hands from the grate lest I call the Cross on you," the neokóros said with a grin. "Now, I'll kindly ask you *civilians* to leave."

* * * *

For the third time in his career, Taki found himself held at bayonet point by the authorities. Except this time, they were intent on shooing him out of the Temple as quickly as possible rather than trying to herd him into a cell or onto a scaffold. A hobnailed boot pushed roughly against his rear end, and he stumbled to the dusty ground outside the iron gates. Lotte followed right after, although without a kick to the buttocks. One of the Black Cross dumped a stack of vellum rolls on the ground, spat, and then turned his back. Taki slowly got to his feet and turned just in time to see the gates shut with an ear-splitting clang.

"Captain," Draco said. He sat on a nearby boulder, nursing a swollen, purple cheek. "What in Christendom just happened?"

"We've been let go," Lotte said. She pointed at the scrolls strewn on the gravel. "Those are our papers."

"What do you mean 'let go'?" Hadassah said. She picked up one of the scrolls and opened it. "What the hell is this? I thought they only let Natalis out!" Something frantic crossed her face, and she tromped up to the gates. "Hey! Let me back in! There's been a mistake!"

A Polaris walking the ramparts overhead spat at her, and she barely dodged the revolting brown glob. She picked up a handful of gravel and chucked it back. The stones plinked off the walls. "Bastard, let me the hell in right now! My *stuff's* in there! I have a *wheel of cheese* under my pallet! If it goes bad, I'll kill you all!"

"Seems legitimate," Karma said, sniffing at his vellum and pressing a nail into the wax. "Principality's orders, and sealed by the exarch. We're…we're all free men now."

Draco grinned. "Not the way I thought I'd end things. Thought I'd wind up dead in the mud or starving in an alley." He started to pace. "Shit! Now what do I do? I should settle down. Buy some land and become a farmer. Maybe I'll be a burgher somewhere! Captain, where's the pension? I'll take my share right now and…" He wrung his hands and skidded to his knees in front of Lotte. "And I might as well ask now! Will ye marry me?"

Lotte fixed a hollow stare at him. "It's all gone. She walked off with our grad."

Draco chuckled. "I understand if you want to take time and think about it. But I promise you I'd be a dutiful husband and my whoring days are behind me and..." He blinked. "What? The grad's gone?"

"Gone."

"But the Code promised us! I mean, we've just got our clothes and that's it! H-how will I buy my farm? Who the hell took my bullets?"

"Hecaton Mezeta."

"How?"

Lotte rubbed her temples. "She asked for them. She got them. She walked away. She...betrayed us."

Something dark crossed Draco's features. "Where is she?"

"I don't know. She's powerful. She could be anywhere. And you're not strong enough to confront her, even if you somehow found her. None of us are."

"Not individually," Aslatiel said. "But together, with *Ba'gshnar* guiding us, even Hecaton Mezeta will have something to fear."

Taki looked up from where he'd squatted in the dirt. Mounted on a coal-black charger and clad in the regal battle dress of an Imperial officer, Aslatiel looked even more imposing than ever. Taki's heart quickened to see the man and four other Alfa waiting on horseback nearby. Unlike before, however, the sight did not provoke instant visions of death. Instead, Taki felt something else: inspired.

"You!" Hadassah said. She stormed up to Aslatiel. "You made this happen, didn't you? Can't you just stop screwing us?"

"I had nothing to do with it," Aslatiel said. "I have no love for Hecaton Mezeta, and she clearly has no respect for me. We were just here to retrieve Natalis." He gestured to Taki. "Are you ready?"

Taki took a step forward. He forced himself not to look at his former squadmates. Like roaches, they'd find a way to survive. They had their freedom. Meanwhile, his new life beckoned. He would finally gain what he wanted. "I am."

"Then, let's be off. Lucatiel, bring the spare mount..."

"Hold a moment," Lotte said.

Aslatiel cocked his head. "Captain?"

"Do you know where she is? Mezeta?"

"No. But she is a grave threat to my people if she's gone off on her own. We will certainly find her. And if needed, we will kill her."

"I forbid it!"

Aslatiel shrugged. "You'll forbid nothing."

"If anyone kills her," Lotte said, "it'll be *me*. It's my *right*, you godrotting Imperial swine! I'll do whatever it takes. I'll even join your army!"

"Really?" Aslatiel let out a snort. "Will you prostrate yourself before the padishah? Accept me as your superior? Follow my orders? Salute my flag? You'll really debase yourself that much for revenge?"

"Yes." Lotte fell to her knees and pressed her forehead on the dirt. "If that's what I must do to find and kill the bitch!"

"And me too," Draco said. "Mezeta's ruined my life. I aim to ruin hers." He kowtowed beside Lotte.

Hadassah, whose face was streaked with tears and grime, grumbled something unintelligible and did the same.

"I just want my bullets, so count me in," Karma said. He took his hat off and bowed with a flourish.

"Forgive me, but I highly doubt your sincerity. Fare thee well." Aslatiel tugged at his reins.

Taki's hand shot out and grasped the ankle of Aslatiel's calfskin boot. "Sir Aslatiel, I can vouch for them. I beg you to reconsider." He locked eyes with his new commander. *What the hell am I doing?*

"I was under the impression you held them in disdain," Aslatiel said. "Sending Lucatiel to your room instead of the wench you'd hired was their idea, after all."

Taki bit the inside of his cheek. Hard. "Please grant me this boon, Oberleutnant."

Aslatiel chuckled. "Fine, but I've only brought one extra mount. They'll have to walk."

"So be it," Taki said, and grinned.

3

Taki was farther from home than he'd ever been. For the last season, he'd evaded death from storms aboard an Imperial carrack, ridden a rusty iron serpent through the sands of a shifting desert, and itched sand from every possible orifice on the human body. Whatever beauty the Imperium's enormous territories possessed had been overwhelmed by the sheer horror of travel, and there was yet more to come. They headed relentlessly east for a destination deep within the heartland, a place Aslatiel called "Xizhang" but refused to divulge more about.

For the last month, Taki had been tasked with guard duty on an Imperial caravan. With twenty heavy wagons overloaded with supplies, this stretch was the slowest and most monotonous part of the journey thus far. He rode with the crates and barrels, squeezing in wherever he could and sleeping next to the wagons when they made camp for the evenings. He caught himself ofttimes wishing for an encounter with bandits, as there was often nothing to do but watch the sun's slow arc through the sky while inhaling the stench of horses and dust.

At first, Taki had feared that his former squad would cause no end of ruckus once Aslatiel had announced they'd be traveling to the opposite end of the world. But to his surprise, Lotte and the others simply assented and had even made themselves useful. A shadow seemed to have sapped everyone's usual truculence, and Taki could not remember a time when he'd exchanged fewer words with any of them. He spent most of his time chatting with Aslatiel, whose time seemed more and more dear with the passing days. The other Alfa were polite but seemed to avoid him.

A day from the Xizhang border, rain turned the road to mud, forcing them to camp early. Hunting was out of the question, so the day's most filling meal was dried jerky and tea under a hastily erected tarp. Silence and boredom loomed, and the moistness and heat of the air threatened everyone's groins with ulcers.

Taki could take it no more. "Sir Aslatiel, may I impose for a word?"

"Yes, Fahnrich?"

Taki's rank still sounded grating and unpleasant to his ears. "Will you finally tell me what we're meant to do in this land of Xizhang? Why we've traveled east for so long, when the Ursalan front is to the west? I thought we'd be fighting the Rex."

Aslatiel swallowed his mouthful of tea and gingerly placed his cup on a nearby pallet. "Yes, I suppose it's time. You're right. Our coming task has nothing to do with our war with Ursala. Tell me, Natalis, what do you think of traitors?"

"I…" *Hate them?* Taki paused and closed his eyes. Bloodshot, lifeless eyes stared up at him from a ditch. "I think it depends on what they've done."

"You still think about that village, even now," Aslatiel said.

"Perhaps I do."

"There's no shame in remembering that. The murders were a grave injustice on the part of the Kosovar Duke. But we, on the other hand, have been ordered to face those with arms and the will to use them."

Taki nodded. "So we're here to put them down?"

Aslatiel's expression turned grave. "We're to eliminate a group who call themselves the 'Mandate of Heaven.' They're a new organization that probably arose from a consolidation of smaller cells, but they've already caused enough trouble to merit our presence."

"Why have they rebelled?"

"There are always those who hate and fear progress. The Mandate rebels are the remnants of the old, obsolete ways that kept us in darkness for so long. For them, education is a sin, and women are less than slaves. So they targeted a girls' school at Chumi Shengo and took prisoner any students they didn't kill."

"What about the teachers?" Taki asked. "Aren't they soldiers, too? Don't they usually fight these raids off?"

"Most of them died," Aslatiel said. "That in itself is highly unusual and suggests a more dangerous enemy than the territorial garrison can handle, so our kind get called in."

"So we're to go in and throw the rebels in the dungeon?"

"No. We're to annihilate them. The padishah wants every last member of the rebellion killed. We will send a clear message to any who would dare raise a hand against our Way."

Taki scrunched his brow. "Did you just say we're killing *everyone*?"

"Our law is very clear on this." Aslatiel said. "Those who use violence or coercion against efforts to promote education within the Imperium will be annihilated. Attacking a school is on par with assassinating the padishah."

"I understand suppressing a rebellion, but isn't that going a bit far?"

Aslatiel shook his head. "Without the foundation of education, the Imperium crumbles. And trying to make us crumble deserves nothing but death."

Lotte spoke. "I'd suspected as much. This caravan's full of weapons and ammunition, is it not?"

"It is, Captain," Aslatiel said. "I trust you haven't been opening the crates and allowing moisture to rust the ordnance?"

"I have more sense than that. But you can't ignore the smell of cordite and iron everywhere."

Aslatiel picked up his cup and refilled it. "You led the Argead legion at Helicarnassus, did you not?"

"A handful of phalanxes. Mostly wounded men dying of fever and unable to lock shields."

"And with those sorry specimens, you held off three companies of the padishah's own grenadier guards. You probably saved the life of the old basileus with your actions."

"And now he's dead."

"Do you regret that?"

She shook her head. "No. I only regret that not a man under my command made it to the next year."

"Captain," Aslatiel said, "I'll confess that I've never led more than a few squads into battle, whereas you've commanded an army. Our small company can't win against thousands of men on the field, so we'll need to rely on the territorial garrison. Will you help me command them?"

Lotte sighed. "I told you, Imperial, that I'd do anything to take revenge on Hecaton Mezeta. The faster we eliminate your rebels, the faster we can resume the search. I'll do whatever you wish."

"Thank you, Captain. May you walk the Way unopposed."

Taki fidgeted. "Sir Aslatiel, you keep mentioning the Imperial Way of yours. What is it, exactly?"

"It's exactly that: a way of life for those who serve the padishah."

"I figured as much. But I want to know more about it."

"You wish for me to explain the Way?" Aslatiel raised an eyebrow.

"Yes." Taki nodded. "We weren't taught anything about you people."

"We know a bit, Natalis," Draco said. Taki was startled to hear him. Ever-ebullient Draco hadn't spoken in a week. "Common knowledge is that the boys are all gelded and the women control everything. And that's why we should hate and fear the Osterbrand menace."

Hadassah glared at him. "And what's wrong that that?"

"With castration?"

"Don't play coy! I know exactly what part of that you *really* object to."

"I *really* object to having my tender places put to the knife!"

Aslatiel cleared his throat. "I'll explain. We want to restore the glory of humankind by uniting all people under our banner. Every Imperial citizen understands this and desires to serve the greater good. Once this world is whole in purpose, there will be no need for war."

"But you do so through conquest," Taki said. "Enlightenment borne on Imperial cannonballs."

Aslatiel nodded. "Force is the fastest way to bring about change. Or do you think the Duke of Kosovo would have stopped his massacres with a polite request?"

Taki's expression soured. "I'm not that naïve."

"Sorry, that was unfair of me. But if rumors are to be believed, perhaps you understand this simple fact best of all. You *did* assassinate your old liege, right?"

Lotte rose abruptly. "We should resume our posts."

"Please, Captain," Taki said. "I know you're trying to protect me, but I hate being the center of rumors. I can't stand keeping it a secret, and the others already have their suspicions. We're not in the Dominion anymore. I can be honest."

"Natalis, don't be rash."

"It's fine. Let them hear. Sir Aslatiel, and hell, Dassa, Emreis, Gillette…the rumors are true. I killed His Majesty."

Lotte swore under her breath.

Taki cast his eyes downward. "It was an accident. I hit him with a log." He shut his mouth and waited for the inevitable. They'd curse him. Someone would try to strike him.

Instead, Hadassah laughed. "You brained him with a *log*? You're so lame, Natalis. At least dress the story up a bit if you're going to confess to something so dunderheaded!"

Draco sucked his teeth. "You should've let me know a long time ago. Do you know how many women out there would *love* to fornicate with a real kingslayer? *And* his best friend and accomplice?"

Taki stared at him in confusion. "Emreis, you weren't even there."

"Then you'd better start thinking of how you can add me in. And Dassa's right, you have to improve your story. This is something that will go in the histories, after all. 'Log to the cranium' does not a woman's smallclothes remove!"

Aslatiel chuckled. "So we have you to thank, after all. When I saw you at the Hot Gates, I thought something had changed about you, but I knew not what."

Taki threw up his hands. "I didn't mean to kill him!"

"I know," Lotte said, and slung an arm around Taki's shoulder. She stared balefully at the others. "The rest of you are to be silent on this subject. We have enough trouble without miscreants trying to settle scores. And von Halcon, I'll take it as a personal slight if you or your men spread news of this to your commanders. Am I clear?"

Aslatiel nodded and sipped his tea. The patter of the rain against the tarp wore away, and the sun now bore down again. Though his companions smirked to themselves and the Spetsnaz seemed to watch him constantly from the corners of their eyes, Taki found his breathing easier now. As the lethargy of digestion set in, the old choking feeling that had taken up residence in the back of his throat was conspicuously absent.

* * * *

Lhasa, capital of Xizhang, was nestled in a large tributary valley flanked by soaring peaks accented with greenery and capped with white snow at their very tops. From far away on the road, it was a filthy jewel nestled in a palm that held up the blue expanse of the heavens with colossal pillars of billowing white cloud. As the caravan rounded a hill and the city came into view, the drivers erupted in a spontaneous cheer. For many of them, it was home.

Taki peered out from a gap in the canvas of his wagon and spied Aslatiel perched at the head of the convoy, surveying the roadway with binoculars. He turned his attention back to the others who shared the cramped confines with him.

Elsa Rana, a fahnenjunker in Alfa, rode in the back with Draco and Hadassah. She'd crossed blades with Taki at Vergina, then again in Pristina, and then at the Hot Gates. None of those times had afforded him a good look at her features, though. Up close, she almost resembled Hadassah, with a heart-shaped face and wavy, willful hair. Elsa's was kept gathered up in a high bun and was shot through with streaks of gold. So far, Taki had taken her for an aloof type.

"We'll probably hit the city in the late afternoon," she said. "Can you smell it?"

Taki shook his head. "I can't tell. It all seems the same to me."

"I hope you're right, Mistress Elsa," Draco said. "It would be a relief to get off the bumpy road."

"Be careful," Elsa said. "The air's thin here, different than in your land. Using sutra will be much more difficult. You'll lag much easier."

"That so? Explains why I've been feeling tired lately." Hadassah yawned. "Thought it was just my period."

"It's because of the elevation," Draco said. "The land generates air from deep fissures within the earth, and that's why we can breathe. But as you get higher and higher up, the heavens suck more and more of the air away to dissipate into aether."

Elsa seemed to perk up at this. "How did you know that? Most foreigners aren't aware."

"I've read the entire *Corpus Historicus Baudolinum Mundi*. All of the knowledge of the old world, or at least all of it that's worth writing down."

She raised her eyebrows. "Hey, wait a second. If you're lettered, why are you on the front lines with us? Did you screw up and impregnate some general's daughter?"

Draco flushed. "No, nothing like that. I just like to read in my spare time. It's not the manliest thing ever, but…"

She gave him a quizzical look. "I think it's pretty impressive, actually."

"I, uh…well, thanks." He looked away.

She poked him on the arm. "Did the book you read say anything about my homeland? It's the Himal Kingdom, just a few days south of here."

"Yes, actually," he said. "I was most fascinated with the fauna, you know. Giant unicorns with meter-long tusks and snake tails, and men with their faces in their chests. Giants, ogres, and the lost cities of Prester John!"

She grabbed him by the shoulders. "What did the book say about the *unicorns*? Is it true that they take virgins back to their caves and turn them into nymphomaniacs?"

"Absolutely! That's why you can't let one create a burrow around any village with a surplus of young people, or around a nunnery. Suddenly, babies everywhere."

Hadassah poked Elsa's arm. "Before you get too excited, remember that most of what he spouts was written by drunkards and sinners. They always write the most entertaining things—you know, stuff you want to hear."

"Dassa, please," Draco said. "We're having a discussion about *unicorns*. This is *important*."

Hadassah rolled her eyes in disgust.

Taki chuckled to himself at their exchange. One of the unforeseen advantages of such a long and tedious journey was the chance to talk with the individual members of Alfa Gruppe. Once, Elsa had been a vicious adversary, and now she had struck up a strange sort of friendship with Draco—a friendship based on lies written down hundreds of years in the past, but there were more tenuous things to base a relationship on.

* * * *

With the sun less than two fingers away from the horizon, the caravan finally entered the city. For Taki, the entire place smelled of yak butter. It was a sour smell, just shy of rancid, that seemed to suffuse every breath. The smell, combined with the musk of actual yaks, made his nostrils fill with mucus. Now that he was inside, however, he could see that this was really no different from most other cities he had been in. He considered investigating whether he could find grilled harspud on a stick.

"Natalis, we're getting off here," Lotte as she slapped the wooden side of the wagon with her palm.

Taki stepped over the rear grate and carefully hopped onto the packed dirt of the boulevard. It was good to finally be on his feet.

"The wagons will take a longer route to the headquarters, but we've got to make haste and meet their leader before too long," Lotte added.

"Yes, Captain," Taki said. "Where's the headquarters, anyway?"

"There." Lotte pointed, and Taki raised his eyebrows. Looming above the cityscape was the Potala, a massive, blocky keep set atop a hill and ringed with stone walls. Red in the center and white on its wings, it was as striking and overpowering to behold as the open sky.

"There?"

"Yes, there," Aslatiel said, shaking the dust from his cap. "The Korps uses the white parts to house its members and garrison, and the regional government uses the red. It's a symbol of authority for the people. I'm told that it was once a monastery that ruled an entire kingdom."

"Looks like a painful climb," Lotte said.

"It was built for aging monks, so there's gentle stairs everywhere. Let's get a move on."

From the outside, the Potala seemed absolutely massive, but on the inside, Taki found it to be cramped, smoky, and dark. *Just like what Eastern monks—and old Hecaton—would want for their lodgings*, he figured. The compound had also been built to withstand sieges and earthquakes. Redundancy was everywhere, from the thick wooden beams crossing overhead to the walls reinforced with ancient metal bands. Eventually, their Korps escort led them to an office on the top floor, and the two squads filed in.

"Glory to the padishah," Aslatiel said; he saluted a woman sitting at an ancient wooden desk. "I am Oberleutnant von Halcon. We're Alfa."

The woman at the desk did not rise but returned the salute. She was squat and looked to be in her fifties, with the leathery features of one who'd lived at high elevations all of her life. Taki noticed the wheelchair before the others did.

"Rinchen Wangchuk, the rector here. I command the garrison and schools. Zhang here is my second in command." She gestured to a lean-faced man behind her. "Forgive me for not rising to greet you, but I lost the use of my legs long ago. My sincere thanks to you for the quick response to our crisis. Please, sit and have some *pocha*. We always serve it to guests."

Zhang hefted a nearby silver-colored kettle and started to pour into bowls. Aslatiel accepted a bowl and sipped from it. Taki looked down at his bowl and decided not to try the oily, purplish liquid.

"There is nothing to forgive. Thank you for your hospitality," Aslatiel said. "Defense of Imperial education is our most important task."

"Glad to hear it," Rinchen said. "How was your journey here?"

"Uneventful. We look forward to getting to work. At our commander's request, we've also brought supplies and weapons for the garrison."

"Good. Most of our equipment is outdated. It was adequate for a peaceful province, but with the rebels gaining strength, we cannot answer them with mattocks and padded jacks."

"How many fighters do you have ready?"

"A thousand from the province. I have a dozen or so who could be line officers and a handful trained in the use of artillery."

"That's rather few for an army."

"We've never needed more. This is a harmonious place. No one's fired a gun in anger in nearly forty years. We're teachers and administrators first. Soldiers second."

"Your artillery forces? Cavalry strength?"

"A few catapults and a pair of bronze cannon." Rinchen shrugged. "Most people here can ride and shoot from horseback, but we have no armored kataphracts, if that's what you're asking for."

"How about the enemy? Do they use the same equipment?"

"Probably close to two thousand in number. I think they're being supplied by smugglers from the Nathu La pass. The teachers who survived recall seeing relic rifles and plate armor, and perhaps some bombs. When you see the school, you'll understand. We couldn't best them in a fight, not without your help."

"Do you know where they're holding their captives? The girls from the school?"

"Unfortunately, we don't. The rebels did a good job of covering their escape, and the men I sent after them have either been killed or found nothing. The people are scared and upset. There are over a hundred girls missing, and the terrorists are issuing unreasonable demands. They want the Korps to leave permanently and for the region to revert back to rule by the *Lamas*. I've tried to stall them as long as possible, but now they're saying they'll sell the girls off as slaves if we wait longer. We both know what will happen to them in that case. We can't track them all down."

"Rector," Aslatiel said, "I can assure you that we will find and eliminate the Mandate of Heaven. I'll need the full cooperation of your subordinates and the authority to issue orders to the garrison troops. Is this acceptable?"

"Can you rescue the girls?"

"If the rebels are dead, they cannot sell their captives."

Rinchen nodded. "I understand. You will have authority over my troops. Zhang will see to your quarters and allocations."

"Excellent." Aslatiel set his empty tea bowl on the desk. "One more thing, before I forget. A trainee should have arrived here direct from Sevastopol. Do you know where she is?"

"I'm afraid not. I'm told the girl came; however, she's not reported to me. Hopefully, she hasn't deserted."

Aslatiel raised an eyebrow. "Indeed. Thanks for your help. We will unload the supplies, survey the base, and then investigate the school in the morning." He looked back at the others. "Captain Satou and I will stay and talk more with the rector. The rest of you, follow Zhang and assist with the unloading."

* * * *

Strange. I'm the highest-ranking member of my squad right now, Taki thought as he followed Zhang down a side staircase that led back to the White Palace courtyard. Lucatiel followed alongside him. Her presence still raised his hackles. He could tell she still seethed over their duel in Pristina. His only comfort was that if she wished him dead, he would have been so already.

"You look troubled," Lucatiel said.

Taki blushed. Was it so obvious on his face? "Sorry. I was just thinking about the battle to come. Your brother was right. Your Imperium is always at war."

"We don't choose the life given to us."

"I'm curious about something he said. Surely we're also here to rescue the captives and prevent them from being sold as slaves or killed, right?"

Lucatiel shook her head. "No, he never said that. We're here to destroy rebels. If we can free some imprisoned schoolgirls, then we'll do so. If it's a choice between the girls and eliminating the rebels, we'll eliminate the rebels. Everything else is collateral."

"That's fuckin' shitty," Hadassah said. "How are you gonna conquer the world if you can't prevent your own people from getting raped to death?"

"Watch your tongue," Lucatiel said. "If the girls die, they die. But if we don't kill every single traitor, that only encourages more of them to crop up. And then you'll damn many more to the same fate as those girls."

"So we're supposed to turn a blind eye to those girls' right to live?"

Lucatiel spat. "No one has a right to live. Not you, not I, not anyone. Those girls know the risks. And if I need to carve through ten of them to hit one rebel, I'll do so without hesitation."

"You're pretty sick." Hadassah grunted in disapproval. "Maybe if you were better at what you did, you'd be able to save innocent lives."

Lucatiel wrapped a friendly arm around Hadassah's shoulders. "Fight me, bitch. Ten minutes, behind the Palace. Don't worry, I won't kill you. Far too much trouble."

Hadassah grinned and tenderly squeezed Lucatiel's hand. "You're on, girlfriend."

Taki narrowed his eyes. "Mikkelsen, don't you dare."

"No one likes an eavesdropper," the two shot back in unison.

"The caravan's pulled up," Zhang said as they stepped into the courtyard. The drivers had done a painstaking job of maneuvering through the congested and ill-planned streets of Lhasa, and the wagons were now arranged in a circle. "I've ordered my men and some of the garrison to help unload this all. I'd appreciate it if you Spetsnaz would post guard throughout. I'm sure the Mandate of Heaven knows you've arrived by now, but your presence will prevent them from trying anything for now."

"Will do," Lucatiel said. "My people and I will take the east flank. Natalis, you and your inferiors can do whatever. Just don't get in our way."

"They're not inferiors," Taki said. "Emreis and Gillette, watch the rear. Mikkelsen, you're on overwatch. Take turns surveying the base, too. I'll rotate between posts." Part of him expected them to either laugh or simply stare, but to his surprise, the others simply shrugged and went off to their posts.

"Oh, so they *do* listen to simple commands after all," Lucatiel said with a smirk.

As the tarpaulins were rolled back and fell aside, Taki realized: *we've enough weaponry for a small army.* Now he could see that the wagon train had been stuffed with implements of battle: stacked wooden crates of muskets and sabers, pikes and spears tied like cordwood, and sets of boiled leather and cloth armor bundled into sacks. Chattering in their native tongue, the garrison gleefully set to work pitching the valuable arms to waiting comrades.

Zhang flailed. "Careful, dammit!" One of the crates fell and broke into pieces, and cartridges rolled merrily every way. "Clean this up, and don't scratch the bullets. And no filching! This is your only defense from the rebels."

"I'm sorry, where are the jakes?" Taki asked a porter nearby. He would have to check on Hadassah soon, just to make sure she wasn't getting into a dustup with the Prince of Maladies. But first, he needed to attend to his bladder. The porter half nodded, half shrugged, and pointed unhelpfully at the perimeter fence. Annoyed, Taki decided to find the latrine himself.

The search ended up fruitless. Of all the mess of sheds and lean-tos near the perimeter fence, none seemed to have a toilet attached. Taki considered simply going against a wall when a jingling noise nearby quashed the thought. His bladder forgotten for the moment, he peered around a pile of pallets. A girl had scaled the top of the fence, avoided death by impalement on its spikes, and made her way down. Her movements were too feline, too wary, to be anything but a product of martial training. He stepped out to block her way.

"Halt!" Taki said, annoyed that his voice had almost cracked. "Who are you? Why did you climb in here instead of taking the gate?" His hand hovered above the holster at his waist. The girl was also armed—and with a first-class pistol too—but he could still beat her to the draw. She flashed him a look of indignation that quickly turned to sheepishness. As far as Taki could tell, she appeared to be his age or slightly younger, with a rounded face and curly, uncontrolled hair. She wore ill-fitting battle leggings stained with mud and dust and a thin linen top that was nearly translucent with sweat. Taki's eyes strayed involuntarily to her chest, which was still boyish in silhouette. He quickly looked away, hoping she hadn't noticed.

"Not so loud! I serve the padishah." She waved her hands to shush him. "I just got here, myself."

"Where are your papers?"

The girl reached carefully into a leather purse and pulled out a small pamphlet of bound parchment. Taki took it and flipped to the front page. The ink drawing was smudged but seemed to grossly match her features, and he quickly scanned over her name and company standard.

He raised an eyebrow. "You're with Alfa?"

She flashed him a row of gleaming white teeth behind sunburned, chapped lips. "Yep! Enilna Shpejtspate. I'm apprenticed to Aslatiel von Halcon." She saluted stiffly.

"Cornet Taki Natalis." He silently chided himself a moment later for slipping up the ranks.

"Corn? Are you a farmer?"

"No, I misspoke. I'm a fahnrich."

"That's too bad," she said. "An army marches on its stomach, so I thought maybe they'd put tactical farmers in the units. You know, harvest the wheat and thresh the oppressors!"

"What are you talking about? It takes an entire season to grow crops. You can't just plant grain on the front lines—" Taki realized with a start that he had forgotten entirely about preventing whatever mischief Hadassah was planning and also about the need to relieve himself. He shifted his feet, feeling harried again.

"So you *are* a farmer after all! No one else would know the ancient secrets of agronomy."

"What I told you is common knowledge!"

"You shouldn't be embarrassed about your profession. I think it's cool that you can coax food from the poisoned soils and stuff."

Taki waved his hands. "I need to get going. Nice to have met you and all…"

Enilna sidled up to him. "Hey, can you help me?"

Taki blinked.

"Thanks!" she said without waiting to hear his answer. She grasped his wrists and whisked him into a gap between a pair of tin-roofed sheds.

"What's goi—" Taki said.

Enilna clapped a hand over his mouth and pressed both of their bodies into a sliver of shadow. *"Shush! Elsa's coming,"* she whispered.

Taki heard the approaching footfalls of boots in the dust. He had many reasons to simply push Enilna away and report the intrusion. Though she seemed to have proper documents, they could always be forgeries. *Hell, she could have killed the real Enilna Shpejtspate for all I know, and I'm next.*

The logical, proper thing to do would be to shout for the guard and especially for another member of Alfa. But logic was nothing compared to the sensation of her pressed against him. His earlobes felt pleasantly warm, and his heart thudded in his chest. Occasionally, Enilna would press even harder when she heard Elsa stop.

Eventually, the footfalls faded after a tense, pleasant eternity. *I think she forced herself on me a little,* Taki thought as her hand came off his lips. Her fingers smelled earthy and sour but not unpleasant.

"Sorry," Enilna whispered. She looked genuinely apologetic. "I'm really sorry! I mean, not for hiding. I was supposed to be on base waiting to rendezvous with everyone, but I really wanted to explore some nearby ruins and thought I'd have time. Oberleutnant Aslatiel wouldn't care, but Commissar Irulan is a hardass. Okay, I must be off! Thanks for your help." She stepped away, gave a perfunctory bow, and scampered off.

Taki ran his fingers through his hair and blinked incredulously. "What the hell just happened to me?" His bladder twitched painfully, and he cursed his luck.

Hours later, he returned to the mess hall with a sore back and aching arms. Unloading had gone slower than anticipated, and everyone had been pressed into labor to complete the job before sundown. Crates of muskets and sheaves of pikes were surprisingly heavy, especially when there were a hundred to handle. Taki nodded to Aslatiel, who had already started to eat a meal of black bread with pickled cabbage topped with shavings of mutton. Beside Aslatiel was the blond woman, Irulan. Noticeably, they seemed to be playfully feeding each other, and the sight made Taki blush.

Lotte and the rest of his company were absent, save for Hadassah. She sat at the other end of the table, talking excitedly with Lucatiel. Taki furrowed his brow when he noted the bruises and split lips adorning the pair. He shot a warning glance at Hadassah, pulled out a seat across from Aslatiel, and wordlessly sat down to eat. The day had been grueling, and he was not entirely recovered from the journey. The soft glow of the sconces overhead invited dozing, but he resisted the temptation.

"There you are," Aslatiel said.

Taki blinked and realized that someone was standing behind him.

"Oberleutnant, I'm reporting for duty," Enilna said. She stood nervously at attention. It was obvious she hadn't bathed.

"Join us and eat," Aslatiel said, and gestured to the food.

Enilna nodded and took the seat next to Taki. She reached for a slab of bread, but Irulan's fingers caught her ears and twisted.

"Not so fast," Irulan said. "So, did you have fun playing around in the mud, climbing the fence, and molesting an officer?"

Enilna let out a pained chuckle. "Ah, nothing gets by you. I was merely discussing important supply logistics with our unit farmer."

"What are you even talking about? Natalis, you should've shot her."

Taki raised an eyebrow.

"Sorry, sorry. Can you let go now?" Enilna winced as Irulan twisted harder.

"Not until I'm done lecturing you. First, when you're given orders to stay in one place, that doesn't mean go and screw around in crumbling hovels. Second—" The clattering of a metal tray stopped Irulan midsentence.

"You!" Lotte stood wide-eyed nearby with the tray and spilt breadcrumbs at her feet.

Enilna's face lit up in recognition. "Big Sis!" She wormed her way out of Irulan's grasp, bounded over the table, and wrapped her arms around Lotte with crushing strength.

Lotte closed her eyes and smiled. She stroked Enilna's hair. "So you finally made it to Sevastopol."

"I did! I never thought I'd see you again. I thought you might have died. I thought—"

"You didn't lose my gift, right?"

"No. I could never do that," Enilna said and buried her face in Lotte's chest. "It reminds me of you."

Lotte's mouth twisted. "I want it back."

Enilna gasped and seemed about to burst into tears.

"Just kidding," Lotte said. "I had to get you back for shooting me in Kosovo."

Enilna blushed. She stepped back and crossed her arms in indignation.

"Wait," Taki blurted, "is *she* the one who killed Duke Hekmatyar?"

"The one and only!" Enilna grinned. "You got a problem with that?"

"No," Taki said. "Not at all. Actually, I think that's really amazing. It must've taken a lot of courage."

Enilna blushed deeper at that.

Nice to get her back as well, Taki thought.

"Actually, I have a problem," Hadassah said. "Because that asshole duke kicked it, we were all sentenced to peel potatoes while we waited to get hanged. I had to listen to these jokers"—she gestured at Draco and Karma—"whinge about how they couldn't find any privacy to wank it. Can you make me unhear that?"

"Ahem," Aslatiel said, clapping his hands twice. "It's time to return to matters of war. Everyone eat their fill because tomorrow, we start work in earnest."

4

"They opened the perimeter wall here," Aslatiel said. He dabbed at the crumbling, soot-blackened edges of blasted masonry with his fingertips. The hole was as wide as three men standing shoulder to shoulder, and just as tall. "Probably with a horse-drawn cannon firing explosive shells."

"Only a legion would have those," Lotte said. "Further proof that the Mandate is being supplied by someone from outside these parts." She stepped in through the hole, crouched in the dirt, and picked up a scorched brass case. "Rimmed Nagant—brass cases and good powder. Used milligrad to take out the tower watch and punch through the mantlets. Then they had free run of the place."

"Our foe is more dangerous than I thought," Aslatiel said. He crunched through the blackened grass and peered into the collapsed remains of one of the classrooms. Above him, Irulan and Hadassah stood watch on the remaining walls. They swept the grassy tundra with the muzzles of their rifles. No threat would sneak up on the squads under their watch.

"I can imagine how events unfolded," Aslatiel continued. "They rounded up all of the surviving teachers who didn't escape, along with the students tall enough to meet their eyes, and butchered them all against the walls." He pointed to where the concrete was riddled with pockmarks and the characteristic muddy color of old, dried blood.

"God," Taki said. He squatted for a moment to hide the sudden weakness in his knees. Visions of an older massacre started to flash in his mind. Convulsing bodies lined up in a trench to be mummified with quicklime. He shook his head to drive the memories back. This wasn't the time. Now, he had to be strong. "Why couldn't they just take more prisoners? Wasn't that their goal?"

"Because adults and teenagers can fight back," Aslatiel said. "They want helpless victims, not liabilities."

"Strange, though," Taki said. "They wanted to torch the place, so why did they pile up all these books and burn them separately?" He motioned at the charred remains of leather-bound texts in the courtyard.

"Because," Aslatiel said, "they wanted to make a statement." He reached into the ash pile and gingerly opened one of the scorched books. It fractured and fell to pieces in his hands. "To these bastards, learning is a sin, so it must be purged with fire."

"I don't care much about books, though," Lotte said, shaking her head. "I want the girls and where the Mandate of Heaven is hiding."

Elsa emerged into the courtyard through the hole and pointed to the smashed gates nearby. "They loaded the girls onto skid wagons and dusted the tracks. There are ruts nearby on the other side but no trail we can use. These are mountain men we're dealing with, so if they don't want to be found, we're out of luck. I sent Mikhail out there to search. If there's anything to find, he'll find it."

"Mikhail..." Taki rolled the name around his tongue. "The albino fellow..."

"Yes, the albino," someone said softly behind him.

Taki turned and immediately felt embarrassed. Fahnenjunker Mikhail Zhukov bore the most stereotypically Imperial of names and yet looked nothing like any easterner Taki had ever seen. Mikhail's features closely resembled those of tribesmen from the southern deserts, save for a complete lack of pigmentation. The man also never raised his voice above a whisper, forcing everyone else to quiet themselves and lean in if they wished to listen to him.

"Oberleutnant," Mikhail said, ignoring Taki. "The winds have obscured most of the tracks. Still, they couldn't have gone far, not overburdened and covering their trail." He drew a dagger and started to scratch a rough map in the dirt. "There are many ancient ruins out here, all abandoned. Any could house an army without the locals knowing. Five of the ruins nearby will allow quick strikes into Lhasa."

"Aye, thanks, Mikhail," Aslatiel said. "That narrows our search down considerably. There are eleven of us in total now, including the kadet. We should go out in two-person teams to reconnoiter each of the ruins."

"Wait, Imperial," Lotte said. "None of my people know the area well. The enemy does, however, and is expecting us. We'll be snuffed out two by two."

Aslatiel frowned. "But what else can we do within reason?"

Taki tapped him on the arm. "How about the smugglers from Nathu La? The rector mentioned them, remember? They might know where their rebel customers are. We may even catch them meeting with the enemy if we're lucky."

Aslatiel looked at Lotte and then at Taki. "Well, Natalis, it sounds as good as any other idea. Are you agreeable to this, Captain?"

"I am," Lotte said. "Natalis, work with the Imperials who know the area and devise a raid. I want it by midwatch tomorrow."

"Yes, Captain!" Taki puffed with pride and tried not to show it. This was the first time Lotte had asked him to plan a battle since his promotion. It would be a test of not only his reputation but also hers in the eyes of their new allies. *And if I succeed, then…well, I have no idea how to climb the Imperial ladder, do I?*

"I'll help, too," Enilna said. "You know, get you all tea and carry stuff. Whatever you want, Taki!"

"Er, thanks," Taki said. *When did you get so familiar with me? I'm an officer, you know.*

* * * *

A trio of horses rounded the bend near where Taki crouched. He had hidden behind a boulder alongside the trail at the bottom of Nathu La for hours. He unconsciously gripped his flare launcher tight as the hoofbeats thudded closer. Mikhail's hand came to rest on his shoulder.

"Just the scouts," Mikhail said. "Let them pass."

Taki swallowed on a dry throat and nodded. Undue tension would cause mistakes, and mistakes would spook the smuggling caravan and cause his plan to fail. The hoofbeats slowed and then stopped. Taki fought the urge to peek around the boulder.

Keeping his voice low so it wouldn't carry, he asked, "What's going on?"

"Silence. They can tell something's amiss," Mikhail said. He drew his pistol and pushed the slide back a finger's width to check for a chambered cartridge. Brass glinted reassuringly, and he slowly eased the round back into battery.

Taki nodded and clasped a hand near his chest to still himself. If the scouts discovered them or Elsa on the other side of the road, the trap was finished. Lotte's reputation would suffer, and they would not be regarded as equals. He would be disgraced and unworthy of his promotion. *Strange*, he thought. Compared to regicide, the prospect of failing his new task stung more.

A mare drew up on the opposite side and stopped. She neighed in protest while her rider tightened the reins. Taki took a deep breath as it started to step toward the boulder. The new armor he wore irritated his neck, further adding to his discomfort; it was rigid in the wrong places and flexible where he would have preferred a harder touch. He wasn't so sure he could fight in it, which was a growing problem right now.

Voices from farther away stopped the rider's advance. Though Taki could not understand the words, he knew what impatience sounded like. The horse trotted away, leaving dust in its wake.

Taki exhaled through a grin. "That was too close."

Mikhail gave a single nod. By now, Taki was used to the man's reticence. Initially, it had been awkward working with the Imperials instead of his own squad. Elsa seemed to lack inhibition; Mikhail simply didn't speak until spoken to, and even then only when necessary. There was also a palpable tension between the two that wasn't animosity but something else Taki couldn't identify.

A low rumbling in the distance broke into his thoughts. Approaching quickly was the dust cloud of a caravan. He brought out Draco's spyglass and peered through it. "It's them. Four light horse in the vanguard. Three wagons and a large carriage trailing. Probably twenty-five or thirty men riding with an unknown number in the wagons. Two kataphracts bringing up the rear."

Mikhail nodded and started a soft chant to activate his *Phon*. Shortly after, Elsa emerged from her hide and stepped into the middle of the road. She was clad in the robes of a beggar and clasped a small, infant-sized bundle to her chest. Soot and mud applied to her face and hair completed the look of dishevelment and insanity. The vanguard came to a stop and leveled their weapons at her. Its leader held his hand in the air and barked a guttural command that Taki could only assume was an order to halt.

Elsa started gibbering, or at least that's what it sounded like to Taki. The plan they'd worked out was that she'd get close enough to sniff out the telltale signs of weapons and armor and then signal the rest to act. Her disguise had been chosen after extreme deliberation—someone worth neither consideration nor the expenditure of effort to kill.

The leader scrunched his face and tried to spit on her. Elsa whirled away, laughing and jabbering to herself. Another rider huffed in annoyance and leveled a rifle at Elsa. An ax head had been grafted on near its muzzle. The leader put his hand out.

Not worth a bullet, thank goodness, Taki thought.

"Get ready," Mikhail said.

Elsa grasped the end of the cloth wrapping around her bundle and whipped it forward at the men. It unfurled in the air, revealing a brace of flash bombs that hurtled toward the center of the vanguard. Elsa wheeled around, clapped her hands over her ears, and dove away. Before she hit the ground, the world exploded into a storm of light.

"It's them!" Taki bellowed as he spun out from behind the boulder and fired his flare pistol in the air. A burning arc of bright red lanced up into the sky. Mikhail raced past him, opening fire with a self-loading carbine. Smugglers tumbled like cut wheat before they could raise their muskets. When his magazine was empty, Mikhail drew his longsword, charged forward, and plunged the blade into a spearman's chest.

Taki raced over to Elsa, blasted the nearest rider at full force with a sutra, and shot another off of his horse. Hoofbeats made him twist to face a rider trying to thresh him with a flail. Before Taki could raise his pistol, a load of shot turned his attacker's face inside out. He saw Elsa work the lever of her own longarm and blast the remaining horseman in the thigh. The rider screamed and grasped at the bloody stump of his leg before being dragged to death by his panicking mount.

"Thanks," Taki grunted. He braced his spell arm and sent another blast of concussive wind into a charging smuggler swinging a poleaxe.

Elsa loaded her last shells. "Where's our backup?"

"I told them to wait for the right moment."

"This *isn't?*"

The two backed slowly away. In front of them were at least fifty angry men who advanced with spears and muskets leveled.

"No, this isn't," Taki said.

"And *when* will it be just right?"

"Wait for it."

"Oy, no wonder you're still a virgin," Elsa said.

"*Look,*" Taki said, "they're easier for *her* to kill when bunched up."

Before the report hit their eardrums, a column of five men jerked forward with gore spewing from their chests. The bodies had barely hit the ground when another line toppled and fell, followed by the booming noise of a sniper's rifle. The mob of smugglers quavered and then broke and ran.

"See? Dassa's the best godrotting shot in the world," Taki said. "I'd stake my life on her."

"Charge!" Lotte hurtled over the ridge nearby, flanked by her companions. She deflected a thrown axe with her shield and took her attacker's head off in return. Draco whirled around with his fighting iron; the weighted end bashed an enemy's forearm to shreds and ripped the jaw off of another. Karma deflected a mass of spearheads away with a burst of prana and threw one of his spatha into a smuggler's neck. With a flick of his wrist, he retrieved the blade via a thin chain attached to the pommel.

"The flanks!" Aslatiel said to Lucatiel and Irulan. The women shouted and threw themselves into the fray. Aslatiel parried a spear thrust with his blade, pirouetted, and slashed his opponent's throat open. With flick of his wrist, steel opened another smuggler's chest. "Shpejtspate, stay close," he said.

Enilna grasped the hilt of her rapier with a sweaty palm and spun to face a charging fighter. He held a spiked cudgel above his head and swung it down at her head. She thrust. The cudgel fell to the ground, and the man's eyes rolled back in his head. Her rapier was buried in her enemy's chest, right under his solar plexus. She stared at the sight for a moment before twisting her wrist to wrench the blade free.

Yes, it's all coming together! We're going to win this. An unbidden smile worked its way across Taki's face as he beheld the slaughter.

"Okay, okay. Sorry I doubted you," Elsa said. "But seriously, try not to give me a heart attack next time."

Taki nodded. "Yeah, sorry. No surprises from here on out."

The last carriage in the caravan shattered into flying wooden chunks. A creature sprang to its feet amid the remains, stomped, and let out a guttural, viscera-twisting roar. Though humanoid in shape, it was three times as tall and twice as wide. Metal slabs bashed together into a rough suit of plate creaked in protest as the creature moved and flexed its joints. Through a gap in its helmet, a pair of cloudy yellow eyes flashed angrily at the fighters below.

"No! What the *hell* is that?" Taki scrambled away from the wreckage with his eyes wide.

Elsa sucked her teeth. "An enslaved monster!" She took aim at it and fired. Her muzzle belched fire and sent a solid lead slug at the juggernaut's head. It slammed against the helmet and let out an eardrum-piercing clang but did not penetrate.

The beast uncoiled a thick chain looped about its waist and started to swing a large, spiked weight in a circle around its head.

Taki fell to his knees. "We're fucked," he gasped. A moment later, he yelped in pain as someone swatted the back of his head.

"Maybe you'll spread *your* cheeks easy," Lucatiel said, "but not the women! Irulan, with me!"

She charged the beast with twin jian sparking. It swept its chain in an arc to try to pulp her, and she threw herself into a slide. Spikes passed a mere hairs' breadth above her face, and she passed between the creature's legs. She whirled, roared, and swung her blades at the juggernaut's heel. Metal crunched and crimson sprayed. The beast let out a howl of pain and collapsed to one knee. It grasped blindly at Lucatiel, but she rolled away and slashed its palms to ribbons.

Irulan threw her rope dart and sank the barb deep into the creature's neck. She sprinted around it in circles, wrapping loops of fine cord around its body and binding its arms. It struggled to free itself, but this only made the strands cut into exposed flesh. Unbalanced, the juggernaut pitched forward and fell prone. From its throat, a soft, mournful groan cut the air.

Lucatiel alighted on its back, raised her twin steel, and drove them into the base of the beast's skull. The rheumy yellow eyes widened and then closed for good.

"Now you see why they call her the Prince of Maladies," Karma said to Taki. He offered a hand, but Taki waved him off and came shakily to his feet. "We never stood a chance against her. She once fought a thousand Ursalan knights by her lonesome. Killed a hundred of them and set the rest to panic. One monster is nothing for the likes of her."

"What *was* that thing?" Taki examined it delicately.

"Bipedal manticore," Karma said. "Used in battle by the warrior tribes of Hunza before they all got Imperialized."

"I didn't think you could tame something like that," Taki said. He glanced over the rest of the road and spat grit. Their fight was over. Bodies lay sprawled in the dirt or slumped against wagons. Bloody-faced smugglers writhed, dusty and in agony, and sent up moaning prayers that the gods ignored.

"You *can*, it just takes a lot of time and willingness to get your people eaten," Karma said. He wiped down his blades with a cloth and sheathed them. "We're dealing with a ruthless bunch, and wealthy, too."

"Did we take any alive?" Taki asked, suddenly filled with anxiety. It would all be for naught if they had no one to interrogate.

"We have prisoners!" Lotte shouted from farther away. Taki fell to his knees again, this time in relief.

* * * *

It was well after sunset by the time the squads entered the gates to Gangtok. The ambush had netted fifteen captives, many of whom were wounded. A combination of pain and resentment made for a slow trudge to the nearest town with a jail and a permanent magistrate's seat. Much to Taki's surprise, Aslatiel had warned that it was frowned on to flog prisoners to hasten the march. Thus, what they could have covered in six hours took nearly ten.

"Natalis, you're first watch," Lotte said, and handed him the cell keys. Fortunately, the jail was almost empty, and the smugglers could be kept separate from the usual collection of drunks and petty thieves. "The albino from Alfa will relieve you in two bells."

"Who's doing the questioning?"

"Mainly that Rana woman, because she knows their tongue. Emreis also volunteered to assist."

"*Our* Draco?" Taki raised an eyebrow. "I never took him for the type who enjoyed pulling toenails."

"Neither did I. I'm not sure whether to be pleased or put off. Von Halcon and I will make sure things don't become too savage. Again, one of their surprising little rules."

"Captain, can I speak in confidence?"

"Aye, what's on your mind?"

"It sounds like treason to say this, but I'm not unhappy at being a part of their army. Do you think I've gone over too quickly?"

"No, and it's not treason to say so. You had little choice in this matter, Natalis. For you to feel glad of it is good fortune indeed. Sometimes, I wish I could trust as easily as you seem to."

"You didn't have much of a choice, either. I hope we find Mezeta."

"I have a feeling we'll be on her trail soon," Lotte said. "She's the sort who relishes chaos, while the Imperials want conformity above all else. All we have to do is wait and listen."

"Captain, what if Sir Aslatiel doesn't want to act against her? What will you do?"

Lotte laughed. "You don't know Hecaton like I do. The entire world will want her dead at some point. In the meantime, your job is to survive and learn. Remember what I said to you, and try to gain what enjoyment you can from all of this."

"I'm relieved, Captain," Taki said.

Lotte smiled and placed a hand on his shoulder. "You did well today. This is the closest we've been yet to finding the rebels."

"I should've anticipated that creature," Taki protested. "It nearly got us all killed."

"You can't anticipate everything that'll go wrong in battle. The only thing you can do is adapt quickly and marshal your strengths." She leaned in. "Also, you should learn how to take a compliment more gracefully."

Taki blushed.

"Make sure you rest after you're relieved. We'll have to move quickly once the rebels figure out what happened. Hopefully, they won't pull up roots and move on."

She left through another iron door, leaving Taki to his solitude. He breathed to calm himself and opened the door to the cellblock.

The prisoners were housed in a large, communal cell with a latrine in one corner and a few lice-infested straw mats shoved against the walls. Most sat sullenly on the floor or lay on their sides, facing away from the bars. Torchlight on Taki's end was the only source of illumination. A simple bench and long table, along with a rack of leather-wrapped cudgels, were the only furniture present. Though he expected jeering and cursing, Taki only found silence from the men. He sat on the bench facing the prisoners and already wished for Mikhail to relieve him.

"Young master?"

Taki started at the voice and instinctively reached for his saber. *Silly. No one's escaped.* He scanned the cell and locked eyes with the man who had spoken. He looked to be either a Chung-Kuo or a Tatar, middle-aged but still fit, with a lean, lined face accented by a short goatee and waist-long hair in a ponytail.

"I startled you. My apologies, young master," the prisoner said.

"Yes?" Taki chose his words cautiously.

"If it is not an undue burden, may I ask for you to pass that bowl through the bars?" The prisoner pointed to where some yak butter tea sat unattended. The brew was cold and had separated, giving it a nasty look. "One of my companions suffers a fever and thirsts badly."

"I'll call for some water," Taki said. For some reason, he felt guilty at hearing the man's words. "Or get some myself."

"My people prefer pocha, actually," the man said with a smile. "I also do not wish to cause you anxiety over leaving your post. Your companions are resting, and the local guards are off drinking, so who will watch us? Just that tea will do. Tea is cleaner than water, after all."

Taki rose from his bench, took the bowl, and motioned for the man to step back. Satisfied that no one could grab him, Taki carefully placed the bowl on the prisoners' side. The goateed prisoner bowed, waited for Taki to step back, and then took the bowl. The man knelt near a companion on one of the straw mats and carefully tipped the fluid into his mouth. The stricken prisoner shivered and coughed, but the tea seemed to calm his rigors.

"My sincere thanks," the goateed prisoner said, and placed the empty bowl on Taki's side of the bars.

"Not a problem," Taki said.

"You're not from a spetsgruppa I'm familiar with."

Taki raised an eyebrow. "How do you know I'm one of them?"

"I was a hauptmann in the army. The Alfa standard is well known among the troops. And if you were fighting alongside them, I assume you are also Spetsnaz. Am I correct?"

Taki shrugged. There was probably naught to gain from lying, as the prisoner posed little threat behind the bars. "You are."

"You also have an Argead accent, young master. Are you of the Cloud Temple?"

"How do you know of the Temple?"

"I was among those sent to take eastern Ursala. We were prepared to fight your kind and take your holy site. From what I've heard, the Dominion has fallen already. You have my condolences."

"I don't mourn for it much, despicable as that may be."

"All mourning must be earned. What's your name, young master?"

"Natalis."

"Are you a foundling?"

"Yes, I am. How did you guess that?"

"It was no guess. 'Natalis' means 'a birth' in many of the old tongues. A name often used for children with no parents."

"And what is *your* name?" Taki's expression softened slightly.

"Jamukha."

"Why did you turn to smuggling? A captain earns a decent wage."

"I grew disenchanted with the army." Jamukha wiped at the corner of his mouth. "Well, that's slightly unfair. To be more accurate, I grew weary of the Imperium itself."

"How?"

"My people are born riders. We can burst the eye of a sparrow a hundred meters away with a carbine, while riding at full gallop, without killing the bird. For three thousand years, we lived on steppes as proud warriors, and even more so, as proud *men*. My father was a noyan of a minghan, or what you would call a captain of a hussar division. His men, who later swore loyalty to me, fought in countless battles from Pokhara to Gdansk, all for the glory of the padishah. And though we subjugated countless cities and crushed countless armies, we never once set foot in the lands of our births. I was actually born in Donetsk, and until I was a full-grown man had never set foot in my own homeland. But my father and his attendants always told me stories about this place and made sure to teach me the language and customs of my people. I grew up a warrior and rose in the ranks."

"I don't understand," Taki said. "It sounds like the Imperium was nothing but good to you and your family."

"It was, for a time. Eventually, my father died in battle. Only then was I allowed to return to my homeland for the burial. When I returned to Lhasa, however, I saw the wages of occupation. The place my father had promised me since my birth was disfigured beyond recognition. No longer were boys taught to ride and fight like their proud fathers were. No longer were we warriors of the steppes but, rather, docile, servile sheep.

"The only remaining *men* were in my unit, with fewer and fewer boys joining every year. We were always told that there was simply less and less interest in our honorable life, and when I went back home, I saw why. Imperial schools had killed our culture, while we remnants of honor were sent out to die in the borderlands, fighting against our mirrors. We were always sequestered from our homeland, so we could not spread our ways back at home. This was a slow but sure way to eliminate us. Not just our bodies, but our *memory*."

Taki bowed his head. "I'm a foundling. My life wasn't mine to begin with. So for me, things like honor and culture aren't really important."

"Then what *is* important to you, young Natalis?" Jamukha crossed his arms.

Taki remained silent. The door unbolted, and Mikhail stepped over the threshold.

"You're relieved."

"Try not to stay so malleable, young master," Jamukha said with a bow and a smile. "It will take a greater sense of purpose to survive the fight to come. The Mandate of Heaven is named so for a reason."

"You misunderstand me," Taki said. "I don't care about traditions and ideals, but I do care about my companions." He rose and left.

Talking with Jamukha had stoked his appetite, and Taki thought about finding the kitchens to see if there was anything but repulsive tea to fill his belly. Trail rations of nut flour and suet were available, but they caused terrible binding in his guts.

"You can have this," Enilna said, as if reading his thoughts. She stepped out from an alcove in the wall and proffered half of a stuffed bun. It was cold, but the odor of the minced meat and scallion filling made his stomach growl. He started to take it but noticed the bite marks.

"Are you seriously giving me this after you *ate* half of it?" Taki pouted.

Enilna laughed. "If you don't want it, I'll finish it off. But you know, there's only pocha otherwise. That or the nut bars."

Taki sighed. "No, I'll eat it, but don't expect me to praise you." He bit into the bun and savored the gaminess of the meat.

"It's all right. Seeing you get grease on your face is good enough." Enilna clasped her hands behind her back and swayed slightly. "So, I've got to ask, what's our prisoner's deal, anyway? 'The Imperium is killing my culture!' and stuff. That sounded dumb as hell!"

"Hey!" Taki frowned and wiped his cheek with a sleeve. "Were you eavesdropping?"

"What else?" Enilna blinked. "I can't read thoughts like *Ba'gshnar* can."

"Weren't you supposed to be on guard duty?"

"I *was*. Aslatiel put me outside as backup in case you got overpowered in there."

"Now I'm insulted," Taki said.

Enilna frowned. "Why? Because I'm a girl?"

"No, because apparently Sir Aslatiel thinks I can't fend off a dozen men dying of their wounds."

"I'm sure he didn't mean it like that. Besides, everyone else is at the interrogation, and there'd be no help if something unexpected were to happen. I hear the questioning is absolutely horrific, by the way."

"Spare me the details, please."

"If you insist." She looked disappointed. "Besides, this is all the fruit of *your* labor. You should be more proud of yourself."

"It was really the others who did most of the work. I just thought of the basics."

"And don't forget, I provided tea."

"I remember." Taki brightened. "I appreciated the fact that you made us normal tea, not that oily stuff. Though I did kind of float out on a wave."

Enilna smiled. "I can't stand yak butter, either. I want to go fight Ursalans so I can drink beer again."

"Aren't you a little young for beer?"

"I'm old enough to kill for the Padishah. The least that geezer can do is allow me to drink whatever booze I want. Besides, you're not much older than I am."

"Fair enough. You're Kosovar, right?"

"I was. But fuck that place. I left and never looked back. I hear they still haven't expelled the Khazari."

"I wasn't there when you killed the Duke," Taki said. "How did you do it?"

"Maybe some other time," Enilna said, looking aside. Taki blinked and decided to leave it at that. For all of her bravado, that still seemed a touchy subject. He poked her playfully in the arm.

"So why were you listening in? Aren't all soldiers supposed to learn how to shut their ears off?"

Enilna shrugged. "I was bored. But you see, I'm glad I did it."

"Oh?"

"Before you got that other guy tea, I expected you to make him beg or gloat over him. But you didn't. It kind of made me feel funny inside. I realized you're a nice person."

Taki blushed again. "I am *not* nice," he grumbled.

"*M'qifsh karin!*" Enilna rolled her eyes and laid a dramatic hand across her forehead. "Big Sis was *right!* You'll stay a bachelor *forever* at this rate!"

Taki reddened. "I'll tell Lady Irulan you've been slacking off instead of keeping watch!"

"Oh no you won't!" Enilna whirled around to face Taki and planted a kiss on his lips.

His eyes widened, his pulse throbbed in his ears, and he felt overcome with the urge to faint. Her lips were chapped but also intoxicatingly soft. She smelled of sweat, as he did, but for some reason her odor was pleasant, sweet.

"Ew, *gross*," Hadassah said as she emerged into the hallway.

Enilna backed away with her face hidden. Taki lurched forward and stopped himself from falling.

Hadassah stuck her tongue out. "I deign to come get you, only to catch *Chomeo and Juliet* live in theater!"

Taki frowned. "Who or *what* the hell is 'Chomeo'?"

"It's a por...a porm...a *portmantle*! A combination of 'child molester' and 'Romeo.' You know, the hero from that famous play by Elvis of Murricania," Hadassah said, clearly reveling in the chance to show her newfound knowledge.

"Has Emreis been feeding you blasphemy again?" Taki placed his hands on his hips. His heart still pounded against his skull despite his best effort to seem nonchalant.

"I know better than to listen to that windbag. But Prince Lucatiel is actually quite the woman of letters. She introduced me to *Romance of the Journey to the Western Kingdoms* and the works of Confuseus. You could learn a lot from her, but you have to beat her in arm wrestling first. Took me a few tries, but it's possible." Hadassah flexed her right bicep into an unexpectedly large knot of muscle.

"Wait," Enilna said, with a quizzical look to the ceiling, "wasn't *Romeo and Juliet* actually written by Bacon of Ursala?"

"Hush, Chomeo," Hadassah sneered.

"Shouldn't *I* be the male?" Taki objected.

"*As I was saying*"—Hadassah cut him off—"we're getting ready to ride. We got a prisoner to spill his guts, so we're moving out quick."

"Where are the rebels?" Taki asked.

"Some fortress I can't say the name of without eating rocks at the same time. Just come along. Godrotting kids."

"Okay, old biddy," Taki muttered.

"Butt-boy."

"Poseur."

"Philistine."

Enilna rolled her eyes at them.

* * * *

With much jangling of irons, the shaking smuggler was led away by two of the local gaolers. Aslatiel had forbidden any locals from being within earshot of the interrogation, for fear of eavesdropping by spies and sympathizers. To smooth bruised egos, Aslatiel passed a round of milligrad to the master jailer and bowed.

"For your men's lunches," he said. "You may let the magistrate proceed with charges."

"Much appreciated, Spetsnaz," the master said.

Taki ducked into the chamber as the man left.

"Good," Lotte said. "Everyone go use the jakes once last time if you need to. We'll be riding all night back to Lhasa, and you can't piss off the side of a horse without making a mess."

"Where's the rebel base?" Taki asked.

"Gyantse Dzong. The prisoner also says that's where the students are being held. We need to get back to Lhasa and mobilize the army. Time for a good old siege!"

Aslatiel tugged at the heels of his gloves. "We must make haste. Word of our battle will spread quickly, and the rebels will pull up roots the moment they hear the smugglers have been captured. Move out."

"Oh, Emreis," Lucatiel said. She placed a hand on Draco's shoulder just as he was about to step out. "I...I apologize."

Draco flinched. "You, er, what?"

"Until now, I thought you to be delicate and lacking in conviction. A preening beauty unsuited to the rigors of war. But after witnessing your true brutality, you have my lasting respect."

"Oh!" Draco chuckled weakly. "I don't know whether I should be mortified or scared or pleased."

"*Pick the third one, moron,*" Hadassah said.

"Shush! I mean yes! Yes, I'm pleased! I accept your apology and such," Draco said with a sweeping, awkward bow.

"I expect great things from you in the future," Lucatiel said with a smile before leaving to make ready.

Taki's jaw dropped slightly. "What the hell did he do to the man? Do I even want to know?"

"I've interrogated a lot of people," Elsa said, "but this was like nothing I ever saw before."

"He sat down in front of the man like this," Hadassah said, miming a bow-legged seat on a stool. "He pulled a knife and just stared at the prisoner for a while. And then, he took a potato and just started silently peeling it. When he was done, he just started on another. Had the rest of us start a fire and find some cooking oil."

"And all this time, he does nothing but stare at the guy and peel," Elsa said. "Not that I'm flirting with you or anything, but that gave me shivers, Emreis."

A frown crossed Mikhail's features but dissolved quickly.

Elsa continued: "About a half bell later, the prisoner broke down and told us everything. Where Mandate of Heaven is based. How many of them there are. Even that they were intending to use that manticore for a siege of the Potala."

Taki shook his head. "I still don't understand, but I guess I missed out on something. What'll happen to those men now?"

"Smuggling carries a five-year sentence," Elsa said. "Knowingly aiding rebels and foreign aggressors can get you ten. You can reduce your sentence if you agree to join a liberation army or row for the navy. It's a rough life, either way, but fair, considering what they've done."

"So what gets you splattered?" Hadassah asked.

"The usual. Rebellion, rape, desertion, various murders. It's all done with one rifle shot to the head and another to the heart. The first padishah outlawed all other methods. I hear you Argeads did things like having horses tears limbs off and boiling in oil. Totally medieval."

"But don't some crimes deserve a bit more suffering than that?" Hadassah frowned. "If someone killed my child, I'd want him to roast in his own juices. Then I'd eat him, because nothing says 'fuck you' like eating your enemy."

"But who decides what deserves certain punishments? Besides, all that gory stuff makes you crazy to look at overlong."

"Perhaps they should just make you padishah, Dassa," Karma quipped. Hadassah nodded solemnly and then pinched him hard on the arm.

5

For the tenth time that day, the Lhasa battalion not only had failed to mimic the basic maneuvers of a pike phalanx but had also tangled the long shafts so badly that two of the troops had been trampled and needed to be sent to the infirmary. Marching on Gyantse Dzong by the end of the week was looking less possible by the day. With a wave of her baton, Lotte signaled for the formation to halt.

Taki's throat burned. He'd run himself hoarse barking out commands all afternoon, and his feet ached from constantly flitting in and out of the phalanx to correct their errors. His head also throbbed from one too many impacts of errant pike shafts. He was beginning to suspect that some of those hits had been deliberate, though the garrisoners only had bemused smiles for him. All in all, he had become much less enamoured of his title as a line officer. *Because if this is all there is to it, I was better off as a mere grunt.*

"Natalis!" Lotte shouted. "Get up here!"

She's pissed, Taki thought, and cringed. He knew that the blame for the men's failure to drill would fall on him. *Godrotting peasants! Why can't they just do shit right?* He trudged over to the podium, where Lotte fumed and Aslatiel stood silent and grave.

"It's hopeless," Lotte growled. "If the enemy goes for a push of steel, our side will get massacred."

"I'm sorry, Captain," Taki huffed.

"Shush, Natalis. I didn't call you up here to speak."

Aslatiel was impassive. "Can *any* of them drill to your satisfaction?"

"Precious few, and only with good line support. Perhaps enough for *one* square, and a small one at that. The rest, I wouldn't trust to march in formation even if I threatened to string up their mothers. We have to think of something else."

"What do you suggest?"

Lotte narrowed her eyes to slits and scanned the awkwardly positioned men and women. "I know we were given enough to equip several tercio, but these people simply *won't* fight like one. They're skirmishers and horsemen at heart..." She trailed off.

"Continue. Please," Aslatiel said.

"We should ditch the heavy armor for all but the actual pikemen. Let the rest wear their usual cottons and leathers, because they need the mobility. Use the surplus equipment in trade with the local merchants to exchange for more horses, muskets, and even bows and arrows if we have to. The bulk of our forces should be either mounted light cavalry or skirmishers who can harass their flanks and retreat quickly if needed."

"And if the rebels deploy heavy cannon?"

"Then it'll be up to our squads to stop them. We'll need to have everyone mobile and ready to take down any that crop up."

Aslatiel nodded. "Then we will do as you say. I'll talk with the rector. Hopefully we can complete the barter in less than two days." He made as if to leave.

"Wait, Imperial," Lotte said. "Are you sure about following me blindly on this?"

"We're running out of time, so we have little choice. I received word from the magistrate at Gangtok that a handful of the prisoners escaped. If they make contact with the rebels, then we're out of luck. And I also trust you. You have much greater experience with field maneuvers than I, and you have a gift for discerning the character of your troops."

"Oh," Lotte said. "By the by, do you remember much from our battle in Pristina?"

"I do."

"I insulted you then."

"What of it?"

"I'm not sorry for it, of course. But perhaps I disparaged you too much."

Aslatiel smiled. "We are both warriors. Your taunts did not cost me any sleep, but...I appreciate your sentiments. And I would like for you to call me Aslatiel. We are peers and fellows in arms."

"Fine, I'll call you Aslatiel. I suppose in fairness you can call me by my name, too."

"Do you still distrust me?"

"A little. Old habit, I guess. You know, I was once an archangel of the Temple. We prayed every day for the death of your people."

"Do you still wish for that?"

"I'm not an archangel anymore. I prayed, and no one answered. So it's a little hard to throw myself behind your Way or your padishah."

"You were a worthy opponent and now are a worthy ally. That's all I could ask for."

"Right," Lotte said, and clenched her jaw.

"I'll be off, then," Aslatiel said. With his characteristic efficiency of movement, he turned and left.

Lotte marched over to Taki and shook him by the shoulders. Despair was written on her features. "I didn't expect it to go that way!" She threw up her hands.

Taki stared back, dumbfounded. "With all due respect, Captain, it sounds like you...got your way. Why do you look so flustered?"

"I'm not flustered! *I'm angry!*"

"But he agreed to your suggestions."

"And that's what pisses me off! And the fact that he was so civil about it and listened respectfully. I wanted to crush his gob!"

Taki gasped for air, as she was now clutching him by the collar of his jerkin. "Captain...did you need me for anything?"

"I wanted your support, damn you. For when he inevitably tried to belittle me."

Taki swallowed. "But he was right. You *are* a fine warrior. The finest I've ever served."

To his surprise, Lotte's cheeks reddened for a moment. She let him go and turned away. "Go dismiss the men. See that they put their pikes away properly this time. Then make sure the rest of the squad's not just dithering away."

"What should I have them do?"

"Something. Anything! Just leave."

* * * *

Much to Taki's great lack of surprise, the majority of his squad was nowhere to be seen, save for Hadassah, who appeared to be lounging in the shade. One glance from her, though, and Taki decided against ordering her to some menial task. Instead, he simply sat down nearby her on the same bench and rested his head on the ramshackle table before him. Irulan sat across from the two Polaris, hard at work on sharpening her blades.

"You know, I thought Aslatiel von Halcon had the world's biggest stick up his ass when I first saw him," Hadassah said. "But in reality, he's a total gigolo. All 'I trust you, and you have a gift.' How utterly shameless! But then again, Lotte needs to get laid more than any of the rest of us, so it's cool."

"He's not trying to flirt with her," Irulan said. "It's just that Asl—the oberleutnant is earnest, and he gives praise where praise is due." She whisked the blade of her rope dart against a sharpening stone, but her distraction made her furl the edge.

"I see. So how long have you been sleeping with him?" Hadassah winked conspiratorially.

"Don't be rude," Irulan sniffed. "We're intelligent, powerful women. Probably the most powerful warriors in the world. We can talk about something *other* than men."

"And what do you wish to discuss that doesn't involve dongs?"

"Actually, I wanted to ask you why you insist on wearing a dress at all times. Isn't it a bit cold up here in the mountains?"

"It's a code." Hadassah said. "Deuteronomy forbids me to wear pants, just like Natalis and Draco can't wear skirts, though they'd look super cute in them."

"But leggings are better for mobility and comfort, especially in our trade."

"When wearing a dress, people can't foresee your movements as much in a fight. Also, it's also a matter of modesty. My fine legs can't be shown to any old asshole, just like my hair shouldn't be seen by anyone but my husband."

"You're not married, though."

"Maybe I just like wearing a hat?"

"Are you sure it's not to hide animal ears?"

"I'll bite you."

"Sorry, it was a bad jest."

"Oh, it's fine. People have said my vagina has fangs and that I drink the blood of babies. Compared to that, I actually don't mind when people ask me about this stuff."

What, you don't have a vagina dentata and drink blood? Taki huffed to himself, but decided against actually saying anything.

"So do you eschew pork as well?" Irulan asked.

"No, because *you* try turning your nose up at old bacon grease when you're starving in some shithole fortress trying not to get screwed sideways by Templars."

Irulan shuddered. "Ugh, Templars. Those *things* are creepy. Do you think the rumors are true? That they're made of the sewn-together parts of other people?"

"That's what Draco said. Though I never got to check, because the only time I had a downed one in front of me, I couldn't pry his armor off. There were a ton of landsknecht after me too, so it's not like I could rig something up to do the job. Still, it just didn't look human at all. Not what I was able to see."

"After we've crushed the rebels here, we'll probably be facing Templars in battle." Irulan shook her head. "I've seen a few before, from afar. They filled me with a really loathsome feeling. I wish I could be totally fearless about it, like Lucatiel."

"Speaking of the Prince, do you also have a cool title?" Hadassah asked, eyes widening.

Irulan laughed and shook her head. "No, that's only Lucatiel. I wasn't in Alfa when she earned it."

"What did she do? I must know!"

"You should ask her."

Hadassah slapped the table. "I tried, and she won't tell me. She just acts all demure and shit. It pisses me off."

"She's a modest person. She doesn't like to brag."

"Just tell me what happened so I can get a title before Draco does."

Irulan looked around first, as if to rule out an eavesdropping. "All right. The story is that she was tired of the slow progress of the siege on Hisn al Akrad. It was a brutal fight, with lots of wounded on both sides. She walked up to the gates and demanded to challenge the fortress commander to a duel. The Shah of Halab, who held the fort, looked over the walls and shouted that he'd commit various obscenities on her body, to which she responded: 'But it is *I* who will be raping *you*! Prepare your anus, shitlord!'"

Hadassah smacked Irulan on the shoulder. "Now you're lying. I can tell."

"On my honor, I tell the truth! Anyway, the Shah opened the portcullis to let his men sally out and take her. Well, that's exactly what she wanted. She charged in, massacred the chevaliers, and confronted the Shah on the walls in full view of the Liberation Army. When he tried to plead for mercy, she chucked him off the edge and into the moat. The moat, of course, was a dry one lined with spikes, so you can predict what happened. The impenetrable fort that had never bowed to an aggressor had just fallen. From that day onward, the Ursalans called her the 'Prince of Maladies.' Because, you know, it was obviously her cock that was responsible for that entire thing!"

Hadassah laughed out loud and then sighed. "Well, at least I know Draco won't get a title. Even if I can't."

"Luca's the only one that I've heard of. We still don't know much about the Ursalans. Like why they seem to take such glee in making their people suffer, or why their princesses all end up killing themselves rather than be captured. In al Akrad, they found that the girl had *disemboweled* herself with her bare hands."

"The Rex must be a virile bastard to sire all the daughters he has."

"And we've not managed to take a single one alive, even with one in every fortress."

Hadassah shook her head. "It's damned creepy. Well, maybe when I see one, I'll make sure to buttstroke her before she gets any fancy ideas."

"It would help the cause."

6

Hecaton Kheiris Mezeta cackled with glee as she hurtled down the ancient roadway at a speed commonly held by the alchemists to result in death by liquefaction. She was strapped to the inside of a wheeled relic named the "Cura," which was the last of its kind in Dominion lands. It had cost her five hundred rounds of Luger milligrad, down from the thousand that the artifact thief had initially wanted. A mix of bargaining, threats, and old-fashioned stubbornness had done the job, and now she owned the clattering deathtrap for as long as she could find fuel.

A waning river of asphalt connected the Dominion to the southeastern reaches of Ursalan territory. Unlike the normal packed-dirt paths, those roads were perfect for wheels because they did not become an impassable morass whenever it rained. On occasion, Hecaton had found her path blocked by shot-up metal carcasses from ancient battles, still bleeding rust centuries later. When faced with one, she merely sucked the power from the earth around her, focused her will, and swept the brittle heaps aside. She resolved to send a bill for her services to whoever governed these stretches. If the noble refused to pay, she'd come back and simply move the debris right back to where it had originally rested.

Most of all, Hecaton found herself enjoying the long stretches where she could depress the stubby pedals as far as possible and enjoy a thrill that would have been unimaginable to her while growing up in the Ring. She had ridden trains before, but they were slow and inelegant compared to her new purchase. Truly, the ancient people had known how to live.

Suitable fuel was a rare commodity, and the Cura would only choke on the thick, gloppy oil commonly used for cooking or warfare. Thus,

Hecaton had made sure to purchase additional amphorae of heady-smelling gasoline from another merchant, who had taken a handful of vials of glowing rock as payment. It would last her long enough to make her rendezvous—an Ursalan term she rather liked. On the fourth day of her journey, plodding along on fumes, Hecaton pulled her Cura up to the great iron portcullis of the golden city of Astarte. It had been named after a goddess of love and death, and within its walls, plenty of both transpired.

"Who goes there?" a guard shouted down from atop the city wall. He wore the bright green and red of the city militia and shouldered a Kalash. A crowd of farmers with carts of vegetables and peddlers laden with fur also stopped to investigate the strange sight of a woman leaning on the sputtering relic.

Hecaton lazily whisked her tinted lenses aside and inhaled the stench of rotting fish. "Open the gate, mongrel, and take me to your leader! I bear a gift."

She pointed to the Cura, and its engine shut down with a final, flatulent sputter.

* * * *

Primate Alesso of Astarte's throne room was a chaos of rococo and menace. Green marble pillars shot through with bulging golden veins supported a ceiling painted on every surface with a scene of hundreds of people copulating in positions both imaginable and unimaginable, with animals and even horribly mutated chimerae joining the orgy. Ornately engraved clocks standing sentry at the walls boasted hands shaped to resemble a man with an oversized phallus and a woman kneeling to receive it as the hands crossed. Golden chandeliers piled with innumerable candles cast flickering light on the court below, dripping a shower of hot wax onto heads and backs. Servants, seemingly about to fall to their deaths at any given moment, teetered on high ladders, constantly replacing spent candles. A throng of courtiers and courtesans, a mass of silks, velvet, ermine, and billowy wigs, mobbed the floor.

"Your Highness," a high-coiffed herald bellowed. "Representing herself, Lady Hecaton Kheiris Mezeta of the Former Argead Dominion!"

76

The man bowed and backed away, and Hecaton pushed through the crowd to approach the throne. She did not bow when she stood before the primate, and the courtiers pointed at her, aghast.

"As I recall, I banned you from coming here ever again," the primate said. An obese, balding man in his fifties, he wore a greatcoat of seal fur over his shoulders and a heavy crown of silver on his brow. His face was simultaneously pudgy and deeply lined from a life of extreme indolence and constant courtly intrigue. His lips thinned to near nothing when he smiled. "However, your gift was satisfactory, so I've overlooked your presumption. What brings you here, Mezeta? Have you been thrown out of the Dominion? Will you get on your knees and beg to serve me again? If so, then proceed already. I haven't got all day!"

Hecaton stifled a laugh. "My dear, dear Alesso. I serve none but myself. I've come with a proposal for you."

The primate raised an eyebrow. "Oh? What's your proposal?"

"Give me what I want or lose your city to the Imperium."

The court erupted in angry roars and calls for Hecaton's head on a pike. A pair of massive Templars standing at the primate's flanks silently tensed in anticipation of the order to cut the interloper down; their crimson-painted platemail creaked at the joints. With an impassive sweep of his hand, the primate ordered silence. The Templars remained ready to strike.

"Why, Hecaton, I had no idea you wished to become my jester." The primate snickered. "I urge you not to quit as a sellsword, though. You're a much better killer than you are a humorist."

"She speaks the truth." The woman sitting next to the primate fixed her gaze on Hecaton. She sat on a bulbous throne of intricately engraved metal that seemed to shift and undulate of its own accord. Except for a delicate crown of drawn gold wire on her head and thin metal bands running under her breasts and around her thighs, she seemed virtually naked. Her golden, utterly hairless skin glinted not from perspiration but from a fundamentally mineral quality. She rippled with muscle and power, and she was as tall as the Templars behind her. Even by the unreal standards of the court, she seemed alien. Hecaton tilted her head and locked eyes with Princess Sophie Troiscent, daughter of the Sanctissimus Rex.

"I assure you, my beneficent darling," the primate sputtered, "that Mezeta does *not*. I know perfectly well that the Imperial dogs have designs on my city, but I have taken the utmost of measures to assure that we will not fall to an attack. My army can meet any siege, and any man who attempts to breach the walls will be greeted with the kiss of the Lamed Goddess!"

"Princess Sophie, you look shiny as always," Hecaton said. "And Alesso, my dear fat little man, you know she's correct. You also know what I'm capable of. Just ask the men whom you sent to kill me. Or did their *coglioni* not satisfy your question?"

The primate thrust his hand into a bowl of fruit nearby and grabbed a ripened fig. He cocked his arm back as if to throw it at Hecaton but seemed to relent. Instead, he simply crushed the fruit in his fist until fragrant pulp oozed between his fingers. "Have you spewed enough filth in my court? If so, then get out."

"Not so fast," Hecaton said. "I have a plan to repulse the Imperium once and for all. To even take out their capital and end the threat permanently."

"And how would you even begin to do that? Do you plan to set my city ablaze with tires like His Holiness did to Berlin?"

Hecaton erupted with a full-throated laugh. "Nothing so comedic. My methods are more mundane. Now, have you ever heard of the God Hand?"

7

The Fifty-Fourth Suppression Army of the Imperium began its march from Lhasa in the foggy darkness before sunrise. Though a mismatched and barely drilled force with only twelve hundred soldiers at most, they were the discipline of the padishah himself. And they were not to return home until either the Mandate of Heaven was wiped from the face of the earth or until they were all dead.

"So how about the fifty-three before us?" Draco asked Elsa, whom he rode next to. "I mean, were they larger? Small like this?"

"Well, the largest one ever was probably the Twentieth, which went out to crush the Sons of Qin three-hundred-odd years ago. I think it was close to two million on our side."

"How many did the Sons of Qin have?"

"Double that. It was a big deal, that rebellion. Nearly half of the eastern territories sided with them, all trying to reclaim the glory of their ancient times. But we won, although at great cost. One of the padishah even died during the last battle, too. They still teach about it in the schools."

"Six million fighters going at it." Draco whistled. "Boggles the mind."

"And in those days, they still used tamed chimerae and relics from the Fall. You had these gigantic colossi totally beating the shit out of each other and falling over and crushing people like ants! And metal birds swooshing around breathing fire and farting cannonballs."

Draco gaped. "Where can I read about that?"

"There's books and stuff about it in Sevastopol. I'll take you to the library sometime."

"I'll hold you to that," Draco said, and extended his hand. Elsa clasped it, and they shook.

"Well," Karma said as he watched from behind, "I never thought old Draco would find someone to nerd out with like that. Elsa didn't strike me as the type, either. I imagined someone more reticent. Or just plain wacko."

"Bunch of perverts is what they are," Hadassah said. She tugged at her horse's reins to keep it from veering off to sniff and bite a mare alongside it.

The army marched as a column of horse, leading a snaking way through the cloudless Lhasa Valley. Behind the horses marched the heavy infantry and skirmishers, adept at the use of bows and antique muskets. Finally, the artillery consisted of three trebuchets and a pair of bronze mortars manned by a merchant named Fang, his wife Borte, and their many children.

Taki rode silently at the rear. Though doing so meant coughing on the dust raised by an entire army and plodding through the truly monstrous amount of horse and human droppings left in its wake, he was far from the boisterousness of the vanguard.

His plan had been successful, and he had earned praise and esteem not only from Lotte but also from the officers in Alfa. And yet his stomach churned and his hands sweated uncontrollably. *Because of her, of course.* The memory of Enilna's scent and, more so, her touch, lingered on his lips no matter how much he tried to rub it away. It was a silly thing to worry about, he knew. He was riding into battle, where his heart's panging was the least important thing in the world.

In a stroke of bad luck, Enilna was in the rear guard, too. Taki had noticed earlier and had attempted to blend in with a group of lancers. So far, the plan to avoid her seemed to be working.

"My favorite farmer!" Enilna cantered up alongside him, clearly enjoying herself.

Fuck. He cringed and made no effort to hide it.

She giggled. "Were you hiding from me?"

"No."

"Whatever, I forgive you. Anyway, get this. Old Fang over there has been with Borte for thirty years, and they have so many kids that they can't actually remember the names really quickly. So instead, they just call the kids by number. Oldest son Bo'er is Fang One, youngest daughter Xixi is Fang Twelve. It all makes sense now, because when I was in Sevastopol, there was this other kadet named Fang Fifteen and for the longest time I thought he was just a fantasist trying to look cool."

Taki's jaw hung open slightly, and he forced himself to look ahead.

"Anyone there?" she said, and flicked him on the forehead.

Taki winced and swatted her away.

"It lives!" she gasped.

"God rot you, I'll just say it!" Taki said. "Why did you kiss me back in the prison?"

At this, the lancers started to chuckle. Taki glared back at them, and they slowed their horses while smirking. Surprisingly, Enilna reddened.

"Ah, that. You know…" She seemed to stumble over her words. "It was to shut you up. I heard that it's a great way to 'terminate thoughts,' as Irulan puts it. She uses it on her lover when he's being unreasonable."

Hearing her words only made Taki grimace. He spurred his horse into a canter and barged up the column. Enilna let out an exasperated breath and looked to the sky.

"We'll support you, sister!" whooped one of the lancers. *"You and that stupid kid look cute together!"*

She laughed and narrowly avoided a clump of manure on the road.

* * * *

By the time Taki wended his way through the unruly stream of part-time warriors to rejoin the vanguard, the sun slumped low in the west. Riding—even at a slow and comparatively leisurely pace—was still a tiring affair. Secretly, he hoped that there would be time to camp, sleep, and eat. When he drew closer to Lotte and Aslatiel, however, he realized that such pleasantries would not come to pass.

"The bastards were ready for us all along." Lotte passed the spyglass to Aslatiel, who peered through them at the valley floor in the distance. The bone-white fortress was perched on a colossal spur of brownish-gray rock, only accessible via a steeply inclined path. Arrayed in front of Gyantse Dzong stood the army of the Mandate of Heaven.

"It's to be expected," Aslatiel said. "Though I'm surprised how fast the escapees made it across the steppes. We'll have to fight on their terms. We can still win."

Taki looked out at the opposing army and silently cursed to himself. Who had been to blame for the smugglers' escape in the first place? Had he left a weapon too close to the cells? Or somehow misplaced a key? *I only gave that man some pocha for his ailing friend.*

Lotte ground her teeth. "More than we estimated. Lots of infantry arranged in forward and reserve squares, a good amount of dismounted archers and riflemen, and the rest light cavalry. Nothing heavy."

"Suspicious," Aslatiel said. "Where's the artillery?"

"I'll bet they're up in the fortress. But you can't take much more than light guns up that path, so we should be able to withstand a barrage. Still, they outrange our own cannon a fair bit. We'll have ours stay back and engage only enemy trying to flank our main force. Harass their infantry with horse archers and dragoons. Turn our heavies on theirs." Lotte turned her head to face the woman next to her, who also surveyed the scene through a spyglass. "Rector, you should probably remain here with the supply train."

"Absolutely not," Rinchen said with a glare. "I'm in charge of the garrison. What sort of unworthy leader hides in safety while her men are cut down defending her ideals? I won't be a burden, if you're worried about that." She patted a pistol at her waist and the steel cuirass covering her torso. Four burly, well-armed men hoisted her sedan chair until she was slightly over Aslatiel's eye level. "These are my nephews. They wished to support their aunty in her fight. If we die, it's going to be glorious."

"I can't disagree with you, Rector," Aslatiel said. "We should make ready for battle. Have your line officers ready the flanks and wings. Tirefire will man the center."

"Always," Lotte said.

"Then I'll be off with the cavalry," Aslatiel said, and rode down the path to rejoin the columns.

Lotte waved to Taki. "Natalis, where were you all this time?"

"Manning the rear guard, Captain."

"I hope you weren't back there flirting with the new girl. Mikkelsen told me you two were petting instead of watching the smugglers."

Taki's cheeks reddened. "I wasn't doing anything with her! And Dassa needs to mind her tongue."

"I don't blame you, Natalis. The girl's young and pretty, but mind you that we're at war."

There was no arguing with his captain, who clearly seemed to enjoy piling on the ridicule, along with Hadassah and everyone else. *Why did I stick with this lot, anyway?* He swallowed his pride and nodded.

"You haven't been in a fight like this before, have you?" Lotte said.

"No."

"This won't be like the times we faced Sir Aslatiel and his men. You survive by staying close and covering your neighbor's flanks. In turn, she will cover yours. If she dies, you die. And try not to brain yourself on a pike shaft. It's really embarrassing when that happens."

"Sounds like death can come from anywhere," Taki said, and chewed on a cuticle.

"Aye, it can. And that's what makes an open battle so damned fun."

"That doesn't sound fun at all!"

Lotte laughed and set her horse to trot. "Oh, but it is! Otherwise, why would we do it all the time?"

Within two bells, the Fifty-Fourth Suppression Army started its advance. From behind the Mandate lines, a low, mournful horn sounded, and their center started to close the gap. Well-clad in half plate and helmets and wielding axes and picks, they swaggered forward, almost jauntily, and drew to fifty meters. With another note of the horn, the men charged.

Taki tried to slow his breathing as the malevolent human wave edged closer. He shifted his musket on its rest and aligned the smoothness of the top of its barrel with the torsos of the charging rebels. Unnervingly, the musket had no sights to speak of, unlike the pistol holstered at his side. But at this range, perhaps precision wasn't needed as much as an overwhelming hail of lead. Next to him, Draco and Karma dug their heels in and braced their longarms. They stood at the head of a tercio— a square of pikemen fronted by gunners who also served as skirmishers able to blend in and out of the tight-knit spear formation.

"Fire!" Lotte shouted.

Taki squeezed his crude, curved metal trigger. A terrific chorus of gunpowder erupted almost in unison, and the first line of enemy fell convulsing to the ground.

Taki scooted back to allow the second line to step forward and fire. He shifted his musket off its rest and set its butt on the ground before slamming its ramrod down the barrel several times. This served to extract the cartridge casing stuck in the breech, or the next round wouldn't fire. Cursing the inefficiency of the whole process, Taki plucked the burnt casing off the end of the rod and then slipped a fresh round primer-first into the muzzle. With another push of the ramrod, the musket was ready to fire again. In the time he'd taken to reload, he could have fired off an entire magazine from his Temple gun. But Lotte had warned him specifically to conserve his ammunition. Open-field warfare was a trial of endurance, not strength.

The gap closed to twenty meters. Taki scooted forward, braced his musket, and let off a hurried potshot that felled no one.

"Muskets withdraw! Center to the ready," Lotte commanded.

Around Taki's head, pike shafts descended in synchrony and, to his relief, did not bash him or his companions in the skull. The charging rebels, flush with rage and hormones, could not stop their momentum. They hit the bristling mass of spear points and died to the sound of crunching metal and squelching flesh.

Engaging the enemy at this distance with a musket was futile now. Taki turned and passed his weapon to a man behind him and drew his saber. Rebels ducked under the row of pikes and slashed at the shafts overhead.

Lotte slapped Taki on the back. "Counter them!"

Taki let out a shout and shuffled forth with his blades at the ready. He swatted a sword thrust away and slashed his saber at his attacker to open the man's arm near the shoulder. The rebel howled and tried to shoot him with a muzzle-loading handgun, only to be run through.

To Taki's left, Draco crouched and darted toward the fighters, tackled one of them to the ground, and stabbed the man in the neck. Karma followed and sunk his short swords into a pair of chests. Screams gave way to gurgles and finally silence. Overhead, the pikes continued to thrust and clank against armor and squish against flesh.

"Give me some cover," Taki shouted to his companions. "I'll blast 'em all!"

He knelt and placed his saber on the ground and then closed his eyes. Power welled within, and he channeled it to his hands. Then, he pointed his palms at the rebels and let the surging energy loose. A concussive blast of freezing air lanced forward and blew a channel in the middle of the packed enemy. Shattered men, armor, and weapons flew through the air, and a cry of panic sounded from the line.

In an instant, the attackers wavered and fled. Taki let out a breath from his nostrils, picked his saber up, and stood. As he did, his vision blurred, and he dug his point into the ground just in time to avoid falling. Elsa's words about getting winded easily in these lands came back to him now.

"Ha! That's our wizard for you!" Draco said, and clapped Taki on the back.

"I'm the *best* wizard," Taki said, and wiped away a line of spittle from his face. He stared at the carnage before him and whistled. Despite his earlier misgivings, Lotte's words from earlier sounded truer than before. Repulsing the charge had been unexpectedly exciting—even enjoyable.

"Give us back our daughters, you sons of bitches!" rang out from the left and then gave way to the thunderous hoofbeats of a cavalry charge.

Taki spun and was nearly knocked aside by the horses. Behind him, Lotte cursed and fired her gun in the air in a vain attempt to signal a halt.

"What the hell?" he shouted.

"Our flankers are *charging without orders!*" Lotte said. "Hold the line, damn you!"

The remnants of the rebel charge dissolved under an onslaught of arrows and lances.

"Wait," Taki said. "Do you suppose it'll work? Should we capitalize on the momentum?"

Lotte shook her head.

From the top of the outer wall of Gyantse Dzong came flashes and puffs of smoke. The wayward riders and their horses were tossed in the air as cannonballs skipped along the ground. Horses fell apart, and human torsos popped like overripe grapes between teeth. The survivors of the rashly executed charge stopped in their tracks and disappeared under a river of rebel lancers.

"Shit. What now?" Taki asked. White smoke erupted from the walls of the fortress.

"They're shelling us! Get down!" Lotte bellowed.

A ball whizzed by Taki's head and smashed into the pikemen behind him. Men spun in the air like figurines batted aside by a child. Other balls hit on both sides, blowing torsos apart and taking off limbs as they bounced. The phalanx reeled. More than anything, Taki wished to turn tail and run, but the sight of his captain standing firm in the face of pounds of lead slinging along shamed him into stillness.

Hadassah was the first to notice the enemy cavalry stirring. "Horsemen!"

Lotte waved her baton. "Make square!"

With surprising deftness, the pikemen rushed to form a hollow square with each side three deep. Spearheads poked out from all sides, ready to deter any cavalrymen foolish enough to charge headlong into the mass. The rebel lancers made a disciplined split before they would have hit the front row of spears. They circled the square closely and threw lances or fired short muskets into the gaps.

Taki picked up a musket and fired at one of the lancers. The man slumped and slid from his horse, but another rider managed to swat the pikeheads aside and bore down to spit Taki through the chest. He tried to swing the barrel around to fire, only to remember that it could not.

Lotte whirled and buried her flamberge deep into the charger's chest, and the lance went wide. The beast groaned and went down but wrenched the massive sword away. She drew a side sword and stuck the struggling rider in the throat.

"Thanks, Captain," Taki said, and tossed the musket aside in disgust. He wiped the grime from his brow and drew his pistol. It was no longer time to skimp on ammunition, especially because the ground had started to shake. To the front of the tercio was an enemy pike phalanx with its points lowered. They inched forward as a gut-churning wall of sharpened steel.

"A push! Make a push!" Lotte shouted. Pike shafts leveled themselves around her to face the oncoming tide of iron points. She dropped her shield and drew a main gauche.

The two phalanxes edged delicately toward each other in a grim mirror of courtship. Opposing spear tips glided and clinked against each other for a brief moment and then thrust in earnest.

Taki clenched his jaw and drove forward again with his companions in tow. He hacked and stabbed and shot at rebels who tried to split him with axes and impale him with rapiers. Pikemen on both sides dropped broken shafts and drew muzzle-loading pistols. A ball smashed against the side of Taki's helm but did not penetrate it. The divot made by the bullet pressed uncomfortably into his scalp, so he tore the helm off and tossed it into an attacker's face to smash the man's nose.

In the corner of his vision, he saw the rector take a round to her chest. Rinchen gasped and spat crimson and thick pink chunks. A returning horseman trampled one of her nephews and tried to lance her, but she fired a round into his face, and he fell from his mount. Taki wanted to help but knew he could not. A Mandate fighter leapt at him while he was distracted and almost knocked the wind from him. They rolled for a while before Taki managed to wedge the muzzle of his Herstal against his enemy's gut and pull the trigger. The rebel rattled and croaked in Taki's ear for a few moments and then moved no more.

"They withdraw!" Draco shouted from out of sight.

Taki groaned and tried to ease out from under the corpse. The prana use and subsequent fighting had drained him. It was tempting to simply play dead and go to sleep, but he knew he could not. Reluctantly, he shuffled the burden off and pulled himself to his knees. Bodies lay sprawled out around him, staining the dirt crimson. Lotte stood over him and offered a hand.

"Are you hurt, Natalis?" she said.

"Nay, just tired is all." He took her hand, and she pulled him up.

The cries of the wounded and dying were the same regardless of native tongue. What soldiers could be saved had been dragged over to the surviving part of the phalanx, where they were attended to with care, if not necessary supplies or knowledge. In the distance, the Mandate army loomed—injured, surprised, and angry.

"Captain!" Draco rushed over with Hadassah in tow. "There's a party approaching. White flag."

"Say the word, and I'll mow them down," Hadassah said.

Lotte shook her head. "No. They may violate the rules of decent conduct, but we will not."

"Except when convenient," Draco added solemnly.

Lotte glared at him and rose to her feet. "Natalis, with me. The rest of you, patch up."

The Mandate party numbered four, and at first glance seemed to follow the promise of their flag. The lead rider, a wizened monk in lamellar and hide, signaled a halt. "We are impressed by your valor, woman. Because you fought so well, we will allow you and your army to retreat with your lives and your weapons." The horse stamped at the ground, and the monk grasped the reins tighter.

Lotte crossed her arms. "Tell your master that I appreciate his offer. However, we are proud and honorable warriors of the Argead Dominion. The day will not end until you have been routed from the field."

The monk scowled and reared his horse. "Know your place, wench! Turn back, or we will stain your souls to ruin! You will spend a thousand kalpa in the world of hungry ghosts!"

With that, the Mandate party turned their horses and galloped off.

"What the hell did he mean by that?" Taki asked as they trudged back to the battle line.

Lotte furrowed her brow. "I'm not sure, but I don't like it. We'd best head back and prepare for another fight."

Soon, something stirred among the rebel lines. At the front of the army was a cart. In it were three girls with their hands tied behind their backs. The seemed to be hungry and thirsty, with sunken eyes and lined faces. Their legs were smeared brown from dysentery. Armored men dragged the girls from the cart and forced them to their knees. They faced the army.

"No," Lotte muttered under her breath. "Natalis, don't look."

"I'm not a child—" Taki started to say, but the next sight made him wish he'd obeyed.

The rightmost of the captured students barely had time to scream before one of the men drew a knife and started to saw away at her neck. Crimson streamed from her throat and slowly dripped down from her rags to the dust while she struggled and shook and then fell still. Murmurs of shock and anger started to swell from the Imperial ranks.

"Captain, it's a clear shot from here," Hadassah said. "I'll get the motherfucker before he does the next one in."

"Hold your fire," Lotte said. "They'll just get another to do it, and another, and another, and you'll be out of ammunition for when you need it most."

The second captive writhed as her throat was slowly sawn apart. Some of the pikemen shouted for an attack while others knelt and wept.

"Lotte, *come on!*" Hadassah's eyes were teary.

Lotte inhaled sharply. "If you won't follow orders, *go to the rear!*"

Hadassah gnashed her teeth and slammed the butt of her rifle into the ground. The third girl flopped to the dirt with her lifeblood spilled on the sand. Two Mandate fighters stepped forward and unfurled a long banner, upon which was written: *"Three will die at every half bell. The next will burn."*

Aslatiel rode up and dismounted next to Lotte. "What should we do?"

"This can't go on," Lotte said. "If the enemy carries out the threat, our men will charge without orders or just rout. We either advance on the fort and get torn to pieces by their artillery, or we do nothing and lose anyway."

"Can we spread out to reduce casualties?"

Lotte shook her head. "It'll save us a few deaths from cannon, but then their cavalry will shred us."

Taki cleared his throat. "If I may make a suggestion."

"Speak quickly, Natalis," Lotte said.

"We need to cut off the head. Get into the fort somehow and take their guns out, or kill the rebel leader and make sure their army knows it. Only then will our men have a chance to survive."

"Aslatiel, can you spare any of your number?" Lotte asked.

Aslatiel nodded. "We'll have my cavalry dismount and serve as extra musketeers. I'll lead a group to circle around the rear and infiltrate. There's no guarantee it'll work, but it's better than sitting around. Lotte, you have to keep them distracted on the field, or we'll be overwhelmed inside."

"We'll gut as many of the bastards as we can. Also, take him with you." She pointed to Taki. "He's our best caster."

"Will do," Aslatiel said. "Natalis, mount up and follow me. We have less than a half bell to do this."

"Captain, wouldn't I be better by your side?" Taki said. "Especially because we don't have artillery?"

Lotte shook her head. "Nay. You said it yourself. We need the serpent's head off. You've seen what our enemy's willing to do. I'll take care of things down here."

Taki swallowed. "Promise you won't do anything rash."

Lotte laughed. "I refuse to die today. I still have debts to call in."

* * * *

Taki struggled to control his ragged breaths as he skittered up a rocky incline and into a scrubby trench to join Aslatiel. The last hundred meters had to be crossed on foot, as the horses were spent from a merciless gallop. Soldiers on foot were much harder to spot, anyway. Their efforts had paid off, however, and now they were at the base of the Gyantse Dzong's rear wall.

"Climb it. Ten meters apart," Aslatiel signaled. Taki nodded and crept along the trench while hugging the wall. There were sentries pacing overhead, though they would hopefully be distracted by their desire to observe the battle. Taki opened his gates and started his ascent. The walls of Gyantse Dzong were in rather good condition for their age and only offered miserly handholds at best. He huffed and continued to pull himself up.

Enilna climbed nearby. *Why her?* Taki wondered. *Why not actual hardened killers like Elsa or Mikhail? At least the Prince of Maladies is with us. Concentrate on the mission.* Footfalls overhead made him freeze, and he heard the rustling of clothing. To his horror, a stream of golden-yellow liquid flew by, barely missing him.

Enilna's eyes widened, and she looked as if she were about to go into convulsions. Taki glowered at her and continued his ascent. Near the top of the wall, he again heard footfalls. When they moved away, he decided to act.

Silently, he pulled himself over the edge and crouched behind a sentry clad in a leather jerkin and a loincloth. Taki slammed his knife home into the man's kidney, withdrew the blade, and then sank it into the base of the skull. Brown slurry dripped from the sides of the sentry's loincloth, and Taki stepped back in disgust. He looked around and noticed that Lucatiel had also made the ascent. Two heads rolled at her feet. Aslatiel and Enilna climbed over the wall a second later.

"That door," Aslatiel whispered, and nodded to an open entrance nearby. *"From here, split up. Luca, you and I look for the powder magazine. Natalis, you and Shpejtspate head up to top. Find and kill their leader. Dangle his body over the walls. Now go!"*

Taki nodded to Enilna, and they made their way inside.

The interior of Gyantse Dzong was similar to the Potala: dank, dark, and smoky. Inside, they could hear the sounds of men scurrying back and forth. Cannon fire reverberated through the halls. Taki suppressed the sick realization that his companions were being shelled. *If we hurry, we'll screw up. Breathe.* He turned to Enilna and pointed at a set of stairs up. She followed, rapier in hand.

The first Mandate fighter they encountered was behind a doorway, squatting over the jakes. Taki's blade pierced him true, and the man's eyes rolled back in shock. The second, Enilna got from below with a rapier thrust that entered his lower back and came out his chest. The third, Enilna also claimed when she bashed his face in with the butt of her sword and then opened his throat. Taki felled the fourth through seventh by blasting them with a *khala* timed for the roaring of the cannons. So far, neither had heard gunshots, which meant that the von Halcons had managed to keep quiet.

At the top, Taki crouched near a large wooden doorway and silently gathered his prana. The door wouldn't budge, so there was no other option but to blast it down and enter shooting. Enilna had drawn her Colt and clutched it to her chest. There was always the possibility that causing a ruckus would make things harder for the siblings below them, but Taki figured that Aslatiel was the type who would anticipate such an event.

"I'll start," he whispered. With his Herstal ready, he placed his left hand on the door right over where the bar would have sat on the opposite side. He started to chant. There were mantras that would enhance the power of most sutras. Those required time to prepare, but the effects were spectacular. With any luck, the ensuing blast would kill everyone in the next room with wood shrapnel. The thought of prisoners on the other side crossed his mind. He shook his head to clear away the thought. They were all dead if he did not succeed.

"My body is pierced by swords and fire, and thus I wake from this fleeting dream called life. My child, I beg of thee to bury me near water. I will rise again as a Sea Dragon and fight the hated aggressors from the east."

The doorway shook, seemed to stretch, and exploded inward along with a good chunk of the stone around it. Taki whirled around and took aim. His bullets ripped into a man wearing dented plate and charging with an axe and also downed a tribesman trying to aim a swivel gun. Enilna's Colt spouted fire and blew out the back of the last man's skull before he could stick her with a spear. The dust started to settle, and Taki quickly looked around at the bodies. Besides the three who tried to attack, there were two others who'd been standing near the door and absorbed the brunt of the shrapnel. They were almost unrecognizable as humans.

"Which one?" Enilna asked.

Taki shrugged. "All of them, I guess. I don't know which one was the leader. It's disgusting, but we should start hacking off heads to display before anyone else comes in here for backup."

Downstairs echoed the faint roar of gunfire. Probably the siblings' handiwork, he reasoned.

"Yeah, that's super gross, but you're right," Enilna said. "I have to find something better suited than my sticker." She holstered her pistol and picked up the broad-headed spear she'd been threatened with.

Taki put his gun away and looped his arms under one of the corpses to drag it closer to the others. Too late, heard the rustling of fabric behind him. He whirled, only to face Jamukha.

"Hands on your head, Natalis. Turn to face the girl."

Taki weighed his options. Jamukha pointed a sawn-off rifle at him; it looked like a butchered version of the Nagant that Hadassah had once used. A hit from that gun would easily pierce his armor and kill him. At this range, there was little hope of being able to dodge the shot. He put his hands on his head and faced Enilna. Her eyes narrowed to slits, and she shifted her grip on the spear.

"You're no smuggler," Taki said.

"Correct, Natalis. I lead these patriots. Like-minded souls who seek to restore the old ways." Jamukha drew closer and grasped the back of Taki's jerkin near the neck while pressing the gun into his spine.

"The three girls on the field," Taki said. "Were you responsible?"

"I was."

"Why the messy execution?"

"I wanted to send your leaders a message. The battlefield is no place for a woman."

"So you stoop to barbarism? I thought you were a prouder man."

Jamukha inhaled sharply. "Of all the indignities I suffered in the army, do you know what the worst one was? Having to take orders from a female. Really, when you give them that much power, they let it go to their heads quickly. Everyone suffers as a result. They have no sense of—" His words ceased abruptly as the tip of Enilna's spear slammed into his face and split his head open.

Taki felt the spray of warm blood against his scalp and instinctively lurched away and tumbled to the ground. Madly, he slapped his palms against his chest to feel for a wound that didn't exist.

"Sorry, I just couldn't stand the rambling!" Enilna bent over and offered her hand with a smile.

Taki blinked and allowed her to help him. "Who the hell *are* you?"

"You don't have to be so sour about it," she pouted, and crossed her arms.

"I'm not being sour!"

"Yes, you are!"

"You could've killed me."

"But I didn't."

"You're too reckless."

"You're pissed off because you were saved by a girl. Admit it."

"I'm angry because I almost died! Look, let's display his body and be done with it."

Enilna opened her mouth to retort but then started to laugh. "I just noticed something," she chortled.

"What?"

"When you get flustered, your lips twitch."

* * * *

"So what now?" Draco asked.

Lotte narrowed her eyes. "We advance. We win, or we die." She gazed at Irulan. A ragged hole marred the front of the woman's chestplate. "How badly are you injured, Surenovna?"

Irulan smiled and shook her head. "It's not even worth—" She was cut off by a coughing fit and hacked up a line of blood into the sand. Elsa rested a hand on her, trying to stanch the hemorrhage.

Lotte shook her head. "Gillette, get Emreis and put her on a litter..."

"You'll not keep me from the fight," Irulan chuckled, and wiped her lips. "I have a bet with the rector. If she kills more of them than I do, I have to marry one of her grandsons."

Lotte resumed her place at the front of the tercio and raised her baton to command them. "Those who can fight, to the front! Wounded, to the rear!"

"Here they come," Draco said. He shoved a clump of rags beneath his armor to stanch the blood from an earlier spear thrust and straightened his posture. The last column of rebels began to move, preceded by a line of horse gunners. At a slow trot, their aim was impeccable, and they methodically fired and reloaded with practiced ease. Lhasa pikemen started to fall.

Draco spat. "I guess this is the part of the story where we all die, eh?"

Lotte stared ahead, pointing her swords at the oncoming army. A ball smashed into her shoulder, and she stumbled but regained her footing. The main gauche fell to the ground, but she held her thrusting sword firmly. Her wounded arm felt as if the flesh were boiling under her steel, but she bit her tongue and endured the pain.

Karma fell, clutching his midsection. The cavalry now broke to the sides, satisfied that the tercio was softened up. The Mandate infantry quickened their pace in anticipation of an easy slaughter. Lotte let out a throaty roar and lunged forward.

A high-pitched whine struck their ears before the ground seemed to well up and burst like a pustular boil, sending Mandate men and pieces of men flying. Lotte could barely comprehend the sight before there was another whine and another explosion, and then another, and another. An endless stream of explosions that turned the world white and orange and unbearable. When Lotte opened her eyes again, where the enemy had stood, there was now only smoke and crater.

Scattered pockets of rebels wheeled around in a fugue. Fewer still attempted to run back to the fortress, only to fall to their knees at the sight of a man's body suspended over the parapets by his ankles. Beneath Jamukha's corpse was an unbroken red stripe over immaculate white.

8

After the bones were set, bleeding stanched, and infections burned away, it was time to lay the fallen to rest. Whether friend or enemy, the bodies had to be burned. Otherwise, the spread of plague would cause tenfold more deaths in the months to come.

Before the row of blazing funeral pyres was a small altar to Tengri, the omnipresence who oversaw the endless plateau from on high along with his riders. Piled on the altar were bowls of rice and handfuls of fruit. Countless joss sticks smoldered atop it and released a sinuous cloud of perfumed smoke. Flanking the altar in two lines, saffron-clad monks beat against wooden fish, sending an undulating beat into the surrounding night. They chanted in a throaty basso, in a language at once familiar and ancient.

Taki knelt at the altar, feeling awkward. What he was doing would have counted as blasphemy, were he still in his homeland. *But I'm not there anymore. I'll probably never return. Just like so many in this army won't.* Only a sliver of the Fifty-Fourth Suppression Army had escaped harm. It seemed like a greater blasphemy to abstain from paying respect, even in a heathen fashion.

He glanced at Lotte, who knelt beside him. To his surprise, her face was streaked with tears. As long as he had known her, she'd seemed like one who only took enjoyment from battle. He chanced a whisper. The others wouldn't be able to hear over the monks' droning.

"Captain, do you feel ill?"

She turned her head to face him. "No. Why do you ask?"

"You look morose."

"And what of it?"

"Beg your pardon. I didn't expect you to…"

96

"Oh, Natalis." She shook her head. "Tell me honestly. Do you think me a monster?"

Taki flinched. "No!"

"Many times, I've been given lives to spend. Every officer has. But I've spent frivolously. I've squandered. I can't stop. I cost all of those garrison men their lives. One day, I'll spend you."

"That's fine!" Taki snapped, despite his best efforts at restraint. "I owe you my life. Everyone else does, too. You're my captain, and I'll follow you to the end. Spend me without regret. I could ask for no more honor."

Lotte fell silent but slid her hand over to rest on his. Their fingers intertwined. Overhead, the night sky seemed to swallow the earth and all of the people who lived and died upon it.

* * * *

The next morning, a massive object in the sky darkened the Potala and obscured the sunrise for a wide swath of Lhasa. Taki stared up at it, agog, his watch duties forgotten.

"Marvelous, isn't she?" Aslatiel said.

Taki nodded, his neck aching from tilting his head back for so long. "But just what is it?"

"A zeppelin. A secret of the old world brought back to us by the padishah's wisdom. That one is the *Lyudmila*. She will take us from here to Sevastopol, as we are conveniently on the way."

"Can it fight?"

"Yes, though she is better used for scouting. I've been told the crew is transporting a survey team sent to explore the waters east of the Goryeo Peninsula. Perhaps we will get to talk with them."

Taki had to stop staring for fear that his neck would start to spasm. The ship was slowly descending, and the tiny forms of the crew were starting to become more visible. Mooring lines fell like silvery threads onto the roof of the palace. The Imperium had fearsome resources at its disposal. *But they lacked a God Hand, and thus I'm still alive,* Taki thought. He looked at Aslatiel. Normally unflappable and almost inscrutable, the man seemed anxious. Like everything else about him, however, the effect was subtle.

"Are you thinking of Lady Irulan?" Taki asked.

"I'm thinking of all who were injured in that battle," Aslatiel said. "She is one of the severe cases."

"I guess I meant on a more personal level."

Aslatiel raised an eyebrow, and his lips thinned with a smile. "You're very perceptive. I'm glad I didn't kill you the first time we met."

Taki's scar throbbed. "You were close. I was worried I'd be crippled for life."

"Being unable to eliminate your squad was a source of aggravation for my sister and me. We were convinced that you were all protégés of the Agia Triada. Imagine our embarrassment when we learned the truth."

"That's a bit unfair."

Aslatiel bowed. "My apologies. I didn't intend to demean you or your fellows."

Taki cast his gaze downward. "No, it was I who reacted overmuch. It's just that, in the past, we suffered greatly because of your actions. My captain most of all." A shiver coursed through him as he recalled his hatred of Archangel Jibriil.

"Captain Satou is one of the most formidable warriors I've worked with in my career. You are lucky to be one of her soldiers. And I am lucky to have her on our side."

Taki nodded and turned his toes inward. "Do you believe in fate?"

Aslatiel shook his head. "We make our own destiny, within certain limits."

"I agree, but I also disagree. How would I have ever ended up here other than through some great design that I can't even fathom?"

"Keep in mind that I've never claimed to have all the answers to those questions. Just because I don't believe in a guiding hand that controls our destiny doesn't mean I'm right."

"May I speak frankly?"

"Always."

Taki felt his cheeks redden and his heart quicken to meet Aslatiel's gaze. "Part of the reason I believe in fate is that—I couldn't have ever imagined myself saying this—I like serving with you. Now that I've seen what you fight against, perhaps the Way is something worth defending.

I've never felt proud of my nation until now." Taki paused and shook his head. "Then again, your nation really isn't *my* nation, is it?"

Aslatiel placed his hands on Taki's shoulders. "Wrong. You followed the Way long before you even knew it, and when asked to uphold our principles, you did so willingly. That means you are a true citizen of the Imperium, and I'm pleased to have you, and even your companions, as its defenders."

Taki felt a strangely pleasant heaviness in his chest. *He always knows what to say at the right moment. Dassa was right: he really is a gigolo.*

"Of course, while you are very perceptive, Natalis, I am as well," Aslatiel said. "I've noticed that Shpejtspate harbors some affection for you."

"Did—did she go around spreading rumors?" Taki said indignantly.

"She comports herself better than that. But it's quite obvious when she pines. I haven't intervened because nothing has happened yet. However, keep in mind the fact that you are a junior officer and she is merely a kadet. Such an imbalance in rank makes for an exploitative relationship."

"I'm not exploiting her," Taki grumbled. "Besides, I wish she'd lay off me. I'm not even sure I really like her in that way."

Aslatiel chuckled. "I know you mean no harm, and I know you haven't inflicted any. It's just that you're both very young. Though we may compel you to fight and kill, we also want you to lead fulfilling lives, as hypocritical as it may be. You don't have to grow up too quickly."

"With all due respect, how old are *you,* sir?" Taki pouted. *Gigolo, my ass!*

"Twenty."

"I'm seventeen, you know."

"And cute as a button." Aslatiel walked away and left Taki fuming.

* * * *

A fortnight later, cabin fever had dampened everyone's spirits. Taki had taken to spending long hours on the top deck practicing his swordsmanship, which he had come to realize was lacking. If his track record from before wasn't proof enough, having Aslatiel as his opponent was.

"Argh!" Taki grunted in pain as the kriegsmesser scored a hit on the meat of his shoulder. A blotch of crimson stained his padded jerkin. Aslatiel had volunteered to teach both him and Enilna the finer points of blade combat, and Taki soon found that his teacher had no compunctions about cutting flesh to teach a lesson. The wounds were all superficial but stung fiercely, and the itching from his scabs added to the torment.

"Focus on me, not my blade," Aslatiel said. "You tripped up and got lost in the footwork, and you didn't see my hips telegraph the strike."

"Sorry, master," Taki said.

"No apologies. This is to aid your own survival. Again."

Aslatiel drew back into a low *posta coda.* They had been at each other for a full hour by now, but Taki's desire to score even one hit overpowered his urge to rest. This time, he approached head on but feinted first, as if he were trying a wide slash. Midway, he drew back against the expected counterstrike and pirouetted to close the gap and try to nick his teacher's thigh. Aslatiel twisted aside and smashed his fist into Taki's solar plexus. Taki collapsed, sputtering for air.

"You…you didn't say we could use fists."

"I did not. You must be ready to use every weapon at your disposal, including your bare hands. Still, the fact that I was forced to use mine means that you are doing better." Aslatiel offered his hand. Taki took it, considered trying a throw, and decided not to. He was tired and did not want to turn a small victory into a major defeat. Despite overwhelming soreness, he smiled at the compliment.

"Natalis, take a break. Shpejtspate, your turn," Aslatiel said.

Breathing heavily, Taki reclined against the deck railing and watched Enilna spar. For a mere kadet, she was surprisingly adept at swordplay, more so than he. This only meant that Aslatiel could lay her out in six seconds as opposed to three. *How did I ever survive the likes of him,* he wondered. Enilna's rapier clattered to the deck, and she raised her hands to yield.

"The enemy will give *no mercy* if she disarms you! Fight!" Aslatiel said, and came after her with his sword. Enilna scowled, hopped to her feet, and charged. She dove under the arc of his blade and tried to tackle him by the waist. Aslatiel drove an elbow between her shoulders, and she convulsed and dropped to the deck. She had barely rolled over before he threw her across the deck to skid next to Taki.

He sheathed his sword. "That's enough for today. You both need to concentrate on the fundamentals, though your blade control has improved. You're at liberty until supper."

"You okay?" Taki asked, and extended a hand to Enilna.

"Ugh, I think he broke something I can't even name." She struggled to her feet.

Taki smiled. "At least he didn't nick you this time."

"I thought Irulan was a hardass, but Aslatiel's a *sadist*."

"He's a hard taskmaster, but I'm also getting fewer scratches these days. Here, let's go back to quarters. This canvas is itchy, and I'm getting blood everywhere." Taki chuckled as he led Enilna below decks. At her quarters, he was about to take his leave.

"Wait. Help me, and I'll help you," Enilna said. She pointed to the back of her training jerkin. Designed to protect vital organs from an errant sword thrust, the jerkins laced up in back and were as cumbersome to remove as they were to put on.

"Fine," Taki said, and started to undo her knots. Halfway down, he realized that she wasn't wearing a camisole underneath. He averted his eyes, and his fingers became clumsy as a result.

"I'll take the rest. Here, turn and I'll get you started," Enilna said. Relieved to not be facing her anymore, Taki acquiesced and let her fingers work at the cords. She was far more dexterous than he, and the vest was off before he knew it.

"Thanks, I'll see you," Taki said.

She stopped him. "That's a nasty one." Her finger traced the cut over his shoulder. "Here, an old-fashioned remedy."

Taki's eyes widened as he felt her place her lips to the wound and start to suck. "What are you doing?" He turned and stumbled when he saw her vest was off entirely.

"Isn't it obvious? I like you. I want you," she said. "And I'm sure you're tired of being a virgin."

Taki felt his heart thump in his chest. A pleasant, irrational fog suffused his brain. It was unlikely anyone would catch them, and there was no telling when another opportunity like this would come up. She was beautiful and willing. Now he would really become a man. He hoped he wouldn't finish too early and disappoint her. He stepped closer and placed his hands on her waist. She raised her head and closed her eyes for a kiss.

She was trembling. Aslatiel's words from earlier nagged at Taki and wouldn't let go. But even more than that, he sensed something strange, whether from her demeanor or her touch. What was the best word for what she emanated? *Fear*, he realized.

"No. Not like this." He backed away and hurriedly gathered his jerkin up. Enilna opened her eyes and blinked in confusion.

"Don't you like me?" she asked, looking wounded.

"I think so, but I want to do this *right*." Taki clenched his teeth and left without a word.

The next time they trained, Enilna didn't speak with him once. For the rest of the journey, their exchanges were terse at best, and she chose to spend all of her spare time anywhere but with him. Taki considered talking with Aslatiel but decided not to. He didn't want to see her disciplined or pulled from a choice apprenticeship. And he didn't want to arouse suspicion of being—how had Hadassah put it?—a "Chomeo." *Fuck my life,* he thought to himself as he gazed over the wastelands.

* * * *

"I never thought I'd see it in my life, and certainly not from on high," Lotte muttered as she surveyed the city below from the top deck of the *Lyudmila*.

Taki raised a brow in concern, for his captain seemed apt to pitch over the railing she leaned over. He considered grasping the back of her shirt to steady her, but reasoned that there was an equal chance of mistakenly pushing her to her doom by mistake. "Captain, is this really Sevastopol?"

"Aye," Lotte said, and pointed. "See the white obelisk rising from the water, near the harbor mouth? Do you see the stone griffin perched atop it?"

Taki squinted at the monument. "I…I'm sorry, but I can't make it out from here."

"Where's Emreis and his spyglass when you need them?" Lotte said. "You'll just have to take my word for it. The griffin is the city mascot, and the the symbol of the Imperial Spetsnaz. No Argead has ever seen this place and survived. The city's a giant fortress entirely dedicated to rearing soldiers like von Halcon and his ilk. If there's any place the Imperials consider sacred, it's here."

"Like their version of the Cloud Temple, then?"

"You could say that, though the Imperials are a godless bunch, in case you haven't noticed. They don't think they need to repent."

Taki found himself reflexively shaking his head. Polaris like him or Lotte were the descendants of the demons who'd ended the golden age of man. It was impossible to absolve such a crushing burden of sin within one life, let alone a thousand. Thus, it was only right that the demons' children paid for their parents' sins. The fact that the taint of prana had grown so weak over the ensuing centuries of Polaris existence was proof that little by little, the debt was being repaid. *But then why would God let us lose to the Imperials?*

He promptly forced himself to ignore his own question. One of the unforeseen downsides of spending time with Aslatiel had been an increased propensity for blasphemous thoughts. Draco was already a lost cause on that front and Hadassah was given a pass because she was one of the chosen, but Taki was resolved not to fritter away everlasting life for stupid reasons. "It doesn't look like a fortress from here," Taki blurted out. "Hell, it looks like any other burg viewed from a mountainside. I'm sure we'll live."

Lotte chuckled. "I won't let them murder us before we've sampled the famous pump showers."

"What're those?"

"I don't actually know. I was hoping to find out, myself."

As they conversed, the *Lyudmila* began a rapid descent toward the city, into a large clearing encircled by a high curtain wall backed by an imposing keep that bristled with cannon and overlooked the eastern sector of the city. Before long, the zeppelin was securely moored to the ground by lengths of braided metal rope. Crewmen delicately lowered the ship's ramp to the ground, taking extra care not to let the metal slab slam against the packed earth. Taki and Lotte moved toward it when Aslatiel tapped their shoulders.

"Hold, you two. Do you not see what's before us?" Aslatiel pointed. "We've got an honor guard. And not just any honor guard. Those are attendants of the Imperial Cult."

Standing in perfect formation nearby were dozens of soldiers armored in shiny black plate and veiled by crimson niqab. Each hefted an ahlspiess taller than a man, and slung on their backs were pristinely-cleaned and oiled rifles. And each one was completely silent and still, to the point where it was hard to tell if they breathed. Taki whistled softly to himself. "Did you just say 'cult?'"

"Aye, though it's an archaic and outdated name for the padishah's personal guard. Remember, he isn't a god and doesn't wish to be thought of as such."

Taki bit his lip. "If they're here, then is the padishah with them?"

"Yes," Aslatiel said. "And I need you to answer me sincerely. Will you bend the knee to His Majesty?"

Lotte raised an eyebrow. "Do we have a choice?"

"No. But I don't wish to pick needlessly at old wounds. If any of your number are thoroughly opposed, then I will give them leave to stay aboard the ship until the padishah has departed."

Lotte smiled. "That's…kind of you, Aslatiel. If our positions were reversed, I'd make you kowtow to the basileus whether you wanted to or not. You'd also be in chains, and quite possibly naked. I will bend the knee, as will my men. We'll do anything to find Mezeta."

Aslatiel nodded. "I thank you for your cooperation. I only hope that one day, you'll kneel out of love of the Way, and not lust for revenge."

"Get us our woman, and I'll love whatever you want me to," Lotte said.

Taki's cheeks reddened again, and he turned and made his way to the ramp. Despite Lotte's sentiments, Taki was flush with anticipation. He'd known and served two Argead basileioi, and had even killed one of them, but the Imperial padishah decided the fate of millions across a land the size of hundreds of Dominions. And unlike the basileioi, the padishah seemed to hold the welfare of his subjects close to his heart. Perhaps one day, Taki hoped, Lotte would find happiness in her service as well.

The two squads slowly marched their way toward the Imperial Cult until Aslatiel stopped, thrust out an arm, and knelt with a flourish. Taki immediately followed suit, as did the rest of the Alfa. The remainder of Tirefire the Lesser gracelessly got to their knees a moment later.

The Imperial padishah sat on a gilded, velvet-upholstered throne that glided along on spoked wheels. He wore a mink greatcoat draped over the shoulders of an Imperial officer's dress tunic, and on his head was a thin circlet of unadorned white gold. His features, however, were anything but elegant or imposing. A pair of sunken and clouded eyes spoke of blindness, and the skin over his drawn features was thin to the point of translucency.

Yet it was not the decrepit Imperial ruler that set Taki's heart pounding, but Chronicler, who pushed the man's wheeled throne. The mere sight of the wizened easterner made Taki's throat want to close, and he quickly averted his eyes. He'd not yet forgotten what it had felt like to stand in the man's soul-draining shadow.

"His Imperial Majesty wishes to commend you, Aslatiel, for a job well done in Xizhang," Chronicler said. "He wanted to personally view the heroes who punished the vile rebels who threatened our honored teaching men and women."

Aslatiel pressed a fist to his chest. "Your presence is too high of an honor to bestow on us, Your Majesty. We merely did our duty to preserve the Way for others."

Chronicler chuckled. "Needless self-effacement is tiresome to hear, my boy. But your work speaks for itself." He glanced at Tirefire the Lesser. "And it seems we weren't mistaken about your valor after all, Argeads. Tell me, Taki Natalis, what does it feel like to be a hero of not only your land, but ours?"

I really wish I hadn't told him my name. Taki cringed as he felt the stares of his companions, the Imperial Cult, and the padishah all drill into him at once. He raised his head and cleared his throat. "With all due respect, Your Majesty, and Sir Chronicler, I am no hero. That sort of title belongs to people like Enilna over there, who had nothing and came from nothing, but stood up to evil men anyway. She shot Duke Gul Hekmatyar in Kosovo when I didn't have the guts to do it. She also speared the rebel leader Jamukha, who had me helpless at gunpoint because of my own carelessness. Actually, she's super effective at killing in general, and…"

The padishah slowly motioned to Chronicler, who bent down to put an ear next to the padishah's lips. A few seconds later, Chronicler nodded and stood straight again.

"His Majesty enjoys your candor, Taki Natalis. He will reward you and the kadet you mentioned with a sum of milligrad for your efforts. Unfortunately, His Majesty tires and must withdraw for the day. Now rest, my disciples, and enjoy a moment of impermanent peace. War is coming soon."

Chronicler wheeled the padishah around and pushed the throne back toward the keep. The Imperial Cult followed in perfect silence, without any of the normal clanking or grinding that always came with wearing plate. Once the entourage was a safe distance away, Aslatiel rose to his feet.

"As our liege commands, all are now at liberty until summoned again. Captain Satou, the hauptmann quartermaster will see to your lodging and sundries. I must accompany our wounded off the *Lyudmila* and cannot tarry."

Taki let out a breath that he hadn't realized he'd been holding. Then, he buried his face in his hands. Once again, he'd failed to make a good impression on royalty. Officers needed to be erudite, not ramble on about inconsequential matters. *And why in the hell was I babbling about stupid Enilna, anyway? At this rate she'll never talk to me again!* He let out a groan.

Hadassah clapped him on the back. "Natalis, if we'd known that you opening your mouth could drive away the Imperium, we'd still have a country to go home to. Talk about shit luck."

Taki squatted where he was and wished with all his might for a deep hole to throw himself into.

"He did well, Mikkelsen," Lotte said. "Milligrad from a king is about as good of a reward as any soldier could ever hope for. And Sir Chronicler violated basic etiquette by talking directly to Natalis. I can't believe the padishah would let the smug old bastard speak on his behalf."

"Captain," Hadassah said, "the padishah seriously looks like a random dead guy they dug out of the graveyard this morning. Just looking at him gave me age spots and lumbago. The guy's brain has got to be nothing but squid cock at this point. I bet Chronicler's just using him as a puppet and saying whatever the hell sounds cool."

"Though I might share your opinion, you should keep any mention of that to yourself," Lotte said. "We've made it this far, and we're not about to get strung up for treason or blasphemy." She grasped Taki's arm and yanked him up. "And you, stop sulking. Go get your reward and buy us some fried treats. If we're in Sevastopol, we're going to try all the terrible food."

9

Sir Ringo Trevelyan lazily yawned and flicked the pommel of his dagger. It spun haltingly on its crossguard atop the oaken table. He had not touched the salted bread and greasy brisket or the spiced ale in front of him, though the smell of rendered fat and alcohol was sheer ambrosia. Partaking of the meal would render him beholden to the one who offered it, and that was simply unacceptable. He gazed disdainfully at his peers. Sir Janus Eicke had already helped himself to a copious amount of beer like the besotted Teuton he was and was practically eating from—Ringo shuddered—*that woman's* hand.

It was one thing for the primate to summon them to gather but another entirely to expect them to serve a commoner, a foreigner, and especially a wench. And especially Hecaton Kheiris Mezeta. In addition to being a common, foreign wench, she was also the sworn enemy of every chivalric order in the Serene Kingdom. Had the others forgotten that basic fact?

In a show of the extreme cruelty of fate, what the horrid woman proposed was actually the solution to all of Ringo's problems. Like the others, he had deserted his order to seek fortune amid the excitement of the divine city's court, but he only found poverty outside the cloistered world of the barracks. Parasitic courtiers and amoral courtesans were always scheming to swindle him, and it was not long before he had fallen into destitution. He could not return and beg forgiveness from the master. The fate of those who did involved a lot of screaming and roasting flesh. With horror, Ringo realized that the memories of burning human fat were making him salivate. He could take no more. Hunger was driving him to insanity. What Hecaton was saying seemed to make sense. He only needed to listen to her and he'd be rich, not to mention satiated.

"Unacceptable!" he screamed, and slammed the point of his dagger into the table top with a resounding thunk.

"Oy, Ringo, what happened? You catch a bug?" Hecaton said, followed by laughter from the others.

Ringo rose from his chair and tipped it over. "Shut your mouth, witch, or I'll put it to better use."

"My friend, that is no way to address a *patrón*," said Sir Juan Diaz de Villavilla. He extended a hand.

"Quiet, Espinard, and if you lay a hand on me, by Jove, I'll gut you." Ringo focused a wrathful gaze on the assembled. "Lest you all forget, we are right honorable chevaliers. We're not slaves of the primate, and we don't serve some Dominion hag just because His Holiness has a hair up his arse! Stay and be her puppets if you wish. I'm leaving."

Hecaton laughed and glanced at his plate. "You want yours to go?"

Ringo gritted his teeth and wrenched the dagger out of the table. His gut ulcers throbbed painfully. "Fuck off."

"Guess I'll feed it to the dogs, then," Hecaton shrugged. "A pity. I heard you haven't had a decent meal for months. I bet it came as a shock that, despite your skills as a cartographer, there was no employment in Astarte. Was it hard on your manly pride to subsist on charity and the occasional bout of hired thuggery? Looks like that's your future now. I'll find someone else to take the God Hand and someone else to share in the rewards. Now, who wants seconds?"

Ringo wished more than anything that he had the strength and the pride to march out the door and return to his hovel outside the castle walls. Later, he'd have to bribe the guard to return to the court, where he would scrape and grovel before sneering dandies and lower himself to beating shopkeeps for protection money. This would be his life until he perished, and that time was coming soon.

He smashed a fist into the wooden doorframe and turned around. He silently righted his chair, sat, and tore into the bread and meat like an animal. Tears of self-loathing coursed down his face. He'd serve Hecaton Mezeta...for now. Later, he'd torture her to death.

"And that makes four. Back to business," Hecaton said. Janus raised a hand. "Yes?"

"*Frau* Mezeta, your plan does not lack for audacity, and yet I can see a problem."

"Go on," she said.

"Let us say that we are successful in raiding the Sepulchre and opening the Ooss inside. How are we expected to take the God Hand back here? From what you describe, it is at least ten meters long and weighs *thirty thousand kilograms*. Four men and a grandam cannot simply strap it to their backs and make the walk. How would we even move it out in the first place?"

"*Sí,*" Juan said. "And that assumes, *amigos,* that we even have the time to think about such engineering feats. I promise you that the Argeads will be on us with full force of arms the second we defile their holy ground. And if not them, certainly their Imperial masters."

Hecaton cracked a smile. "Sir Janus, you are an engineer with a talent for the repair of ancient artifacts, are you not?"

He nodded.

"And Sir Juan, you are a master navigator of the seas, correct?"

"*El mejor.*"

"And Ringo is supposedly one of the best mapmakers in the kingdom."

Ringo seethed but remained silent. He still felt starved but did not wish to give Hecaton the pleasure of seeing him ask for more food.

Hecaton smirked. "There's a reason I asked Primate Alesso for you three in particular. You are all skilled fighters but more importantly, you have the collective means to bring a ship across the sea without sinking it. What do you all think the Ooss really is?"

"I think I know what you imply. But even if so, it has no sail, no rigging, and no cannon," Juan said.

"It's a special sort of boat that doesn't need sails or masts. A rare type made to sail both on and *under* water. It not only houses the God Hand but also serves as a means to launch the Hand. The basileoi of the Dominion are a direct line from the original crew of the Ooss, and that is why one of their many pointless dictums is to make sure that the Hand can be made ready to fire at any time. The holy Ooss must always be kept in good repair for the day when they make their final journey back home. I aim to exploit their tradition. We are going to steal not only the God Hand but also the holiest relic of the Argead Dominion."

* * * *

Despite how much he wished to disembowel Hecaton, it was not without some satisfaction that Ringo departed his dingy hovel for what he knew would be the last time. It was a miserable existence, shivering night after night under a holey plastic roof propped up against the walls of the gatehouse. The closest place to shit was a horrific-smelling ditch on the side of the road that always overflowed and left indescribable filth where he should have slept. His belongings were constantly subject to theft by packs of feral children who populated the ghetto. Once, he had caught one in his grasp and was about to cut its throat when the other hovel dwellers suddenly surrounded him with cudgels in hand. One day, when he was a rich man, he would return and kill them all.

It was a half bell's walk to the docks, where Hecaton had told the crew to assemble in the morning. His remaining possessions all fit on his person, for they were the only things he absolutely could never sell. Besides the brigandine, coif, greaves, and boots, he had a steel dagger. Two reloaded rounds were all else he had to his name. In the service of the Ordo Anglia, he had carried a rifle, but the gun had been pawned a long time ago.

"Sir Ringo, I beg a moment," muttered someone at his right.

"Not interested," Ringo murmured back and kept his eyes ahead.

"An Old Nayto Standard for your time."

Ringo edged closer to a nearby tavern and crouched as if to tighten his lacings. His stalker dawdled nearby. He pressed his back to the wall and peeled back the lip of his right boot to further expose the hilt of his dagger. He would not be caught unawares by some wretched plot. Imbecilic Hecaton had of course announced her plan to steal from the Dominion in front of the entire court. Now, there were hundreds of swirling schemes centered around that fact. Ringo knew he was a target in at least a few of them.

"Drop the grad where I can see it," he said. "Regardless of what you say, I take it and leave. If you follow me, I'll tear your head off."

A cartridge plinked onto the cobbles. Ringo picked it up. It seemed to be true milligrad, but even if it was a gilded reload, it would still represent more wealth than he had possessed in a long time. The headstamp was marked with the circled cross of Old Nayto, and the primer seemed to be original brass. Ringo shoved the round into his leggings for safekeeping. He glanced to his side to make sure the stalker wasn't edging closer; that would earn him a gutting.

"I speak for the primate alone," the stalker said. "Mezeta has no intention of delivering the God Hand to His Holiness as promised. Once the Hand is secured, eliminate her. His Holiness will pay a hundred thousand rounds of Old Nayto for this, divided between survivors."

Ringo's lips thinned into a smile. "And if there is only one survivor?"

"He would gain the full sum."

Ringo stood without another word and walked away. *I'd have done her in for free, but if I can off Eicke and Diaz, I'll be a wealthy man indeed.* He turned to assure himself that he wasn't being followed. The stalker had disappeared. The milligrad had not. Ringo made his way to the docks.

Cobblestones gave way to wooden planks, and the omnipresent odor of human excrement was quickly replaced by that of decomposing fish. According to the old hag, they were to board a trade ship to Korinthos and from there would travel through Dominion territory to the outskirts of Athenaeum, where the Sepulchre waited. Ringo quickened his pace when he saw the masts of the trade ship. He would not suffer the humiliation of being tardy.

Ringo grunted when he collided head on with something heavy. Fortunately, he slightly outweighed whatever or whoever it was, and he did not pitch backward into a pool of oily filth. He tensed in indignation and glared at a boy—actually, a girl—sprawled out in front of him. She was of middling height and plainly featured, wearing a servant's attire, her hair drawn tightly into a small bun. Around her were scattered what appeared to be metal tools, both new and ancient. She raised her eyebrows in alarm and scrambled to her knees in supplication.

"Damned wench, are you blind?" Ringo drew back a hand to slap her.

"Stay your hand, good sir!" Janus, fat and out of breath, bounded up to them and stood in front of the servant girl. "I shall recompense you for the inconvenience, of course, but she is *mein* servant alone, and thus I demand you not to beat her."

"*You* have a wench?" Ringo had to chuckle. He dropped his hand. "And I thought you weren't into rutting, Sir Janus."

"She carries my bags and helps with calibrations. More like a squire, really."

Ringo rolled his eyes. "A *squire*. Right. You into boys?"

Janus glared at Ringo and turned to the servant. "Come, Samara, pick this up, and we'll head to the boat."

Ringo left the embarrassing spectacle behind and walked up the gangway to the *Cuenta Cuesta*. Hecaton leaned against the mainmast and winked at him. Juan was busy schmoozing with the captain at the helm. He ignored them in favor of laying claim to a comfortable spot below decks. It would take at least a fortnight to reach their destination, and though seafaring usually meant intolerable boredom for a passenger, he could use the time to think about how to eliminate Hecaton once and for all. And how to obtain the full hundred-thousand-round prize.

10

"You never realize that you smell like a million unwashed assholes until you actually get clean again," Draco said. He raised his right arm and pressed his nose to the pit and inhaled deeply. "Like a rose, I am."

"Roses smell like dogshit," Hadassah said. "And do you really need to sniff yourself in public?"

"How else would I know? Not like I can ask anyone else to smell me."

Lotte clamped her hands on Draco's shoulders and sniffed at the nape of his neck. "Yes, like farts."

"Am I the handsomest of roses, Captain?"

"Definitely the stinkiest," Hadassah said.

They grouped together while they walked down the busy corridors of Sevastopol Fortress. Around them flowed a current of Imperial troopers and pages laden with dispatches. The distant thumping of artillery practice made the less acclimated wince with every discharge. A sense of frenetic foreboding stirred the air. Battle was imminent.

"I'm just glad for the pumphouse," Karma remarked. "I never imagined I'd have my own little rainstorm to wag my manhood around in."

"Aye," Draco said, "it's the best place to spend some alone time in."

Lotte nodded her approval. "I've never loved our creator much, but then I found the detachable showerhead."

"It's much better than any fingers," Hadassah said conspiratorially.

"Remember, you lot, we're in their house now," Taki said on seeing the titillated expressions of two kadetten who were obviously eavesdropping. "We've got to comport ourselves respectably."

Draco laughed. "Did Natalis just act like an officer?"

"I didn't mean—"

Hadassah knelt with exaggerated flourish. "Yes, sir. We're sorry, sir. We'll stop talking about wanking now, sir. There will be no discussion about choking the chicken, beating the exarch, firing blanks, riding solo, dancing with oneself, teasing the bearded clam, or plain old diddly-winks…*sir*."

Taki tried to bury his face in his collar.

"All right, lay off him," Karma said. "He's right, too. We represent the Dominion, like it or not."

"I thought you didn't give a damn about the Dominion," Hadassah said. "Or are you taking your crown princeliness too seriously?"

"Am not!"

Compared to the sweltering, crowded barracks within the Cloud Temple, their new accommodations were shining emblems of comfort, with individual chamber pots and partitions between their beds. Lotte's rank rewarded her with private quarters on the floor above, but out of habit she continued to share a bed with Hadassah. By now, they had gotten used to the stares and whispers and made sure to always travel in pairs or as a group if possible. Just as there had been Polaris itching for payback, there were Imperials with similar sentiments. The fencing or sparring rings were just invitations to trouble, so none of them set foot in those places.

"We're here," Lotte said. "Everyone suck in your guts."

The sentinels at the door bowed and opened the way. The Imperial contingent had already arrived, though Irulan was absent due to fever from her wounds. Taki's eyes flicked around the chambers. They belonged to General Reinhard, a bear of a man who was Chronicler's second in command, and also the castellan of Sevastopol keep. The space was spartan in its adornment, much like Reinhard's features.

Reinhard sat at his desk, nursing a pipe. He looked up. "Argeads. Does the name 'Hecaton Kheiris Mezeta' mean anything to you?"

The explosion that followed left Taki's ears ringing.

"Where is she?"

"Have you seen her?"

"I'll kill the bitch!"

"I'll take that as a 'yes,'" Reinhard said, and he shook his ashes out.

Lotte marched up to his desk and slammed her palms on it. "Don't jape with me. I just helped your people put down a peasant rebellion at the cost of too many godrotting lives. If you've seen Mezeta, then tell us where she is *right now!*"

"I intend to," Reinhard said. "Von Halcon says you want revenge on her, and this may be your chance. We can help you do that and in turn, you can help us."

"Lotte," Aslatiel said. "Hear him out. Please."

"Thank you," Reinhard said. "Spies have spotted Mezeta in Astarte. She's apparently living in the lap of luxury and employs a squad of chevaliers as her bodyguards."

"That doesn't make sense," Lotte said. She crossed her arms. "The primate banned her from the city on pain of death. I was there when it happened."

"And that's what worries me," Reinhard said. "Pacifying Astarte is vital to the campaign. Unless we either kill its leaders or buy them off, we won't be safe on the march to southern Ursala. But the spies tell me that Mezeta has offered her services to the primate against us. This cannot be allowed. She's a greater threat to the padishah than she ever was before."

"She's always a threat," Lotte said. "But how to take her down…"

"You mentioned buying the ruler off," Taki said. "Is that even possible?"

"Yes," Reinhard said. "The primate may have sworn fealty to Ursala, but he's a disloyal subject who wheels and deals with his enemies on a regular basis. He had an arrangement with the Argeads and is open to dealing with us, so long as it benefits him. I want you to sneak in and meet with the man. Find out what he wants for his allegiance and what it'll take for him to deliver Mezeta into our hands. She may be powerful, but she can't win against an army. And if needed, *Ba'gshnar* will deal with her."

Aslatiel furrowed his brows. "How will we meet with the primate?"

"Vympel Gruppe has put in a lot of hard work to arrange an audience. Alfa's job is to make absolutely sure he comes to an understanding."

"We'll make it happen," Aslatiel said and bowed.

"I have faith in your people, von Halcon. The city's on the brink. See to it that we push it over. You're dismissed."

Taki glanced over at his compatriots. Their excitement over the chance for murder was almost palpable. Hadassah seemed to positively glow. Disturbingly enough, it made her look quite lovely. He shuddered and turned to Aslatiel.

"Sir Aslatiel, are we to assassinate this primate?"

Aslatiel shook his head. "Only if all else fails. If that were to happen, then we'd be on a suicide mission."

"So what can we offer that Mezeta can't?"

"I don't know, but I have a feeling he'll demand discreet service. He has enough grad that anything we can offer won't make a difference. But the primate is still an Ursalan subject and answers to a daughter of the Rex. Whatever he wishes will have to be accomplished beneath her notice."

Lotte put an arm on Taki's shoulder. "I forgot that you haven't traveled much in your life."

"I haven't, Captain."

"Astarte is a beautiful place. But you'll drown in intrigue there if you're not careful."

"Have you visited there, Captain?"

"Once, when I was Archangel Yuriel. Mezeta was there, though I didn't serve her at the time. I wonder if the primate will recognize me."

Taki worried at a cuticle. "So we'll walk in and meet the man, then?"

"Not if we want to keep Princess Sophie in the dark. If we don't do it discreetly, we'll have every royal assassin in the place up our arses." Lotte looked at Aslatiel. "But knowing your people, there's a plan in place already."

Aslatiel winked. "Aye, the Imperium always has a plan."

* * * *

A woman whom Taki had never seen before reclined in one of the oversized oaken chairs in the study. Aslatiel had ordered everyone to meet there on one of the middle floors of the keep but had kept his reason for doing so a secret. The more Taki saw of the new arrival, though, the less he wished to stay, especially when she winked at him and licked her lips. A deep, crudely healed scar etched into her right cheek turned half her face into a ghastly, fanged rictus. Taki turned his eyes away.

"Alfa," Aslatiel said, "this is Brigade General Chang of Vympel. She arranged our meeting with the primate. Her intelligencers will also disguise us for entry to Astarte. Follow her counsel as you would mine own."

"If you don't, you'll not only die there but also make a foolish-looking corpse," Chang said. She rose and started to pace. "You are to meet the primate in the Tintoretto. Think of a gaming hall mated with a brothel. We have chosen that place because Princess Sophie does not accompany her consort there. In addition, this is festival season for Astarte, so her agents will be overwhelmed by the number of visitors to the city."

"I assume we're entering in disguises?" Lotte said.

"Aye," Chang said. "You'll be replacing a nobleman and his entourage. They had an unfortunate encounter a fortnight ago. Highway robbery with no survivors. So very, very, sad."

Jesus, Taki thought as Chang cackled at the last part.

"So we need to pick who plays what part." Chang leaned over, pierced Draco with a stare, and gently traced the line of his jaw with a fingernail. "*Yes*. This beautiful buffoon will play the part of *le Vicomte de Bretagne.*"

Draco tensed, and his cheeks reddened. "The victim de what?"

Aslatiel cleared his throat. "The Viscount of Brittany, a man of the Ursalan court. That means the rest of us will play servants and bodyguards. General, I suggest that Rana plays the viscountess."

"A fine choice, von Halcon. Make it so," Chang said.

"Wait a godrotting second," Hadassah piped in. "Why does Draco get to be the big shot here? I'm not going to bow and scrape to him, let alone serve him cheese on a platter."

"I don't want your cheese, you wanker," Draco said.

"That's fine. You make plenty of your own."

"You're disgusting."

"Says the man with a foreskin."

"That's sexual harassment, I'll have you know. I don't have to take it."

"I enjoy a double standard, sheepfucker."

"Captain!"

"Shush, both of you," Lotte said. "Von Halcon is right. Emreis has the most stereotypically Ursalan features of any of us. He can easily pass for one of their inbred nobles."

Draco looked wounded.

"I didn't mean it in a bad way!"

"Mikkelsen, your people are nonexistent in the Serene Kingdom," Aslatiel said. "In fact, it's risky to even take you."

Hadassah crossed her arms. "So why does *Elsa* get the part of lead actress, huh? I call discrimination."

"This isn't playacting for fun," Aslatiel said. "We're trying to sneak into a pleasure palace in the middle of a city full of spies and soldiers for an illicit meeting with its leader right under the nose of his consort. I suggested Rana because she looks so Anglian, and Anglia is close to Burgundy. It's more plausible."

"Dassa, you think I *want* to be dressed in frilly bullshit and paraded around as a boutonniere for a sack of shit?" Elsa said.

Draco's lips quivered. "I'm a *sack of shit* now?"

"She's just getting into character," Lotte said.

"I'm not calling him 'Your Grace,'" Hadassah sniffed.

"You will if you address him," Aslatiel said. "Ursalan protocol rules the day. Especially for you, Emreis. Knowing how to speak correctly and conduct yourself with flourish is the most important thing to any member of the court. Flub it, and we'll be outed. Then, we'll be tortured to death."

"They'll remove your manhood first," Chang said matter-of-factly. "Speaking of which, Captain Satou, does his work? Have you tried it? And will you lend him to me tonight?"

Lotte shook her head. "No on all counts, Madam General."

"Of course, mine works!" Draco insisted, nearly in tears.

Taki cleared his throat. "We're getting off track here! Sir Aslatiel, will we be allowed arms inside?"

"No," Aslatiel said. "Only Emreis and his bodyguard would be allowed swords. Ursalan law demands death for commoners and slaves found with weapons."

Chang nodded and clapped twice. A press of Imperials entered the room. "Everyone, get changed. My intelligencers will assist you with all of the details. We'll see how you do in costume."

* * * *

A bell later, Taki nearly collapsed with laughter when he saw Draco in full costume for the first time. The intelligencers had spared no effort to paint a convincing picture of an indolent, pleasure-obsessed courtier. Draco sported a ruffled silk shirt under a velvet doublet, along with tightly drawn silken hose and a wide-brimmed felt hat embellished with a brace of peacock feathers. The caked-on powder and rouge, along with a waxed moustache expertly adhered to his upper lip, completed the picture.

"Draco, it's so *you*!" Hadassah slapped her thighs and doubled over. Instead of finery, she and Karma had been given plain-looking servants' clothing.

"Oh, stuff it up your poopers!" Draco said. "I'm not the most ludicrous-looking one here." He pointed his emerald-headed cane at Elsa, who threatened to topple at any moment under the strain of her hooped ball gown. Her face was flushed red due to a a corset that had been applied without mercy.

"If I could breathe…I'd kick you," she said.

"I think she looks beautiful," Lotte said.

"Thank you. You're quite…handsome yourself."

"Aye, thanks…" Lotte's eyes were downcast. She cut a dashing figure with a sweeping, high-collared velvet greatcoat festooned with brass buttons, braids, and a long pair of tails. Her chest had been bound with linen, and the shape of her waist was hidden with a broad leather satchel belt. Her hair was drawn tightly back and oiled, and she looked every bit the part of a swaggering mercenary contracted to guard the viscount.

"Captain, you don't seem too pleased," Taki said. He tugged at the hem of his page's doublet. It fit well and would have been stylish if not for the Ursalan standard adorning the breast.

"Oh, I'm pleased enough," Lotte said. "It's just that Rana's dress is pretty, and I could never really fit into it."

Taki tilted his head in confusion. Why would such a fierce warrior wish to dally with frilly silks and cambric? "I think boiled leather and steel go better with you."

Lotte shot him an exasperated look.

"We'll be wearing these disguises all throughout," Aslatiel said. "So you need to get comfortable moving in them."

"The things I do...for my country," Elsa huffed. She tried to take a wider step and ended up pitching backward from the imbalanced outfit. She spread her arms in an attempt to direct her fall but ended up in Mikhail's arms.

"Make sure you all practice fighting in those clothes," Chang said. "Or at least know what to tear away before you get into it. Spend the rest of the day in your disguises to get used to them." She turned to leave. "Don't fuck up, by the by."

"Oy," Draco said. "Where's the Prince of Maladies? Shouldn't she be suffering along with the rest of us?"

Hadassah stuck her tongue out. "You just want to see her in a cute dress, pervert."

"No! It's just that, you know, maybe I wanted to see another side of the fearsome Prince." Draco's ears reddened through the powder.

"My sister is too recognizable to the Ursalans," Aslatiel said. "She'll stay back for this one."

"Makes sense," Draco said. "They titled her."

Taki yawned and righted himself. He saw Enilna staring at him while she squatted against a corner. She was attired as a lady-in-waiting, and though her finery lacked the expense of Elsa's or the striking appearance granted to Lotte, it lent Enilna a certain air of delicacy that Taki found himself appreciating. He met her eyes, and she looked away. He went to her, sick of feeling blamed for everything.

"What's your problem?" he snapped. Immediately, he regretted his words.

She glared at him. "I have no problem. I'll be off now."

"Wait. Sorry, I didn't mean to insult you," Taki said. "If I did, I'm sorry. But I'm not sorry for turning you down aboard the zeppelin."

"You're impossible to figure out, Natalis. It confuses me, and when I get confused, I get angry. And you're making me *really* angry!"

"We're about to do something dangerous. We can't be pissy to each other like this."

"Then give me a straightforward answer. Am I not good enough for you? Is there something about me you dislike?"

"It's not about you."

"Then what is it? Do you have a dysfunction? Do you fancy older women? Do you want to rut with your captain instead?"

Taki grimaced and shot a glance toward Lotte. When it looked as if she hadn't heard Enilna, he sighed in relief. "No, and be quieter, damn you."

"You don't even know what you want. No wonder you're still a virgin."

Taki clenched his fists. "You hit me with that whenever you feel stung. Everyone mocks me all the time. It's not like I *want* to be ridiculed forever! I wanted to take you, but you were scared out of your godrotting mind."

"So?"

"It's not supposed to be that way! You shouldn't have offered yourself if you weren't ready. And if I'd done it anyway, then I'd be even more pathetic for it."

Enilna punched him on the arm. "You're so annoying! I hate you!"

Taki shook his head. "The real problem is that you're still a *child*. Well, I'm no molester." He turned to leave.

Enilna grabbed at his sleeve.

"What?" he spat.

"When…when you were all awkward with the padishah, did you mean what you said? About how you think I'm heroic and good?"

Taki sighed. "Yes, I did. You're braver than most people have a right to be."

"Then I guess I can forgive you a little. Can we stay friends?"

Taki threw his hands up in frustration. "Of course we can."

11

Lotte breathed in through her nostrils, held her breath, and let it out slowly. She closed her eyes and grasped the hilt of her side sword. "I know where she is."

Hadassah grinned and smacked her fist into her palm. "Then let's start the hunt. Hear ye, Mezeta, I'm going to find you. And then I'm going to eat you."

"You say the same thing when you've got a finger in your nose," Draco said.

She reddened. "I do not!"

"No cannibalism! And pipe down, you're arousing suspicion!" Taki focused on holding his studiously bored expression. They had barely gone a dozen steps past the grand portcullis of Astarte, and everyone was already breaking character. Everyone in *his* squad, anyway. *Why can't they just be good?* Meanwhile, the Imperials seemed to blend perfectly into their roles.

"Even if Hecaton Mezeta were to pass right in front of our noses," Aslatiel said, "we're in no position to face her. You know this, Satou. Follow the plan, or we all die. Viscount of Brittany, control your horse."

Draco tugged at his reins and prevented the mare from snapping up an apple from a nearby street vendor. "Damnable beast," he muttered.

He alone rode while the others walked. They were disguised as a standard, if somewhat small, noble's entourage. Aslatiel had beaten it into their heads: the Viscount of Brittany had journeyed to Astarte to dice and enjoy blood sport at the Tintoretto.

"My apologies, von Halcon," Lotte said. "Mezeta didn't just steal from us; she ruined our lives. We were cast out of our home with only the clothes on our backs. We'd have ended up as beggars or highwaymen if you hadn't taken us."

"And if Natalis hadn't vouched for you," Aslatiel said. "There's no love lost between Mezeta and me, either. We will face her again, I'm sure, but on our terms. For now, let's obtain lodging and a place to rest our horses. Viscount, you remember how to comport yourself, right?"

"Aye," Draco said. "I don't touch grad for any reason. I leave it all to you, and the other servants carry the bags. I'm to hit them with my cane if they tarry. The long and short of it is: I'm to be a giant dick."

"Precisely. And if someone of noble blood should insult you at any point?"

"Challenge him to a duel, to be held in the morning. He picks the seconds."

"Don't forget to throw your glove down."

Enilna tugged at Aslatiel's sleeve. "Can we attend the festival? I've always wanted to go to Korbo's Feast, ever since my mother told me about it."

Around them, the city buzzed with preparation for the ancient rite. Paying homage to a harvest god whose worship even the Santctissimus Rex could not stamp out, the festival was one of Astarte's most popular. Brightly colored banners unfurled from high windowsills, and towering effigies of saints and devils received finishing touches from attentive craftsmen. Eventually, they would all burn for the culmination of the festivities. Enilna eyed a three-meter-tall caricature of the padishah, with comically oversized and sore-ridden genitals, and laughed.

"No," Aslatiel said.

Enilna looked crestfallen but did not protest further.

"Sir Aslatiel," Taki said, "I mean no insubordination, but becoming familiar with the city layout and hearing the local gossip would only help us in the end. We all know better than to become intoxicated, too."

Aslatiel scratched his chin in thought. "I hadn't thought of that, Natalis. Very well, I'll allow some of our number to go."

"Thank you," Taki said. He glanced over at Enilna. She frowned at him...but insincerely.

* * * *

Despite Taki's misgivings, he was still glad for the chance to explore the festivities, even for a limited time. He had also heard about the processions and parades, with their dueling effigies and bawdy bards that whipped the crowd into frenzy. Now, he could get to see it for himself. He strolled down the boulevards close to the inn and let himself gaze in wonderment at the multicolored lanterns strung out between rooftops like flies caught in spider webs.

"Call me a child, will you?" Enilna laughed and poked his cheek. "You've gone all goggle-eyed, there."

Taki sniffed. "Remember, we're actually supposed to be scouting. I'm not excited. I'm trying to blend in."

"You expect me to believe that?"

"I'm the responsible one, here."

Enilna put her hands on her hips. "You're fighting a smile. Why are you always so stiff? Just enjoy the chance to have fun."

"How can I enjoy myself when I'm saddled with watching a kid?"

"Are you surly because you're not arm-in-arm with your captain right now?"

"Enough about that. I respect and admire her, that's all."

"After I shot the duke in Kosovo, guess what I did? I stuck my hand under Lotte's cuirass. I felt her *boob*!"

Taki blushed. "Just lay off me."

"I'm not jealous, just so you know. I also hold her in high regard. You'll never tumble with her, though, as high strung as you are."

"I said lay off!"

Enilna raised her hands. "Fine, I yield. But I do think you worry too much about stupid things."

"Then that's my problem, not yours."

"Look, I was going to thank you for convincing Aslatiel to let us go to the fest. Do you know what this whole celebration's most famous for?"

Taki scratched his cheek. "Er, not really."

"Pickled apples!"

"Sounds unpalatable."

"Not at all. They layer slices in honey and add ginger and cardamom to the mix. My mother told me that my father got some for her once, and it was the sweetest and best thing she had ever tasted in her life."

Despite himself, Taki found his mouth watering ever so slightly at the description. "I suppose that sounds tasty," he said. "But where do you think we'll find some?"

"I don't know. That's why we have to ask around," Enilna said, and twirled on her feet. Her dress puffed outward in a swirl of color.

Taki started to smile. *She's pretty, too.*

"Oh, come on," he said. "Let's go look for those apples. But we can't get separated." He extended a hand, and Enilna grasped it.

"Your hand's cold," she said. "But that's fine; it'll warm up. Just like your withered, old, bean-counting heart."

"You want apples or not?"

She giggled, and they set off. Eventually, after inquiring at a few beer stands, they were directed to the only stall that had any preserved apples in stock. For the ruinous price of two rounds of Luger milligrad, they found themselves in possession of the dregs of the vendor's last barrel of the honey-pickled treat.

"I got us some drinks," Taki said. He sat next to Enilna on a bench and passed her a tankard. They were at the periphery of one of the city's squares, facing a bubbling fountain.

"I thought we couldn't have booze," she said.

"It's a smallbier. Really just malt boiled with some hops. I'm not about to disobey my captain's order. She'll smack me, and it'll hurt like hell."

"Irulan tugs at my ears," Enilna said.

"You'd better not have eaten all of it already," Taki said, eyeing the treat. "We paid far too much for too little."

Enilna rolled her eyes. "What do you take me for, some kind of gourmand? I'm going to savor this slowly, especially after the highway robbery we just went through."

"You know, this stuff is usually reserved for the nobles. They just make an exception during festivals. Allows the merchants to dump stock that's going bad and make room for more."

"You mind not shitting on my enjoyment?"

"I'm still the purser for my squad. It's my job to shit on everyone."

"I liked you better as the unit farmer."

"I was never a farmer!"

"If you were, you'd enjoy this every day."

"I'd work my hands to the bone without any assurance of survival."

"Nothing's guaranteed in life, Taki. That's why you have to just let loose and enjoy things like this. Dance and drink and get in bar fights!"

"I've been in a bar fight. It was horrible."

Enilna laughed. "I guess there's no arguing with a masochist. Well, shall we?"

Taki dipped a wooden spoon into the wax-paper cone his companion held. He struggled to maneuver a small piece of apple onto his spoon without losing the fruit in the gooey mess and brought it to his mouth. Strands of stickiness hit his chin, and he wanted to wipe them away. As he had suspected, the fruit had been kept overlong and now tasted more like alcohol than apples. But the honey and spices still caused a pleasant, sweet burn in the back of his throat without being as cloying as he'd feared.

"Not terrible," he said, and looked over to his companion.

Tears streaked down Enilna's face as she chewed and swallowed. Taki raised an eyebrow. Surely she didn't find the taste *that* offensive?

Her words about her mother and the taste of pickled apples came back to him. *She's a war orphan.* The Duke of Kosovo had killed her entire family. *Of course she's crying.* What human or witch wouldn't? He set his tankard and spoon down and tentatively brushed her hand with his.

"You, uh, miss them, right?" Taki said. He immediately cursed his ineptitude with words, but Enilna did not seem to care. She nodded and turned her face into his shoulder. With trepidation, he started to stroke her hair. He hadn't needed to do this before. He didn't know if this would help her or if it would simply confuse her more. "I also lost my parents. It happened a long time ago, and I don't even remember their faces, and I certainly don't know their names. And in truth, I never really cared to find out." He looked down, unsure of where to go next. "But I know that if my squadmates were to perish, I'd miss them terribly. They're kind of like family now. I don't know what I'd actually do if I saw them fall in front of me. I think I'd go crazy, or I'd disobey orders if I thought I could save them. Once, I'd have gladly dumped them to get promoted, but I was foolish then and didn't know a damned thing. I only thought of myself. Sorry, I'm rambling. I guess I wanted to tell you I could understand what you're going through, or something. Forgive me. I'm probably making things worse."

Enilna shook her head, her face still buried in the cloth of his shirt. She finally drew back and chuckled. She wiped a sleeve end against the moistness of her face.

"You definitely lack Aslatiel's way with words, but thank you. I guess I wasn't ready for this." She was flushed. "My mother was right, though. This is the sweetest thing I think I've ever eaten so far. I'm glad I got to taste it with you. Thank you, Taki. One day, I'll make it up to you. I'll give you something far sweeter."

She leaned forward. Taki tensed. He did not know what to do if she wanted a kiss. He would be unable to resist her a second time. Her lips veered to the side of his, and she planted a peck on his cheek.

"We're friends, remember?" Enilna squeezed his hand and let go.

Taki nodded in relief. "Aye, we're friends." He stood up and offered her his arm. "Shall we go back?"

"Let me finish my b—" Enilna started to say, but she was cut off by a belch. Taki laughed and gazed up at the night sky.

* * * *

Draco leaned on his jewel-headed cane and twisted his moustache. He huffed and stamped his feet, mimicking the mannerisms of an indolent playboy. A footman in front of him pored over a large, open text mounted on a pedestal. The man's eyes flitted between the book and a dog-eared sheepskin festooned with dozens of wax seals, smeared annotations, and obscene doodles disguised as scrollwork.

"Canst thou not read? I tire of thine fumblings," Draco sneered. "Let me to the tables else I beat thee with mine cane!"

"Master, I beg you to relent," Aslatiel said. He had donned a robe of brocaded silk, and his queue trailed almost to the ground. "The honorable servant must confirm every man of high stature against the holy primate's record, else it's his head!" He shuffled up to the footman and bowed yet again. "Prithee, sire, is there a problem?"

The footman rolled his eyes and shoved the counterfeit letters of nobility against Aslatiel's chest. "None, save for the mongrel in front of me. Takee thine scrollee to thine Lordee and tell him he may pass."

"Thank you, thank you, sire." Aslatiel bowed again, stepped back, and then turned to Draco. "Master, you shall win big tonight, yes. Shall I order the maids to take the viscountess to the powder rooms?"

Draco nodded dismissively and flipped the end of his powdered wig. Aslatiel gestured for the servants to make haste. Taki groaned inwardly as he shouldered one of the ends of Elsa's palanquin again. Taking it through the city had made his body ache, and when he complained about it, Elsa had smacked him with her fan. *She's enjoying this way too much.*

Thankfully, soon after they passed through the iron-reinforced wooden doors, he laid down his burden. With great ceremony, Elsa stepped out of her gaudy carriage and went with all of the women toward the powder rooms. Taki followed along after Lotte.

The pavilion reminded him of a gaudier version of the Duke of Kosovo's throne dungeon. A riot of chandeliers swayed overhead, showering hot wax onto those below. Gaming tables hosted games of dice and cards where whole belts of milligrad were wagered without a care. Servants of the gaming lords plied their masters with a continuous stream of drinks and bloody meat. Gorging seemed to be as much of a competition as baccarat. A string quartet on an elevated platform provided strains of tinny music, but their efforts were overshadowed by the main attraction in the center of the room.

Within a cage of wrought iron, a nearly naked man was fighting a bear. The bear stood on its hind legs and tried to bring its massive bulk down on the human fighter to crush him, but he rolled and evaded the strike. The crowd, desirous of blood, booed. The fighter grinned, spat, and started to pummel the bear with his fists. The bear in turn tried to swipe at him with its forepaw and narrowly missed.

"It's all an act," Lotte snorted as she witnessed the fight.

"How do you figure, Cap—I mean, Sir Gunther?" Taki asked.

"Why did we pick *Gunther* as my name?" Lotte sighed. "Anyway, the bear's holding back. The man is its trainer. Whoever runs this show tries to entice people to bet against the human and profits immensely."

"Ah, then I shall lay a clip on the line for the man," Draco said. "Make the arrangements."

Lotte smiled and brushed his sleeve with her fingertips. "You're a dab hand at this, Viscount. Sadly, there's no time to bet."

"Aye," Aslatiel said. "We must go down. Natalis, you're dressed as a page, so you'll come along too."

The human fighter in the cage pranced victoriously around the bear, which lay still and seemingly too exhausted to fight. The crowd simmered with disgust.

"Is that it for the show?" Draco asked. He twiddled with his moustache and squinted at the cage.

"No," Lotte said, "they're going to put in someone the bear doesn't know. It'll be a bloody mess. Let's go down. That's where the primate is."

They came to the top of sweeping marble stairs cordoned off by velvet rope and manned by guardsmen. One undid one end of the rope to allow Draco and the entourage to pass. Their boots clicked on stone before crushing fine velvet.

Draco gasped. *"Sweet Jesus!"*

The basement was a domeless rotunda with multiple halls branching off like spokes of a wheel. Marble pillars held up the ceiling, covered with snaking, flowering vines. Torches cast a soft, red glow that flickered over the proceedings below. The very center of the wheel was a stepped depression piled high with pillows on every available surface. Lying upon them were dozens of courtesans on display: a curling, gliding mass of limbs and torsos and flesh to rile even the most devout.

"Control yourself," Lotte said.

Past the orgy was a massive metal door the height and width of two men from end to end. It was closed save for a small, barred portal through which a pair of hands passed out boxes of gleaming, brass-cased ammunition to waiting footmen who disappeared into a nearby servant's passage.

Taki's eyes bulged in their sockets as he took in the sights.

"You too, dammit," his captain said.

"Sorry," Taki said. "Er, where's the primate?"

Lotte scanned the writhing pile and then pointed. "In the center. Come now, let's greet him." She descended the marble steps into the depression, and the mass of flesh parted before her.

The buck-naked primate of Astarte reclined on a pile of cushions as Lotte approached. An attendant knelt with a goblet of pungent, resinous wine perched on a golden platter. The primate took the cup and drained it in one messy gulp while rivulets of purple ran from the sides of his mouth.

Taki scrunched his eyebrows. Whatever features the primate might have been born with were entirely enveloped in sweaty rolls of pannus. *This is the city's high priest?*

"Fat man, cover your shame before I relieve you of it!" Lotte snapped.

Taki felt his knees go weak. Aslatiel winced and opened his mouth to speak, but the primate cut him off with a deep belly laugh.

"A raging bitch as always, Archangel Yuriel," he said, smacking his thigh in amusement. "But that's why I like you so much. No one else talks to the holy diver of Astarte like that and lives!" He waved idly to the stunned crowd around him. "Continue."

Strings and drums, which had abruptly stopped at Lotte's greeting, immediately picked up where they'd left off. The orgy resumed its sinuous waves as if nothing had transpired. Aslatiel stepped forward and knelt.

"Your Excellency, we are Alfa Gruppe of the Osterbrand Imperium. We humbly request the right of the Liberation Army to traverse your demesne—"

"Shush, bootlicker. I was talking to Yuriel here," the primate said.

Lotte rested a hand on Aslatiel's shoulder before addressing the primate. "You know I do not answer to that title anymore."

"Yes, I know. 'Twas a damned shame you couldn't punch through the Teufelsbrucke like you claimed you would. If it's any comfort, the bastard Duvalier and his shitty little tollbooth have also given me endless grief."

"Well, you *are* a big apostate," Lotte said.

"Do you see, bootlicker?" The primate winked at Aslatiel. "She gets booted right in the cunt, and she still struts around like a big shit. That's what a true archangel of the Temple acts like, which is why I shall always call her by her title. But we're not here to reminisce. I let you all interrupt my fun because you can do a few things for me. In exchange, I'll make sure my cannons stay silent when your army mucks up my highway."

"And what about Hecaton Mezeta?" Lotte said. "I heard you're letting her step all over you again. I thought you had better judgment than that. But don't fear. We'll take her head if you give her to us."

The primate frowned. "If only you'd been here earlier."

"What do you mean?"

"Mezeta left my city yesterday. You know how the woman is. Fickle and not a shred of honor or decency. She stole my grad, gorged on my fare, and then seduced my best retainers."

Lotte's face reddened. "Where did she go?"

The primate's lips curled into a triumphant sneer. "I'll tell you *after* you perform those favors for me."

For a moment, Taki feared that Lotte would simply run the corpulent priest through. To his surprise, she simply laughed.

"If your information's garbage, I'll grind your manhood underfoot," she said. "So what do you want from us?"

"Two things, the first of which should be easy enough for you lot. If you can't handle it, then there's no point in telling you the second."

"Get on with it. What's the first task?"

"Simple. Kill my wife."

"By *your wife*, I hope you mean Princess Sophie and not some common girl you've knocked up."

The primate snorted. "I have dozens of starving, trained killers for the latter. Yes, I'm talking about my dear princess. I can't make any deals with her around, lest she spike me from ass to mouth for disloyalty to her father. She also commands the loyalty of every idiotic royalist in this city. Once she's gone, I'll purge them all, too. Then your padishah and I can come to an agreement."

"Then where is she?" Lotte sniffed. "We'll do it tonight."

"Oh, Yuriel, I've longed to hear you say that," the primate cackled.

From above came an unmistakable rumble that Taki knew too well. *Gunfire,* he realized, and he instinctively reached down to his hip for a side arm that wasn't there.

"Shit Christ!" the primate said, and nearly bowled himself over in panic. "She found out!"

"Betrayal?" Aslatiel also reached for his absent side arm.

"No," Lotte said. "He hates the princess with a passion. We've been found out somehow."

"Then…Mezeta?"

"We'd already be dead. And she doesn't use guns. Hates the things." She pointed at the primate's entourage. "Hide him in the treasury! We'll deal with the threat!"

The man's attendants and guards wasted no time in hauling the corpulent priest up by his arms. Sweating, they dragged him from the center of the orgy pit to the vault door. Metal creaked as the door started to swing open.

Karma was the first to stumble through the velvet curtain. Mikhail's arm was draped over his shoulders, for the albino had been struck in the leg and hopped along painfully. Karma's shirt was also stained with blood.

"Report!" Lotte commanded.

"Chevs!" Karma said. "Assholes poured in and started shooting and hacking at everyone! The albino's hit bad."

"I can still fight," Mikhail said.

Enilna was next through. Her face was speckled with blood and her dress torn, but she had a rifle slung over her shoulder. She raced over to Taki and cupped his face in her hands.

"You okay?" he asked.

"No," she said. "Sorry, you can't have my gun."

"I wasn't asking for it!"

Another staccato press of fire from above, and the last two finally pushed through. Elsa's finery was in tatters, and she bore a cut across her side. Hadassah stuck the barrel of a musket through the curtain and fired a shot before retreating to where her companions huddled.

"There's a ton of them," Hadassah said. "All shouting *Pour Sophie!* and stuff."

"All of you get guns and ammo from the vault before they lock us out," Lotte ordered. "And save a few rounds for yourselves if the princess gets her hands on you!"

Taki raced through the vault and skidded to a halt, amazed at what he saw. Countless glinting brass cartridges overflowed from bulging boxes on shelves like lethal cornucopias. Ancient guns—Temple guns—lay haphazardly against each other like so much piled-up firewood, and an entire row of shelving was devoted solely to cannon shells.

The primate's footmen had already taken the heaviest and best guns of the hoard for themselves and seemed in no mood to share. Taki, however, had neither desire to carry the heavy deathbringers nor knowledge of how to use them. A Herstal pistol on the ground nearby caught his attention. He picked it up and raced back outside.

The velvet curtain at the base of the stairs caught fire. Taki raised his pistol and focused on steadying his aim. Any moment, dozens of soldiers could come pouring into the rotunda. Something Draco had once muttered came back to him unbidden: *Once more unto the breach, dear friends.* The smoldering cloth finally fell apart, and in stepped a pair of Templars.

While his compatriots had faced these foes before, Taki had not, and his first impulse was to gawk. Each fighter was a behemoth, standing easily two meters tall. Deeply pitted metal armor covered almost every surface save for the joints, which were encased thickly in chainmail and aramid. Their helmets were fearsome, horned things with a demonic visage formed on the faceplate with only a single, tiny eyeslit. Each carried what looked like the end of a hose apparatus, fed by a massive pair of canisters hefted on their backs.

The naked, huddled courtesans tried to make a break for it. Shouting their loyalty to the crown, they ran toward the Templars. Without a word, both monoliths raised their hoses and spewed fire at the crowd.

Taki's jaw dropped as bodies toppled and the stench of burnt hair hit him full in the face. His legs buckled, and he vomited all over his own feet. Heat washed over him like a smothering current, and his throat closed against it. *This isn't real. That didn't just happen. Thou shalt not be affrighted by them, for the Lord thy God is among you, a mighty God and terrible...*

Lotte grabbed Taki by the back of his coat and pulled him behind a pillar. "Natalis, compose yourself!" She let out a burst from her rifle, and one of the giants stumbled back but quickly righted itself. The creatures shed their strange fire weapons and drew greatswords.

"Everyone watch your ammunition!" Aslatiel shouted from the next pillar over. "Shoot their vulnerable parts. Joints and heads!"

Taki struggled to raise himself and wiped foulness away from his lips. He fired with his pistol, and the round splattered against a horned helm. Despite the superior marksmanship on his side, the hail of bullets didn't appear to be seriously harming the Templars, though they seemed reluctant to advance.

"Natalis, flank and cast a sutra," Lotte ordered. "We'll close in and finish them off."

Taki nodded and slunk out of cover. Though nauseated, he managed to slip behind a crumbling dais to the right of the Templar duo without pausing to vomit. In his peripheral vision, he caught sight of a pair of charred bodies. The corpses were stuck in an embrace, one of them trying to protect the other's head. Taki clenched his fists. He remembered how impotent he had felt back in the Kosovar lands. Not anymore. Now, he was free to act. *Vengeance is mine. I am he who will repay.*

He let his gates open, and his power bounded and frothed. He murmured a strengthening mantra and then stepped out from cover and extended both arms. The Templars turned to bear on him, and he released his anger. Twin streams of blazing air lanced out from his palms. One punched through a Templar's groin and severed his legs. The other Templar caught a blast full in the face. It dissolved the metal visor and punched out the back of his helmet. The behemoth fell back, smoking dead.

Almost instantly, his companions were on the wounded Templar. Lotte stomped on the hulk's wrist and wrenched the greatsword away. Hadassah jammed the muzzle of her rifle against the eyeslit and pulled the trigger again and again until dark paste splattered on the floor. Taki fell to one knee, breathing heavily. Save for the sound of licking flames, all was silent.

"Natalis, you're burned," Lotte said as she grasped one of Taki's arms. He gasped. Blisters had sprung up on the sensitive undersides, and some were already leaking. She let go. "Sorry, I didn't mean to cause you pain."

"All's well, Captain," Taki said. "I just got a bit too angry when I cast the sutra. It'll be a lesson." He wiped his eyes with the dirty hem of his page's shirt.

Lotte gently helped him to his feet. She leaned in closer, and her breath tickled his ear. "I'll help you wash up later."

"Captain," he groaned, trying not to flush even harder.

"Did I say something wrong?"

"I'm just glad we're all going to make it," he said with a smile.

"We got company!" Hadassah shouted from afar. She trained her rifle on a new arrival.

"*Infidels. Defilers.*" Princess Sophie Troiscent slowly descended the stairway and stood at the threshold. "Cast your arms aside and beg forgiveness."

Hadassah spat. "I ain't doin' *shit* for someone in a chainmail bikini! Put your fucking hands up and...and stop *objectifying yourself*! It's gross!"

"If you will not accept purity, then you must be purged," Sophie said, and knelt. Before anyone could comprehend her actions, her body started to change. Her arms stretched and dislocated, and her torso arched back in extreme lordosis. Silvery rivulets coursed over her skin to cover her exposed flesh. A pair of spiny legs erupted from right below the junction of her chest and abdomen and punched spiked ends into the marble. Where her hands had been were now scythes of chitin. Her jaw split down the middle to become a pair of mandibles, and her screams and moans took on a newly guttural, alien-sounding quality.

"Did she j-just turn into a gigantic f-fucking *bee*?" Karma asked. He raised his carbine and fired. "I *hate* bees!"

Sophie sidestepped his shots and leapt through the air to latch on to one of the pillars. The end of her reticulated abdomen swept in an arc. Karma bent back just in time to avoid having his face taken off by a meter-long metal spike. He tumbled to the floor, and the stinger whipped around and plunged right at his chest.

With a vicious clang of metal, it ground against the edge of a greatsword before it could impale him and then punched a hole in the stone floor. Lotte whirled around to slice Sophie's guts open and put a deep rent in the armor plate. The princess let out a warbling shriek and skittered away to hang from the ceiling.

Something protruded from where Sophie's pelvis had once been. It gave off a metallic whine but then issued forth a molten stream that carved a smoking trench up the center of the room. Another long burst sawed into one of the pillars and caused it to buckle and collapse. The pillar's inside was filled with tightly compacted limestone powder, and the impact sent a great plume of choking dust into the air to fill the rotunda.

"Back to the vault! She can't fit through!" Aslatiel shouted.

Sophie dropped to the floor and lashed her spiked tail at whoever she could.

"What the godrotting hell is that?" Taki sputtered.

"An Ursalan princess," Elsa said. She had propped herself up next to him and busied herself trying to stanch the bleeding from Mikhail's wound.

"That's a princess?"

"Aye. Ursala makes 'em strange and deadly."

Christ, there's bone sticking out of Zhukov's leg, Taki thought. *He'll lose the limb for sure...if we don't die here.*

"Elsa, the monster must be killed," Mikhail said. He charged his rifle on a fresh magazine.

Elsa squeezed his arm. "I know. We're working on it."

"I have a plan," he said. Before Elsa could react, he reached out, cradled her face in his palms, and pressed his lips to hers. After a few seconds, he broke off the kiss and rose to his feet with rifle in hand.

"What're you doing?" Elsa cried as he limped out of the vault. She started after him.

"Stop her!" Aslatiel shouted.

Taki gritted his teeth and tackled Elsa in a bear hug. She struggled against him, making his joints burn.

Mikhail fired blindly and wildly into the dust. Sophie dropped from the ceiling and plunged her stinger through him. He groaned, dropped the rifle, and tightly grasped the metal spike.

Sophie thrashed from side to side, trying to shake Mikhail off, but he held firm. Finally, she drew her belly in to bring him closer. He was ashen from blood loss but still would not let go. She seemed to stare at him for a moment, and then she brought her mandibles to his neck.

Mikhail's eyelids fluttered open, and his free arm whipped out to shove something between her pincers and down her throat. Sophie clamped her jaws and chopped his arm away neatly at the elbow. Blood splattered her face, and Mikhail's eyes rolled back in shock. He let go of the spike, and his body slid off the stinger to drop to the floor with a dull thud.

Elsa screamed and thrashed against Taki's arms, but he held firm. She sank her teeth into his arm, and the pain made his eyes water. She bashed her head against his nose, and Taki heard a crunch as it moved out of place, but he still held firm.

"Let me go! Let me go!" she screamed. They both went rolling on the floor, right in front of the vault opening.

Sophie clacked her mandibles together and went prostrate on the ground in front of them. Her back arched, and the contraption on her abdomen whined as its barrels started to spin. She swung it to aim into the vault.

Shit, Taki thought—they were right in the line of fire.

Before Sophie could rake them with lead, white-hot metal erupted from her chest and spewed all over the floor. Her limbs thrashed violently, and she curled into a ball. A few seconds later, she went limp.

Taki grimaced and let Elsa loose. She kicked away from him and rushed past the princess's grotesque corpse and over to where Mikhail lay. Something made Taki pick himself up and bound over to where she was.

She cradled the albino's head in her lap, rocking back and forth. His color would have made it hard to tell whether his blood was still in his body, had it not been for the large crimson pool around him.

To Taki's surprise, Mikhail's lips were moving.

"Don't," Elsa said to her stricken comrade. "I hate good-byes. See you next life."

Mikhail smiled and was still.

Taki knelt. He heard Lotte bellowing commands but couldn't understand her. He wiped the blood away from his face. He'd triumphed. An Ursalan princess lay dead before his feet, and the Imperium was that much closer to victory. Mikhail had been a valuable companion during the raid in Lhasa, but he hadn't known the man very well. There were a thousand reasons to be happy, but for some reason he felt only hollowness and bile.

12

The clouds hung low in the sky, pregnant with rain, but failed to deliver while Astarte smoldered. The streets continued to overflow with human waste while rats tore each others' guts out, but now a newer contaminant flowed into the trenches: human blood.

Taki shook his head as he peered out from the window of his room at the inn. Since the battle with Princess Sophie, the streets had become an impassable morass of checkpoints, barricades, and clashes between armed men bearing a multitude of standards that Taki had never seen before but could only assume were some flavor of Ursalan. Thus, for the time being, everyone was stuck indoors at the rooms they'd rented before visiting the Tintoretto. The inn was a large establishment that could hire its own private guards, which suited everyone just fine. Below Taki's window, a lone, cloaked figure furtively made his way down the avenue, only to be set on by two others. The two dragged their mark into the darkness of an alley, and he heard squelching sounds.

A knock sounded at his door; Taki tensed and reached for his Herstal. "Yes?"

"It's me," Lotte said. She pushed the door open without waiting for him to invite her in.

"Captain," Taki said. He rose to salute, but she dismissed the gesture with a headshake and went over to sit in the casement next to him.

"Believe it or not, this is a peaceful coup for Astarte," Lotte said. "Many of the Rex's die hards perished in the Tintoretto. Now, the primate's followers will take care of the others. And loot and rape and murder for fun on the side."

"I thought we were here to be discreet," Taki said. "I didn't know we'd set off a bloodbath."

"The Ursalans can kill each other off to the very last man, as far as I'm concerned," Lotte said. "Better their lives spent than ours."

"Guess you're right," Taki said. He looked at his hands.

"These aren't poor peasants," Lotte said gently. She squeezed his shoulder. "Everyone in this place has a gun behind his or her back and plenty of sins to defend with it."

"I've gotten over that," Taki said.

"Feeling morose over the albino?"

"Perhaps. Zhukov was a good man. I'd never known a Moslem before I met him."

Lotte smiled. "If it's any comfort, they believe that when one of the faithful dies in battle, he's greeted by seventy-two virgins in paradise."

"That sounds apocryphal," Taki said with a sour expression.

"You're just jealous. How are your wounds?"

Taki drew his sleeves up and showed her. The blisters had all ruptured and sloughed off, leaving grainy scabs. The swelling and redness from the burns, however, had disappeared.

"You never took me up on my offer," she said.

"You were just teasing me, Captain," Taki said.

"You shouldn't always assume the worst, Natalis. You'll be a virgin for the rest of your life that way."

"And now you *are* teasing me."

"Is that new confidence I hear from my awkward little cornet? Did you, perchance, tumble with the Kosovar girl who likes you?"

Taki turned red around his ears. "She's immature. I don't really fancy her in that way."

Lotte laughed. "It seems I hit a nerve. Not to worry, I won't tease you more."

"Thank you, Captain. And forgive me if I presume too much, but you've also been in higher spirits these days."

"Perhaps I am." She paused. "I remember you asked me if it was treason to find contentment fighting under the enemy banner. Once, I'd never have imagined such a thing possible. Now, I'm not so sure. Imagine that: an archangel of the Temple serving the hated Imperium with pride. I don't know what's become of me."

Taki frowned. "If I may speak frankly, I'm just glad to be rid of the Triada." He spat as the last syllable left his mouth. Like any other clueless Polaris freshy graduated from the academy, he had once held the Agia Triada of the Temple in fearful reverence. After all, the three archangels—Michail, Yuriel, and Jibriil—had been the infallible personification of Temple Law and the Hoplite's Code. That is, until Taki had actually met them.

"Mezeta told me, by the way. You asked her to kill Jibriil. Practically twisted her arm, too."

His heart started to race. "I only spoke in the heat of anger…"

"That was truly bad form, and it could have earned you the gallows, Natalis."

Taki bowed his head.

"And yet…" Lotte sighed. "I was also pleased. I didn't think anyone cared."

"I was impulsive. I know better, these days."

She ran her fingertips across his cheek. "You've a kind heart. You make me regret things."

Taki noticed that her hand trembled. "What do you mean?" he asked.

"I've been overly harsh with my words, and many times, I struck you all when I should have shown restraint. I treated my men the same when I was Yuriel, and now they're dead. I can never earn their forgiveness."

Taki clenched his fists and was silent for a moment. "Captain, when I asked Mezeta to kill the Archangel Jibriil, she told me that the only reason we hadn't been hanged for our failures was because of what you endured. You saved our lives so many times. I have no right to judge you. I can only praise you."

"I merely did my duty. And did it poorly, at that."

"Now you're the one morosely refusing a compliment." He cracked a wry smile. "You'll be a spinster forever at this rate."

Lotte's lips parted in disbelief, and she pushed Taki hard enough to bowl him over on the floor. He started to laugh. Her face flushed, and she crossed her arms. "No one likes a smartass!"

"Aye, there's nothing more useless than a man like me."

Her expression softened, and she bent to help him. "Do you really think I deserve praise, Natalis?"

He clasped her hand and pulled himself to his feet. "I do. I've never met a warrior as fierce and courageous as you. I wouldn't want to face Mezeta without you."

"And to think we were so close to her," Lotte said. "I should kill that old fat bastard primate, but Sir Aslatiel won't allow it. I've about had it up to here with the Imperials."

"It's not their fault that we missed Mezeta by hours."

"I don't know about that."

"Surely you're not suggesting they're in league with her?"

Lotte shook her head. "It's no coincidence where she's supposedly gone."

"The Teufelsbrucke." Taki looked at Lotte. "Where you…"

"Lost miserably and got my life ruined." She laughed. "It's also the gateway to southern Ursala. The Imperials want it badly. That Reinhard wants me to lead the battle to take it, promising that I'll corner Mezeta for sure. It wouldn't surprise me if they'd told her to go there."

"But he said Mezeta's a threat," Taki said. "Why would they let such a threat simply walk away?"

"Because they only think of their own campaign. They don't care much for our pain. But fine. I'll take the damned fortress if there's even a chance of sticking it to the old witch."

"And I'll follow you there as well."

Lotte pursed her lips. "You might eat those words later."

"Captain, are you worried about the fight?"

"Aye. Von Halcon is under the impression that I should lead the battle because I've been there before. I've told him I never got past the bridge, but he's stubborn."

"I think he's a good judge, though."

She smiled. "You've taken quite a liking to him, and he to you."

"I suppose," Taki said. "But I said once I'd follow you to the end. I won't renege on my promise."

"Natalis, you make me regret many things." She leaned forward and pressed her lips to his.

Taki tensed but relaxed quickly. His shaking hands went to just under her chin, and he brushed the tips of his fingers against the sides of her neck. He heard the footsteps from the hall too late.

"Taki, the fat man sent someone, and he's asking for—" Enilna let out a squeak as she entered.

Lotte immediately broke off the embrace. Gooseflesh erupted on Taki's neck, and his mouth went dry.

"Tirefire." Enilna croaked. She averted her eyes from either of them. "He's...he's waiting in the stairwell."

"Thank you, Shpejtspate," Lotte said. "Send him up."

Enilna turned stiffly and bounded away.

Taki started after her, but Lotte grasped his arm.

"The new caller first," she said.

He had no choice but to agree. *Enilna's just a friend, anyway. We made sure at the festival.*

Heavy footsteps sounded from the stairs. Taki checked again to make sure his Herstal was at his side. Why would a messenger from the primate wish to talk to Tirefire specifically, and not Aslatiel or the rest of Alfa? Before he could muse further on this question, the Archangel Jibriil stepped in.

Taki's hand instantly shot to his side arm, and he freed it from its holster. He aligned sights on the man but stopped when Jibriil knelt in supplication.

"I'm unarmed! Stay your hand." He raised his chin and locked eyes with Taki. "Please."

Lotte gently pushed the Herstal's muzzle down. "We won't hurt you, Jibriil," she said. "Unless you try to hurt any of us."

"I swear on my honor, though I know it means little to either of you," Jibriil said. "I come in peace, as a messenger of His Holiness the primate of Astarte—"

"*Your master is the exarch,*" Taki spat with vehemence that surprised even him.

Jibriil cast his gaze down. "Nay, Sir Taki. I am a dog of Astarte now. I no longer hold the title of archangel or the name Jibriil."

Lotte sucked her teeth. "Tell me what happened, Sion."

Sion? Taki reeled. *That's the name of the soldier she chose to live! The one she sacrificed her betrothed for!*

Jibriil shook his head. "It's far too shameful, Lady Lotte."

Lotte squatted and stared at him. "Humor me."

"After Mezeta deserted, the Usurper Amilia was furious. I'm told she raged for a day straight. Soon after, she forced Exarch Constantine to abdicate his post. I'm told he digs for potatoes in Thraike now."

Lotte slowly shook her head. "At least he wasn't killed outright. Did a similar fate visit you three?"

"No, milady. We were spared. We agreed to govern the Temple as a triumvirate, with plans to choose a new exarch once things quieted down. Then, Michail and Yuriel plotted in secret against me. I woke up one night in shackles with a blade sunk in my chest. My own men laughed while they stuffed me into a coffin and nailed it shut. I feared they'd bury me alive but instead, they chucked me into the sea. I must've floated some way, because when the lid came off it, I saw chevaliers. They brought me to the primate as a prize, and he's sheltered me since. The man's a sinner, but he's honorable enough."

"So Michail and Yuriel are in charge now?" Lotte chuckled. "What a ludicrous couple."

Jibriil shook his head. "Michail's exarch now. Yuriel's body was found soon after my 'funeral.' I'm told the corpse was only recognizable by a jeweled piercing on the...pudendal area."

"That's her, all right," Lotte said. "So, what did the new basileus think of this? Will Michail get chopped soon?"

"The Usurper seems not to care," Jibriil said. "The Temple survives. Perhaps it's better off now. I wouldn't know."

A grim smile crept across Taki's face. Jibriil had finally gotten his just deserts, even if the new exarch had failed to actually kill the man. The fallen archangel kneeling before Taki had none of the self-assured swagger that he'd possessed before the conquest. The man's hollow cheeks and dulled eyes were in stark contrast with the pride and power that he'd held. Once, Taki had prostrated naked and freezing and contrite before Jibriil. *And now...*he let out a soft chuckle.

"Natalis." Lotte shot him a chastising glance.

"Milady, he has every right to gloat," Jibriil said. "Sir Taki, your scorn is justified. I treated you and your fellows very badly. I was arrogant and spiteful, and for that, I apologize. I beg your forgiveness, and I'll work hard to earn it if you'll give me the chance."

'Fool. *I'm* not the one you should be bowing and scraping to," Taki said, and crossed his arms.

"Indeed. The one I've treated most terribly is beside you," Jibriil said. He lowered his head to Lotte. "While I recovered from my wounds, I reflected heavily on the actions that brought me here. I acted in an uncouth and abusive fashion to you, milady. I failed to pay you the respect you deserved as a warrior and trod on your liberty. I...I forced myself on you many a time."

"Sion," Lotte said, "it wasn't that way. I could've killed you at any time had I felt you were..."

"Milady, I call it what it was. It was coercion, even if only backed by words. It was rape. I don't expect you to forgive me, and I won't ask for it."

With a sound mimicking an explosion, Draco and Hadassah burst into the room. Jibriil barely had time to turn his head before the pair set on him with their fists and feet. He curled and did not resist.

"Stop this at once!" Lotte bellowed. She took each of them by their collars and flung them into separate corners of the room. "That's an order!"

"He admitted it!" Draco roared. "He finally fucking admitted it! Lemme at him!"

"Cut the shitlord's balls off, and I'll be happy!" Hadassah said.

"I won't repeat myself," Lotte said. "Move closer, and I'll break your faces. This man is here as a messenger of the primate of Astarte. He may be essential to our mission here. No one is to mistreat him. Especially not you, Natalis."

Jibriil pulled himself to one knee and wiped the blood away from below his nose. "Thank you, milady, though I understand their sentiments. My presence disturbs many, so I'll be brief. The primate is ready to consider an alliance."

Taki glowered. "We killed his princess and lost one of our own, and he's ready to *consider* an alliance?"

"His words, not mine, Sir Taki. He had two requests of the Imperium, and the Imperium has fulfilled one. The second is thus: your forces are to venture north, to the lands of the Ulrichtochten."

It was Lotte's turn to glower. "The Cantons? What could the primate *possibly want* with those barbarians?"

"His Holiness predicts the Imperium's eventual victory. Thus, he would like to establish an agreement between the mountain women and Astarte in the interest of continued trade and peace."

"So he wants them to not kill his traders when they venture too far off the path," Lotte said. "But there's a problem. None of us know the area well, and I doubt that any in Sir Aslatiel's company do, either. We'd be killed quickly."

Jibriil swallowed. "That, milady, is where I come in. I happen to know those mountains more than most, as my father was an Ursalan mountaineer. I'm to serve as a guide for a small group. No more than two others."

"And who is to accompany you?"

"That is for you and Sir Aslatiel to decide. The primate expresses that the sooner the mission starts, the sooner he will allow the Liberation Army to cross unmolested. And the sooner you'll be able to find...*her.*"

"I'm not going with this asshole. Neither will Karma," Hadassah said.

"I'll go with him," Draco said, "but I'm coming back *alone.*"

Lotte pointed at the door. *"Leave."*

The two tromped out, casting toxic glances at Jibriil. As they did so, Aslatiel stepped in. Following him was Enilna.

"Satou," Aslatiel said, "this man has been vetted by General Chang. He tells the truth, or what passes for it these days. We must move the army soon, before the Teufelsbrucke becomes impassable for the winter."

"Of course," Lotte said. "The campaign *must* go on. Who really cares about the greatest threat your Imperium has ever faced? What if Mezeta decides to kill your padishah? Meanwhile, we're being used as *pages.*"

"And what would you have us do instead?" Aslatiel said. "If you have a better idea of where to search for her, then I'm listening. But by squabbling here, we are wasting our time and effort."

"I can't believe you trust that fake priest."

"I never said I did. But right now, he's our only lead. I also wish to see Mezeta eliminated, but victory comes first!"

Taki's hand shot up. "I'll go. We'll have our alliance and be one step closer to Mezeta."

Lotte shook her head. "Natalis, you don't have to—"

"I *want* to." Taki crossed his arms. "How else will I make leutnant? And more important, no one in Sir Aslatiel's company knows just how treacherous the arch—this man can be. He could easily endanger them if given the chance. So I'll go. I'm stronger now. I can defend myself from the likes of him if needed." He fixed a glare on Jibriil.

Lotte did not relent.

"Duly noted, Fahnrich Natalis," Aslatiel said with an approving nod. "That leaves one spot to fill. Most of my squad is injured, and I must remain here for diplomatic reasons, so I suggest taking my sister. I will request her transfer immediately."

"Sir!" Enilna piped up. "I volunteer. Lucatiel is all the way in Sevastopol. It would take her at least a fortnight to arrive, even if she took *Ba'gshnar's* personal flying thingy."

"You're too inexperienced," Aslatiel said. "Though you do have a point about the travel time. Rana it is, then."

Enilna stamped her foot. "She *just* lost her lover! She's in no shape to climb mountains and fight monsters! Don't be a huge dick, sir!"

Taki tensed. Such words would have gotten her a drubbing from any officer.

Aslatiel drew in a breath and locked his gaze with Enilna's. "Watch your words, kadet." He sighed. "But yes, you're also right for the second time. You'll accompany Natalis and Sir Jibriil, then. I only permit this because we're so undermanned right now. You must be careful. Understood?"

Enilna clasped her hands together. "Thank you!"

"Very well, then. It'll be Shpejtspate joining you, Natalis. Remember that much hinges on your decisions."

Taki nodded. "Aye, I know."

Jibriil rose. "Thank you for your trust, milords. There is no need to worry about the actual dealings with the Ulrichtochten. The primate has drawn up an irresistible offer for them. The hard part will be getting there."

"When do we leave?" Taki asked without making eye contact.

Jibriil bowed. "Preferably tonight, under the new moon. The streets are less restive, but there's always risk of being mistaken for royalists. I'll be waiting in the tavern. Take as long as you need."

"First," Taki said, "let's get one thing straight. This is an Imperial mission. You may be our guide, but I am the one in charge. If I think for a moment that you mean us harm, Shpejtspate and I walk away. I'm sure your new master wouldn't look kindly on that. Do you understand, Jibriil?"

No indignation or raged marred Jibriil's features. The man only smiled, bowed again, and backed out of the door.

Taki let out a slow breath, now aware of the fact that he'd been holding it for a while. Lotte clamped a hand on his shoulder. Not caring that others were watching, Taki placed his hand over hers. She'd been right about the city: it was indeed a treacherous place, and the primate was more dangerous than any opponent they'd ever faced, though he wasn't even an enemy. Still, there was a mission at hand. Taki steeled himself and resolved to complete it, even if it meant working with a man he'd hated so much. For his career, for his honor, and for his new nation, he'd endure anything.

13

Ringo hated ships and seafaring. Spending weeks in constantly heaving, claustrophobic monotony had been a special type of torment best inflicted on true monsters: regicides, cuckolding wives, and Hecaton Mezeta. He especially despised that, out on the ocean, whether he lived or died was entirely out of his hands. A storm or an encounter with a sea beast would snuff his existence as casually as stepping on a roach near the jakes, and with just as little consideration. On land, he stood a chance; on land, he could rise up again even if he fell. But at sea, there was nothing but an inky void to drown in. What also peeved him was that all sailors clearly enjoyed the superiority that their knowledge and skill gave them onboard, whereas he was a clueless landlubber. Even their language was incomprehensible: port and starboard, mizzenmasts and spinnakers, and tacking and jibbing. None of the bastards probably knew how to ride.

The monotony would have been less stifling if he had come with peers to drink, gamble, and sing with, but Janus had been busy with his ancient knickknacks, and Juan had spent the entirety of the voyage suckling Hecaton's shriveled teats. The idiotic Valencian was firmly under the witch's spell, and thus he would be the first to die after Hecaton. However, the individual who had rattled Ringo the most was actually Janus's servant girl, the one he called Samara. She had not spoken once during the voyage, leading Ringo to believe that she was a mute and most likely touched in the head. Strangely enough, he had never seen Janus grope her for amusement as one might expect from a bored man on a long journey. Once, Ringo had attempted to pick through Janus's luggage to see what manner of ancient tools the man had brought along, only to see Samara holding a belaying pin, ready to strike. He had sometimes sensed her presence in the shadows, especially when he was alone. Whenever he had tried to flush her out, however, he had found nothing.

Thus, Ringo was glad to be back on land, where a man of honor and means could truly be a master of his world. The port of New Korinthos smelled like stale urine and thrice-digested fish, but he did not mind. In fact, the first thing he had done after tromping sullenly off the boat was to find a tavern to binge on real food—anything besides watered-down grog and hardtack. He had considered buying a girl, but harbor whores were universally infected with the pox. Wenching could wait until they were further inland. A fortnight at sea had killed his libido, anyway.

"Ale, your freshest meat, and fluffy bread. Keep it coming, too," Ringo said, and slammed the round of Old Nayto on the bartop. The tavernkeep picked up the round, inspected the headstamps, and shook it gently near his ear to check for the subtle swish of smokeless powder grains. Satisfied, the keep brought out a tankard of hoppy ale, a plate of just-made blood sausage, and a warm wheat boule. Ringo attacked his meal, drained the ale, and felt human again.

"Did you come here on the *Cuenta* from Astarte?" the keep asked.

Ringo nodded.

"Oy, it was good joss to come here then."

"How so?" he asked through a mouthful of bread.

"You've been at sea, so you couldn't have heard. We just got word from the clipper captains a day earlier. Astarte's gone over to the Imperium."

Ringo's eyes widened, and he straightened to let out a gasp, only to be interrupted by beer-soaked crumbs that tumbled down his trachea. He doubled over, coughing and gagging and pounding his chest. The tavernkeep reached out, but Ringo angrily waved him off.

"What do you mean, *gone over?*"

"I mean what I said, Sir Knight. The city's run up the Osterbrand flag beside its own."

"Who fucked up the siege?"

"There was no siege. I'm told assassins took Princess Sophie's life, and in the chaos the Liberation Army entered."

Ringo squeezed his temples in disbelief. "They killed Princess Sophie? The animals! The fucking spetsnaz were involved, I bet my life!"

"Sir Knight, I must decline the wager."

"Oh, shut up," Ringo snarled. Goose bumps erupted on his skin. If Astarte was lost, that meant his promised reward had evaporated, too. His dreams of a hundred thousand rounds of Old Nayto started to dissolve into excrement. There was no work for a chevalier in the Dominion—no, the Imperium—and he lacked the funds to return. He was marooned in enemy territory. *I'm ruined! I'm fucking ruined! Mezeta, you bitch, did you plan this? Why not just kill me instead? Damn you to hell!*

"Sir Knight?"

Ringo's face contorted into an agonized rictus while he dug into his scalp with his nails. His lips twitched, and he frothed from between clenched teeth.

The tavernkeep sucked his teeth and started to slowly back away.

"The primate," Ringo said. "What of the *primate*? Does he *live*?"

The tavernkeep cringed. "I'm told, Sir Knight, that the man was named a viceroy by the Imperium. He's their dog now. Just goes to show that the nobles always come out on top regardless of who wins, eh?"

Ringo wiped tears away with his sleeve. If the primate still lived—and more importantly, if he still had wealth—then perhaps there was some merit in following Hecaton for the moment. The chance to salvage even a small reward was better than the execrable, short future he was otherwise left with. Besides, there were probably others who might wish to reward him for the witch's death. Perhaps someone might even seek to hire him as a bodyguard, for the man who took down Hundred-Arms Mezeta would earn fame beyond imagination. He resolved to bide his time. He'd suffer the misery of being Hecaton's man for a while. And then he'd pull her intestines out through her mouth.

"I'll take my change in Luger," he said, and stuffed the last of the bread in his mouth. The keep hastily returned five rounds.

Ringo was still jittery when he left the tavern. Nausea coursed through him, and he ducked into a side alley where he retched his lunch all over the bricks. He punched the wall in impotent anger: at the primate, at Hecaton, at his compatriots, and at his own body for rejecting a meal that he had paid too much for. He squatted, brought his hands up to his face and started to sob in earnest. His master at the

Ordo had told him once: sometimes it was better to weep rather than keep his rage contained. But *only* in private.

When he was done, he rubbed at his face and stood. Samara knelt almost right next to him, petting a stray kitten and feeding it morsels of jerky from a pouch. Ringo's jaw dropped. She had seen the entire thing. She had seen him wail like a woman.

"You bitch," he snarled, "how long have you spied on me?"

Samara blinked and shook her head.

"Don't play coy. The others are too stupid to notice your snooping, but I do. What's your aim? Are you telling Janus my secrets?"

Samara scooped up the kitten, curtsied, and started to walk away.

Ringo had tolerated enough. He could always pay Janus back for property damage, and this damnable wench more than deserved a split lip and a broken tooth. He stepped forward and clamped a hand on her shoulder, intending to spin her around and into a proper slap. For a moment, he was struck by how *muscular* she felt underneath her habit.

Ringo's world exploded in white. His perspective upended itself, and he landed face down in the soft dirt of the alley. Before he could fully process what had happened, he felt the unmistakable sensation of a knife-edge against his throat. Someone's knee was on his back, and his wrists were caught in an iron-vise grip. The kitten peered at him and started to lick his nose.

"Don't worry. I won't tell them that I saw you have a good cry," a woman purred in his ear.

"Sa-Samara?" Ringo gasped.

"Hey, sexy."

He struggled, only to feel the knife press harder. "Who...no, *what* the fuck are you?"

"Not so loud, boyfriend," Samara admonished. "I really didn't want you to see this side of me, but I won't tolerate abuse in our relationship. So, no more hitting, and no more cursing. If you're good, I'll do something nice for you."

"Godrotting..." The curse died in his mouth as she put more weight against his spine. He relented when his fingers and toes started to tingle. "What do you want?"

"I know you were promised an idiotic sum for some dagger work. But face it—you don't stand a chance against her. When you try to scheme against the likes of old lady Mezeta, you're drowning in a nightmare you can't possibly comprehend, let alone survive. So back off with your retarded plan, let me keep an eye on her, and we'll strike when the time is right. But *only* then, and *only* on my say-so. If you play your cards right, you'll get much more than the measly hundred K that the primate wasn't going to give you anyway. Believe it or not, I'm on your side, *Ringo dearest*. Understood?"

He swore under his breath but nodded. "You're spetsnaz, aren't you?"

Samara laughed and let off the pressure from her knee. The blade slowly retracted, gliding menacingly on his skin without breaking it. "Let a girl have *some* secrets. I don't need to tell you what happens if you spread rumors, do I?"

"No, you don't," Ringo said, and rose to dust his breeches off. *Damnable bitch, I'll kill her first.*

"Oh, and from now on, we're lovers on the side."

"What?"

"You heard me," she said. "Now, get a move on. We don't want to keep the hag waiting."

14

There were great tracts of land where the skies still rained ash. Rifts in the earth belched fine dust, like suppurating wounds that refused to heal, and formed giant, fragile white dunes that migrated slowly to an uncertain end. Humans could not farm or live in these places, though they could certainly die in them.

Taki stared blindly at the beauty of the toxic landscape outside his train window. Flurries of choking particulates blew past the glass, pantomiming snow. He would have closed his eyes and dozed away the boredom if not for the fact that Jibriil snoozed nearby. Though the man's chest rose and fell as if he were in sleep, there was no way to be sure. Earlier, Enilna and Taki had set up a watch system so that one would keep watch over the former archangel at all times. It had been Enilna's turn to nap, and thus Taki resolved to stay awake for her sake.

He turned his attention again to the outside and wondered when—and how—the rails had been laid in the first place. He knew he was lucky to even have the option of riding the ancient relic, else the journey north would have taken weeks, if not months. The world, scarred as it was, was still terribly large.

The unlikely trio had ridden the train for two days from Astarte's outskirts and, based on their location in the ash plains, would arrive at the Salted Fortress in three more. That was assuming that they didn't run out of fuel early, that enemies hadn't sabotaged the tracks, or that bandits weren't foolish enough to try to rob a train flying the primate's banner.

And how ludicrous this all is, Taki thought as he glanced over at the other passengers. All of them were Ursalans, whether they were merchants, messengers, or mercenaries. Though the primate had purged the loyalists and had a princess killed, he still flew the Ursalan crest over his own. The fortress that was the train's destination had only passed into Imperial hands within the last season, and though Aslatiel had assured everyone that spetsnaz agents would send advance notice, Taki wasn't sure he would receive a welcome devoid of bullets and explosions. He squeezed his eyes shut to try and force the thought away. He drew in a breath and held it. The resultant exhalation fogged the window. *Strange. It's not really snowing.*

Something bumped him, and he looked over to see Enilna's head resting on his shoulder. He'd noticed that when the girl slept, she slept hard. Her lips were parted, and she snored softly. A line of drool connected the corner of her mouth and the canvas of his brigandine. The sight made him cringe, but he decided against shifting away. It was unusual to see her so unguarded. He wanted to reach out and run his fingertips through the auburn waves atop her head but didn't.

Just friends, he resolved. He touched his lips instead, savoring the memory of when Lotte had come to him. If Enilna hadn't barged in so boorishly, would more have happened? Might he have tumbled in bed with his captain? The thought brought a smile to his face, and yet for some reason, Aslatiel's words came to mind again. But was it really so terrible to consort with someone of a different rank? *I'm a man, dammit. Not a servant girl being victimized by some overlord.* It was easy to despise himself in these weak moments. He gnawed on a thumbnail and turned his attention back to the silent storm outside.

"Want some?"

Taki started at Jibriil's voice, and he bumped Enilna's cheek. Jibriil squatted in the aisle with his hand out to offer a strip of thick, dried beef encrusted with peppercorns. It took Taki a few breathless seconds to realize that the man wasn't armed. "No...thanks," he muttered.

Jibriil shrugged. "Thought I'd ask."

Enilna's eyes had fluttered open when Taki had shifted, but she had fallen back into slumber just as rapidly.

"I had a meal already," Taki said, feeling relieved that he hadn't entirely spoiled her rest.

"I, uh, noticed that you rip your cuticles," Jibriil said.

Taki hardened his features. "And that's your concern because?"

"Don't misunderstand—I wasn't criticizing you. I actually had the same problem for a long time. My fingertips looked like worm-eaten bark, and people would recoil if I showed them my hands."

Taki blinked. "You said you had the problem. So did you beat it?"

"Whenever I caught myself with my fingers in my mouth, I substituted something else. After much trial and error, I found beef jerky to work best. Probably because the texture was similar. Sorry, I know that's disgusting."

"No, I can see that working quite well," Taki said. Despite his apprehension, he let out a chuckle.

Jibriil cracked a wry smile. "I always made sure I had some in my pouch. Within a season, my fingers were whole again. It took some getting used to, having nails again." He offered the jerky once more. "So, want any?"

Taki started to reach for it but stopped. "It's...uh, too much."

"Don't worry, I take no offense," Jibriil said, and bit off a small piece near the end. "Not poisoned. Better now?"

"Yes, thanks," Taki said, and took the strip.

"Hope it works for you. Wenches—not to speak of respectable women—won't let your fingers anywhere *near* their nethers in that state," Jibriil said with a laugh.

Taki reddened but let out an inadvertent snort of amusement. "Aye, I'll keep that in mind."

Jibriil nodded and eased back into his seat. He cozied up against the bulkhead and closed his eyes. Within minutes, he snored again.

Taki looked down at the jerky in his hand. Part of him wanted to cast it aside and tread on it. Not for suspicion of poison or spoilage, but because of whom it had belonged to. The cuts on Taki's back from the cat-o-nine tails had long since faded into tiny pink lines, but when he regarded Jibriil, they throbbed. *Silly. It isn't the meat's fault. I'm stronger now, and he's weaker.* After a moment more, Taki opened a pouch on his belt and slipped in the jerky. Perhaps he'd give Jibriil's method a try. After all, if he ever got to tumble, he didn't want his partner to be disgusted.

* * * *

The last bits of clinging ash fell away as the train slowly rumbled to a stop. A whistle sounded, long and mournful, to announce the train's arrival to the nervous Imperials in defilade nearby. Taki held his breath as he waited for the pings and thumps of a full-out assault, but they never came.

"Looks like your officers pulled through on their end," Jibriil said. "We're not dead ten times over."

"Aye. Sir Aslatiel's a responsible sort," Taki said. He pulled his pack out of the netted pouches overhead and checked for the hundredth time that he was still armed. His saber rattled reassuringly in its sheath, and his Herstal was snug across his chest. Then, he got up from his seat. It was liberating to be on his feet again after all that time riding.

Jibriil trudged on ahead, awkwardly hefting his own kit. Taki had made another unspoken rule that the archangel was never to see their backs if they could help it.

"Hey." Enilna tugged on Taki's sleeve. "So is this place really made out of a huge block of salt?"

"I don't think so. More like there were probably salt mines around the place. Far as I know, the walls are stone."

"That's lame if true," Enilna said. "I kind of thought we'd get to see cooler places, like Vistula. I hear it still gives off smoke from the walls, kind of like Berlin."

"That sounds less likely than a castle made of salt."

"You know that thousands of our boys lost their lives to take the smoking fort? But then the old general who used to lead Alfa Gruppe—before Aslatiel did, but he's dead now—stayed up for a straight fortnight to prevent his men from just sacking the place and raping all the women inside. I wish I'd met the guy."

Taki chuckled. "Sounds like something the old exarch would've done."

"Well, all old bearded men look the same, so maybe they think the same."

"That's really simplistic."

"You're just jealous you're not an old bearded man. Actually, I don't think I've ever seen you shave."

"Because I don't," Taki said with a shrug. "And you shouldn't be spying on me."

"I'm an Imperial kadet. Spying is my job," Enilna said.

As he stepped off the train, Taki was immediately struck by the omnipresent smell of sulfur in the air. He hoped he'd get used to it quickly. If nothing else, Jibriil did not plan to tarry here for long. Beyond the loosely gathered bunch of Imperial porters and musketeers that had come out of the portcullis to meet the train, there was little evidence of life around the Salted Fortress. The ground was barren, and not even crows circled overhead.

The actual walls were of sloped brick and built as a many-pointed star. At each point were a pair of long-range cannons for distance and a mortar for close-in work. Ravelins and tenailles completed the defensive array. Almost obscured by smoke and fog, the keep itself loomed high on a nearby motte.

After a cursory inspection of his papers, Taki passed by a pair of janissaries with halberds and came out on the other side of the gates. The inner courtyards smelled strongly of wood smoke from countless cookfires that rose from brick stacks attached to hastily erected housing. It appeared to him like a smaller, ramshackle version of the Temple, complete with enterprising soldiers selling snacks and copies of the on-base gossip rag.

"The latest news from the heartland and annexed territories! A twenty-two will do!" one of them cajoled in a singsong voice.

"Can we?" Enilna said.

Taki shrugged and handed a dusty cartridge to the merchant girl, in exchange for a flimsy sheaf of onion paper. One of the larger lines of print caught his notice. *New Head for the Polaris.* Jibriil's story had been true, as far as he could tell. The Archangel Mikhail now called himself exarch. There was no mention of the rest of the Triada. For a moment, he almost felt sorry for Jibriil.

"Hey, let me see that," Enilna said with a tug of his elbow.

Taki handed it over to her. "You can read?"

"Aye! Though not all of the words. They taught me how, in Sevastopol. I hated it, though. Too many smacks."

"But that's how you learn best."

"All it did was make me hate the instructors."

"When I taught Emreis and Mikkselsen, I did the same. Now they fill their heads with new blasphemies every day. If you wish, I could teach you."

Enilna stuck her tongue out. "If you ever smack me, I'll take your hand."

Taki sniffed. "Perhaps I won't, then."

"Yeah, I'm kind of a bitch like that."

"I don't think so. You're just spirited. I like that about you."

"Mmm, you're getting better at interacting with women," Enilna said as she sagely flipped through her periodical. "You might be able to sweet-talk Captain Lotte into bed in about a decade."

Taki fumed. "Shut up! I'm much closer than that. You...you saw what we were doing!"

"Yeah, and it was *gross*!"

"Maybe to a runt like you."

"You're calling me a runt? You're the manlet here."

"Big words from a kid I rejected!"

At that, Enilna growled and kicked at Taki's shins. He hopped away and stuck his tongue out at her; she threw a clod of dirt at his head before trying to tackle him. Taki pivoted and avoided the missile but failed to step out of Enilna's way and found himself with his back on the ground. His pack made it hard for him to right himself, and before he could roll away, Enilna was on top of him. She smacked him across the face with her sheaf of papers, and he grabbed her wrists to restrain her. She hissed and struggled.

"Hey!" Jibriil snapped. "Take your petting inside. We're in public here!"

Taki looked up, and his face reddened, as did Enilna's. A small crowd of Imperials had gathered to point and laugh. Enilna rose to her feet and dusted herself off. Taki pulled himself up and tried to mime nonchalance.

"Well, uh, where to?" he asked.

"The quartermaster's. The primate paid for our horses, provisions, and ammunition for the journey. After we've equipped, we'll head west."

"No more trains?"

"Nay, we're on foot. This is a contested borderland, but we'll be in the heart of Ursala soon. There'll be no reinforcements if we get into a fight, so we must be discreet."

Taki let out a small sigh. Despite the monotony of the train, it had been far more comfortable than riding could ever be. But more worrisome was the fact that now, he and Enilna would truly be alone with Jibriil. Back in Astarte, and even aboard the train, there had always been others around, but in darkest Ursala, there would be no one to help. He nodded and brushed his fingers over the grip of his pistol. If nothing else, steel was always dependable.

15

Taki's eyes flicked up and down, alternating between the corpse and the gray chunk of decaying matter beneath it. The woman's body was one of at least a dozen strung up on the low boughs of the dead oak. Judging from the amount of flesh already torn away by carrion, the hanging had taken place within the last week. The congested pattern of boot prints and hooves in the mud underneath suggested that the tree was a popular spot for executions.

The three had ridden hard for two days and had ventured near a few other killing grounds, but they had not strayed as closely as they had to this one. The shifting borderlands between the Imperium and the Serene Kingdom were a foggy, drab-gray hell where it was common to run across crows and vultures too fattened on corpses to fly. Even common game animals seemed to have changed their diets. A day before, the squad had hunted a deer, only to discover that its belly was full of human flesh.

Though Jibriil had maneuvered to avoid known patrol routes, it seemed as if the party constantly ran into the smoking remains of battles and skirmishes. Bodies, both Ursalan and Imperial, unburied and often desecrated, dotted the roadways. The farther in they'd ventured, the more corpses they'd found. These were not soldiers, though.

"Peasants," Jibriil muttered as he surveyed the swaying, ghastly fruit. "Ursalan dirt farmers." He tightened his reins to prevent his horse from drawing too near. He narrowed his eyes as he spied the same fleshy mass Taki had seen, and spat off to the side. "At nine months, too. What foul joss to see this!"

"Who did it?" Taki growled.

Jibriil shrugged. "Might've been Liberation Army, but we're deeper in than they ever patrol."

"Then bandits?"

"Highwaymen would just leave the corpses on the ground. Soldiers did this. Most like Ursalans against their own."

"God! Why?"

"Chevaliers don't need a reason. If you're not one of them, you're just practice. Livestock's more valuable. You don't kill those until they're well fattened."

Taki made a fist. "Whoever it was, they'll pay."

"They won't," Enilna said. Her voice sounded far away. "They never do. They just go around and rape and maim and kill, and then kill some more."

Wait, Taki thought. *She came from this same sort of hell.* He reached out to her, but she shrank away. He decided against trying anything more.

"Come, Sir Taki," Jibriil said. "We'd best move, and off the main paths from now on. 'Twas my error to guide us so close to one of these."

"Nay, Jibriil, I'm actually grateful you did."

"Huh? Why?"

"Because when I signed up for this, I did it in hopes of a promotion. I hoped that Sir Aslatiel would be impressed by my bravery. I only thought of my own interests, but after seeing this…this bullshit, now I know that what I'm doing is right. We have to beat the Ursalans and destroy their entire godrotting nation. Now I know they all have to die."

* * * *

Days later and farther west, the fog finally lessened. The question of food, though, was becoming more important. Even after trying to supplement rations with game or forage, the trio's saddlebags hung limp and empty.

"Finally, a homestead," Jibriil said. "We should raid it."

A thin column of smoke rose from a decrepit collection of huts and a barn in the distance. The horses dipped and bobbed slightly to steady themselves on the jagged crest of a shale ridge that jutted from a floor of clustered pines below. According to the maps, the squad was on the outskirts of a massive forest, well away from the usual army routes and surrounding patrols.

Taki nodded. "Aye, though only preserved meats and foods. Take nothing we have to go through great pains to prepare."

"I'll find a spot to tie up the horses," Jibriil said.

"Wait," Enilna said, "are we really stealing from them?"

"Yes," Taki said.

"But we have milligrad to spare. Can't we just buy whatever we need?"

Jibriil shook his head. "If they see our faces, they *will* report us to the next Serene Kingdom soldiers they see. It's a death sentence not to."

"Can we at least leave them something? A bullet or two?"

"Lady Enilna," Jibriil said, "a peasant who flashes grad at the market is instantly regarded with suspicion. Everyone will assume he stole it from his betters, and he'll be worse off for it. Better to just take what we need and leave them enough to survive. And if they don't have enough to survive after a small loss, they were dead, anyway."

"Taki, you can't possibly agree with that!"

"I do," Taki said. "We have to survive and succeed. If we don't, then our companions will suffer."

"Aye, sir," Enilna said, looking away.

They scouted a small depression containing young trees and tied the horses to their trunks. The contour of the land hid the animals from casual view, and it was a clear break from the farmstead if the trio were forced to run. Taki crept silently through the leafy woods and stuck to the shadows. They had all invoked the *phon* sutra on each other, to keep the need to speak to a minimum. The forest floor was covered in a volatile carpet of shed pine needles, he noticed. A single errant flame would burn the entire place to the ground.

"*Split up,*" he muttered once they drew closer. The buildings were the typical ramshackle expected of isolated farmsteads, where the need to secure food for the table was at constant war with the need to keep everything from collapsing. The place was definitely inhabited. Smoke issued from a stone chimney attached to the main house, and goats chewed blithely out in the muddy yard. "*Jibriil, look in the root cellar. Enilna, keep watch on the road.*"

Taki slunk around to the opposite side of the house and tried to peer in through the gaps in the slat walls. The house hadn't been daubed in some time. Whatever family lived here would have to take care of the chore lest they freeze solid in the coming winter. He slowed his breathing and found a good-sized hole where a rat had chewed through. It gave him a view of the inside, where four peasants were sitting down to sup. Three women and a man, probably the patriarch. He didn't relish the thought of stealing from them, but theft was far better than murder.

"*Hark!*" Enilna's voice quavered with a mix of fear and excitement. "*A company of horse approaches from the road. Sigil is a red shield with a golden fleur-de-lis. Six men, chevaliers, lightly armored.*"

"*Arms?*" Taki whispered.

"*Swords and maces with bucklers. Three muskets, a few pistols, none true relics.*"

"*Everyone conceal yourselves. Let them pass.*" Taki held his breath to slow his heart. Six chevaliers weren't insurmountable, especially with a former Triada under his command. But it would make noise, expose their presence to the farmsteaders, and leave Taki with bodies, equipment, and horses to hide from view if more chevaliers dropped in.

"*Uh, Taki, this is bad. They're coming in,*" Enilna said.

Taki swore under his breath. This would complicate things. The men had likely come for sport and plunder. While the former was detestable, the latter meant that his squad would get nothing for their trouble and time. It meant much more risk and much more of a chance of failure. They would have to retreat and try again at another farm, and that was assuming they ran across one before their rations ran out. Hunger meant they couldn't travel, much less fight.

"*Your orders?*" Jibriil sounded impatient.

Taki steeled himself. "*Stay calm. Report Ursalan positions as they change. Jibriil, hide in the cellar if you can't make a clean break. I'll watch the far side of the house. Defend yourselves if needed, but see if they'll just leave.*"

"*Three coming to the house,*" Enilna whispered. "*One making his way to the barn. Another scouting around. Last one is lashing the horses to the gateposts.*"

Taki heard a chevalier bang his mailed fist against the door before Enilna stopped speaking. The peasants in the house fell silent. Even without the aid of prana-sense, Taki knew they were trembling in fear. A few seconds passed, and he heard the door crack and fall off its hinges. He cautiously raised his head back to the rat hole and peered in.

The old man with swollen, arthritic joints knelt with his eyes firmly fixed on the dirt floor. "Milord, you honor us with your presence!"

The chevalier had his weapon out and scanned the room with a suspicious glare. Taki pulled his head away to avoid it. After he heard a sword being sheathed, he returned to watching.

"Shut it, sniveling cur. You address Sir Silas of Rouen, not 'milord,'" the chevalier said, and plopped down on a stool at the table where the peasant and his family had supped. He was stocky, with mean black eyes and a large red beard that looked like a bloody waterfall. "It smells like pigshit in here. Give us ale and have your lumpy wench feed my men, else I'll cut your throats."

Two other chevaliers loomed in the doorway. One was a lanky blond with an axe, and the other a redhead who carried a flanged mace. They strode in, casting menacing grins at the three women in the hut. One of the women was older and obese, with muscly arms from churning and milking. *Probably the wife,* Taki thought. The other two were younger and shapelier, and that meant they were in greater danger. For now, though, the men seemed more focused on eating than anything else.

The farmer's wife rose to her feet and shuffled to the stove, where she started to stir porridge. "Cosette, Babette, slaughter and prepare a pig for your lords," she said.

Trying to distance them from the men. Cover them with blood and feathers and excrement to make them less appealing. How the wife remained so collected while being so helpless impressed him.

"No," Silas said. "The comely one stays here and sings for us. We've been traveling long on the road, defending you ungrateful vermin against the ravenous Imperial hordes." He rose to his feet, stomped over to one of the daughters, and grasped a handful of her hair.

The girl started to quake in fear.

"When the Imperium takes a town, they like to cut off all the girlies' titties and serve the boys their own balls," Silas purred. "They want to make everyone into a eunuch. That's the sort of monster we protect you from every day. So, sing sweetly for the brave knights, my darling."

"Babette, *get the pig,*" the wife said. The other daughter, who was more pockmarked, squeezed her sister's hand, rose shakily, and headed out the broken front door with her head bowed. As she passed, the lanky blond chevalier swatted her rump with a mailed hand. She remained silent.

Taki rubbed his temples. *I have to do something, and soon.* He knew what fate likely awaited the comely girl, but at least she would probably live. If the pockmarked one was messy enough with the slaughter, she might sustain a few cuffs but avoid being violated. *Why do I care? I'm here to steal from these people, too.*

"One's coming up to the cellar entrance," Enilna whispered.

Taki clenched his fists. The moment had finally come. *"Jibriil, one's coming to you. Kill him silently. Enilna, to the barn and kill the other. Watch out for the girl there."*

"With pleasure, Sir Taki."

Taki let himself form a smile. Violence wasn't the solution to all problems, but it was a sufficient answer to most. He resisted the temptation to talk while the others carried out their grim duty. The effects of *phon* allowed him to hear every stab, strangling, and thump of flesh against flesh well enough. Within the house, however, things were becoming more dangerous by the moment.

"What's taking the girl so long, old wench?" Silas snarled. "We're hungry."

"Please, Sir Knight, partake freely," the wife said, and bowed as she placed three steaming bowls of porridge on the table. "Lord Husband, more ale!"

Silas lowered his head and sniffed the bowl. His face scrunched with displeasure, and he casually tipped its contents onto the floor. "This smells suspicious. I won't have it."

"Forgive us, Sir Knight," the wife said. "I'll pluck a fresh chicken immediately."

The younger, red-haired chevalier rolled his eyes and rose from his seat. "Oy, Father, these vermin have nothing we really want. Well, maybe except for that," he said, and flashed a scraggly grin at the remaining daughter.

"You may have your way with her. Perhaps I will, too," Silas said.

"Please, milord, I beg you not to," the farmer cried and tried to kiss Silas's mailed boots. Silas kicked out and sent the man sprawling into a corner.

"She has...she has the pox, good sirs," the wife said. "That is why she stays here and has no husband. I beg you not to endanger yourself."

"Oh, well, so does my son." Silas laughed. "Girl, meet Sir Giles. He'll show you attention you haven't had for a while."

The wife rushed over to her daughter's side and threw her arms around the girl's shoulders. For her trouble, the blond chevalier knocked her to the ground. "Oy, Gilly, pray tell if she really has the pox or not. I want seconds if she's clean," he said.

"Oh, shut it, Oxney. You always want to stick it where I've been, you cur," Giles said. He dragged the girl away by her arm into the adjacent sleeping room and slammed the door shut.

Damn you, fucking Ursalan swine. Taki shook his head and slunk along the wall. When he came to a windowsill, he carefully rose and slipped into the darkness.

Giles the chevalier faced away from him, leering at the girl, who huddled against a corner. Taki slapped one hand over the man's eyes and then drove a knife through the base of his skull. The knight went limp, unable to speak and unable to breathe. Taki eased the body gently to the floor, looked at the girl, and motioned for her to keep quiet.

"Osterbrand! *Osterbrand!*" she shrieked.

Taki's jaw dropped in amazement and disgust. "Really! Are you fucking *kidding* me?"

The blond knight barreled in with his axe held high. Taki jammed his forearm into the knight's wrists to prevent the axe from falling, drew from a holster, and fired three rounds into the man's gut. Oxney staggered back and dropped the axe. Taki took aim at his enemy's forehead and pulled the trigger.

Behind Oxney's falling body, he saw Silas pull out a brace of muzzle-loading pistols. Taki pirouetted to dodge a shot and sent a round into the man's thigh. Silas groaned and pitched forward while trying to bring the other pistol to bear, but Taki was already on him. He grasped Silas's beard and gave it a yank to slam his head onto the table. Then, Taki pressed the muzzle of his Herstal against Silas's temple and fired twice. As the armored body slid off the table, Taki aligned sights on the farmer and his wife.

"Sir Taki!" Jibriil stormed in with his carbine at the ready. When he saw the chevaliers' bodies, however, he lowered his weapon and started to laugh. "By the Usurper's shriveled titties, I thought this was a burglary mission, not a massacre!"

Taki threw him a poisonous glare. "Keep the commentary to yourself."

"Everything all right?" Enilna was breathless as she also peeked in.

"No," Taki said. "They've seen us."

"Should we?" Jibriil pointed his gun at the family.

Dammit, Captain, what would you do? What would Sir Aslatiel do? Taki fixed a stare at the old farmer, as if daring him to move. He couldn't leave witnesses. The trio would be hunted relentlessly, and by far more capable soldiers than the ones they'd just killed. But the family hadn't asked for this, either. They weren't soldiers, or rebels, or smugglers. They were just like the people he'd seen mowed down in a similar shithole long ago. *But this is also war, and I know I'm no hero.* He raised his gun again and tried not to look at Enilna.

"Forgive us, Imperials," the wife said, and touched her forehead to the ground. "I know not for what purpose you came here today, but I thank God for you. We all do."

Taki sucked his teeth. "Is this place often visited by patrols? Are there more on the way?"

"Nay, milord," the old farmer said. "Those men were a prank of the devil. We are simply poor folk who can live nowhere else, so we live in seclusion. You've done us a great service, milord, and we do not believe the slander spread about your nation."

Taki lowered his gun. *Fuck it, I'm no war criminal.*

"Fine," he said. "But you will give us supplies and help hide the bodies and horses."

* * * *

Before long, the two daughters were happily bleeding and plucking a pair of chickens in the yard, while the old farmer and his wife set to work bundling together sacks of gruel and dried vegetables that could be made into porridge.

Enilna picked through the small mound of equipment scavenged from the enemy. Most of the weapons and armor had been poorly maintained, but there was a good amount of milligrad and some reloads.

Enough to make up for what Taki had spent, in any case. The rest would have to be burned or buried. She had driven the Ursalan horses away after stripping them of their reins and saddlery. Meanwhile, Taki and Jibriil had grown sweaty from the arduous task of toting the dead bodies into the root cellar. When the sun dipped against the horizon, the trio convened again in the main house.

"If you go south, there will be a shortcut to the Cantons," the old farmer said. "But the Schweizmadchen are fearsome and unruly. Even you, our saviors, might not be strong enough to overcome them."

"My thanks," Taki said. He tore into a chicken half with his teeth and fingers. It was hot and gamey, with a pleasing golden hue. "We'll be the judges of that."

Jibriil shook his head. "The old man's right, though. Chevaliers are one thing, but those warrior women are another. If we engage them in combat, we will die. I also don't enjoy the thought of fighting women."

Enilna winked at him. "Don't worry, Archangel, I won't let them rape you."

Jibriil chuckled. "I'll seriously hold you to that, Imperial."

"M-madame?" Cosette said.

"Huh?" Enilna said. "Me?"

"Does the Osterbrand king let all women have…guns?"

"Child," the farmer's wife admonished, "don't bother our saviors."

"Oh, it's fine," Enilna said. "Basically, yes. The padishah is kind of like this big floating head that flies around, and when we bow to him, guns come out of his mouth!"

"Don't feed the girl lies," Taki said.

Jibriil finished off the last of his broth and sucked cartilage off a bone before standing. "We should be on our way, Sir Taki. While we have the cover of night."

Taki considered telling Jibriil to shush, but he knew the man was right. It was comforting and warm in the house, but there were more chevaliers around, and the peasants weren't exactly friends. "Very well, we'll go. And, good sir, I advise you to remove the bodies and stow them far from here, for fear of dogs."

"Thank you, milord," the farmer said.

By the next bell, the trio headed out at a brisk canter through the trees. The night was pleasantly moonlit, and the horses were laden with food, perhaps overly so. Taki occasionally looked over his shoulder, expecting to see the torches of an Ursalan cavalry column in the distance, but so far there was nothing but silence.

"Did you sense it?" Jibriil asked, finally.

Taki blinked. "Sense what? You think they were going to report us?"

"Nay, but I believe something else might have been afoot concerning that family. I didn't want to say it at the time because I had no proof, but when scouting to find a place for our horses, I encountered a great many bones hidden under the leaves. Based on the shape, probably human."

"Bones litter all battlefields, though."

"I know, but I also saw no clearings or fields around the homestead. A farmer must clear trees and rocks away lest he ruin his plows. And yet there was no sign of such activity."

Taki frowned. "Are you accusing them of cannibalism?"

"I don't know," Jibriil said, "but I am glad that what we ate was prepared in front of us. And I wouldn't worry overmuch about taking so many of their winter stores. We might have left them a surfeit of meat in exchange."

"Cannibals or not, I didn't sense evil. Perhaps they were driven to desperation and lost their way. Many Ursalans seem to be."

"Somehow, I get the impression they weren't luring in armed patrols," Jibriil said. "I only hope they haven't been enticing too many innocents. Lonely woods like these hold many terrible secrets."

Taki laughed. "You're a suspicious sort, aren't you? I didn't think so back at the Temple. I always imagined you more self assured."

Jibriil winked. "And I never imagined myself being stuck between chevaliers and wendigo. But I'm glad, though."

"For what?"

"That you are a capable commander after all. I feared you would be bloodthirsty and weak willed. But I was proven wrong. I'm glad to serve you, Sir Taki."

Jibriil extended his hand, and Taki shook it.

16

By the valley entrance was a tower of skulls. Skulls stacked on top of long bones stacked on top of yet more skulls, with the smaller bones—phalanges and vertebrae—used to fill in gaps. Some still wore rusting helms and decaying chain cowls, but nearly all of them were marked with the same feature: bullet holes.

"What the hell is that?" Taki asked.

"A welcoming sign," Jibriil said. He unslung his carbine and chambered a round. "It means we're in the right place."

Enilna's eyes widened like saucers, and she trotted over to the ossuary, where she started to poke at the exposed ends of old bone.

"What the hell are you doing, milady? That's dangerous!"

"I'm just looking!" Enilna said. "They told me about the famous greeting towers, but I've never seen one in real life. It's really impressive. I wonder how long it took to make. How many bodies are in this thing, anyway?"

Jibriil wrung his hands. "The natives introduce themselves by shooting you in the head from a kilometer away. Our only chance for survival is to constantly watch each others' backs and stay discreet. That tower was our last warning to leave."

"So how are we to avoid trouble?" Taki said.

"Same way anyone does. A bribe." He reached into his saddlebag and withdrew a bulging sack. Holding it high in the air, he wheeled his horse around and then slowly trotted up to the skull tower. Finally, he set the bag on an altar of ribs and let it fall slightly open.

Taki drew in a sharp breath when he saw what was inside: glinting rounds of Old Nayto Standard. "Will it work?" he asked.

Jibriil shrugged. "It should prevent the older clanswomen from attacking us outright. They're the better shooters—the ones we should be especially concerned about. The younger goats might still try to kill us and loot our corpses, but they're nowhere near as fearsome as the nannies."

Enilna snorted. "They charge a hell of a toll, and we're still expected to defend ourselves from raiders *and* not do anything to offend their sensibilities. What a ripoff."

"Better than getting picked off while you're taking a shit," Jibriil said.

Taki shook his head and pulled ahead. In his peripheral vision, he spied the glint of sunlight reflecting off a rifle scope hidden in a copse of trees on the mountainside. Knowing that he was in someone's sights unnerved him greatly, but there was nothing to be done about it. If the sniper had wanted him dead, Taki would have already been face down in the mud. Hopefully, the payment was enough. If not, then the trio would not only be dead, but poor.

Over the next three days, they endured the agony of traversing a mountain range. The horses tired easily, the air was chokingly thin, and the evenings were never restful. Every distant howl, flap of a wing, or shift of the logs on their fire was enough to induce an anxious wakefulness. In the distance, pairs of eyes glinted in the trees but vanished when focused on. Mornings brought relief at having survived another night in this savage hinterland. On the fourth day, as they crested the peak of yet another endless series of hills that barely failed as mountains, they saw the town of Ulrichtochten.

"Remarkable, isn't it?" Jibriil said. "Like the Fall just didn't happen in this corner of the world."

"You're right," Taki said, "it's too pristine. I thought no one had been spared the wrath of the demons."

"This land has always been strange," Jibriil said. "Even before the Fall, they were an isolated sort that didn't care for the demands of their neighbors. It's plausible that they may have defended themselves successfully. I don't know."

"But we're not all speaking their language, so something happened to make them perish, anyway," Taki said. "Anyone within?"

"Assuredly," Jibriil said, "and the matron is down there somewhere. They're testing our resolve. Do we go through and start looting and get shot, or do we go around in fear? It's a game for bored locals to play on the tourists."

"But these are the people your master wants us to bargain with, so we've got no choice. They think we've got grad, so they'll be willing to talk."

Enilna huffed. "Do we have enough to just buy them?"

Jibriil shook his head. "There's not enough grad in the world for that. We'll need to find the matron and come to another arrangement. Be careful, though, and prepare to fight your way out."

"Sounds like if it comes to a fight, we're dead," Taki said.

"Perhaps, but we'll take out a lot of them before we go down."

"I like the way you think, Jibriil."

After a short hike down the hillside, Taki set foot on the first paved surface he had seen since leaving the Salted Fortress. When he realized just how well preserved it was, a chill went through his core. Intricate architecture overlooked expertly planned avenues lined with well-manicured trees, and the storefronts still had glass in the windows. Like all glass, it was distorted from centuries of slow melting but still glistened attractively in the light.

"It's so beautiful," Enilna whispered. "Did everyone in the old world live like this?" She twirled around and inhaled the apple-scented air.

"Stay alert," Taki said. A scowl marred his features as he regarded the rooftops and alleys.

"Look, if anyone wanted to actually attack us here, we'd be dead ten times over already. We're in five killzones at once right now. This is the worst possible place to be trapped, so just enjoy yourself, okay?"

"I still prefer to be prepared."

"You know, if a man's too stressed, he'll find it hard to get it up."

"Christ! Enilna!"

"Company," Jibriil said.

In front of the squad stood a pair of women cloaked in hides fringed with ragged tufts of burlap. They carried rifles with immaculate wooden stocks and not a trace of rust. Taki recognized the guns as Gewehr rifles that only shot the best types of milligrad and always hit their targets. The Temple had possessed a few examples, but those had been considered too precious to take into battle.

Jibriil gestured for the others to stand back and approached with his hands calmly at his sides. "I speak for the holy diver of Astarte. Please, show us to your matron."

One of the women spoke. "For what purpose, male?"

"His Holiness wishes to enter an agreement. One bullet turns to a thousand."

The two women started to murmur to each other. After another tense moment, the women simply turned and gestured for the trio to follow. Eventually, they led the band to the outside of a massive granite tower in the middle of a tiled courtyard. One opened the door. Jibriil made to enter, only to find rifles aimed at his chest.

"Males may not enter," one of the women said.

Jibriil scowled. "I said I speak for the diver. If I cannot enter, I cannot speak for him."

"Your *mistress* may enter."

"What?" He looked around and then at Enilna. "You mean her?"

"Who else?" the woman said.

"She's not of Astarte! She knows nothing of His Holiness's plan—"

"Wait, Jibriil," Enilna said. "Didn't you have a scroll or something that the primate gave you? Surely you didn't just memorize the entire agreement?"

"I...I do, but he entrusted me to handle it," Jibriil said, scratching his head.

"But if they won't let you in, then nothing will happen."

"Then we'll leave," Jibriil said, and crossed his arms. "I don't like this one bit."

"It's not up to you, anyway," Enilna said, and crossed her arms too. "It's up to our leader. Well, what say you, Taki?"

Taki furrowed his brow. "Jibriil, you said you were only to be our guide. Did the primate expect you to negotiate for him?"

Jibriil grimaced. "No. He only wished to have the matron sign the agreement."

"So there shouldn't be a problem with giving it to Enilna. Besides, if she has a question, she can always take her leave and come out here to ask you."

"But..."

"We went through a lot to get here. My captain, Sir Aslatiel, and all of my friends are depending on our success. We lost one of our own for this, and I won't have his life be spent in vain." He locked his gaze with Jibriil's. "Give her the scroll."

For a moment, something inscrutable flickered in Jibriil's eyes, almost so quickly that Taki wouldn't have caught it if he hadn't been staring the man down. It wasn't hatred or contrition or anything so obvious, and by the time it had even registered in Taki's consciousness, the look had long faded. Jibriil's eyes flicked down and then back to Taki's. Then, he extended the scroll to Enilna.

"Have the matron seal it with her personal chop, too," Jibriil said. "Tell her if she dislikes any of the terms, they're all negotiable later. If you have questions, come out and ask me as Sir Taki said to."

Taki nodded, and Enilna took the leather-bound scroll. She strode into the building and disappeared from view. The cloaked women also turned and entered. The door closed with an ominous clanking sound. Now, the two men were alone again.

Taki spoke first. "Thank you, Jibriil."

"Beg pardon?"

"I said thanks. For being flexible and patient. I know you were loath to part with the scroll, but sending Enilna was our only option."

Jibriil chuckled and stretched. "I still have misgivings. The madchen are notorious bandits, and not simply because of the sniping. They use their tongues to steal, even more so than their guns. But as you said, Sir Taki, you're in charge. I must abide by that."

Taki bit his lip. "Yes, that's right. But you still have my thanks."

"I remember the first time I saw you. You were a fresh corporal then, were you not?"

"I'd graduated the academy only a fortnight before the fall of Vergina."

"Your type of power is rare, and I heard you were a gifted student. I'd have scooped you up into my unit in a heartbeat, had I the choice. How did you end up stuck in Tirefire the Lesser?"

Taki let out a half smile. "It's a long story, but suffice to say, it was mostly Hecaton Mezeta's fault."

"The old bag sure liked to screw with people." Jibriil snorted.

"The last thing she did was steal our pensions."

"Really now? That's…" Jibriil counted his fingers. "Five hundred rounds. I heard you all were after her like hungry dogs. Now I see why."

"Well, the captain said that next time we see her, Mezeta's dead no matter what."

"If I'm around, you'd better let me in on the slaughter," Jibriil said, and extended his hand.

"Aye to that," Taki said, and shook it.

For a moment, both were silent. Jibriil sighed. "Don't misapprehend me, but how is Lo—I mean, your captain?"

"She is well." Taki toed the dirt. "Perhaps better than she has ever been before. Certainly happier to be away from the Temple…and away from you."

Jibriil smiled, though sadly. "Then I am happy for her. I always thought her destined for better things."

Taki wanted to stop there but found himself unable to. "Then why did you mistreat her so?"

"Sir Taki, you may never believe this, but I did—and still do—genuinely love her. Lady Lotte is a woman unlike any other. She's strong of body, heart, and mind. She possesses valor to rival the exarch's, and I mean Choniates and not Michail when I say that. She's…" He paused. "If I'm not mistaken, you're also acquainted with her virtues as well."

"You still haven't answered my question," Taki said, trying not to redden.

"Sir Taki, do you know aught about these parts?"

"No. I don't see what that has to do with—"

"I told you, my father was a mountaineer. My mother was one of the madchen, who are a strict matriarchy. It's what naturally happens in a society where everyone's armed to the teeth. Regardless, there are no adult males around these parts. Clanswomen will occasionally meet with men from greater Ursala to procreate, but they only keep the girl children. I was lucky and was given back to my father. He was a lout. His answer to disobedience was a fist or a boot. The same applied to the women he kept. When I was finally taken to the Temple, I knew nothing else. I knew nothing of how to court, so to speak.

"I joined the Lotte's unit right out of the academy. You know how brutal and yet tender she can be. Because of that, I worshipped her, perhaps literally. Then, she saved my life and lost everyone else. I finally had my chance, so I took it. I thought I'd treated her fairly and shown her my love. I had done no wrong, and my power confirmed it. But then we lost to the Imperium, I woke up to my own burial, and I had to start over from nothing. I lost her, and deservedly so."

"You sound as if you blame your father for your actions."

"No, I do not. I have only myself to blame. I was happy to see her again and finally apologize. It does little to mend things, but words are better than nothing."

"You've still a long way to go to deserve her forgiveness."

"As I said, I don't expect it."

"Then take my advice, Jibriil. After our business here is concluded, don't approach her again. Even if you've changed, none of us need suffer the memories your presence brings."

"I'm glad, Sir Taki."

"For what?"

"That you serve her now. You're a good commander and a brave fighter. And, take no offense, but I can tell you have more than simple devotion in your heart. In return, I shall give you advice."

"And what would that be?"

"Don't two-time her. Don't make her share your attention with Lady Enilna."

Taki crossed his arms. "Enilna's just a friend."

Jibriil snorted. "Is she?"

The door to the granite tower creaked and drew both men's attention. Taki rested a hand on his pistol grip. Visions of Enilna's severed head presented at the tip of a pike drove him to a cold sweat. *I forgot, dammit. I forgot to tell her to take their salt and bread first. Shit!*

"Okay," Enilna said, and stepped out. Taki unclenched to see her. His breathing returned to normal. "I got her to sign and seal it, but we've got to pay her now."

"Pay her?" Jibriil threw up his hands. "The primate specifically said *no concessions!*"

"And that's what pissed her off!" Enilna crossed her arms indignantly.

"We used our funds to bribe our way in here. We've got nothing."

"I'm way ahead of you. Instead of 'grad, we'll provide services instead. So, uh, we've got a feast to attend. And a monster to, uh…kill."

* * * *

Later, in the smoky, high-ceilinged hall of the grand lodge of the canton, Taki feasted. He sat cross-legged on a pile of hides in front of a low-set table piled high with roasted cuts of venison and blackened pheasants. Enilna sat next to him and busily devoured a shank crusted with salt and whole peppercorns. They tore into drumsticks and thighs with relish and mopped up the grease on their plates with chunks of coarse bread. Wine, tapped from ancient casks, flowed freely.

"Enilna, I never knew you liked rare meat," Taki said between bites and swallows. "Thing's practically running out of your grasp!"

"It tastes better when it's bleeding," she retorted before upending her plate against her lips and slurping down the shallow crimson pool.

"Gross!" Taki stuck his tongue out.

"Sir Taki," Jibriil said, "a woman who likes bloody meat is the most desirable of all. She won't make you slave away overlong in the kitchen."

"Like I'll ever cook again." Taki snorted.

"Lady Enilna," Jibriil said, "the feast is nice, but what does the matron want with a monster?"

"From what I understand, about a half-day's ride from here, there's a giant that lives near the road. The matron called it the 'Wailing Lady,' and apparently the thing can speak. Sounds like it's hell of depressed, too. She wants us to put a bullet in its head. But from the way she described it, I don't know if a bullet will do the trick."

"Christ," Jibriil said, and rubbed at his eyes. "She wants us to kill the Wailing Lady of Lucerne. Of all the rotten luck..."

"Jibriil, do you know something of this?" Taki asked.

"Aye, though not much, and I've never seen her in person. All I know is that she's supposedly fifty cubits tall and wields a club. Never knew she could speak. Titans are horrible opponents, though. Forget shooting them or even hitting them with sutras. You have to do it the old-fashioned way."

"Ooh!" Enilna said. "You mean climbing up their dangly bits while they try and smash you like a bug, and then sticking them in their crystals?"

"Yes. Exactly that."

"How are we going to *do* that?" Taki said. "Why the hell did you agree to this?"

Enilna scowled at him. "Give me a break! I'd like to see *you* deal with high-pressure sales tactics!"

"I'm an expert at those!"

"Are not! Otherwise you wouldn't be a virgin anymore!"

Jibriil started to laugh. "It's fine, you two. We'll just deal with the titan. It'll be a bit easier with three of us, anyway. The matron could've demanded much, much worse."

As if on cue, two clanswomen came up on him from behind, pressed their hands on Jibriil's shoulders, and started to squeeze. He turned his head in confusion and was met with a pair of sultry smiles.

"I am Hilda Head-Taker, and this is my sister, Salia Throat-Ripper," said the crimson-haired of the pair. "We defeated many others to claim your seed."

Jibriil's jaw dropped, revealing a mess of half-chewed pheasant and bread. Hilda stuck her nose in his hair and inhaled deeply.

"Yes, it was worth it. Now come with us, male." The sisters looped arms under each of his arms and started to drag.

"Lady Enilna, you sold me out, didn't you?" Jibriil huffed.

Enilna chuckled nervously and waved.

Taki glowered at her. "Did you barter him off to be made into meat?"

"Not *literal* meat!"

"You're really bad at negotiating, aren't you?"

She glared and swatted at him with a piece of rib. The glaze left a sticky mark on Taki's nose.

Taki chortled as the realization hit him. "Then I guess I'll just wait around for a clanswoman to come get me, then. It's not how I imagined my first time would go, but it'll help their people and be fun for me, so there!"

"Oh, that won't happen," Enilna said. "You're safe tonight."

"Wait, what? But they *fought* to claim the likes of Jibriil..."

"Well, I told the matron like it was. We'll kill any monster she wants, and her daughters can bang the hell out of smelly Jibriil all night long, but I won't let them lay a single finger on you. The old hag tried to boss me around and threaten me to high heaven, you know. She even offered to let the titan thing go if I offered you up, but I held firm! So don't ever call me bad at negotiating. I know where to draw the line!"

Taki's jaw dropped. *"Are you serious?"*

Enilna cupped his face in her palms. "Very serious. I won't let a bunch of horny, murderous bandit bitches pass you around like a bent reload. You, Taki Natalis, are special to me. You're my precious friend. I thought you'd…you'd kill those poor people in the hut back there, but you didn't. It meant a lot to me, and I think I've fallen in love with you a little. So I'd hate for anything bad to happen to you." She leaned forward and kissed him on the forehead. "Now, let's eat until we're in pain."

17

Taki heard the weeping first. It sounded strange, though, and unlike any other he'd ever heard in his life. An ululating basso throb battered its way into his skull and echoed unceasingly within. He held up a fist to signal Enilna and Jibriil to be vigilant. None of them could see the source of the weeping, but all knew they were close.

The matron's directions had led them to a place nearly overtaken with tangled, ancient trees and littered knee-deep in dead brush. Thick fog sank the forest into a lulling darkness that seemed to invite sleep. Not an ideal place to have a fight, Taki reasoned, but on the other hand, the oppressive overgrowth would help his soldiers evade an angry titan.

"One last time," Jibriil whispered. "If the thing attacks..."

"Enilna and I will bait it on the ground," Taki said. "You'll climb and target the crystals on its body."

"What if it has no crystals?" Enilna hissed.

"Then we're basically dead," Jibriil said with a shrug. He trudged forward, obviously limping.

"You sure you're okay to fight?" Enilna asked.

"I'm fine," Jibriil said. "Just sprained a few things."

Taki grimaced and forged on, unsure of whether to be envious or relieved. The weeping grew louder and more distracting the closer they advanced, as did the thickness of the brush. Just before it became impossible to tread farther, however, he spotted the opening to a glade.

"This is it," he said. "Enilna, stay hidden as we planned. Jibriil and I will go forth. If we're killed, do not fight but retreat." Something told him not to enter the clearing with a weapon drawn. No individual bullet, milligrad or reload, would probably help much anyway. *Lotte, Sir Aslatiel, watch me,* he thought, and stepped into the open.

The glade was really part of the grassy bank of a lake, and its far end was bounded by rippling, murky water. It was impossible to tell how large the lake really was since everything else was shrouded by fog. Twisted ruins of a bridge jutted from the ground like gray saplings that had died without the chance to bud. Kneeling at the water's edge was the Wailing Lady.

It would have been easy to mistake the titan for a colossal pile of fallen, mossy tree trunks. Her overall shape seemed to be humanoid, but much like an ancient woodpile, her profile was broken by jutting, branch-like structures. Her skin, if it could be called that, had a close resemblance to slate rock and boasted centuries of lichen and mats of velvety green moss.

Taki held in a breath, walked forward, and considered how to get the creature's attention without getting smashed to paste. It occurred to him to leap onto it, try to find the head, and stab the hell out of everything, but he recognized the idea as similar to the sort of compulsion that made one want to jump off a high bridge. When nothing else came readily to mind, he simply cleared his throat and spoke.

"Er, milady Titan…"

The ground trembled as the Wailing Lady straightened her torso and shifted around on her knees. Birds' nests and accumulated detritus plummeted to the ground around her. The titan's face could not have been said to be human in appearance, with block-like features and eyes like deep, dark pits.

"You," the titan said in a rumbling voice that reminded Taki of millstones grinding grain. "You're not from around here."

"I am not," Taki said. "I am Taki Natalis, fahnrich of the Imperial Spetsnaz. The matron told me where to find you."

"Are you here to laugh at me?"

"No. I was sent here to…to kill you."

The Lady let out a baritone laugh. "Plenty have tried, all have failed. I will not move from this spot until my dear husband comes for me. Neither of you puny men look like him."

Taki gritted his teeth. As predicted, there was a small area right on top of the Lady's pate that seemed less slate-like than the other parts of her body. Most of the larger monstrosities had similar chinks in their armor, though the Lady's was placed in a location impossible to hit from the ground. Fortunately, she was also encrusted with stringy vegetation and harsh outcroppings that could serve as handholds. It was just a matter of not getting crushed first.

"How do you know that your dear husband will come back to you?" Jibriil shouted. "For all you know, he is dead or has gone back on his word."

The Lady slammed one of her blocky fists into the ground, and Taki nearly fell over from the ensuing temblor. "Imbecile, you know him not! My dust will be mingled with his, forever and forever and forever. Why should I climb the lookout? Leave!"

Shit, she's fast as well as strong, Taki realized as he reclaimed his footing. He glanced at Jibriil, upon whose face panic was spreading. According to Jibriil, the inherent weakness all titans had was their relative sloth in comparison to their strength. But the Wailing Lady was different. She'd crush them all like bugs.

"While your hair was still cut straight across your forehead, you played about the front gate, pulling flowers," Enilna said, as she stepped out of the brush.

"The hell are you doing, girl?" Jibriil shouted at her. "Get back!"

The Lady stared at Enilna, her dark pits possessed of a menacing intensity. "How? How do you know this?"

Enilna put her hands on her hips. "He came by on bamboo stilts, playing horse. He walked about your seat, playing with blue plums. And you went on living in the village, two small people, without dislike or suspicion. At fourteen, you married him, your lord. You never laughed, being bashful. Lowering your head, you looked at the wall. Called to, a thousand times, you never looked back. At fifteen, you stopped scowling. You desired your dust to be mingled with his, forever and forever and forever. But at sixteen, he dragged his feet as he departed into the river of swirling eddies. He has been gone for many months while the birds make sorrowful cries overhead. And now, by the gate, the moss is grown too deeply to clear away."

"What sort of gibberish are you spouting?" Taki said. Enilna shushed him with a glare.

"The leaves fall early this autumn, in wind," the Lady said in a gravelly whisper. "The paired butterflies are already yellow with August over the grass in the gardens. They hurt me. I grow older."

"He told you once," Enilna said, gathering her fists over her chest, "that he would let you know beforehand if he came down through the narrows of the river. So that you could meet him, as far as…"

"As Sanct Gotthard," the Lady concluded. She bowed her head. "How did you know this? How did you know what my dear husband confided only to me?"

Enilna lowered her arms. "It's an old poem, written by Master Li long before the Fall. *Ba'gshnar* loves it because it's by his favorite smut writer. A romantic but ultimately tragic tale. Your husband probably wanted to tell you to give up hope and move on but could not do so directly. He wanted to free you from his spell."

"Nonsense," the Lady said. "He clearly told me he'd send me word of his return. Even if this is an old poem and not his creation."

"I am truly sorry," Enilna said. "But when Master Li wrote the poem, it was because he wanted to tell a tale of two people caught in a love affair that ended too early. Two humble folk separated forever by distance and the cruelty of death. Your husband wanted you to move on, to climb the lookout. To search for your true purpose and worth. That is why you must leave this place and break free to reclaim your pride."

"And what do you know of love?" the Lady snarled. She brought her face close enough that Enilna's hair was blown back from her breath. "Have you a dear husband?"

Enilna let out a nervous laugh. "Well, funny you should ask! The thing about that is…you know…" She shrugged. "No."

The Lady let out a wailing roar, twisted, and plunged a hand into the murky water. A mussel-encrusted, twenty-meter-tall pillar of stone leapt from the depths and sprayed foulness high in the air. She raised the giant club high in the air and threw a glinting arc of water droplets into the fog. Then, she swung it straight down.

Taki leapt without conscious thought and barreled into Enilna to push her out of the way. She let out a yelp when his shoulder crashed into her gut, and they rolled painfully on uneven loam speckled with fist-sized rocks. Behind them, the earth heaved as the titan's club smashed home and sent pieces of turf flying.

"You okay?" Enilna asked.

Taki blinked. He lay on his back with a rock grinding on the small of his back, and his limbs felt on fire. Enilna lay on top of him, covered in green foulness from the bottom of the lake. He wanted to laugh at her appearance, but behind Enilna, the titan's outstretched hand reached out to crush them.

He intoned a breathless incantation and stuck a palm out. A shimmering burst of compressed energy spat forth and smacked into the monstrous hand to repulse it. The Lady let out a high-pitched roar, and the earth heaved again as she stumbled.

"Dammit!" Jibriil shouted. From what Taki could see, the former archangel swung perilously by one hand from a ledge near one of the titan's hips. Jibriil's face contorted in consternation as he tried to latch his other hand on to anything else. "I said distract her, not piss her off!"

"How the hell do I do that?" Taki yelled.

"Like this!" Enilna said. She took aim with her Colt and fired.

The Lady howled and smacked at her face as if swatting flies away and let out a roar. She lifted her club again and took another swing. This time, both Taki and Enilna dove the opposite way before the massive stone pillar turned them into paste.

Taki glanced over at Enilna to make sure she still stood and then knelt to invoke another sutra. Enilna's gun barked as it discharged lead at the titan's newfound sensitive spots and drew the Lady's attention away. Just as she was ready to try for another swipe at Enilna, Taki stretched out both palms and let the energy flow.

"*Pyr!*" he shouted, and sent out a blast of hot plasma that hit the Lady in the back of her leg.

She howled and stumbled. Jibriil, who had made it midway up her back, let out a melodic stream of curses. The Lady issued a piercing, tree-shaking roar and rounded on Taki. She twisted her hips and swung in a wide arc, which he barely ducked under. Ancient trunks behind him snapped like stalks of wheat hit by a flail, and a cloud of angry birds erupted from the destroyed greenery. Yet more gunshots rang out from Enilna's direction.

Taki tried to pull himself to his feet, tired beyond measure. His prana was waning fast. He found no success, though, because one of his ankles had been trapped by a pair of massive, fallen boughs. With growing panic, he tried to wrench his leg free. Suddenly, Enilna's gunshots stopped. *She's run out of ammunition,* Taki realized. The Lady let out an angry roar and raised her club again. This time, Taki wouldn't be able to dodge the blow. He grimly drew his saber. Survival demanded he lose his foot, but it was better than dying meaninglessly...

A pair of deeper gunshots rang out from on high. The titan faltered, fell to one knee, and jammed the end of her club into the ground to save herself from falling over. She let out a deep groan and reached for Taki to crush him. Before her fingers could close, she stopped and went silent.

Taki let out the breath he'd been holding and tried desperately not to piss himself.

From atop the titan's head, Jibriil's head poked over. "You okay?"

"Yes!" Taki said. "Another second, though, and..."

Jibriil looked over the scene and grimaced. "Don't even think about it. I'll get you free in a moment."

"I think...I think you saved my life."

Enilna bounded over to where Taki was and scampered over a fallen trunk. "Taki! Oh God, Taki!"

He waved weakly. "I might've shat myself, but I'm good."

She wrapped him in a frantic hug, and Taki almost vomited from the smell of the lake-bottom muck. "Never make me worry like that again!"

"Y-you're the one who made us have to do this!" Taki said.

"Yeah, and we won! So shut the hell up!"

"You're impossible!"

She took his face in her hands and snarled at him, to which he snarled back. Then, she leaned in and kissed him deeply and fiercely.

"Break it up, you two," Jibriil said. "We're not out of the woods yet."

Taki blinked and sputtered and swatted Enilna away. "Is she dead?"

Jibriil knocked against an outstretched stone finger and shrugged. "Probably?"

"You sound unsure."

"Because I am. I found what looked like a crystal, and so I shot it, twice. Thing stopped moving soon after. It's not like I can take its pulse or anything."

Enilna frowned. "It's still kind of sad, what happened to her. Monstrous titan or not, she still got dumped by some asshole and didn't have the sense to move on."

"Perhaps it was better we killed her, then," Jibriil said.

"I know she tried to mash us, but I hope she's not really dead."

Taki shuddered at the thought. "Let's get away before we find out. Someone help me with my leg."

* * * *

Later, when they'd gone some distance away from the Wailing Lady's glade, Taki finally allowed himself to collapse from exhaustion in the grass under a tall tree.

Jibriil sat nearby in a meditative pose. "We might as well rest here. I'm running low as well. I also started with a slight handicap." He scowled at Enilna.

She flipped him off. "Oh, whatever. You were all smiles and sunshine this morning."

"Thanks to your shenanigans, Hilda and Salia might each end up with triplets. What will I do if they're all boys and I have to raise them?"

"Not my problem," Enilna said with a shrug.

Jibriil sighed. "Regardless, we must plan our way back to Astarte."

Taki lifted his chin. "We can't retrace our steps?"

"No, it's too dangerous, especially since we took out that group of chevaliers and left the farmsteaders alive. We'll have Ursalans up our arses day and night. The Salted Fortress might not even let us in."

"So what do you propose?"

"If we go but a day's march south, we'll end up in Uri, where there's lodging, food, and most importantly, beer. Farther south, and we'll be in the primate's domain again."

Enilna pointed an accusing, tremulous finger at Jibriil. "What? Why didn't we just take that route in the first place?"

"Because," Taki said, "that way we'd have to pass through the Teufelsbrucke. Isn't that right, Jibriil?"

"Yes," Jibriil said. "There was no way we'd have made it through there coming from Astarte with an agreement scroll and a sack of grad, but look at us now. We're poor, covered in shit, and out of options. Basically, we'll pass inspection without a problem."

"What about the castellan? They say he can sniff out a spy leagues away. What makes you sure we'll escape his notice?"

"Because," Jibriil said, "there's something different about us now. We trust each other. Don't we?"

Taki blinked. Only a week ago, he'd have never agreed to that statement. In fact, he'd have gladly put a bullet in the former archangel's head. But Jibriil had just saved his life. It would've been easy to let the Wailing Lady crush Taki, and no suspicion would have ever been cast on Jibriil. Tentatively, Taki nodded. "Aye, we do."

18

Taki rubbed his upper lip and frowned as his fingers came away feeling simultaneously slick and sticky. The cold, dry air of the Lepontine Alps made his nose run continuously. So much so that his handkerchief was already saturated, and now he was forced to use his bare hands. One thing that Jibriil had failed to warn him about was the danger of drowning in his own snot. He leaned over the top of the stone railing on the bridge and gazed miserably down at the rapids a hundred meters below. Astarte, even with its intrigue and terrible memories, was becoming quite appealing. Enilna, on the other hand, seemed to be enjoying herself immensely and was entirely unaffected by the weather.

"You mind?" Taki said as she jostled him.

"I don't mind at all," Enilna said. She grinned to show him the food stuck between her teeth. In her hands was a steaming potato, freshly plucked from a bed of coals and dusted with salt and coriander. Around them was a crowd of several dozen packed on the Uri side of the bridge, gathered in the hopes of passing through the Teufelsbrucke.

The Devil's Bridge was infamous. The sole pass through an otherwise impenetrable mountain range, it was the gate to the Ursalan heartland and the best-defended toll fortress in the Serene Kingdom. Stretching thirty meters high in the air, its stone face was riddled with arrowslits and murder holes and permanently blackened by centuries of battle. But the real source of the fort's brutal legend was the man who controlled it.

"Take this a bit more seriously," Taki said. "You're just stuffing your face and making an ass of yourself."

"I'm blending in," Enilna said. "You're the one acting all rigid, like some sort of enemy spy."

"Can you not say that word here?"

"Spy?"

Taki crossed his arms and glared at her.

"She has a point, Sir Taki," Jibriil said. "The key is to be relaxed. I know that doesn't come easy."

"No, I can do it," Taki said. "Not like our lives are on the line or anything."

Before arriving in Uri, Jibriil had suggested the trio discard and bury their arms and armor. He had gone so far as to suggest the guns meet the same fate, but Taki and Enilna had refused. Jibriil had ended up burying his carbine with many promises to return after the Imperium stormed the fortress. Despite the comforting weight of his Herstal, Taki still felt naked without his brigandine and saber.

"Where the hell is this Doohickey guy, anyway?" Enilna asked.

"Duvalier," Jibriil said.

"Doodoo, whatever. Isn't he supposed to judge all who try to pass the bridge? We've seen lots of people go across and nothing."

"Be patient," Taki said. Enilna had been right, though. *Perhaps he died or moved on. Or perhaps he never existed at all?* The last thought he quickly pushed down into the rubbish bin of his consciousness. Of course Duvalier was real, or Lotte wouldn't have ever lost her status as archangel.

Enilna broke his thoughts by tugging on his sleeve and thrusting the half-eaten potato at his face. "Want a bite?"

"No."

Enilna seemed taken aback, but her eyes quickly lit with realization.

"Oh," she said with what seemed to be genuine contrition. "I forgot about your trauma. Do you want to talk about it?"

Taki rolled his eyes. "I *don't* have potato trauma!"

"That's classic denial. Do you startle easily when you see a root vegetable? Irulan tells me that's one of the cardinal signs to look for."

"Commissar Surenovna needs to stop pretending she's a surgeon," Taki said, and turned with his back to the rail. "I'm just…worried. I'd almost rather the castellan be present than hidden."

"True, but isn't it nicer this way?" Enilna smiled. "Soon we'll be across the bridge, and it'll be easy travel to Astarte. You should feel lucky to spend a few peaceful days with a cutie like me."

"You? Cute?"

Enilna flicked him on the forehead. "Don't push your luck, V-bag."

"You're horrible, you know that?"

"For a small fee, I won't teach that word to Dassa."

"How much?" Taki sighed and fished around in his money pouch to buy her silence. Of course, it was a lack of funds that had driven the trio to try passage across the bridge in the first place.

"A round of Old Nayto."

"That's extortion."

"We're up next," Jibriil murmured. *"Remember the plan."*

Taki swallowed, gritted his teeth, and trudged past the thick iron bars that made up the portcullis. He was in a small square courtyard ringed by a raised stone platform with a tall archway at each corner. The walls of the fortress loomed high above him and were also ringed by torches. In front of him was another portcullis, similar to the one he'd passed under to enter this place. And past that gate was freedom.

A sentry raised his hand. "Halt."

With a rumble that Taki could feel through his feet, the gates behind and in front of him closed. The trio was now trapped inside the fort. From the archways, Templars stomped out and assumed a silent vigil. They hefted poleaxes, dark and stained with grease.

Enilna's eyes widened. Taki saw her reach, unconsciously, under her poncho to where her Colt was. Quickly, he put a hand on her forearm and stroked it reassuringly. She in turn intertwined her fingers in his and squeezed. Together, they stood in silence.

"Kneel for inspection by Lord Duvalier!" the sentry said.

Yea, though I walk through the valley of the shadow of death, I will fear no evil. Thou art with me. Thy rod and thy staff, they comfort me...

From a darkened archway above emerged a man of middling height and great beauty. Blond and smooth faced, the castellan carried himself with the surety and grace of a man who not only accepted but actually embraced his station in life. He stepped up to the edge of his perch and peered down at the group.

"Pray, tell me your names and destination," Duvalier said.

Oh fuck, it's him.

Jibriil raised his head. "Milord, I am Sir Silas of Rouen, a poor knight-errant in search of employment. I beseech you let me pass to Astarte, where I may petition the primate for work."

Duvalier sniffed. "Pray tell, Sir Knight, what Ordo did you forsake?"

"The Ordo Draconis, milord. I am…not proud of my misdeeds, but I aim to regain my honor through virtuous employment."

"And those two?"

"My squire is Giles of Rouen. The girl is a farmer's daughter he has ruined and taken ownership of."

"Her name?"

"Cosette, of no special origin."

Duvalier nodded. "You know, Sir Silas, I also have need of men skilled with arms. If you wished, I would extend an offer of work as a sentry. I pay better than the apostate in Astarte, too."

Jibriil bowed his head again. "My thanks, milord. But…I have family in Astarte. My father has perished, and my poor mother has none else. She is the reason I left the Ordo in the first place."

"How virtuous of you." Duvalier smirked. "How about we have a test of sorts? If you can defeat one of my guard captains, then I will let you and your dependents pass unmolested. If not, then…well, you weren't strong enough to survive the intrigues in Astarte anyway, and neither was your mother."

"Milord, I beg you!" Jibriil balled his hands into fists. "I have no sword, shield, or armor! Surely you, who are the epitome of justice, will not make me fight one of your men, naked as I am?"

"You raise a fair if cowardly point, Sir Silas. If you don't wish a trial by combat, then my men will simply take the wench off your hands. Unlike you, my guardsmen are brave and deserve comfort. And by your admission, she has no virtue to ruin. When they are done with her, she will be returned to you. Not to worry. They won't kill her, and they'll pay her well for her services."

Enilna clenched her jaw and tensed. She gripped Taki's hand until his knuckles turned white.

"I won't let them!" Taki stepped forward and rolled up his sleeves. "If J—Sir Silas won't fight, then I will! Who wants it first?"

Jibrill glared at him. *"Quiet!"*

"Ah, Sir Giles, it seems your squire has more sand than you," Duvalier said with a chuckle. "Perhaps there is some hope for the youth of Ursala after all. Due to your stirring display of valor, young squire, I will allow you, your wench, and your cowardly master to pass. Raise the gates and send in the next group."

With that, the castellan turned and disappeared back through his archway without ceremony. The Templars tromped back through their passages as well. And with another rumble, the portcullises began to open. With his legs feeling leaden, Taki grasped Enilna's hand and trudged forth without checking if Jibriil accompanied them.

The crowd of onlookers on the Astarte side of the bridge murmured excitedly, and some reached out to try and touch the trio. Taki shrugged off the grasping hands and continued to walk. He walked silently until they were in the middle of a town center, where inns and taverns offered weary travelers rest and liquid courage.

"Taki!" Enilna jerked his sleeve. "You with me?"

Taki blinked and forced himself to turn. His heartbeat throbbed all the way up to his ears. *How the godrotting hell did we manage to survive that?* He brought a thumbnail to his teeth and started to chew frantically.

"Is this the mental sickness of a virgin?" Enilna asked, rapping on his skull.

Taki glared at her and stopped chewing. "No, it's not! We were nearly discovered! You were nearly...ugh, I don't want to talk about it! Dammit, Jibriil! What happened to your grand plan?"

Jibriil rubbed his face. His palms were smeared with sweat. "I'm sorry. I didn't expect a trial by combat! I'd forgotten what a twisted bastard the man was." He clapped a hand on Taki's back. "Look, though! We're through the gate. We're home free! We're alive, and that's what matters."

Taki twisted away. "We need to leave. I want to get as far away from here as possible, right now."

Jibriil hung his head. "Can't. There's a blizzard cresting the horizon. The roads will be naught but death within a bell. Our best bet is an inn. It'll be warm. We can eat and then leave early in the morning. Besides, the castellan's done with us. He doesn't have jurisdiction over these towns, just his fortress."

Taki cursed but knew Jibriil was right about the impending blizzard. The clouds overhead were starting to darken, and the air had taken on an unfriendly chill.

"I'm with Jibriil on this one," Enilna said. "Besides, my feet are cold."

"I suppose we can hunker down for the night," Taki said. "Do we even have enough for a room, though?"

"I, uh, know an innkeeper here," Jibriil said. "She'll accept forms of payment other than grad."

Taki scrunched his brow. "Other forms?"

"I'll pay her back with certain favors."

"What sort of favors? Jibriil, be clear."

"Taki, he means that she'll make him rub her feet all night long," Enilna said. "Isn't that right, Jibriil?"

"Absolutely," Jibriil said with a smile.

"What the hell is it with women and their feet?" Taki said, feeling slightly better.

A silver dusting of snowflakes had already settled on the rooftops in announcement of the storm to come. Taki drew his cloak tighter. Though it was damnable luck that they couldn't leave until the next day at earliest, Enilna's presence lessened some of his worry. She was ill mannered and impulsive, but that in turn only warmed him more. *Damn you lot,* he thought to his companions in Tirefire the Lesser, *you've all made me a masochist.*

* * * *

Jibriil's promised lodgings were more humble than Taki had expected. *Actually, it's more like a cell,* Taki thought as he rearranged the embers in the meager hearth. He looked at their dwindling stack of wood and regretted not having the funds for more. Jibriil was absent, having disappeared into the innkeeper's chambers to pay off his debt.

"It's so godrotting cold! Maybe I should've taken up the castellan on his offer," Enilna said.

"Ugh, why did I ever try to stand up for you, again?" Taki said.

"Oh, hush. You know I'm just japing." Enilna sidled up next to him on the edge of his pallet and slung her blanket around his shoulders. "Here. It'll be warmer if we're like this. We'll save body heat."

"I think you're the one draining most of it," Taki said.

Enilna scowled and shoved her hands under his jerkin and shirt. The chilliness of her fingers against his bare belly made Taki want to yelp and wiggle away, but he controlled himself.

"Thanks for the warms," she said with a sardonic smile.

"My hands are cold, too. Maybe I should do the same to you!" Taki said. A moment later, he blushed in realization. Hadassah would have slapped him for that. He did not want to think about how Lotte or Lucatiel would have reacted. To his surprise, Enilna moved her hands from his skin, grasped his, and guided them under her shirt. "I w-wasn't being serious..."

"I lied earlier," she said. "I don't see you as just a friend. I like you, Taki Natalis. I desire you as a man. I want you to see me as a woman, not as the scared little girl I was before. You told me I shouldn't offer myself until I'm ready. But I'm ready now." She locked her eyes with his. "Please, believe me this time."

Taki swallowed. The terror that had been in her eyes on the zeppelin was gone. He inched his trembling hands up her torso, and she smiled and kissed him. Again, his heart fluttered as it had when Lotte had done the same. Unlike many times before, he felt truly at ease. It did not matter that he was a virgin and inexperienced. It did not matter even if his comrades were somehow eavesdropping and making jests at his expense. It did not matter if he was Enilna's superior by age and rank. It did not matter that the castellan of the Teufelsbrucke had almost slaughtered everyone. For once, everything was right. He drew closer.

"Can I...take you?"

Enilna's lips tickled his ear. *"Yes!"*

An axe head crashed through the thin wooden boards of their door, and Taki scrambled for his pistol. Enilna was slower but raised her weapon a moment later when the door shattered on its hinges and a pair of footmen rushed in with cudgels raised.

Taki's head throbbed painfully as he shot the closest intruder, but he only gritted his teeth and continued. Enilna's pistol belched fire as it discharged and bowled the remaining man over. Two more, this time in stiff boiled leather, charged in with spears. Curiously, the tips had been blunted. One of them caught Enilna in the side and knocked her back. She crashed against the shutters of their window, clutching at her ribs, and the aged wooden slats fell to pieces.

A howling gust from outside dusted snow in Taki's hair. He knocked one of the spears away and sent the last round in his pistol into another man in armor. Enilna seemed to want to bolt out of the door, but a deep thudding sound stopped her.

A fully armored Templar ducked into the room wielding a bar mace wrapped in leather thongs. One of the wounded Ursalan footsoldiers tried to reach out for help, only to have his hand crushed under the Templar's boot.

Taki swore and flooded his prana gates. *They're trying to capture us alive!*

"Out the window!" he ordered Enilna. "Take the roof and get out of town. I'll hold them here!"

"No! We're leaving together," she said.

Taki whirled around and leveled his side arm at her. *"Do not question my orders!* If we don't get back to the captain, we're dead for nothing!"

Tears streamed from Enilna's eyes, and she gnashed her teeth, but she slipped into the icy gusts. Taki turned back to face the Templar. He wondered why it had not simply clobbered him yet. Taki thrust his right hand forward and braced his elbow with his left hand.

"I see," he said. "It's me you want, after all. Well, I don't have all night. Come at me, man!"

The Templar raised its mace to attack. Taki let out a grin and started his incantation. A second later, the swirling whiteness of the blizzard was saturated with blinding light.

19

With the one eye that wasn't sealed shut from bruising, Taki stared at the rat with a mixture of fascination and dread. It was one of the largest he'd ever seen, almost the size of Babu back at the Cloud Temple. How the rat had gotten so large was no mystery: it obviously had a taste for human flesh. If Taki wasn't vigilant, if he fell asleep, then the biting would begin anew.

It was surprisingly hard to figure out how much time had passed since his capture. Enilna had fled, and then he'd woken up in a gaol, bound in chains and encrusted with filth. The first thing he'd seen clearly in the darkness was a yellow-hot iron going into a dirt-encrusted slash on his thigh. He had pissed himself and passed out. When he had woken up again, it was to the pain of a rat trying to tear into his jugular.

He wanted to just strike the creature, but his hands were chained tightly and his feet were manacled together. The rat was his only roommate in a small, squarish cell devoid of even a decaying pallet of straw. Flickering torchlight filtered in from a tiny cutout window set in a thick wooden cell door banded with iron. He wondered if he was in the Teufelsbrucke, but there was no way to be sure. What was obvious, however, was that he was at the enemy's mercy.

Weakened as he was, there was no hope of casting. Escape was impossible, and he knew better than to expect his comrades to try to rescue him. Even if the primate had been convinced to let the army march, the Imperials were at least a fortnight away. If the rumors were true, the Ursalans would have a slew of tortures planned before they executed him. He wondered if the Templars would want to harvest his corpse for parts, and if that would happen before or after he died.

If any of them see my manhood, I'm in trouble! Remembering Draco's words from long ago made Taki smile. *Well, mine's never been used. Get it while it's fresh,* he thought. Letting the rat tear his throat open might be less painful than what his captors had in store and would ensure that he did not betray his comrades while maddened with pain.

He wondered if Enilna had made it back to safety or if she'd died. Sending her out into a mountain blizzard was a stupid idea in retrospect, but death from hypothermia was much gentler than anything that awaited her here. If she had been captured, though…Taki clenched his jaw and bared his neck for the rat. It was better to die not knowing. *Kill them for me, Lotte. Kill them for me, Sir Aslatiel. I'm sorry I failed.* The creature inched forward with its teeth bared and tail flicking in anticipation of blood.

The cell door opened. The rat whirled and hissed at whatever was coming to steal its prey and was promptly crushed by a massive iron boot. A Templar reached down, grasped Taki by his wrists, and jerked him upright. Taki gasped as his shoulders bent at an unnatural angle, and he retched bile all over the Templar's gauntlets.

A man sucked his teeth and shook his head. "My dear squire, you're filthy."

Taki raised his head. He recognized the voice from before. It was the castellan, Duvalier.

"You'll get nothing from me," Taki said. His voice was weaker than he would've wanted for this show of bravado.

Duvalier smiled. "Are you talking about your plan to entice the primate into Osterbrand clutches? I knew what that apostate was up to before your little trek to the Cantons. I also know the Liberation Army's on its way, but none of that is of any consequence. My humble fortress is located in quite the natural bottleneck, so it matters not if the padishah sends fifty men or fifty thousand. We're well prepared for any attack and always have been. So I need no betrayal from you, little squire."

"Then just kill me."

"That simply won't do," the castellan said. "You've attracted the interest of my princess. Her Highness was quite attracted to your display of chivalry, no matter that you're a deceitful Polaris serving the

Imperials now. She could barely contain her excitement. I was obligated to follow her wishes and retrieve you for further study."

A princess? Like that monster in Astarte? And one who can smell us?

"Oh, and the girl you were with," Duvalier said, licking his lips. "If it consoles you somewhat, we found her frozen corpse being gnawed on by wolves. A pitiable sight."

Taki lowered his head and stared at the grimy cobbles below. *Thank God.* His teeth began to chatter, and tears dripped to the floor.

"Now, time to make you presentable for Her Highness," Duvalier said. "She simply cannot wait to begin. Templars, take him to the chamber."

"I'll have you know something, milord," Taki grated.

"Yes?"

"We don't have fifty, or fifty thousand, or fifty million coming for you. There are *seven* of us." He looked up and met the castellan's gaze. "And I give you my word that those seven are going to come here and kill you. Then, they'll tear down your capital and kill the Sanctissimus Rex. They're going to destroy your putrid society and spread the Way to all corners of Ursala. We're going to liberate the shit out of you."

20

The Holy Sepulchre of the Dominion had once been a pilgrimage destination, but now its gates were closed to all. Angry devotees had raged that the usurper basileus had ceded to Imperial mandate and shuttered the site to all, for the Osterbrand oppressors hated all things built on faith. The booming towns built on the pilgrimage route had since fallen into ruin, and only brothels and alehouses remained.

Ringo regarded his dingy surroundings with disinterest and disdain. The Argead Dominion was little more than a buffer state and a knockoff of true Ursalan cultural glory. The only thing that had prevented the Rex from simply unseating the pretentious basileioi was the God Hand. But if the Argeads truly worshipped their precious God Hand and its vessel, the Ooss, then they were doing a poor job of showing proper reverence. Now, he no longer felt any twinges of guilt about the impending theft. *These people don't deserve nice things.*

"This is a place of ill repute," Sir Juan Diaz de Villavilla said. He stroked his goatee and peered at the front of the Admiral's Club. The sole surviving inn of the Sepulchral Burg, it reeked of opium. The chevalier sniffed deeply. "Such blasphemy, and yet it is our transgressions which make life enjoyable, *tambien.*"

"It's certainly not the Tintoretto, but if the rooms have locks, then perhaps we should count our blessings," Sir Janus Eicke said.

Samara, who stood beside him, looked pleased to have a chance to set down nearly fifty kilograms of her master's possessions.

Ringo smirked at the sight of her burden and made sure that she could see him. Even though she could snap him like a twig, she still had to keep up appearances as a servant for the fat Teuton, and thus carried a heavier load than the rest. After what had transpired in New

Korinthos, he had been in a spiteful mood, especially where she was concerned.

Hecaton emerged from the inn with smoke billowing at her feet and a coarsely rolled cigar clamped between her teeth. She had gone on ahead a few hours ago, with the ostensible purpose of scouting the Burg and securing their lodging. Simply holing up in one of the abandoned properties was not an option: thieves were everywhere, and the chevaliers needed a decent rest. Yet, Ringo noticed with annoyance, Hecaton had obviously just been gambling or indulging in opium or both.

"Hey, boys," she said. "You can come on in. They won't bite. Rooms upstairs at the end of the hall."

"You're a sodden mess," Ringo said.

Hecaton rolled her eyes. "Chaperoning you all drives a woman to drink."

"Milady, I would be honored to join you in your libations," Juan said with a wink.

Hecaton beckoned for him to join her and disappeared back into the den.

Janus looked at Ringo and shrugged. "Well, shall we go upstairs?"

Hecaton's promise of rooms had not been a lie. Ringo claimed one immediately, flopped into the bed without taking off his boots, and slumbered like the dead.

Later, he awoke to the sound of knocking. He cracked an eye open and quietly drew his blade. Slowly, he sidled up to the door. Robbery was common in lawless burgs like this.

"Aye?" He tried to sound noncommittal.

"It's me," Samara said.

Ringo did not sheathe his dagger but eased it to his side. He unbarred the door and opened it to allow a sliver of light in.

"Put your stupid pigsticker away and let me in," she said, and pushed the door open.

"What do you want?" His gaze fell to an oblong object wrapped in canvas that she carried.

"This is for you," she said, and pushed the parcel into his hands. "You're the least well equipped of all of us. I can't protect you all the time."

Ringo scowled at her temerity, but she was right. Unlike Juan and Janus, he only had a small blade to fight with. He started to undo the canvas and tried to suppress his anticipation. A broadsword would be nice, or perhaps even a matchlock to give him distance. The sight of oak and forged steel quickened his heart, and he pulled her offering fully from its wrappings.

"An Enfield!" He cradled the rifle with relish. He grasped the fore end in one hand and worked the bolt with his other. The action was impossibly smooth. "I carried one in the Ordo," he said, boasting like a new squire. It was really someone else's gun and not his, but simply holding one again was welcome balm on the ulcers of his soul. He had hocked his old rifle to avoid losing his hovel; that day, the world had darkened permanently.

He sensed Samara smiling, and his own smile soured. Surely she wasn't feeling happy to see his reaction. No, this was probably something to draw him further and further into her witch's web.

"Where did you get this?" he said, and hurriedly shut the door. The last things he needed now were prying eyes.

"From a drunken praetorian, of course."

"How did you…" He stopped. "No, I don't want to know." He looked down at the rifle and then back at her. "I hope you don't expect me to kowtow."

"A simple 'thank you' will suffice." She looked downcast.

To his surprise, Ringo found himself feeling contrite. He set the rifle near his bed, got to one knee, and kissed her hand. *How many years since I did this as a squire?* Strangely, as hackneyed as it was, the silly old ritual felt fulfilling. "You have my sincere gratitude, milady."

Samara blushed. So there *were* things that could unsettle her, after all.

"It'll help the mission," she said, and turned away.

Ringo rose, filled with new energy. A brief glance through a sliver of open shutter told him that it was firmly evening. "Where's everyone else?"

"The knights are gaming. Old Mezeta is having a grand old time sharping them."

"Then I shall also try my luck." He patted his money pouch and was rewarded with the clink of milligrad. Even a single round of Luger could carry an evening of cards, and a few reloads were enough for a quick roll in a brothel afterward. He went for the door.

Samara cocked her head. "What are you doing?"

"What do you think? I'm leaving to go find some grog and some company," Ringo said. "Don't worry, Imperial. I'm not the sort who blathers while in his cups. Your secret's safe."

"I didn't say you could leave."

"Be reasonable, wench. I'm a healthy man." Ringo shook his head and reached for the handle.

Samara's hand clamped around his wrist. "Don't call me that."

He winced. "Ah, right, I'm sorry, milady. I'll be going now."

"But I want you to stay."

Ringo sucked his teeth. "And do *what?* I'm not pretending to be a servant like you. I have the right to enjoy myself about town."

Samara eased her grip. He again reached for the door, only to stop when her hands settled on his chest.

"What are *you* doing?" He didn't like what her demeanor suggested. It wasn't menacing, but rather, disconcertingly lonely.

"Keep me company. Please."

"We have little to discuss."

She rolled her eyes. "Do I have to spell it out for your stupid ass? I want you to pleasure me, Ursalan. That's part of what you agreed to."

"Huh? I never…godrot you, that's just a farce for if the others get suspicious. Besides, aren't you supposed to be Eicke's toy?"

"No, but you're mine. So do your duty." She reached to her neckline and pulled open the lacing of her shirt. The linen fell about her shoulders.

Despite his indignation, Ringo still felt his heart quicken. After misery on a boat and a week of travel without any chance to stop at a brothel, he was indeed in need of respite. And no matter how much he despised her, Samara was still a woman. *I'm being used like a common wench.* He stopped himself. The thought was too humiliating to dwell on. *Godrot it, as long as I'm stuck doing her bidding, I might as well have some fun.* He sighed, and his hand slipped from the door handle. Reluctantly, he reached to her waist and put his lips to hers.

* * * *

The next morning, Ringo shivered in the chilly air as he trudged toward the Sepulchre. Underneath his homespun, he wore brigandine and greaves, but the wind still found a way to his sensitive skin. Juan and Janus were also dressed as ragged, traveling pilgrims. Samara, disguised as a young nun, walked ahead. She turned her head to peer at Ringo, and he angrily looked away. The shame of last night burned brightly still.

To stifle his self-loathing, he focused his wrath on Hecaton. Everyone else was rightfully tense, save for her. The old hag traipsed along in her mismatched outfit of an Argead officer's blouse, clam-digger pants, and decaying ancient sandals with pink plastic thongs. *An officer, my ass!*

If all went smoothly, Hecaton would pull rank on the praetorian guard at the entrance and allow them all to pass under the guise of an escorted religious mission. If the guards did not allow this, then the chevaliers would simply take the men out with a minimum of noise and quietly sneak onto the premises. It was risky, but better than simply rushing in.

Ringo exhaled in relief when he saw that the Sepulchre was only lightly guarded: four bored-looking praetorians with Temple guns that weren't likely loaded. Other members of that elite cadre patrolled the rooftops but seemed disinterested in their tasks. Notably, the Imperial flag was absent from the premises. The praetorians manning the gates tensed and raised their rifles as Hecaton strolled up to them.

"Halt," a lieutenant ordered. "The Ooss is closed to pilgrimage by order of the basileus!"

Hecaton stuck out her tongue, raised her arms, and blasted the man to nothingness. His companions were flung aside by the impact and broke into ash dust when they hit the ground. The iron gates of the Sepulchre glowed red-hot at ragged edges, which curled apart like opening petals of a chrysanthemum.

Ringo's jaw dropped. "Oh, for Christ's sake," he snarled. He curled his fingers under the clasp across his throat and pulled his cloak off. "I thought we were going to *sneak* in!"

Hecaton looked at him as if he were the stupidest man alive. "Where'd you get that idea? I'm a hundred arms of destruction! I don't *sneak.*"

She aimed her palm out at a small group of praetorians, who rushed out with halberds, and snapped her fingers. The ground erupted underneath them with teeth-shattering force and flung bodies and weapons aside like broken staves. With her other hand, she pointed at another squad of defenders and sent a bolt of lightning that seared the air and turned men into bloody steam.

By Jove, Samara was right. I don't stand a godrotting chance against this monster. He unslung his Enfield and regarded it for a fraction of a second. Against a seasoned fighter, it was a formidable weapon; against this horrific biddy, it might as well have been a broom. Hecaton sauntered in through the mangled gate, and a chorus of gunfire and screaming erupted from within.

"*No mames,* Sir Ringo!" Juan shouted at him. "We're going in like real men!" The Valencian drew a pair of finely engraved rapiers and charged the entrance. Janus followed, shuffling and out of breath.

Ringo clenched his jaw to still his trembling. Through the gaping mass of twisted iron was a smoking abyss of flying bullets that only a complete fool would dare enter. If he wished, he could always simply retreat back into the cover of the surrounding brush and escape. None of the praetorians who had seen his face were still alive.

"Don't even *think* about running, you pansy," Samara said, and pressed her back against his. In her hands was a Temple gun.

Ringo wheeled on her with ferocity that startled even him. "Damn you, I'm no coward!"

Samara blinked and wiped a fleck of spittle from her brow. "Easy there. Are you still upset because you cried after we did it?"

"I did *not* cry." He flushed crimson. "It was all the dust in the mattress."

"It's nothing to be ashamed of! And maybe I like that side of you."

"Godrotting witch!"

Samara laughed and dragged him into the Sepulchre.

The inside would have been an awe-inspiring, even faith-stirring sight if not for the pitched battle that raged within. The Ooss was an alien-looking monolith that rested on its side like a giant in repose. Squat keel blocks, blackened from age, suspended it off the ground. Most of its body was obscured by wooden scaffolding for laborers to lovingly rub its surface with anointed oil and priests to bless the work with a kiss and a wave of the censer. The rituals, repeated faithfully every on every seventh day since the founding of the Dominion, had kept the sacred coffin from rusting apart and releasing the dangers sealed within.

Ringo's eyes tarried on the Ooss for longer than necessary. Samara yanked at the back of his jerkin, and he stumbled just in time to avoid a bullet. Chastened, he took cover behind a keel block. Bodies lay sprawled about, some charred beyond recognition. Though he should have been thinking solely about survival, Ringo instead wondered why there was no water around; Hecaton had told them all that the Ooss was supposedly a boat.

Silly me, it's a dry dock, he realized as he glanced about. *Their holy site is a giant slipway. Past the far doors is probably a sea channel. But we'll never move the damned boat with just four! These things take entire legions to budge!* Nearby, he saw Hecaton smirking as she puffed on a cigarette with irritating disregard to the battle going on around her. The sight infuriated him: Had she just led them in here to die, after all?

"Damn you, Mezeta! What the fuck do we do now?" He heard the sound of shuffling in the periphery, however, and the need for self-preservation outweighed his need to berate her. He peeked around the edge of the block and spied an approaching praetorian. He leveled his rifle and blew a hole in the man's chest and then returned his ire to Hecaton. "Did you just bring us here to die?"

"Have the manners to let me finish my cig, you dogsbody," Hecaton said with a roll of her eyes. She drew in a lungful of smoke and then tossed the butt aside. She exhaled through her nostrils, reminding Ringo of a surly dragon. "There. Now, give thanks to your deity, for you are about to witness the true power of a twice born!"

She closed her eyes and turned her palms upward. She seemed to shimmer, and the smell of ozone became unbearable. Air contorted in an expanding sphere around her.

Ringo grimaced and wanted nothing more than to scurry away with all haste. The field menaced him, threatening to suck his life away. Bullets whizzed at Hecaton and yet seemed to drop harmlessly to the ground in midflight, as if robbed of their will to press on. As the undulating edge of her influence reached him, Ringo could do naught but cower while clutching his rifle to his chest. He closed his eyes and prepared to die.

Golden Peach lay motionless in the fountain, congealed globs of blood snaking slowly toward the bottom.

"Why is she burned?" Celmeg demanded.

"I called its name," Sirin said. "I called for the lightning, and it came. The g-great god answered me. And filled me with light, and I burned her."

Ringo guffawed at the sight, even as he felt his consciousness fade. Why was there a fountain present in the Argead Sepulchre? Who was this murdered girl lying about? Why was Hecaton Mezeta so young? He wanted to approach them, but he was too weak to continue and impotently dropped to his knees.

Steel wailed in protest and played a horrific note as it drew against unyielding wood. Scaffolding shuddered and collapsed, adding to the hellish overture. The walls of the Sepulchre convulsed, sending stone and metal crashing from the roof to the ground and scattering the praetorians. Those who were not crushed by debris fled in panic. The reason why became obvious to all who stuck around to watch: the Ooss itself was moving.

Hecaton's eyes were closed, and her expression was untroubled, but the muscles of her neck were drawn tight, and the lines of her face seemed as deep and ancient as arctic crevasses. She slowly swept her arms, and as she did so, the Ooss shifted reluctantly toward a massive pair of doors at the end of the Sepulchre. When the bow reached the end of the keelway, Hecaton raised her other hand and, with strain deeply graven in the lines around her mouth, pushed.

The enormous steel slabs whined as if the metal itself was in pain but started to swing open while the Ooss pushed through. Salt water lapped at the keel, which only plunged further into the waiting waves. In only a few meters, momentum took over, and the massive submarine slid completely into the sea channel.

"You emptied yourself?" Celmeg snarled in disbelief. He cupped Sirin's jaw in his hand.

Ringo looked up from the mud and vainly reached out toward the pair. He would not join the corpses around them. He needed to live. To kill Hecaton Mezeta. To gain the reward that would secure his future. His fingers trembled, and the world before him started to fade.

Damn it all, not like this...

His eyes fluttered open, and his pupils immediately constricted as a ray of sunlight hit him in the face. He realized he was staring at the sky, through a gaping hole in the Sepulcher's roof. Nausea washed over him, and he started to choke and gag. Samara glanced down at him and drew back her hand to strike him with her palm. Ringo cringed in anticipation of the impact, which never came. The bile retreated back down his throat.

"Can you walk?" Samara asked.

Ringo now saw that she crouched next to him, and that the hand she would have struck him with gently rested on his cheek. He nodded and shakily got to his knees. He felt drained, in the fashion that only a year of uninterrupted sleep would ever hope to redress.

"We need to get out of here," she said, and pulled him to his feet. With her other arm, she hefted his Enfield and pressed it into his hands. He tottered, but she prevented him from falling back.

For what seemed like an agonizing eternity, Ringo plodded forward. For some reason, he felt as if he were learning to walk again. In the distance, faint cries and gunshots rang out. Able to bear no more, he buckled and fell to his knees. They were less than ten meters from the edge of the water. Through bleary eyes, he could see the Ooss bobbing in the channel. Janus's head poked up from a hatch atop the large sail tower near the bow. The Teuton was firing his rifle over their heads to cover their escape, while Juan waved frantically from the top of its hull and tossed a length of rope their way.

"Leave me!" Ringo said. Tears welled in his eyes. "I can't go on. Mezeta killed me."

"No," Samara said with sudden vehemence. "There's another way." She inhaled, tensed; her skin started to glow.

Ringo's eyes widened as he saw it: *prana* coursing through her body. He had no time to marvel at the sight before she threw him over her shoulders and sprinted down the last bits of concrete toward the edge of the water. Stone shattered under her feet. They flew through the air, weightless for a brief moment.

As soon as he could comprehend the new sensation, it came to an abrupt end. Ringo slammed face down onto the cold steel of the hull and rolled into the sail tower. He felt his ribs crunch and the breath leave him.

The Ooss let out a deep, rumbling moan, and water at the stern bubbled and frothed.

Dazed and drooling from pain, Ringo raised his head and cast a glance around him. They were moving out of the channel. A body lay next to him: Samara. She groaned and whispered something that he could not hear. Ringo choked back an unseemly cry of relief, took her hand, and refused to let go.

* * * *

Samara flashed a condescending leer at Juan and spat a crimson stream of spittle at his boots. Juan's lips curled back, and he punched her again. Suspended by her wrists from rusting ductwork, she swayed gently in the still, sterile air of the Ooss.

"I'm warning you, Sir Knight, *watch the teeth.* I'm the only one in my company with a perfect set."

"Indeed, *señorita,* you do have a very fine set of pearly whites," Juan replied. He wiped a fleck of her blood away from his cheek. "May I ask how you preserved them for so long?"

"It's simple, really. Scour them with a bristle brush dipped in a solution of natron after meals. But you must be consistent about it and never lapse. If you forget, the rot will set in."

"Is that what they taught you to do in the Spetsnaz?"

"Aye, but regulations only demand it once a fortnight."

"I do not like how your sort tries to deny the natural order of this world. Teeth are meant to rot and fall out. I should really remove yours. It would make everyone more comfortable, *sí?*"

"But, Juan, my darling," Samara said, "how would I tear out your throat, otherwise?"

He replied with a haymaker to her gut. "Try it, bitch."

"I won't tolerate name calling. You've been warned."

"Sir Janus, have you in your tool set a pair of pliers?" Juan asked.

Janus nodded.

"Well, get them," Juan said. "This Imperial wench thinks she is above us because of her fiendish dentition, and I as a proud chevalier of Ursala cannot abide this insult to our honor."

From his corner, Ringo fought the urge to avert his gaze. That Juan was brutalizing Samara wasn't the issue. Spies deserved much worse than mere death. The only reason she wasn't being boiled in oil or gutted round a tree was because there were none of those things to be found in the cramped quarters of the Ooss. No, what bothered Ringo most was that he still felt *obliged* to her, though she was an enemy and an informer and had seen him cry.

He stared at Hecaton out of the corner of his eye. Stupidly, he had expected her to voice some opposition to Samara's execution by torment. Instead, Hecaton looked bored out of her mind. The woman's nonchalance infuriated him. Would she have reacted the same had Samara gone and murdered the entire Ursalan contingent? Just as long as someone was around to keep the ship clean? *Bloody hag-bitch. Does she see us as merely ants? Does she even need us for anything but amusement?* He swallowed back a rush of bile. *No, she doesn't.*

Hecaton was the reason the Ooss moved. Through devilry that none could explain, she had somehow breathed life into the dead reliquary. It hummed with energy where she touched it. Panels and buttons and switches lit up like little jewels surrounding tiny suns. Ancient motors dead for centuries hummed happily, as if they'd been made the day before. And most ominously, the resurrected vessel contained the legendary Argead God Hand, which had cowed the Liberation Army at Thermopylae. Hecaton Mezeta was now the most powerful being in the world, and Ringo hated her.

"Sir Juan." Janus handed a set of small iron tongs over.

Juan took them with relish and grasped Samara's jaw. "Where do you want me to start?" he asked.

"Up your behind, Sir Juan," she said.

Juan squeezed with his fingers and forced her mouth open. He shoved the tongs in, and she started to hyperventilate and struggle.

Ringo looked away. Much as he hated to admit it, he had always disliked watching the sort of prolonged execution that his peers had in mind. He could watch miscreants being hanged, shot, immolated, and beheaded all day, but not this. Once, his master had ordered a deserter to die by cutting and cautery. Ringo had barely made it through the day and had later been unable to eat supper. But even more distasteful was the fact that *Samara's* suffering affected him so. She had threatened him, humiliated him, and spied on him. She was one of the elite forces of the heathen Imperium. She had also saved his life. They had…

He found himself staring at Hecaton. She mouthed something at him. He focused and tried to comprehend.

You. Are. A. Pussy.

He gripped the edge of his seat, livid. Hecaton needed to die. She needed to die, but he wasn't strong enough to do the deed himself. With Samara's aid, though, there was a chance. There was a chance that, one day, he would hold the foul witch's severed head in his hands and laugh at her. The Doge's promised reward didn't matter anymore. Hecaton's death would cleanse all sins. The mere chance of bringing it about was more than enough to justify what he was about to do. He rose from his seat, suffused with absolute clarity.

"Sir Juan, cease your inquest," Ringo said. *"Immediately."*

Juan blinked. "Sir Ringo? What is the meaning of this?"

"I said, cease the inquest. I'm laying a claim to this woman as my betrothed. If thou touchest her, I shall seek satisfaction."

The stunned silence was broken by Hecaton's laughter.

* * * *

Samara shivered under the blanket draped round her shoulders. She sipped haltingly at a mug of diluted grog and grimaced at Ringo. They were alone, in a small alcove at the bow that Ringo had chosen as his living space. The Ooss had clearly been meant to house more than a hundred men at a time, but with a crew of only five, everyone had enjoyed the ability to spread out.

"Bastard cracked it," she said. She winced as she took another sip of the grog to be sure.

"Cracked what?" Ringo sighed.

"My tooth. Maybe I should've let him pull it entirely."

"You've got a lot of gall to complain, you wretched spy."

Samara laughed. "That's not a nice thing to call your fiancée."

"Shut up. It was all I could think of to save you. There is *nothing* romantic between us. You barely qualify as a woman as it is."

"You thought I needed to be saved? How cute."

Ringo wanted to slap her but refrained from doing so. Even injured, she could likely best him in physical combat.

"You sure looked like you were in control there, all panicky and struggling not to scream," he said.

"Relax. I'm not saying I'm ungrateful," Samara said. She smiled softly at him. "I confess, you did look quite dashing there."

"I wasn't trying to impress you, nor did I feel any sympathy. I only did that because I can't kill Mezeta on my own. I need you. I mean, I need your help."

She laughed. "That's the most romantic thing anyone's ever said to me."

"Enough impertinence. As my wife, you're beholden to me. Your only purpose is to help me kill the bitch. I'll present this relic to the Rex, and he'll make me an earl. Then, the engagement's off!"

"There's a problem with that plan, Lord Husband Master Sir."

"What problem?"

She rolled her eyes. "You continue to assume that killing Hecaton Mezeta is a matter of sticking a knife in her back while she slumbers."

"She bleeds, does she not?"

"She *doesn't*. I've come to the conclusion that she's basically untouchable, at least to mortals like us. The surest way to kill her is to sink this boat in the middle of the ocean with her inside. Seal her forever beneath the waves."

"What will happen to us, then?"

"We'll die, of course."

Ringo sighed, collapsed on a nearby bench, and rubbed at his eyes. "Fuck my life. Fuck everything!"

"There's another way, though. At some point, she needs to get off the boat. I suspect she wanted the Ooss not for its power but solely as a means of transport. She has a destination to get to, and it's on land. When she's off the boat, we can use the God Hand to burn her off the surface of the earth."

"That'll never work."

"No, it's possible. We just need to bide our time. We'll wait, and only when the moment is right will we strike. Now, where does she want Juan to pilot this thing, anyway?"

Ringo looked up, too sore to jape. "Due east, to some blasted heathen shithole I've never heard of. The coordinates are real, though, and we should be able to get there within a season."

"What's the name of this place?"

"The Blue Sky Land."

21

Taki's eyes weakly fluttered open under white light. His body ached, and he felt thirsty although he was pretty sure he'd drunk his fill earlier. He tried to lift his head from a down-stuffed pillow but found that he could not. *Down?* He could have sworn that he'd spent the last few days on a grimy piece of slate.

Enilna stared back at him. Taki opened his mouth to speak, only for her to shush him. *Wait,* he thought, fighting the haze brought on by her touch. *Didn't I send you into a blizzard? Aren't you dead?* It was becoming an effort to stay awake. *Damn that Jibriil! I knew I shouldn't have trusted him.* He tried to rise up out of bed, and Enilna pushed his head back down onto the pillow.

"No, wait," Taki said, rolling away. "We need to tell Lotte. Warn her about Jibriil, that we've been had." With titanic effort, he managed to sit partway up.

"There's no need, Natalis," Lotte said. Taki looked up to see his captain's face mere fingerbreadths away from his. She straddled his hips. Her fingertips gently pushed him supine, and the strength evaporated from his core.

"Captain, he's a traitor!"

"My poor, loyal soldier. Rest now. Let me reward you."

"Wait," he moaned.

Lotte seemed not to heed him but instead, buried her face against his neck. He felt her breasts press against him and her flesh touching his loins. Teeth ripped into the meat of his chest, and he gasped in pain. Warmth covered his torso, and he sank into contented, glassy stupor. But he could not sleep, as something continued to nag at him.

"Rest," Lotte said, and kissed him. Her breath tasted of iron.

But you smelt of cordite. Taki's eyes widened as the floor rumbled. He could have sworn that at the edge of his fraying consciousness, he heard gunfire and shouts. "Captain, something's wrong."

Lotte looked up, and her expression changed to annoyance. Her irises went from brown to red. Her features changed now, to elongate in certain areas and soften in others. The woman who stared back at him now had the perfect proportions for beauty and yet seemed incredibly cruel. She had the face of a princess.

Taki tried to push her away. "You're not my captain."

"And you are becoming troublesome," the princess said. She drew back, and her jaw seemed to dislocate to accommodate an expanding maw full of spiked teeth.

Taki tried to scramble away but found his limbs too weak to move. The princess wrapped her spindly, clawed fingers around his throat. Her teeth started to close on his face. He screamed.

A sharp crack interrupted Taki's death, and the princess's body suddenly went limp and fell by the wayside. Her head flopped at an unnatural angle and sprayed crimson into Taki's face. A booted foot crashed into the dead monster's side and punted her off the bed. Taki wiped the blood away from his eyes and saw Jibriil standing over him.

"Uh...hey," the archangel said.

Taki blinked. "You killed her."

"Well, *yeah.* I've never liked Ursalan royalty, and she was about to bite your face off." Jibriil knelt and pressed a hand to Taki's chest.

Taki instinctively flinched but soon felt the familiar warmth of prana suffusing his core. Sensation returned to his limbs, and his fingers and toes tingled, almost painfully so. He hungered for more, so much that it embarrassed him to remember the source. But in the state he was in, Jibriil's touch was pure succor. Before Taki was satisfied, Jibriil lifted his hand away.

"I can't give more, sorry. Spent a lot getting here," Jibriil said.

Taki slowly sat upright. He scanned his surroundings and grimaced to see the princess's monstrous corpse laid out nearby. Though her face had possessed a chilling cruelty, it had been comely. *Well, before the teeth and claws came out.*

The room he'd woken up in was a far cry from the miserable, rat-infested cells on the rest of the block. It was cavernous and appointed with silks and goosedown pillows strewn over the marble-tiled floor. Taki sat in a four-poster bed with a gossamer canopy hung over a mattress of ermine and sealskin throws. It was the very picture of a princess's inner chamber, and it reeked of lavender and dried blood.

"What the hell happened to me?" Taki looked down and blushed as he realized he was naked. "What is this place?"

"It's what it looks like," Jibriil said. "A princess's chambers."

"Why the hell would there be a princess here?"

"The Rex has a daughter in every city and keep," Jibriil said. "Helps him keep all of his castellans, barons, and counts under watch. The Teufelsbrucke is no exception. The bitch here has been draining your blood for a week. I'm not sure how you managed to wake up. Thought I'd find you more…husk-like."

Taki patted his chest where the false Lotte had bitten him. He winced to palpate a pair of wounds similar to holes left by fangs. "How did you get here?"

"Snuck in, killed some chevaliers, and then killed her." Jibriil fished around in an open chest and pulled out a tunic, which he tossed into Taki's lap. "Here, get dressed. If these aren't your size, I'm sure there are plenty more to choose from. There's also boots and tabards, too. Goddamned man-eater, this one was. Can you walk?"

Taki slowly eased off the fur mattress and found his footing on the chilly floor. "I think so. Give me a minute." He pulled on the tunic and noted with some distaste that it was indeed property of a former Ursalan squire. He stumbled over to where Jibriil had pointed and gritted his teeth as he beheld a pile of discarded outerwear. How many others like him had fallen victim to the monster? *She collected their clothing.* The thought made him want to retch.

"Try to be quick about it," Jibriil said, tapping a foot. "Won't be long till they discover the bodies. I don't want to be here when they do."

Taki grunted and obliged. He threw on a richly embroidered, padded tabard and secured it with a thick leather belt. After he tried on a few ill-sized boots, he found a pair that seemed to fit. As he rummaged further, a glint caught his eye. It was a small dagger in a leather sheath, and the only weapon he'd seen in these chambers.

Jibriil seemed busy poking at the corpse. Taki silently reached into the pile, took the sheath, and secreted it under his tabard and out of sight.

They made no sense, Jibriil's actions. *First he gains my trust, then he sells me out, and now he's come to rescue me? For what purpose?* The dagger's weight reassured him. When the moment was right, he'd use it to kill the archangel and be done with everything. *But right now, I need to get out of here, and he seems to know the way.* Just to be sure, he patted the weapon's hilt under his clothing. "I think I'm good," Taki said. "What now?"

Jibriil nodded in approval. "Now, we get the hell away from here, sneak outside the walls, and hope that your friends don't blast us on sight."

"Wait! What about my friends?"

"Ah, you can't hear it down here because we're so deep in. Sir Taki, the Teufelsbrucke is under attack. The Imperial Army's at the gates."

* * * *

High above the Devil's Bridge, blazing jars of pitch arced from catapults, leaving smoky contrails in the air. The missiles smashed against the Teufelsbrucke and sprayed liquid flame through its gunports. The men hiding behind were turned into a screaming mass of melting limbs.

On the ramparts above, a Templar swiveled an ancient relic around on a pintle, aimed at an advancing column of Imperials, and pulled the trigger. On the ground, troops wavered, fell to their knees, and burst into flames. Others rolled on the ground, screaming and choking as their vestments smoked and their blood boiled. The Templar swiveled the contraption and took aim at another group; before it could fire again, the back of its head exploded in a cloud of spall and brain matter.

Hadassah whooped in triumph at the hard-won kill. She worked the bolt on her rifle, and a smoking, hand-length cartridge plinked onto the rubble nearby.

"Direct hit, enemy helmet!" Irulan shouted, and swept the crenelations with her spyglass.

"Helmet?" Hadassah sniffed. "I turned his brains to baba friggin' ganoush!"

"That's what you *should* be doing, anyway!"

"Did we scare 'em off the death ray?"

"Aye. We've got to move, though. Their muskets are taking shots at us, and it's only a matter of time until the cannonballs follow."

The women turned around and skidded down the gravel rampart and into the trench behind it. They trudged past battered pavisiers and dusty laddermen, all lined up for a turn at the grog trough. It had only been a day since the siege began in earnest, but the strain of fighting in the thin mountain air was already taking its toll. Hadassah stopped, took a swig of cold tea from her skin, and spat.

"Doesn't feel like we've got a thirty-thousand-strong army with us," she said. "Damned bridge is no closer to the taking."

"It's because we're bottlenecked," Irulan said. "Only a few hundred can squeeze into the front lines."

"What a shithole. I bet the entire castle's full of traps and no naked maidens to save, either."

"Well, there *is* Natalis."

Hadassah spat again. "I swear, if we take this thing and some cock-puncher tells me my princess is in another castle..." She hefted her behemoth of a gun over her shoulders, almost knocking down a pair of fighters. They cursed at her, but she silenced them with a glare. "To the breastworks, spotter. We've got shitlords to remove."

Nearby, Lotte crouched with Aslatiel and two leutnants behind a battered mantlet. Bullets smashed into its pockmarked face in chaotic rhythm, and the men flinched to hear it. Lotte peered around its side and quickly pulled herself back to avoid garnering attention.

"Just as before, there's no end to them," she said. "Can we use the mortars yet?"

"Aye, *effendi,*" one of the officers, a janissary, said. "But they are too far back. We would hit our own men while we bombarded the fortress."

"I won't allow that. At least not without a good trade in Ursalan lives. Von Halcon, how fares the engine?"

Aslatiel seemed to disregard her at first. He knelt with his eyes closed and his palm splayed out on the ground. Before he could be accused of rudeness, he emerged from out of his trance and nodded to her. "It's ready. It will be coming up the road to the bridge within minutes!"

True to his word, the ground started to rumble, and gravel danced in place. As the siege engine came into view, a roar of approval rippled through the entrenched mass of Imperials. Standing twenty meters tall, it was clad in thick metal scales and boasted carronades to spray a castle's defenders with grapeshot. A tower that heavy would have been impossible for men or horses to propel, but this one was powered by fuel and the knowledge of the ancients.

"A fine and terrible beast! If only I'd had one the first time," Lotte said, shaking her head.

"Infantry Commander," Aslatiel said. "Withdraw the ladders but keep up your fire. Draw the enemy's wrath away from the tower."

"Effendi," the man replied.

"Are you ready, Satou?"

"Aye," Lotte said. "I've waited for this day for years. Now I'll show you the wrath of an archangel."

Aslatiel clapped her on the pauldron. "For the glory of the padishah. And, for your revenge."

"I'd best not keep my date waiting."

As the siege tower rolled past, Lotte emerged from behind the mantlet and hopped up to the lower deck. Berserkers in plate twiddled axes and halberds and shifted restlessly in anticipation of the fight to come. As she strode through the mass of fighters, they wordlessly parted to allow her passage.

At the base of the stairs up, a hulking commander blocked her passage. Twisting braids of coal-black hair spilled from beneath the rim of his sallet.

"Yuriel of Cloud," he said in a gravelly baritone, "you have killed many of our number on the battlefield. Now you direct us to our deaths. Will you promise us glory and bloodshed?"

Lotte smiled and rested her palm over the pommel of her greatsword. "You do me honor to remember my deeds. Yes, it is true that you may die under my command, but I can only promise you bloodshed. I cannot promise glory."

"Then why should we follow your lead?"

In a flash, she had her greatsword out to chop at the man's neck. The blade stopped just short of his ringmail.

"Glory is yours to take by the throat and not mine to spoon into your mouth like your mother," she said. "Now stand out of the way, or else get thee off my beast!"

The berserker's eyes glinted under the slit of his visor, and he stepped to the side. "We look forward to spilling Ursalan entrails with you!"

With his words, the berserkers let out a roar of approval and clanked their weapons against their shields. Her path unobstructed, Lotte wound her way up the planks and then reached the top. Bullets and stones clanged loudly against metal scales as the siege engine rolled across the bridge. Under its solid metal wheels, the bodies of the fallen burst against unyielding stone.

The swarm of berserkers tensed for action, with Lotte in the center. Ominously, the patter of bullets started to die down. She knelt and started her incantation. No sutra would protect her indefinitely or completely, but she didn't intend to stay still.

"Ready your shields!" Lotte shouted as the tower finally ground to a halt. "They intend to meet us with lead! In turn, we will give them steel!"

A carronade broadside thundered above, and one of the men blew a shrill whistle before kicking a massive latch open. With a creaking sound, the main ramp fell forward and slammed against the lip of the fort's ramparts.

Flashes of light burst through the smoky haze, and charging berserkers dropped. Bullets whizzed by Lotte's head and gouged her armor. She held her blade high, leapt from the edge of the ramp, and swung. A chevalier tried to block her strike with the shaft of his poleaxe, but her blade simply cut through the wood and split him from helmet to crotch. She whirled and slashed away at a thicket of spearheads before bowling the men over like so many ninepins.

Metal boots clomped against stone in eerie rhythm. The ramparts shook, and she realized that their small foothold was now surrounded by demihuman giants. Armed with armor-shredding guisarmes, the Templars also hid behind slab-like pavises. Lotte cursed. A shield wall was the hardest formation to crack.

Her greatsword cut deep into the soft iron face of one of the shields and forced the Templar behind it to stumble back. In retaliation, two of the guisarmes lashed out from either side to gut her. One of them she deflected with her blade, but the other caught its hook on a gap in her armor and tore a ribbon of metal away. She hopped back, dismayed to find blood welling up from under the gash. Her side throbbed, but she paid it no further heed. The circle was closing.

A few of the berserkers charged together, only to end up torn to pieces by the spears. Lotte cursed and tried to drag one of the wounded away, only to have a pauldron torn away and the side of her neck gashed open for her trouble.

At Lotte's side, Elsa clamped a hand down on the wound and started to infuse prana, stemming the blood. "It's no use, we have to retreat," she said, and tugged on Lotte's arm.

Lotte drew her pistol, aimed, and squeezed off a round at a gap in the shield wall. The slug downed one of the giants, but his compatriots simply rushed to fill the gap.

"Now," Elsa said.

Just as Lotte was about to sullenly agree, she heard a woman roaring.

Her features blurred and her limbs like small maelstroms, Lucatiel leapt off the top of the siege tower and landed in the middle of the shield wall. The Ursalans in her path shattered like chaff knocked aside by a flail. Crenellations nearby turned to dust, and great chunks of stone and mortar tumbled from the outer walls. The Templars shared the same fate, and giants hurtled to their deaths at the bottom of the ravine. Lucatiel straightened her posture, splayed her swords in outstretched arms, and turned her head to wink at Lotte.

"Hey, Big Sister!" Lucatiel said. "You look to be in a jam! Never fear, I've come to unfuck you."

"Then don't just pose there! Press the attack!"

Lucatiel flipped her off and then drove her swords into a nearby Templar's gut. She scissored them, and the behemoth fell apart at its waist. Another Templar tried to bash her with the face of its pavise. Lucatiel kicked the massive shield aside and sank a blade into its faceplate. She let go, drew one of her pistols, and blew a charging chevalier's brains out. Finally, she wrenched her blade out, and the Templar clattered to the ground.

* * * *

Taki kept his gaze lowered and his helm on, as Jibriil had instructed. In the chaos of an enemy attack, the usual vigilance of the keep's guards had gone by the wayside so long as the pair of men walked with purpose. For now, Taki was glad he hadn't simply stabbed Jibriil in the chambers. The Teufelsbrucke was a fiendishly twisting hell, especially in its lowest levels, where the princess had made her nest. Rows of cells all held emaciated prisoners who regarded the two with sunken eyes, but there was nothing Taki could do to help. He was barely strong enough to keep pace with Jibriil.

After they'd climbed a few spiral staircases, the sounds of battle were more apparent. The sound of stone crunching under leaden balls took on an almost rhythmic quality, and the keep seemed to shake with every hit. Dust and smoke swirled in the air and plunged even well-lit halls into a murky twilight that Taki almost felt he could simply push aside. The acridity of burnt human flesh stung his nostrils and made him gag. Jibriil wasn't immune, either.

"We can't go out the front," Jibriil said. "Gates are closed, and that's where the fighting's heaviest. Best bet is to reach the roof. Then we'll try our luck with the nearest Imperials we see. Hopefully they're not of a mind to execute prisoners."

Taki glanced at his surroundings: a ruined servant's barracks, well away from the press of chevaliers and guardsmen rushing to and fro. Now was as good a time as any to ask the question. "Jibriil, before we go on…"

"I know what you're going to ask," Jibriil said. He chuckled. "Yeah, I betrayed you to the castellan. In fact, I'd arranged for his men to seize you and the girl right at the gates, but then you pulled the big hero card, and it threw off plans a bit."

Taki wheeled around and smashed Jibriil right in the chin. The archangel fell back against a rotting bunk, and before he could get to his feet, Taki was on him with hands on his throat.

"I never should've trusted you!" Taki roared as he squeezed. "I tried to ignore my instinct! I tried to think you'd changed! But fuck you! *And fuck me for letting my guard down!*"

"I told them not to harm you!" Jibriil sputtered. "I promised Duvalier a seat on the Astartean council for that *one* condition! Please!"

Taki slammed his forehead into Jibriil's nose and was rewarded with a crunch. "So you were in league with him the entire time?"

"Yes! Though not against you, and not against the Imperium! I wanted to depose the primate."

"By killing us off!"

"No! The primate was never going to let your army pass. He planned to eke out more and more concessions forever until your people were dead and the padishah sent someone else. He lied to you about Hecaton Mezeta! The bitch was never here!"

"Bastard! Fucking bastard!"

"I wanted to use you to spur your side to act. Then, I'd start a coup, seize power with Imperial help, and the castellan would've thrown the gates open. No one would've died!"

"You whoreson." Taki sank a knee into Jibriil's gut, and the man gagged. "Because of your cockamamie plan, Enilna froze to death!"

"She's alive!"

"What?" Taki loosened his grip, although only slightly.

"I picked her up after she fled. We went back to Astarte together. Then, Lotte somehow convinced the primate to let the army pass. She told me that if she found your corpse, she'd chase me to the ends of the earth. So I came back."

"I won't let you betray her again," Taki said, and smacked Jibriil once more in the face.

"Then just…do it now. It's my just deserts…"

Taki reached into the folds of his robes and drew his dagger. Then, he slammed it into the meat of Jibriil's arm. Jibriil let out a cross between a groan and a sob.

"You piece of shit," Taki said, and stood.

Jibriil coughed, rolled onto his side, and vomited. Blood dripped from his nostrils and speckled the mess. He spat and then panted for a while before looking up. "Then, Sir Taki, let's move on. We've got a ways to the top…"

Taki wiped his blade off on the hem of his tunic and stowed it away again. "If you've lied about Enilna or hurt my friends in any way, I'll cut your manhood off and feed it to you."

"Aye," Jibriil said.

Overhead, the sounds of cannon fire and explosions rocked the keep. *They're getting closer,* Taki realized.

With some difficulty, the two wended their way through fallen rubble and gingerly toed their way around charred bodies caught in poses of pure agony. There was little time to reflect on the horrific sights. All

Taki could think about was getting to open air, even if it smelled of burning pitch.

"Hold fast," Jibriil said before Taki would have rounded a bend. Around the corner were massed armored chevaliers and their squires facing the entrance of a chamber. The front ranks had set up an overlapping wall of shields and pikes. The men in the rear aimed muskets, crossbows, and even a swivel-gun at the doorway.

"We've ambushed an ambush," Taki said. "Back me, Jibriil. I'll cast. Make them burn."

"Use your head! You don't have the energy," Jibriil said.

"Unlike you, I'm not a greedy coward," Taki said. He clasped his hands together and started an incantation. The air shimmered around him as prana coalesced around his focus point. Jibriil hadn't been wrong: to make a *pyr* strong enough to disperse this formation would likely render him helpless afterward. But if he didn't act, then whatever Imperial soldiers chanced into the room would be turned to mincemeat. The far door opened, and the Ursalans raised their weapons. Taki stepped out into full view, extended his arms, and let loose.

The air thickened to jelly, and a small nova erupted in the center of the formation. It expanded faster than an eyeblink and enveloped the men-at-arms in flames from head to toe before they could even scream. At the same moment, the door burst open to reveal the befuddled sun adorning the face of Lotte's greatshield. As Taki collapsed to his knees, he saw her peek over the top edge with surprise in her eyes, but only for a moment. Taki also saw she was not alone, either. Enilna and Lucatiel rushed in after her and set on the flaming Ursalans with gusto.

The men who weren't immediately cut down either rolled around spasmodically on the floor or pitched themselves out of nearby shutters to smash on the rocks hundreds of meters below. One who'd escaped the brunt of Taki's flames, however, turned and raised his mace to bring it down on Taki's head. Before the deathblow came, a greatsword erupted out of the front of the chevalier's torso and then swept to the side, flinging the man into a nearby wall. Masonry cracked as the body hit and then slid lifelessly to the cobbles.

Taki looked up to see Lotte standing over him. She was covered in gore, and her armor was blackened and gouged. To his eyes, she looked incredibly beautiful.

"Taki Natalis," she said. "You're late."

Taki nodded, his chest too tight for words.

Lotte bent to one knee and extended a hand, but before she could do so, Enilna tackled Taki to the floor. "Dumb motherfucker!" she shouted and swatted at his pate.

"What's your problem?" Taki said. He tried to push her off but to no avail.

"You! Getting your dumb ass captured in the first place!" Enilna said. "And especially for pointing your stupid gun at me and telling me to leave. You damned useless virgin!"

Taki sat bolt upright despite a rush of blood from his head. He was too annoyed to pass out. "That was to save your life! And…and being a virgin is better than settling for your scrawny hide, anyway!"

"That's not what you were saying a fortnight ago, Taki 'my hands are cold so I'll grope you under your shirt' Natalis!"

"Y-you started it first!" he said.

Sounds of a scuffle behind them ended the exchange. Jibriil hobbled into the room with his wounded arm bent backward in a joint lock and the muzzle of one of Lucatiel's guns pressed to the back of his head.

Lucatiel pushed Jibriil prone with a foot on his back and rested a finger against her trigger. "Big Sis, this one was trying to sneak away. Say the word, and I'll turn him into mystery meat!"

Lotte looked at Jibriil, and then at Taki, and then at Jibriil again. "I didn't think you'd actually rescue Natalis. But you did, so you've earned life from me."

Jibriil let out a quavering breath. "Milady, I—"

"But you also betrayed him in the first place!" Lotte said. "So, in accordance with the Hoplite's Code, I leave judgment to Natalis. Fahnrich, he's yours."

"Kil—" Taki stopped short when he saw something flash across Enilna's gaze. Sure, she'd also figured it out, but she wasn't rejoicing to be rid of the traitor. Most of the time, it was difficult to describe the momentary feelings of a glance, but Taki found reading her to be easy. *Regret,* he chose. *She still thinks I'm a kind soul and not a petty bastard.* He would have to disabuse her of that notion. *But not now.*

He cleared his throat. "Stay your hand, Prince of Maladies. This man's a cur, but he's also lost everything."

Jibriil lowered his forehead to the cobbles and squeezed shut his eyes.

"Von Halcon," Lotte said, "I must impose on you once more. Take Jibriil into custody and deliver him to our gaolers. He's strong and wily, and I trust only you to mind him."

Lucatiel groaned and spat but set to work tying Jibriil's wrists together. Then, she pulled him up and kicked his rump to get him to move out the door and back to the rooftop. "Hadassah's right," she said as she passed by Taki. "You *are* lame, Natalis."

Taki couldn't find the words to retort.

Enilna wiped at her eyes and threw her arms around Taki's neck. Despite how exhausted he felt, Taki allowed himself to revel in her warmth. Her hair tickled his nose, and he breathed in deeply. She smelled of sweat and gun smoke, and the scent drove away the nauseating odor of blood still stuck in his throat.

"By the way, are you still *intact?*" she said as she broke the embrace.

He scrunched his brow. "What does that mean?"

"They didn't violate you, did they? I mean, rape you?"

"Now you're being annoying again."

"Well?"

He sighed. "Not that I remember. I think some creature sucked my blood, but as far as I know, she didn't do anything else."

"Good," Enilna said. She grasped at the collar of his shirt and pulled him in so their foreheads collided. "You'd better not screw up and die or get captured again, Natalis. And when you're healed, I'm going to deflower you."

"Not if I get to him first," Lotte said.

Enilna's reply was drowned out by the sound of shouting as Draco, Hadassah, and Karma barged in with weapons drawn. Taki cracked a smile and let them tackle him again. His ribs ached and his limbs burned, but there was no way he'd turn down their affection. Despite everything that had happened, he'd missed his friends.

* * * *

With much hesitation, the impenetrable gates of the Teufelsbrucke rose to the accompaniment of cheering and the popping gunfire. Thick smoke wafted from almost every arrowslit on the walls, and the banners of the noble houses of Ursala were strewn on the ground in tatters. The Imperial standard flapped in the wind amid a swirl of embers. The Liberation Army had ended its month-long siege.

Tirefire the Lesser had nested in a ransacked nobleman's bedchambers with a panoramic view of the mountains near the top of the keep. No one wished to go back to the squalid conditions back at the army camp, and no others seemed to mind or take notice.

Taki winced while Draco clumsily mashed a poultice of herbs soaked in lye against the fang-marks on his chest. "Are you sure you know what you're doing?" he asked while he fought the urge to start scratching his skin off at the edges of the bandage.

"Aye," Draco said. "Elsa's been teaching me the ways of healing. Now, I can bandage, splint, and even suture up a gash." He eyed Taki's leggings. "Say, you sure you don't want me to take a look down below? I know what can happen in the dungeons, and it's no stain on your honor…"

Taki shut his legs together. "It's perfectly fine!"

"Are you sure? I've got a recipe for a soothing ointment, with a pleasant side effect of…"

"He just wants to finger your bung is all," Hadassah said, and set down a basket of gauze strips nearby.

"I'll have you know that men have a certain gland that the likes of you couldn't possibly hope to comprehend," Draco sniffed.

"Ew," Hadassah said with a grimace. She pushed Draco to his feet. "Go be pervy somewhere else. Stimulate Karma's gland if you must! Shoo! Get out of here!"

Taki snickered as Draco left in a huff. Without missing a beat, Hadassah continued to wrap loops of cloth around Taki's chest.

"Thanks," Taki said. "But I think it's a bit too tight."

"You've ever worn a corset?" Hadassah retorted. "This is nothing, so bear with it. And I can't believe your gall. You let Jibriil's head stay attached to his body? What happened between you two? Hanky-panky in the mountains?"

"No, although I trusted him more than I should have in the end. He did save me from the princess in the dungeons. I owed him that. And now he's a ruined man."

"His type never stays down for long. If I get a chance, I'll put a round in his head. You can buy me cheese and beer for it."

"Aye, cheese and beer sound amazing right now." Taki laughed. "I missed you, by the way."

"You'd better not have thought of me while wanking in the dungeon."

"I wouldn't dare."

"Smart lad," she said, and yanked the ends of the bandages into a knot. Then, she put her lips to his ear. "Captain told me not to tell you—seeing as you're one of their officers and all—but I know you'd want to hear it. Jibriil spilled his guts. The primate lied to us about Hecaton, and the Imperials just went along with it. They never wanted us to find her. So we're gonna get them back."

"How?"

"The Imps are hiding the castellan down in the caverns below. He's a valued source of info for them, and they probably worked out a deal allowing him to hide until we're well away. So we're gonna kill him, and there's nothing the Imperials can do about it except get mad. Your choice to come along or not. We'll understand if you don't."

Taki nodded imperceptibly. "Thanks, Dassa."

* * * *

Two bells later, Taki stepped up to Lotte in the torture theatre and saluted. His saber was strapped to his side, his brigandine was taut, and his pistol loaded and chambered. "Reporting for duty, Captain."

Lotte looked at Hadassah and scowled, but a moment later shook her head and smiled. Draco and Karma grunted in approval and patted the hilts of their blades.

"So, where is he?" Taki asked.

"Deep down," Lotte said. "Past where human hands built. The Imperials want him to burrow in safety until we're long gone. But I know where he is. I can tell."

They set off. Past even where Taki had been held and his blood slowly drained, and past where the smoothness of masonry gave way to the jaggedness of rock and the majesty of caverns forged by time. Lotte moved as if guided by some unknowable essence, some connection of fate, even in the overwhelming darkness so thick that five torches held high did little more than illuminate the ground beneath their feet.

After what felt like days on end of treading in the dark, Taki saw something shimmering in the distance. He tapped Lotte's shoulder, and her face turned stony.

"Snuff the torches," she ordered, and then gestured for the others to follow at a distance.

Taki crept around the stalagmites a few paces behind, gingerly stepping through the treacherously sharp stones underfoot. As he drew closer, he could now see a stone grotto dimly illuminated by a pair of torches. Within it was a ramshackle hovel, obviously built without the benefit of a work crew or tools larger than could be carried in hand. From the hovel, a man emerged. Taki recognized him immediately: the castellan.

The man smirked. "Finally. I was beginning to think you Osterbrands had left me to rot. Tell Generalleutnant Reinhard I want my chambers restored to the exact way I had them before. Well, don't tarry. I'm sick of this place already."

Lotte drew her greatsword. "Duvalier."

"That's Comte de Duvalier to you, woman. Put your sword away. There's only molerats down here."

"Do you remember, three years prior, an attack by the Archangel Yuriel?"

Duvalier snorted. "Ugh. So you're not from Reinhard. The incompetent ass." He spat. "There have been many attacks from the exarch, woman. I deign not to memorize my enemies' names. I assume I bested you at one time, yes?"

"You did," Lotte said. "You destroyed my company and then captured three of us, myself included. You made me choose who died." Her greatsword shook.

"I think I vaguely recall that. Yes, that hideous scar of yours. Really, you should be grateful and lower your weapon. I not only spared your life back then, but also an additional man as well. Now take me up to my castle, and I'll reward you handsomely for the escort. I won't even tell Reinhard about your little tantrum."

The gall. Taki's hand went to the hilt of his saber. *The absolute gall.*

Lotte let out a chuckle. "You won't be leaving this place alive, sirrah."

Duvalier snapped his teeth together. "You'll regret that!"

A woman emerged from the hovel door. In contrast to the decrepit surroundings, she was clad in the sort of finery only reserved for royals. Cambric, lace, and velvet, all topped with a heavy veil that hid her face. Taki clapped a hand over his mouth as he recognized the familiar smell of blood and honey.

Lotte leapt forward and swung to take Duvalier's head off, but the princess moved swiftly and blocked the strike with a sword breaker. The clash threw angry sparks in all directions, and the blade fractured. Lotte pivoted and chopped at the woman's wrists to cut them, but the woman parried again and shattered the massive blade at its midsection. In return, Lotte lashed out with a swift kick and pushed her opponent back. The veil fell away from the woman's face, revealing the haughty perfection of an Ursalan princess.

The princess snarled, crouched in a fighting stance, and drew another sword breaker. She murmured a brief incantation, and arcs of current boiled off the weapons' rounded heads. One strike from either breaker, and Lotte would fry. The princess licked her lips and strode forward with a look of feral glee.

Without devoting overmuch thought to it, Taki drew his Herstal and fired. The princess's head snapped to the side, and something splashed on the floor. Her body went limp, and she flopped over on the ground.

"That's cheating!" Duvalier exclaimed.

"Fuck your rules," Taki said.

Lotte dropped her broken sword and pounced on the castellan before he could draw a gun from within his finery. She wrapped her hands around his head and drove her thumbs into his eyes. After a few more minutes, he was still. She let the body drop and turned to Taki.

"Let's go home."

22

Reinhard pushed a small wooden soldier figurine over a large map of the Ursalan heartland. Across from him, Aslatiel sat with his chin rested on folded hands. Standing next to Reinhard was the primate of Astarte, bundled in velvet trimmed with ermine and leopardskin. Torches lit the castellan's former private bedchamber, which had been turned into an impromptu war room.

"We'll push across the Rhone in five places at once," Reinhard said. "The bulk of the offense will be led by three brigades of infantry backed with lancers and mobile cannon—"

Lotte kicked the door open and strode in with Taki in tow. The rest of Tirefire the Lesser tromped in behind him. The primate yelped and stumbled back and fell unceremoniously on his rear. Aslatiel and Reinhard, however, seemed unfazed.

"Captain Satou," Reinhard said. "You're just in time. We're planning the invasion of the heartland. I'd like to make you commander of five tercios, especially after your stunning performance in Xizhang—"

"You lied about Mezeta," Lotte said. "She never came through here."

Reinhard shook his head. "The primate gave you bad information. It's unfortunate, but I promise you that finding and capturing Hecaton Mezeta is a top priority—"

"No, it's not! You just used us to take this place. If you have any sense of honor at all, then tell me where she is. *I know that you know.* Otherwise, my men and I are leaving, and you can shove your invasion up your asses."

Aslatiel rose. "Lotte, I promise you. After we take Ursala, the entire army will be devoted to her capture."

"No, Sir Aslatiel," Taki said. "You're not being fair with us. We helped you take this castle and you just string us along? If so, then…then I take back what I said earlier. I've served leaders without honor, and this feels just like those times. If you won't honor your part of the bargain, then I'll leave as well."

"Taki," Aslatiel said. He opened a nearby wooden box and plucked a silver neck chain from it. "You displayed an astounding amount of valor and skill during your mission. I was going to tell you later, but I might as well let you know now. You're a leutnant now. At seventeen, you'd be one of the youngest ever. Congratulations. Come here, I'll put it on for you."

Taki's eyes burned. *It's not fair.* This wasn't how a promotion of such importance was supposed to happen. Not if it meant betraying Lotte, and hell, the others in turn. All he wanted to do was shrink. Shrink so much that no one could see him.

He felt Lotte's hand on his shoulder and looked at her. She'd be disgusted, for sure. Or at least displeased. But instead, she smiled at him. And surprisingly, so did the others.

"Go on," she said. "Take the chain. You earned it." There was not a shred of resentment in her voice. Draco ruffled Taki's hair, and Hadassah gave him an awkward half hug.

"You know how to deal with a manipulator, right?" Karma chuckled. "You've got to one-up him! Besides, no one else I know has survived a fling with an Ursalan princess. That alone should get you hauptmann or something. Go get the silver, man."

The hairs on Taki's neck rose, and he felt someone behind him. Everyone in the room lurched back. The Imperial brass hurriedly fell to their knees, while the primate simply fainted. Taki blinked and looked down to see a pair of scarred, leathery hands resting on his shoulders. The leutnant's chain was already fastened around his neck.

"Aslatiel, Reinhard." Chronicler squeezed Taki's shoulders. "I thought I taught you both better than that. Hecaton Mezeta *is* your top priority. While you dithered, my wife got her hands on the Argead Ooss. Now, she's headed east and planning all sorts of mischief. But don't fear. I intend to stop her. I've got a plan for you all. *Especially* young Taki."

Taki extricated himself from Chronicler's grasp and edged away. He still hadn't forgotten the time they'd talked near the Hot Gates. He reached for his throat and felt the cold metal links of his rank insignia. How in the world had it ended up there? His heart thudded in his chest.

"I don't think Natalis ever gave you permission to touch him," Lotte said. She had her hand on her sword hilt.

Chronicler bowed. "I apologize. But my offer still stands. Hecaton is a wily woman, and we must move quickly if we're to catch her. It will be a hard, long journey, and you will face hardships and tragedy that will make you long for the simple horrors of starvation and disease. But I will catch her, I guarantee it."

"With all due respect, *Ba'gshnar*," Reinhard said, "the padishah demands your attention in other matters. He does not permit you to chase your...your *ex* halfway across the globe."

"Ah, I suppose I should tell you now, Reinhard. Padishah Imran the Fourth no longer sits atop the throne. He surrendered his authority to me, shortly before casting away the mortal body he'd occupied for eighty years. The Imperial Cult will attest to the truth of all I have said."

"*Ba'gshnar!*" Aslatiel said. "What are you saying?"

Chronicler laughed. "Aslatiel, how dense can you be? *I* am the padishah now."

Keep going for a preview of <u>Prince of Maladies</u>, the story of Lucatiel's rise to power!

Visit www.carsonchoi.com for updates, announcements, and bonus material!

There, you can follow us on Twitter, like us on Facebook, join our mailing list, and be the first to hear of deals and new releases.

Finally, if you enjoyed this book and want to see more in the series, leaving us a review on Amazon is the single best way to let us know.

Prince of Maladies

My sister had sapphire eyes that marked her as a bastard, and thus her stepmother—my mother—hated the hell out of her. Under these circumstances, one might have expected my sister to have spent her time clothed in rags and chained to the hearth until her rescue by a prince, but this is a different type of story. *Our* story ends with Lucatiel becoming a "prince" in her own right and killing a whole lot of armed and dangerous people along the way.

I was ten when Lucatiel was brought to my door. She was one year younger than I and yet carried herself with the swagger of a hard-bitten soldier. My father, a hauptmann of the hussar regiment, rested his jagged, scarred hands on her shoulders and wore a look of contrition. She was a child he'd adopted on campaign, he said.

My mother dug her nails into the meat of my arms. "Who...no, *where's* her mother?"

My father shook his head.

Mother's jaw tightened. "She looks like you."

"She does." Father looked away. "We ride to Gdansk in a fortnight. It'll be a long campaign. She cannot accompany me any further. The law says..."

"I'm a professor of the law. I *teach* our law to every clerk, factor, and army officer in Anatolia."

"Yes, of course. I'm sorry..."

"What makes you think I want to raise your bastard?"

"I will earn double pay for battles," Father said. "I will be sure to send remittance for her education and board."

"Keep it. I make much more than you ever will." Mother's eyes were flinty. "You, on the other hand, should find somewhere else to stay in the meantime."

"Are you divorcing me?"

"Don't be silly. I want our son to have your death gratuity."

Father walked down the path leading to our house and disappeared from sight. He never looked back, so the last I saw of him for many years was a pair of sagging shoulders under a drab hussar's overcoat. My mother stared at Lucatiel, who returned her gaze with equal disdain.

"Aslatiel, show her to a spare room," Mother said to me, and she left to grade exams.

I doddered forth and tried to pick up the small satchel that Lucatiel had dropped at her feet. The need to feign politeness outweighed my growing unease. A premonition flitted through my mind.

Lucatiel grasped my wrist, pivoted, and forced me to my knees. Her grip was as unyielding as iron manacles.

"Stop this now," I yelped, "or I'll tell mother! Mother!"

"You're pathetic." She wrenched my arm, and the pain stole my breath away. "Your mother's not going to help you. Why won't you fight back?" She frowned. "You look like you go to school. The older boys beat you often, don't they?"

I burned all over, and my guts spasmed. I nodded. It was the truth.

She grimaced. "A weakling. I *hate* weaklings."

"I'm sorry." The words came out as a whimper. "I am. You're right."

She released her grip, and I pitched forward into the dirt. Before I could pick myself up, she hauled me to my feet by my collar. My knees still shook.

"Garbage. Disgusting. But Father told me to watch over you." Lucatiel wiped a clod of muck away from my cheek, hoisted her satchel, and then stepped over the threshold and into our house. "Much as I hate it, you're my brother now. I'll do my part. I'll protect you."

Though her condemnation burned my pride, there was a reason for my disgusting passivity. What I couldn't reveal to her, or anyone else, was that I carried a taint. Mine manifested subtly, making me entirely different from children who'd come to attention by incinerating their homes or hefting oxen like playthings. If either of those had happened with me, I would never have escaped detection for as long as I had.

Even without abnormal strength or pyrotechnics, however, I was a descendant of the demons that had once ravaged the world. Though I could never hope to mimic their strength, I still represented a threat.

Were my taint ever to be revealed, I'd be conscripted into the Imperial Army to fight out the rest of my days as one of their witch-warriors: the Spetsnaz. They were hardened killers, feared by all and respected by none. Thrown into the meat grinder of our empire's interminable wars, they used their demonic powers to turn the tides against impossible odds and always at great cost in lives. Though their sacrifices spared the lives of regulars like Father, the Spetsnaz were not part of our Padishah's vision for society. They were tools, not humans, and thus had no rights.

Mother insisted I was one of the lucky ones. I possessed a dangerous flaw, but it was one I could suppress, letting me live a normal life. As her only son, I was meant to join the Imperial bureaucracy and live in peace and for that, she would do anything. But I had to do my part. I had to swear to never place myself in a position where my powers would manifest, which meant I could never raise my hand against another person. If I endured, I'd reap the rewards for sure and make her proud. First, though, I had to survive my education like any other teenager.

* * * *

"Order pikes! Advance!" Our instructor sounded bored already.

I could tell he simply wanted to go back inside to a waiting samovar of tea, and I couldn't blame him. Every Imperial citizen was a reservist in the army, and thus formations and drill were part of every school's curriculum. I shifted my weight, rebalanced the heavy wooden shaft in my hands, and then took a step forward only to feel something heavy bump the side of my head. Having gone through the same motions almost every day of every year since enrolling, my classmates and I were skilled enough to not brain each other during pike drill. At least, not deliberately.

"Stop that, or I'll report you," I said. I knew who'd hit me with his pike.

"We both know shit-all will happen, von Halcon." Feyd turned his head and leered at me. A full head taller than I was and a lot more muscular, he harassed me every day and usually got what he wanted. Most of the time, it was money. Sometimes, he just wanted to beat me up.

"Charge your pikes!"

I lowered mine to fighting position. I imagined Ursalan men-at-arms charging at me with their horrible battle cry and smiled as they collided with the wall of sharpened steel points. Then, I shook the image out of my consciousness. Foolish martial fantasies would only detract from my studies, Mother had often admonished.

"Charge for horse and draw forth your swords."

We all bent, braced the butts of our pikes against the ground, and pretended to draw nonexistent side arms. I felt something metallic and sharp jab my side. I looked over and saw a knife in Feyd's hand. It had sunk partway into the standard-issue bulky jerkin I wore. "What the hell are you doing?"

"My father got it for me," Feyd said. "Nice, isn't it? He killed a bunch of Ursalan wenches with it. Come by later to the back, or I'll use it on you for real."

"You've gone too far this time. You've brought an illegal weapon to school. Toss it, or you'll be expelled."

He laughed, because we both knew my threats were empty. He got away with everything he did because he was the school's star fencer and the top performer for all exams—a genius with a nasty streak. By now, most of the teachers and even the headmaster were unwilling to deal with him. Just wait until he graduates, they'd tell me when I complained. I had no choice this time.

He extorted his victims behind the shed where our drill supplies were stored. It was out of plain view, though I suspected he'd be able to run amok in the headmaster's office if he wished. Later, after lectures were done, I grudgingly counted up my credit slips. That was another week without lunch. And mother always wondered why I seemed so thin.

When I reported to the miserable rendezvous point, I found Lucatiel instead.

"I told you I'd protect you, but I didn't know it was *this* bad." She shook her head and idly picked under her fingernails with a stiletto—the same knife Feyd had poked me with earlier.

"What are you doing with that?" I asked.

Lucatiel grimaced. "He wanted to cut you, so I took it from him."

"Feyd's not serious when he says those things," I said. "Even he has to abide by the law."

"The law?" Her expression darkened. "The law will protect you from *this*? It's solid steel, dumbass!"

I hopped back right before she flicked it at my feet. The blade sank neatly into the ground, right where the gap between two of my toes would have been. "What the hell is your problem?"

She raised her eyebrows. "Wait! How did you know to jump away? You're not that agile or perceptive."

Bile rose in my throat. My power was manifesting again. I'd suppressed it easily until recently, and the premonitions had almost completely stopped. But since Lucatiel had shown up, all my progress was coming undone. "That's unimportant. And why did you get involved? I have a plan, you know. I'll bring him down before the year's over. I just need time."

Before she moved, I knew she'd swing for my nose. Normally, I'd have stood there and taken the blow, but anger made me irrational. I would not be upstaged by a little imp who had called me disgusting garbage. She'd disrupted my peaceful home life, and Mother now drove me relentlessly. I wanted Mother to hit Lucatiel, but it never happened.

I snapped my head to the side and avoided the blow I'd sensed coming. I clumsily twisted and trapped Lucatiel's arm against my body. I drew my fist back. I'd get her for all she'd said and done. I'd bloody her nose, and perhaps she'd stop looking at me with such disdain. Before I could enact my revenge, she slammed a knee into my gut, and I collapsed in agony and out of breath.

"Trash." Lucatiel planted a foot on my chest and pushed me over. "You'd hit your own sister, but you won't raise a fist to scum who steal from you? Humiliate you? Try to hurt you?"

I wanted to insult her—tell her she wasn't family. But what she'd said was horribly correct. In this moment, I was no different from those blackguards who beat their wives and children because they were too cowardly to do anything else. I punched the ground hard as I got to my knees. "Yeah. I guess I'm trash, after all. I'm sorry. Even though you tried to hit me first."

She sighed and paced. "Does it happen every time?"

"Does what happen?"

"I've been watching you, and this confirmed it. You *know* what people will do to you before they do it. Don't you? That's why you hopped out of the way of the knife. That's also why I couldn't lay you out right away."

My stomach turned. "That was just luck. And you're a spiteful sort, so I knew you'd try to menace me somehow."

"You're a shitty liar. Tell me the truth, or perhaps I'll accuse you in public next time. The authorities *really* don't want little demons running free, you know."

"Damn you!" I clenched my fists but decided against simply swinging at her. If I wanted to save myself, I'd need to get on her good side. "Okay, fine, you win. I'll tell you everything, but I need some time to collect my thoughts."

"Stop stalling and tell me now."

There was no evading her, it seemed. "I…sometimes get these visions of what people's actions will be a few moments before they happen. I don't want the visions, and most of the time I'm scared shitless. I'd managed to suppress them, too, before you showed up. Now, I'm having them more often. So please, *Sister*, if you really want to watch over me, help me keep this secret."

"That's the first time you called me Sister…" Lucatiel bit her lip and for a moment, her scowl wavered. "Though I know you didn't mean it. That aside, clairvoyance is a pretty big deal. If you were fighting alongside Father, he'd have a much better chance of survival out there. So why should I do a damned thing to help your stupid cover-up? Why won't you just come out and enlist?"

I clasped my hands together. I looked pathetic, but I didn't care. "Because I don't want to hurt anyone! I just want to be a clerk! Or a scribe or…or whatever! I want to live in peace!"

"That's what your mother wants. Not you."

"I have a good future in the bureaucracy. I won't end up digging ditches. I refuse to end up in the army."

Lucatiel snorted. "I'd love to go back. That was *living*, you know."

"You call starving and killing all the time 'living'?"

She poked my chest. "I call things as they are. And you, *Brother*, are lying to yourself."

"I'm not. I just want to live in peace."

"You *don't*. You actually wish you were out there fighting in the trenches and gutting fools. You're frustrated when you have to hide your gift and rely on the adults to bail you out. You'd kill Feyd without hesitation if you thought you'd get away with it."

I frowned and massaged my sore stomach. "What's your problem? Why are you so violent? Why did you have to come to my house? Why did you have to wreck my family?"

"I didn't ask for any of this," she said. "I didn't make Father carry on with *my* mother, though after meeting yours, I can understand why. But unlike you, I'm honest with myself and know what I want."

"Then go! Run away! Stop making Mother so miserable!"

"I can't." Lucatiel threw up her hands. "Much as I'd like to pack up and leave the bitch, I can't."

"Is it money you need? Take mine, then!" I thrust my handful of credit slips at her.

"The only thing these are good for is wiping my ass. Do you have any milligrad?"

"Of course not. Only yokels pay for things with…with ancient bullets."

Lucatiel rolled her eyes. "Well, I'm just japing, anyway. Even if you gave me a clip of Old Nayto, I wouldn't leave. I have to watch over you."

"I don't want you to. I don't like you."

"I don't like you, either. But I made a promise to Father, and I can't take that back."

I shook my head. "That man abandoned us both. You don't have to honor *any* oath to that deadbeat."

Lucatiel slapped me. "Show some respect. He sacrificed much for me when he didn't have to. And through me, he's watching over you too."

My cheek stung, and I grimaced. "He doesn't care about me."

Lucatiel drew back as if to strike me again but relented. "No, he *does*. He knew you were special, and he knew you'd slip up one day. You'll show everyone what your mother wants you to hide. So he made me promise to not let you die."

"Ridiculous! I'm not going to die. We're in the heartland. This isn't some mudhole."

"You're naïve. Those boys who like to beat you are a bunch of true sickos. Do you realize that any other little thug would've gotten bored with you long ago? Not these assholes. They aim to kill you. Feyd wanted to shove his pigsticker in your gut today."

"That's not true. He's just..." In truth, the beatings *had* become more vicious. And more than a few times, they hadn't even bothered to take my credits. I'd been seeing more weapons as well.

Lucatiel sighed. "If you really used your foresight, you'd beat Feyd easily. Maybe even take on all three of the boys at once and win. I'd love to have what you have."

"I already told you why I can't."

"What a coward!"

"I just want to be a godrotting clerk."

"You may not get the chance." Lucatiel crossed her arms and spat.

"After I broke his face, Feyd swore he'd come back with a rifle. I'm not sure I'll be able to stop him if he does. Watch your back, Aslatiel."

To be continued...